美国文学研究

（2020）

郭继德　主编

山东大学出版社
·济南·

图书在版编目(CIP)数据

美国文学研究.2020/郭继德主编.—济南:山东大学出版社,2021.5
ISBN 978-7-5607-6994-3

Ⅰ.①美… Ⅱ.①郭… Ⅲ.①文学研究-美国-文集
Ⅳ.①I712.06-53

中国版本图书馆 CIP 数据核字(2021)第 094861 号

责任编辑 肖淑辉
封面设计 牛 钧

出版发行 山东大学出版社
社 址 山东省济南市山大南路 20 号
邮政编码 250100
发行热线 (0531)88363008
经 销 新华书店
印 刷 济南新科印务有限公司
规 格 850 毫米×1168 毫米 1/32
10.5 印张 300 千字
版 次 2021 年 5 月第 1 版
印 次 2021 年 5 月第 1 次印刷
定 价 42.00 元

目 录

In Memory of Ihab Hassan: The Selves in Postmodern Perspectives: Theory, Autobiography, and Travel

原 元

A late afternoon in September 2015, my wife and I received an unexpected phone call from Sally and were informed the sad news: Ihab passed away... No Funeral. In November, at "Beyond Crisis: The Humanities in Renewal: An International Symposium Dedicated to Ihab Hassan", a memorial ceremony was held to celebrate his life. Earlier that year in April, in good health and jovial spirit, Ihab and Sally came to visit us in San Diego, and we also made plans for another get-together at Dana Point in the first week of May before their trip back to Milwaukee for the international humanities conference Ihab partly organized. Due to an unforeseeable circumstance, we were not able to meet again as planned; eventually, missing that chance turns to be missing Ihab for life.

My personal relationship with Ihab Hassan dated back to the

middle of the 1980s. I was then a graduate student at The Institute of Modern American Literature, Shandong University. In 1983, Hassan came and delivered a series of lectures on modernism, postmodernism, literary criticism, and contemporary American literature. I had just read his *Introduction to Contemporary American Literature* in translation before meeting him in person—from a distance, i. e. attending his lectures in a large audience. Like most students in the lecture hall, I was totally awestruck by the legendary critic known as "the godfather of postmodernism"and thoroughly enthralled by all the astounding ideas about a postmodern era. Hassan's lectures on postmodernism, though packed with elusive notions of "uncertainties" and "indeterminacies", intriguingly *define* the subject of my scholarly pursuit and *determine* the direction of my academic career in future. Two years later, in 1985, I went to The University of Wisconsin-Milwaukee to pursue my doctoral degree in the English Department. Since then, Ihab became my teacher, academic advisor, and dissertation supervisor, and later, a lifelong mentor and close friend—our friendship lasts over three decades. (Note 1) After leaving Milwaukee in 1991, I regularly went back to visit Ihab and Sally for about ten years; during the last decade they sometimes came to California and we met in San Diego, Santa Barbara, Los Angeles, and Dana Point. This essay is a rewriting, in memory of Prof. Ihab Hassan, of a previous project that was published in a special collection in 2005, *Festschrift in Honor of Ihab Hassan: Return to Postmodernism*, honoring Hasson's lifelong academic achievement on the occasion of his 80th birthday. For me, this re-writing off ers another chance of meeting Ihab "in texts", from both a personal perspective and an academic point of view. As Ihab once mentioned, we can always meet in texts if not in person. (Note 2) Therefore, this essay serves dual purposes: to celebrate Hassan's huge contribution to the broad academic circles and also to retrace my personal memory of Ihab, in a very limited way, with profound gratitude to his generous counsel and kind guidance over several decades. (Note 3)

Ihab Hassan hardly needs any introduction to the academic world, with all the accolades of honorary degrees, fellowships, and lectureships from various institutes of different nations. His contribution to contemporary theories, especially on issues of postmodernism, is widely acknowledged as singularly significant. (Note 4) The endeared term, "the godfather of postmodernism", suffices to attest to his uniquely eminent position in contemporary theoretical field. In his life time, Hassan has published fifteen books and more than 300 articles on theories, literature, and culture. His writings have been translated into twelve different languages. For several decades, he has developed, probed, conceptualized, and queried postmodernism via a variety of different perspectives: a cognitive paradigm, a literary movement, a writing strategy, a cultural transition, an artistic expression, or a way of being. Moreover, he is distinctly credited as the one that brought postmodernism to the center of academic discourse and engaged postmodernism on a global level. Hassan offered over 500 lectures at various universities across continents and the revered title, "Professor of the World", he rightly deserves. (Note 5)

The impact of Hassan's theories of postmodernism is huge and remains to be assessed in many aspects; his enormous accomplishment, a vast and complex body of works, covers a broad spectrum of theoretical ideas and diverse fields of literature, culture, criticism, paracriticism, memoir, travelogue, short stories, and long fiction. Evidently, this essay is hardly the place to account for all Hassan's contributions to literary criticism, critical theories, and cultural studies. Nor is it an occasion to address all current debates on issues of postmodernism, even though deserving our attention in a different context. Instead, I intend to, in a limited scope, mainly focus on discussing Hassan's ideas of the self or selves in his autobiography and travel writings via the lens of his postmodern theories—those areas, I personally believe, have not been addressed sufficiently and remain to be fully explored. For this reason, I will be brief about his theories of postmodernism per se since scholarships abound in this area. At the end of the essay, I will discuss slightly the issues of spirituality and postmodernism, a topic Hassan returns to during the last few years of his life.

> Ihab would joke with Joy, "Call me 'Ihab'", whenever Joy (my elder daughter) stubbornly called him "Hassan". Sally would mock, "Ihab is Ihab". We were all amused. Joy had not read *Moby Dick* yet, nor heard of Ahab—she was only two years old at that time, often sitting on the colossal Webster Dictionary on the floor of Ihab's study. (Note 6)

How to address the self, or the selves, when any position of the subject is not only deemed precariously paradoxical but also gravely anachronic in an age that is generally characterized as an epoch of deconstruction? It is indeed challenging to evoke the controversial topic of the self under the postmodern condition and in the wake of Derrida's hauntology. (Note 7) Despite the rumors that the subject has already been declared "dead" on various occasions and at different fronts, Hassan, however, provocatively insists on a self, or selves, as both a textual and an existential category, and keeps probing this haunted being with an "independent stance", unlike many other contemporary critics who have suspended, dismissed, or dismantled it without any reservation. (Note 8) To negotiate with trendy and prevalent ideas regarding disappearance, deprivation, and dispossession of the subject, Hassan opines, nevertheless, we still engage the lived self in terms of writing, with "a scribbling hand", vaguely reminding us of the paradoxical posture of Becket's end game.

All writing, some critics contend, is autobiographical, relevant to the lived experience of the writing self. From this perspective, the self remains an interesting, pertinent, and tenacious category in contemporary critical debates despite the heavy tolls claimed by all sorts of deconstruction movements. Albeit all kinds of subversive thinkers keep deleting, undermining, and debunking the self to echo the "death of the subject", the specter of the self, textual, pragmatic or otherwise, still haunts us in our writings—not dead yet. In "Postmodernism Revisited", Hassan asserts: "The self remains a vital, existential category, an organizing, pragmatic, if not ontological, principle, keenly relevant to us all..." ("PR" 3).

Indeed, the self from a postmodern perspective is no longer construedunitary, original, or ontological, but rather, in his opinion, multiple, pragmatic, and performative. Departing from the usual position upheld by others, Hassan ventures to make and unmake a different self in plural forms with practical consequences.

In *The Right Promethean Fire*, Hassan inquires: "Who, indeed, is the critic? How many in him speak? Yet 'murmuring in various voices', as Japanese authors say, I cannot pretend to have 'dispersed' or 'displaced' myself entirely: my sense of both self and self's other self, death, *finally* inhabits that game" (*RPF* xvii). Hence, the self, or the selves in the critic, speak in various voices and perform varied acts in different contexts. For instance, Hassan articulates his self in a plural form in his autobiography *Out of Egypt*: "But three hearts beat in me. One existential, a little Faustian; one utopian though politic; one Orphic, almost mystic" (*OE* 27). Possibly more selves, one may speculate, are involved in an array of theoretical, fictional, personal or symbolic undertakings: the self in paradoxes in postmodern theory, the self in allegories in autobiography, the self in displacements in travel, as well as the self in a mythical quest for spirit or self-transcendence.

As noted earlier, due to the unusual nature of this essay, I will mainly focus on discussing Hassan's suppositions of the self in the context of his postmodern theory as well as his views of personal self in the context of his autobiographical and travel writings. (Note 9) I believe, the self in postmodern theory and the self in personal articulation, discrete but inseparable, are defined, to a great degree, by "in determanence", a key concept Hassan coined and developed to characterize the postmodern culture in general. That is to say, to engage the self from a postmodern stand point means to "indeterminate" the subject; it requires both questioning of and questing for the selves. In an allegorical sense, the selves in Hassan's theoretical, autobiographical, and travel writings venture on a groundbreaking journey, not toward the origin, nor the final end, but in an infinite process of mythical quest. Towards "a postmodern spirit" perhaps?

I. Indeterminacies and the Independent Position of the Self

> *In his famous Seminar on Postmodernism, a class taught regularly in the English Department at UWM, Hassan usually started his seminar with a mocking tone: "Postmodernism is an ironic concept; it designates a lineal process that the concept itself denies. The term is a self-mockery."* (Note 10)

In his interview with Frank Cioffi, Hassan declined the assumption that he was the first one to use the term "postmodern". (Note 11) Instead, Hassan was widely credited with conceptualizing, clarifying, and defining the contemporary use of the term "postmodernism". In other words, Hassan translated, developed, and substantialized a random term "postmodern"—a floating signifier without any tangible anchor—into a concrete concept, a specific subject matter, a comprehensive theoretical discourse, and a systematic body of ideas pertinent to literature, art, culture, and writing.

Now the question: What then is postmodernism? An army of negative prefixes? Displacement, decenterment, disintegration, disjunction, delegitimization, de-definition, demystification, detotalization, discontinuity, destabilization, and deconstruction? Or some positive trends: a celebration of openness, difference, diversity, heterodoxy, heterologies, pluralism, and multiculturalism? (Note 12) After decades of animated debates among critics, Hassan reaffirms in "Postmodernism Revisited": "Postmodernism remains an essentially contested category among its proponents, let alone its opponents" ("PR" 2). Indeed, to finalize postmodernism is not only considered theoretically impossible but also denounced entirely contradictory to its basic tenets and fundamental principles. In "From Postmodernism to Postmodernity", Hassan mocks anecdotally:

> The term, let alone the concept, may thus belong to what philosophers call an essentially contested category. That is, in plainer language, if you put in a room the main discussants of the concept—say Leslie Fiedler, Charles Jencks, Jean-François Lyotard, Bernard Smith, Rosalind Krauss, Fredric Jameson, Marjorie Perloff, Linda Hutcheon and ... myself—locked the room and threw away the key, no consensus would emerge between the discussants after a week. But a thin trickle of blood might appear beneath the sill... ("FPTP" 1-2)

Moreover, he maintains that postmodernism is open to change, and "like a ghost, it eludes definition" as it evolves ("FPTP" 1). However, despite all the confusion, rejection, and debate incurred by the concept, Hassan uncovers an unexpected and baffling outcome, "All this has not prevented postmodernism from haunting the discourse of architecture, the arts, the humanities, the social and sometimes even the physical sciences; haunting not only academic but also public speech in business, politics, the media, and entertainment industries" ("FPTP"1). It is entirely startling that his ideas of the postmodernism, disputed and resisted sternly by various groups at the onset, ironically initiated all sorts of other "posts" to follow: postcolonialism, post-feminism, post-Marxism, post-Freudianism, to name a few. For quite a while, the prefix "post", though signifying "after", becomes a signature label that some schools of thought put on in order to fashion themselves as the most avant-garde postmodernists. In response to this farcical situation, Hassan quotes William James' sarcastic rebuttal in his Introduction to *The Postmodern Turn*, "First, you know, a new theory is attacked as absurd, then it is admitted to be true, but obvious and insignificantly, finally, it is seen to be so important that its adversaries claim that they themselves have discovered it" (*PT* xi).

Unlike some theories that are inclined toward a definitive closure, Hassan contests that postmodernism develops toward an openness, flexible enough to allow diverse, heterogeneous, and contradictory elements to cohabit, mediate, negotiate, emerge, and merge without a final resolution or a specific telos. Postmodernism thrives on fragments and incompletes, paradoxes and differences. Hassan suggests: "Perhaps, after all, postmodernism can be 'defined' as a continuous inquiry into self-definition" ("FPTP" 6), or a continual process of self-de-definition and undercutting. That is to say, to come up with a finite closure for postmodernism simply defeats its purpose. Hence, for a concept of such abroad scope and so varied significations in addition to a continual process of revisions since its debut, I apologize I have to limit my scope of inquiry to only several key concepts postulated by Hassan that stand out consistently throughout years of his engagement with postmodern discourse. I am afraid this certainly seems suspect of simplifying and reducing Hassan's theoretical sophistication.

For five decades, Hassan has identified various tendencies of and developed abundant neologies for the postmodern discourse. Among them, one key concept, I believe, remains foundational, central, and seminal to characterizing the basic principles of postmodernism. That is, "Indetermanence", a neology that Hassan fully presented in *The Postmodern Turn*. He coins this term to "designate two central, constitutive tendencies in postmodernism: one of indeterminacy, the other of immanence" (*PT* 92). In the chapter entitled "Culture, Indeterminacy, and Immanence: Margins of the (Postmodern) Age", he proposes that "indeterminacy to be neither a fashionable nor a factitious term but rather a decisive element in the new order of our knowledge" (*PT* 71). Hassan's ideas of postmodernism, in my opinion, is largely anchored in the seminal concept of indeterminacy or indeterminacies—instrumental to his theoretical inquiry.

In *The Postmodern Turn*, the most provocative work that attempts to conceptualize the postmodern culture, Hassan elaborates: "By indeterminacy, or better still, *indeterminacies*, I mean a complex referent that these diverse concepts help to delineate: ambiguity, discontinuity, heterodoxy, pluralism, randomness, revolt, perversion, deformation" (*PT* 92). And immanence intends to "designate the capacity of mind to generate itself in symbols, intervene more and more into nature, act upon itself through its own abstractions and so become, increasingly, immediately, its own environment" (*PT* 93). A decade later, Hassan reaffirms in *Rumors of Change* that the postmodern moment in Western societies is "characterized by its 'indetermanence'—indeterminacy of knowledge, action, and authority lodged in the immanence of languages, symbols, media" (*RC* 130). (Note 13) Therefore, the term "indetermanence", as fundamental and central characteristic of the postmodern discourse and culture, designates a kind of in-completeness, uncertainty, multiplicity, heterodoxy, and constant transformation and re-creation. In "Ideas of Cultural Change" collected in *Innovation/Renovation*, Hassan argues that indeterminacy "reopens or revokes our familiar modes of thought and being" (*IR* 28). In other words, "indetermanence" recuperates the self inconstant displacements and decenterments.

Many are inclined to argue that the self in the postmodern age has already been dismissed as a "dead subject". In Preface to *The Right Promethean Fire*, Hassan observes: "The self, advanced opinion now has it, is a 'fiction'" (*RPF* xvii). And he continues later in the book: "The Self, structuralists and poststructuralists insist, following the intuition of Nietzsche, is really an empty 'place' where many selves come to mingle and depart" (*RPF* 202). In *The Postmodern Turn*, Hassan contends, "The Nietzschean self may be a 'fiction,' an empty space where various person ages come to mingle, squabble, and depart; yet it remains a 'fiction' more dense in its desires—including self-annihilation—than any neutron star" (*PT* 149).

Well, how to revive or enact "the empty subject" in the postmodern age marked widely by words like "end", "demise", and "absence"? Hassan resorts to pragmatism to both engage and disengage the self. In the "Introduction" to *The Postmodern Turn*, he points out: "But a Jamesian pragmatism may permit us to act provisionally, consequently, on beliefs adequate to their circumstances. Such actions, in William James's pluralist universe, avoid the extremes of dogmatism and deferral, though pluralism itself could never become a stable sign" (*PT* xiv). In other words, he collaborates and integrates Nietzsche's skeptic thinking (a nihilistic ethos) with James' pragmatic approach to negotiate with the postmodern condition, thereby invoking a self that is multiple, practical, and creative instead of being ontological, total, imperil, or vacant. By mediating the ghost position of an empty subject—postulated predominantly by French poststructuralists—with pragmatic ideas offered by William James, Hassan attempts to conjure up, arguably, "a postmodern self". In this way, he intends to carnivalize the self with a Bakhtin esque position that could "release us from the prison-house of tribal identity" ("FPTP" 13) according to the "postmodern episteme of unmaking" (*PT* 136). It is evident that Hassan shares Lyotard's vision against "the tyranny of wholes" and James' belief of "an unfinished pluralistic universe." To a certain extent, the idea of "incompleteness of the pluralistic universe" partly forms and informs his postmodern theory of the indeterminant self or selves.

Hassan turns to pragmatism for its positive way of relating thought to existence, principle to practices, theory to experience, for its tendencies of pluralist view, its heed to consequences instead of a *priori*, and its openness to heterodoxies of all kinds. In *Rumors of Change*, Hassan declares: "I needed no ontological self; the lived, pragmatic self, thick with existential pathos, sufficed" (*RC* xv). Thus, the self is performative and pragmatic, re-creative, and multiple, rather than ontological or original; and moreover, the indeterminate self is never fixed in any single position. In this aspect, he resolutely and consistently maintains "an independent stance".

What constitutes "an independent stance"? Hassan elaborates comprehensively his unique position in plurals in *Selves at Risk*, a book exploring the theme of quest by contemporary American writers that resonates with his own sentiment, mentality, personality, and spirit. Hassan writes:

> It means resistance to one's own immediate community... It means certain agility, mobility, nimbleness of spirit, what Lyotard calls "sveltesse", with regard to systems. It means less a position than a process, a continual struggle among

> perspectives. It means recognition of differences, heterogeneity, a way to inhabit the space of otherness. It means acceptance of marginality, knowing how to skate on edges. It means a cheerful skepticism of solidarity, or the raised voice, pointed finger, clenched fists. It means distinctive style, in writing, thinking, acting, in being in the world. (*SR* 15)

As noted above, Hassan consistently upholds a distinctive independent stance in terms of pragmatic pluralism and enacts a postmodern subject in continuous and perilous (ad) ventures towards a heterogenous space of alterity.

II. Autobiography and Unmaking of a Subject

> *Before leaving Milwaukee, in July* 1991, *Ihab and Sally helped plan a driving route on map from Milwaukee to San Diego and told us their own across America drive thirty years ago. At the farewell party, Ihab suddenly asked me, "Yuan, do you keep a journal? You will find it useful in future." Unfortunately, I did not. Now I was full of regret... but not exactly for the sake of myself...* (Note 14)

In general, Hassan's autobiography and travel narratives are intrinsically interwoven. Hassan holds that both autobiography and travel involve adventures of and quests for the self, either metaphorically or geographically; both probe and embody the perplexities of postmodern conditions in respective fields; and both anchor the self at risk, in a perpetual displacement and decenterment towards otherness. In Hassan's words, autobiography and travel require the self, "in letter and deed", to embody "the postmodern episteme of unmaking" (*PT* 136).

What is the connection between self and autobiography? In "Quest for the Subject: The Self in Literature", Hassan insists on a lived and effective self, repelling all previous appeals for totality or stability. He regards the self as "pragmatic act, less fiction than function, a felt agency, personal memory, fiducial force, positing value in the world and immanent in its own effects. The self simply *interests* us, whether in life or in literature. It interests us, especially, in autobiographical narratives of quest or adventure where in an individual at risk enacts our life in myth" ("QS" 437). (Note 15)

Departing from the usual track, Hassan opts for a different path to trace the self and posits the subject in pragmatic terms instead of an ontological category, i. e. , a self in practice that gains the capacity to translate and displace, and a self that straddles and migrates across different borders of culture, nationality, language without resorting to any closure. By embracing disparate selves in a creative negotiation with others, can one expect to find ways to transcend the confinement of identity politics. Likening to a nomadic traveler, the subject in action is mobilized and deterritorilized in a diverse space and in perpetual transition. Henceforth, the subject in autobiography and travel is forever reconstituted by its ongoing encounter and intermixing with others, thereby opening up multiple selves for transformation and displacement.

In "Counterpoints", Hassan identifies autobiography as "a way to enter the subject, a way to question theory, ideology, the pride of mind" ("C" 282). Alas, who would trust autobiography when the subject is already declared dead, dispersed into language, retrieved as a nostalgic fiction, and displaced elsewhere? The myth of the solipsistic subject of primary narcissism is indeed deemed dangerous if not obsolete. Unlike past convention of autobiography, Hassan's *Out of Egypt* is a highly experimental hybrid text interweaving several active and reflexive movements, full of fragments recollected through diverse currents of feelings, thoughts and experiences. It is fraught with citations from other writers, thinkers, and artists, interlaced with theoretical speculations of present cultural debates, personal anecdote of his life, and social commentaries on world politics, scattered with paragraphs of his critical essays of the past—partly personal, partly academic, and partly lyrical. It is an intertext in "disjunction", "in fragments", "in slip of memory, scraps of thought" (*OE* ix). This hybrid or carnival text is both a cultural inquiry and a personal contemplation that link three streams in a mosaic fashion: reflection of his childhood in Egypt, his life in America, and the present writing process in Munich. "All three, in confluence, enter this book" (*OE* 37).

Hassan calls *Out of Egypt* a "fragmentary autobiography", a distinct mode of discourse in the context of postmodern writing that circumvents confines of the traditional genre of autobiography. In other words, as a postmodern practitioner, Hassan puts his theory into practice and translates his postmodern ideas into his writing process. When encountering resistance to his innovative style, he responded in "Introduction" to *Rumors of Change*, "My writing offended most when it addressed postmodernism in paracritical form... . Still I wondered why critics who spoke of 'decenterment' did little to decenter their work. I wondered why reviewers, intimate with every cultural vagary, tolerated no experiment in critical style" (*RC* xiv).

Arguably, Hassan inaugurates the genre of postmodern memoir. Fully resonating with the postmodern narrative technique, his writings in general are highly self-conscious and self-critical; his sense of the self and his theoretical ideas coherently reflect and interrelate each other. Especially, his autobiography *Out of Egypt* is in effect a postmodern intertext wherein he constantly interrogates his perceptions of the selves and queries the complicity of autobiography as a genre in a self-reflexive and self-subversive mode of discourse that posits the subject in perpetual displacement. Instead of constructing the wholeness of a sovereign subjector to cohere those diverse selves dispersed in fragments, he intends to present the inevitable challenge of engaging the subject in an autographical mode and to entertain an innovative discourse strategy to inquire the postmodern conditions of the selves in plural, fragmented, and nomadic manners.

Hassan claims "we choose autobiography because it expresses all the ambiguities of our postmodern culture" (*RC* 188). Autobiography as an allegory of the self translates into an evocative genre that both reflects and engages the postmodern positionality. Fully recognizing the verbal complicity in all narratives, Hassan reminds us in *The Right Promethean Fire*: "Allegory removes, displaces—and returns us finally to language, locus of all displacements" (*RPF* 36). What is autobiography if it is not the self in allegories and self in displacements? The word "allegory" calls for the other in its Greek root, and similar to travel, allegorical narrative moves and displaces the self toward the other.

Autobiography for Hassan does not constitute a backward journey towards home, nor does it anticipate anchoring a self in the origin with the sentiment of nostalgia. In his interview with Lerzy Durczak, Hassan declares: "For me, personally, origins mean little" (2); and also he attests elsewhere, unapologetically: "I feel no nostalgia, almost none" (*RPF* 34). Actually, the postmodern self does not start at home as the originating moment, but elsewhere. The self in retrospect evokes other scenes, other people, other places, and other times. Hassan's autobiography, resonant with Emersonian spirit of self-reliance and independence, is entirely devoid of nostalgic pathos or diaspora mentality, unlike the postures entertained by other "diaspora" writers. (Note 16)

In *Out of Egypt*, Hassan states: "Egypt herself is a palimpsest of cultures, her history an echolalia of conquering tongues..." (*OE* 3). At the hypothetical origin uncovers a cultural process—disparity and multiplicity, a palimpsest of histories written by others: the origin already displaced. That is why he feels himself a "stranger" even in the country where he was born and grew up. As Hassan describes, "My childhood space: it was indeed a palimpsest of styles, babel of tongues, French and Arabic were my first languages; but I liked far more another which I now write; and I speak all with a slight foreign sound" (*OE* 3). In short, the foreign otherness already inhabits the self at the primal space, in effect a space of alterity and displacement, a palimpsest of other tongues, other cultures, and other people at the origin.

Instead of passive recollection, Hassan's autobiography figures as an activating postmodern instrument to probe and invoke the self: an allegorical adventure in the symbolic forest. In *Rumors of Change*, he queries: "Is not autobiography, therefore, itself a quest rather than a record of a quest, a labor of self-creation no less than self-cognizance or self-expression? And does not this quest, this labor of self-creation, in turn affect the real, living, dying subject?" (*RC* 188-189). Apparently, the answer lies in the question. Writing about the self-subject unfolds a process of self-questing rather than simply a nostalgic reconstruction of the bygone. All quest involves risk, so is autobiography as a metaphorical adventure of the self or an allegorical quest for the subject.

In his interview with Durczak, Hassan states: "They say character is fate. Perhaps so, especially if we include in character the possibilities of self-creation, self-renewal" (8). Strong belief of character, or to be precise, of the possibility of creation in character, guides his autobiographical quest for his selves. Not fixity but flux, no home but journey; identity is what we create and re-create on the roads to our different destinies. In his interview with Galdos, Hassan marks his different stance: "most people now around the world are interested in the question of identity—who I am" whereas he enjoys "the idea of displacement, of changeling, and uncertainty about who I am" (98). In other words, while most are infatuated with the identical, he is attracted by differences and indeterminacies.

Further, in *Rumors of Change*, Hassan proposes: "We can suppose, then, that autobiography, adventure, and quest coalesce in a contemporary genre that convey both the perplexities of postmodern condition and the ancient, visionary powers of myth" (*RC* 189-190). Therefore, quest in autobiography not only exposes the postmodern condition but also unveils the mythical power of spirit. In brief, Hassan's autobiography, *Out of Egypt*, marks a personal, intellectual, mythical, and spiritual voyage of a staunch and daring postmodernist.

III. Travel and the Selves at Risk

Sally told me once that Ihab really wanted, if there is a choice, to live in the Age of Renaissances, an age of bountiful opportunities for expeditions and adventures whereas Prof. Mark Krupnick, a former colleague at UWM, used to compare Ihab to the flying Dutchman because of Ihab's untiring travel around the globe, for several decades, lecturing at various institutions across continents. The three postcards from Ihab, each with a decade apart, illustrate the busy schedule of his lectures or his journeys of quest.

For decades, many critics have voiced loudly their theories of displacement and decenterment, but only a few, like Hassan, have engaged their theories personally in practice or acted upon their own hypothetical positions. For many, theoretical schemata remain as abstract conjectures or literary metaphors in a textual space whereas Hassan translates those metaphors into realities, words into deeds, logos into being, by implementing displacement and decenterment in different textual spaces, specific social territories, and varied existential contexts.

Hassan opines: "My own metaphors, I admit, tend to motion, an independent stance" ("C" 293). That is why he insists that "Motion is an intellectual thing, and travel is a metaphor, rife with mischief and right for our times" (*RC* 208). There is an urgency and necessity to travel both intellectually and geographically because, as Hassan observes, nowadays "most of us remain locked, almost locked, into our ideologies, our tribes" (*RC* 241). From this view, travel figures a pivotal tactic in our postmodern age to "displace" the subject so as to overcome ideological sleep, dogmatic fixity, mental paralysis, and the closing of the mind.

While in Egypt, Hassan dreamed about his imaginary journeys in terms of infinity: "I could not resist these invitations to voyage, and promised myself secretly, desperately, to leave some day on an endless journey, and see all the sights and strangers in the world" ("C" 290). He claims travel functions "as a postmodern metaphor of self and the world, thus a kind of transcultural discourse" (*RC* 185). Voyage evokes an allegorical adventure that embodies and enacts the postmodern self as he asserts, "This artist often takes the strangeness and solitude of travel as an allegory of the human condition" (*RC* 209), and in effect, an allegory of the postmodern condition.

Selves at Risk specifically explores the theme of travel, quest, and writing in the context of contemporary American fiction. (Note 17) Hassan views "quest as a vital, symbolic option in the postmodern world" (*SR* 4) and quest signifies "hope, movement, danger, exposure to otherness in alien cultures or natures" (*SR* 4). Travel or quest involves transgression of borders, toleration of uncertainties, and exposure to otherness—a frontier condition. Moreover, Hassan contends that travel and writing, albert distinct in different realms of engagement, interact and reflect one another, hereby "inner and outer world, letter and deed, emerge" (*SR* 28).

In *Between the Eagle and the Sun*: *Traces of Japan*, Hassan states, "I could never decline an invitation to voyage" (*BES* xv). In this travelogue, he cautions that this travelogue is not simply a book about Japan, but also "a book about myself living among others. Living and seeing myself sometimes as another, because in Japan I will always remain a stranger on a far island" (*BES* xvi). In fact, this hybrid book presents not just anthropological observations of "a far island", but also a comparative study of literature, culture, and history between Japan and America. Most of all, it presents Hassan's own self-reflection as the other in a foreign land, or a self-critique in the space of alterity as he notes that "I know that each journey can only confront me more sharply with my own, not Japan's, lacks.

That is well: we grow through the cracks in our being, our lacks" (*BES* 206). Each travel informs and unfolds a process of self-confrontation, self-exploration, and self-creation.

Ultimately, travel involves quest, "an experiment in estrangement" and "a trial by otherness" (*SR* 59), and subsequently "the self opens" (*SR* 60) to embrace alterity and enlarge the mind. Hassan argues, "The seeker, then, is a traveler among realms of being, eternal mediator between our multiple selves and our multiple otherness" (*SR* 76). Travel calls for displacements and movements in multiple environments and spaces, and it "entails encounters between cultures, values, histories, entails frictions between modes of human existence" (*SR* 79).

Hassan shares William James' view: "There is no possible point of view from which the world can appear an absolutely single fact" (*RC* 141). To overcome the paralysis of the single point of view that tends to reduce the world to a single fact, he puts his self in motion to experience difference, i. e., "to indeterminate" the subject position, to borrow his key word here. Hassan announces in various contexts, "I myself insist on an independent, roving, even nomadic point of view" (*RC* 168). In regard to these "solitary adventurers", he has this to say: "In quest or adventure, the self opens, becoming everything that it is not, opens for an instant to the light" (*RC* 192). In other words, travel translates into a postmodern way to negotiate with the subject position, to mobilize the nomadic self toward otherness, and to push the self toward the light and self-re-creation.

In his introduction to "Travel, Autobiography, Geopolitics", Hassan inquires: "Does not travel transgress margins, boundaries, differences, of every kind?" (*RC* 185). Therefore, travel turns into a postmodern strategy to negotiate with margins, boundaries, and differences. What is travel if it is not constantly moving one's self outside the familiar environments and beyond the borders into other space to encounter difference, otherness, and the unknown? Hassan assures us: "Travelers, nomads of every kind, still live closer to our historical energies. Their restlessness and vision make our world more richly interactive" (*RC* 227). Yes, richly interactive: one meets a lot of friends who speak with an accent in Ihab's house in Milwaukee—people he met on his trips. Thus, one always meets Hassan somewhere or elsewhere, or his friends. At his residence in Milwaukee, I met scholars and students from all over the world: Korea, India, Bangladesh, England, Japan, Sweden, Italy, Australia, German, France, China, etc. We come to know each other via "Ihabian" connection. Once we almost started an organization: Ihab International Association at an international conference at Bamberg, Germany in 2001. Hassan established a large global network of scholars across nations, cultures, ethnicities, genders, and continents. In this aspect, he is truly tans-national and transcultural.

Hassan's personal trip from Egypt to America, from engineer to literature, from Arab to French and then English signals his "displacements in space, time and language". But he vehemently denounces: "I will not call it exile" in "Without

Exile, A Postcolonial Intellectual Abroad" (*RC* 243). Why? Because, he inquires: "How else can I speak of exile, real or imaginary, or of a homelessness that is home?" (*RC* 247) In his interview with Durczak (and also in various other contexts), Hassan declares: "I have never felt exile" (3) and "I feel comfortable on margins, probably because I acknowledge no center" (8). In "Postmodern Revisited," Hassan asserts: "For I believe in a kind of homelessness in the world—or rather, at—homeness in the world—a certain ease in travel, transport, crossing borders, living in-between" ("PR" 4). It designates a kind of borderland condition if you will. As he points out in "Globalism and Its Discontents", "Home is not where you are first pushed into the light but where you gather it into yourself" ("GD" 62). Homelessness in his view does not signify loss or absence, but an open and fertile space that frees the self for a expedition of quest, an opportunity to go beyond containment into an unlimited realm.

This accounts for why Hassan constantly travels around the globe for several decades on his lecture tours, absent of any desire for center or home, or the nostalgia for the origin as well as the sentimental feelings of exile shared by romantics, modernist, or current post-colonialists alike. He is an artist/critic on the road—a nomadic traveler. Exile as well may be a wrong term to characterize his position as he observes in "Without Exile, A Postcolonial Intellectual Abroad": For me, exile is a lack of an attitude toward creation, a loyalty narrower than the pine coffin (*RC* 253).

Never at home in Egypt, or anywhere else for that matter,

the post modernist Hassan travels, beyond the mentality or sentimentality of nostalgia for home as origin, but simultaneously at home everywhere and nowhere. Different from the protagonists of modern literature who are estranged and suffering from exile, always traveling backwards toward a home or a recovery of the self, the postmodern travelers never adventure anywhere towards a so-called "home", but enjoy the eternal journey of on-the-road without return, in an infinite voyage of self-re-creation. Modernists move toward self-recovering and closure while the postmodernists travel toward self-creation and open space.

In "Marginal Literature at the Exploded Center: An Okinawan Instance", Hassan announces that he was "born on the margin, living decentered" (13). In *The Right Promethean Fire*, he writes: "I am, it seems, a westering spirit, with back turned on orients and origins. Still, the earth is round: there is never escape in movement or metamorphosis" (*RPF* 34). Never to return, or to put it more precisely, never to return to the same place—the origin, Hassan always re-turns elsewhere: to Africa, Asian, Europe, Australia, and North America as he says in *Out of Egypt*: "Roots, everyone speaks of roots. I have cared for none" (*OE* 4). In "Postmodernism Revisited", he says: "I have never returned to my native land. I regard my birth in Cairo an accident, not a destiny" ("PR" 3), for he believes in "self-creation: a sovereign fiction that yet enabled me to resist, even to remake, 'things as they are'" (*OE* 6). Clearly, his personal "displacements" demonstrate a postmodernist's allegorical excursion towards the otherness: other locales, other borders, and other selves—nowhere near home.

Hassan tends to believe that home is not defined as a locale but as an attitude. In *Rumors of Change*, he remarks: "Homes are not places, and they are where hearts are, since we all carry our hearts wherever we go. Home is an attitude, a readiness for death and dispossession, a kind of self-heedlessness that makes the entire universe a home" (*RC* 249-250). That is why he characterizes himself as a "traveler of eternity" in a "journey, indeed without exile, beyond exile" (*RC* 253). In his view, exile reveals a concealed nostalgic regression toward origin while journey of quest expresses desire for infinite self-displacement. Travel or quest, henceforth, becomes both a postmodern metaphor and a postmodern practice to negotiate with home, identity, and positionality. All human beings have to be elsewhere to be what we are. Who as homos sapiens have stayed in the original homes, the places where we first started? Home is a space you create, not a place wherein you are stuck. In "Travel, Literature, and Spirit," Hassan opines that travels are displacements, "crossing not only cultures but realms of our beings" ("TLS" 191). From this perspective, Hassan indeed embodies, so to speak, "a true traveling spirit" (*IQN* 45).

Autobiography and travel in Hassan's view are either fictional or actual processes of conscious self-displacement, self-inquiry, and self-creation. In *Rumors of Change*, he observes: "But the journey also becomes symbolic of the writing process itself, and of the artist's own quest for self-understanding" (*RC* 209). Here, we see again, through autobiography and travel, letter and deed, postmodern theory and postmodern act cohere to construct the postmodern self. Let Hassan speak here, "Travel and writing engage in profound collusions," and therefore, "Every writing is a journey, every book a trip"; and "Finally, writing itself is a kind of travel, a text of secret displacements" (*RC* 209). Here we may hear a distant echo of a famous Chinese saying: "Reading thousands of books; travelling thousands of miles."

Afterword: Self-Transcendence and Wandering Spirit

> *At UC Berkley, Joanna (previously, Joy) was curious to explore faith. Of course, college is the best place to get lost. We suggested she consult her "godfather". A couple of days later, Joanna told us, "Ihab said he believes in the void". I doubt if that is probably the most intriguing advice anyone can expect from a godfather. In fact, I just finished reading the manuscript of the kenotic essay Ihab sent me several weeks ago.* (Note 18)

Throughout his life, Hassan upholds an independent stance as a spiritual wanderer as he describes himself in the interview with Frank Cioffi as "a wanderer in the cosmos, and so a wondering agnostic" (10). To evoke spirit, I have not left the postmodern discourse, nor has Hassan. I personally believe that silence, void, and spirit map out different stages of Hassan's postmodern exploration as they all aspire toward self-transcendence. Especially during the last couple of decades of his life, Hassan gradually comes to probe the issue of spirituality as the marginalized and unrepresented part of postmodernism or postmodernity in terms of self-voiding, self-overcoming, and self-transcending.

Hassan's inquiry of the spiritual aspect of postmodernism traces back to his early works on silence. He identifies "Something mythic, perhaps a little mystic, inhabited the articulate silence of this early postmodernism" (*PT* 4). In *The Postmodern Turn*, he already intends to disclose an inherent liaison between kenotic myth of self-emptiness and literature of silence in terms of "the impulse of self-unmaking which is part of the literary tradition of silence" (*PT* 86).

In "Joyce, Beckett and the Postmodern Imagination", Hassan unveils a postmodern tendency towards emptiness in Beckett who "restores to words their primal emptiness" (*RC* 103). Emptiness and silence are inherent and transcendent part of speech since silence can speak "across and beyond language" ("PR" 4). Silence—literature beyond words—is compared to a desire in "literature that disdains all but the most primitive and magical use of language" ("PR" 6). Contrary to common hypothesis, a return to silence does not intend to vacate words, but to resurrect the mythical power of words so that silence can transcend language itself.

In "Introduction" to *The Dismemberment of Orpheus: Toward a Postmodern Literature*, Hassan points out that, in both Surrealism and Existentialism, "the destructive energy of the avant-garde seems finally redemptive, the voice of silence assumes a certain fullness of being" (*DO* xviii). Clearly, he locates in silence not only the destructive and the negative, but also promise of a new being, a mystic being that transcends language—a spiritual being perhaps? Therefore, language of silence, Hassan continues in the same book, "conjoins the need both of autodestruction and self-transcendence" (*DO* 12). In other words, two accents of silence seem to persist in postmodern literature: "the negative echo of language, autodestructive, demonic, nihilist" and the "positive stillness, self-transcendent, sacramental, plenary" (*DO* 248). Nihilism and redemption, self-destruction and self-transcendence, though seemingly opposed to each other, are simultaneous processes of quest for a mythical spirit. A paradox thus emerges: silence embodies both emptiness and fullness and "silence itself suddenly turns into speech" (*DO* 8). Inevitably, silence and speech, void and being, though mutually exclusive but inherently interlocked, be get each other. Put differently, silence and void, in an absent status, become instrumental to achieving transcendence to spirit.

How to embody spirit in terms of self-practice? Hassan suggests kenosis, a kind of positive nihilistic tendency toward self-transcendence. In his interview with Frank Cioffi, Hassan identifies a "positive, almost holy or kenotic kind of nihilism" (10), and further he is interested in discovering and"discerning the nexus between spirit, nihilism, and language" (16). This evidently marks the transitional turn of Hassan toward a specific cultural issue, spirit—a postmodern spirit. In "Of Truth and Lying—A Kenotic Essay", Hassan engages the issues of self-transcendence in relation to truth. To disengage the self toward spirit, he suggests the kenotic practice of self-emptiness in terms of void or nothingness. In this essay, he writes: "It is a kenotic claim, calling us to self-emptying, self-dispossession, harder than dying" ("TL" 28). Therefore, the authority of the void, the myth of nothing, and parables of the abyss clear the way paradoxically for the truth of spirit—a kenotic claim, indeed.

Hassan regards nihilism as a typical form of intellectual skepticism, informing the "philosophical unconscious" of the Western culture. He believes the quest for spirit involves a process of self-negation; he proposes: "But I offer this paradoxical guess: *it (the ontological assent) comes from self-dispossession, self-abnegation, self-disregard, kenosis*" ("TL" 33). In this case, nihilism in terms of self-voiding becomes the ground for spiritual quest for truth. To get the truth of spirit, Hassan suggests: "Consume yourself, empty yourself, aspire to zero in the bone" ("TL" 28). As a critic, he has consistently followed the postmodern episteme of self-unmaking and self-recreating. In *The Postmodern Turn*, he holds that "The strongest self is least absorbed; it opens and imperils itself continually. Its achievement, both mystics and nonmystics say, may consist in self-overcoming" (*PT* 166). In the past decade, Hassan's turn to the topic of spirit, for me, signifies both a departure as well as a return to postmodernism or postmodernity—a continuation of his speculation of the postmodern self in a different guise. (Note 19)

Then, what constitutes spirit in the postmodern age? For Hassan, it means, most importantly, a mythical quest for self-transcendence with pragmatic consequences. In "Marginal Literature at the Exploded Center", he remarks: "Spirit is what humanity shares, not this god or that. It moves within the myths of the world... . However we may choose to define spirit, it expresses the most fundamental impulse to be human—or rather, the impulse both to fulfill and transcend ones' community" ("MLEC" 19). In "From Postmodernism to Postmodernity", Hassan further elaborates:

> We need to cultivate a keener, livelier, more dialogical sense of ourselves in relation to diverse cultures, diverse natures, the whole universe itself. And we need to discover modes of self-transcendence... that avoid blind identification with collectives premised on exclusion of other groups.... Still, I would maintain, that is the spiritual project of postmodernity. ("FPTP" 13)

Moreover, he urges, we need to release us from the prison-house of tribal identity, and from the terrible grip of self-concern. That is spirit ("FPTP" 13). Put differently, we need to "indeterminate" our selves towards self-transcendence, to borrow the key concept central to his ideas of postmodernism. No doubt, Hassan suggests we seek modes of spirit as ways to negotiate and transcend identity politics. Amidst all ideological excessiveness and pursuit of power, he translates his postmodern project into a radical position: self-transcendence toward spirit against the solipsistic self and the sovereign subject.

Evoking spirit, Hassan intends to resurrect the "unpresentable" part of postmodernism, via a return to silence and void. In his kenotic essay, he remarks: "The void is unspeakable; its relation to language is nil" ("TL" 28).

Unspeakable but articulate like silence, unpresentable but apocalyptical like void, spirit here resembles Dao, permanently indeterminate and infinitely nameless in a mythical realm. Identical to Dao, spirit is obscure and nameless, beyond intellect and words—beyond the logocentric tradition of the Western metaphysics. Similar to Dao, spirit informs infinite transformation and re-creation of the indeterminate self.

If all writing is autobiographical, then Hassan's self-creative journey begins with radical innocence and ends with holy indifference (self-transcendence), toward a postmodern spirit. A spirit, beyond intellect, of wisdom, of intuition, of new Gnosis. Hassan's postmodern turn from the self toward spirit for the last two decades marks his final intellectual and mythical adventure to explore the unmarked territory ahead of the rest. A voyage not towards a specific locale, a definite closure, or a final telos, but toward an infinite open space and self-transcendence: quest itself is a mission and a destiny, to eternity and infinity.

Ihab started his teaching career at UWM in 1970 and retired in 1999. I got the special honor of being invited to teach the last class on Waiting for Godot to conclude his famous Seminar on Postmodernism that had lasted several decades in the English Department. On that occasion, I joked with Ihab about a "Post-Hassan" era after his retirement while discussing issues of absence in class. Now Ihab passed way, I gradually came to realize the immense loss and the huge void left by his departure and felt strongly what "Post-Hassan" really meant for me personally and for the entire academic world.... But who knows, someday, I might get another postcard from Ihab.... (Note 20)

PS:

Sally passed away two years later, in Oct 2017. During Christmas season in 2016, as usual, Sally sent her greetings, saying Ihab has become part of her life, being with her all the time. I have similar feelings; as Ihab said, we could always meet in texts, as in this dialogic essay.... (Note 21)

Notes:

Note 1. I was very fortunate to get the opportunity working as a research assistant to Ihab for several years and the assistantship provided rare chance to learn directly from Ihab the rigorous research methodology and passionate intellectual inquiry. See "Acknowledgement", *Selves at Risk: Patterns of Quest in Contemporary American Letters* and"Ihab Hassan: Fragments of an Autobiography", *Contemporary Authors Autobiography*

Series. Gale Research, Vol 12: 135-166.

Photo by Sally: Ihab and me in their house, Milwaukee, calling my home in San Diego after my dissertation defense in May 1992.

Note 2. Ihab often suggests, whenever possible, we meet in person outside texts, especially after I left Milwaukee in 1991. One postcard from Ihab:

16 October 2005 from Milwaukee.

Dear Yuan:

Return to Postmodernism has just arrived, with your fine, your touching contribution. I'm so glad we could meet in this book, if not in California, this year. . . .

Thank, again—and let's work on meeting outside

books.

Warmest Regards,

Ihab.

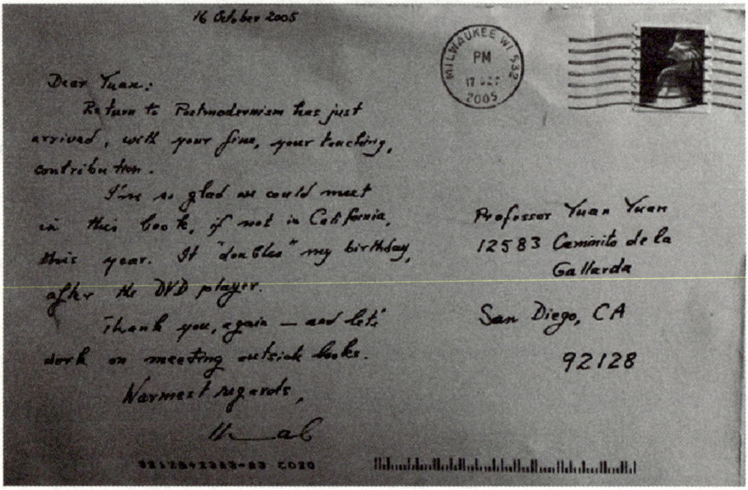

16 October 2005

Dear Yuan:

Return to Postmodernism has just arrived, with your fine, your touching, contribution.

I'm so glad we could meet in this book, if not in California this year. It "doubles" my birthday, after the DVD player.

Thank you, again — and let's work on meeting outside books.

Warmest regards,

Ihab

Professor Yuan Yuan
12583 Caminito de la Gallarda
San Diego, CA
92128

Note 3. Due to the particular nature of this essay—partly academic and partly personal, I will either call him "Ihab" in a personal context or address him as "Hassan" where I assess his scholarly contributions to the academic field.

Note 4. Hassan has a long and distinguished career of publication. Most critics agree that Hassan's research largely falls into three distinct areas or stages. (ref: *Return to Postmodernism*) The first stage or focus includes his early writings on literature: *Radical Innocence: Studies in Contemporary American Novel* (1961); *The Literature of Silence: Henry Miller and Samuel Beckett* (1967). The second stage/focus marks Hassan's most important contribution to academia, inaugurating and developing a new field of study—postmodernism, a concept, a paradigm, a culture, or an era that "he helped to launch into wider circulation" (Stierstorfer 11).

This stage includes these important works that chart the emerging ideas of postmodernism: *The Dismemberment of Orpheus: Toward a Postmodern Literature* (1971); *Paracriticisms: Seven Speculations of the Times* (1975); *The Right Promethean Fire: Imagination, Science, and Cultural Change* (1980); *The Postmodern Turn: Essays in Postmodern Theories and Culture* (1987). The third area focuses on subjects of autobiography, travel or quest: *Out of Egypt: Scenes and Arguments of an Autobiography* (1986); *Between the Eagle and the Sun: Traces of Japan* (1996); *and Selves at Risk: Patterns of Quest in Contemporary American Letters* (1990), a return to literature that integrates ideas of quest in literature, autobiography, and travel. *Rumors of Change: Essays of Five Decades* (1995) collects some of the best essays on a variety of scholarly subjects. Hassan's last book, *In Quest of Nothing: Selected Essays 1998-2008* (2010) includes essays on issues of postmodernism and spirituality, a new direction in his continued exploration of postmodernism and beyond. In addition, he has delivered more than 500 lectures across continents.

Note 5. Nobody knows exactly how many lectures Hassan has delivered in his life time. Someone came with a number—over 500. See "Obituary" published in *New York Times* (Oct 12, 2015): "he has delivered more than 500 public lectures in North

America, Europe, Asia, Africa, Australia, and New Zealand."
Here are three postcards from Ihab:

> In 1987 or 1988 from Stockholm, Sweden.
> Greetings to all the Yuans, Shan Shan, Joy, and Yuan from Stockholm.
> I did three lectures and three seminars here, and will move to Gothenburg on west coast of Sweden, to do the same. All the best. Ihab & Sally. (I was living in that address between 1987 and 1988.)

> May 1, 1996 from Perth, Australia.
> Dear Yuans:
> We write you from Perth, Australia, a lovely city that reminds me of San Diego. We have been for 6 weeks "on the road", for New Zealand, then Australia—for a total of 25 lectures. Next is London, Sweden (for an honorary degree), France, back at the end of June.... We wish we could see you. Keep Milwaukee in mind. And affections to you all from Sally and Ihab.

> April 10, 2005 from Sydney, Austrilia.
> Hello to all Yuans—and greetings from lovely Sydney. We hope you are all well. We had no chance to meet in California this time. But we may go to Japan in October and stay in Santa Barbara on the way. Here I am giving lectures sponsored by various universities in Melbourne and the State of Victoria.... We send you warm regards. Ihab & Sally.

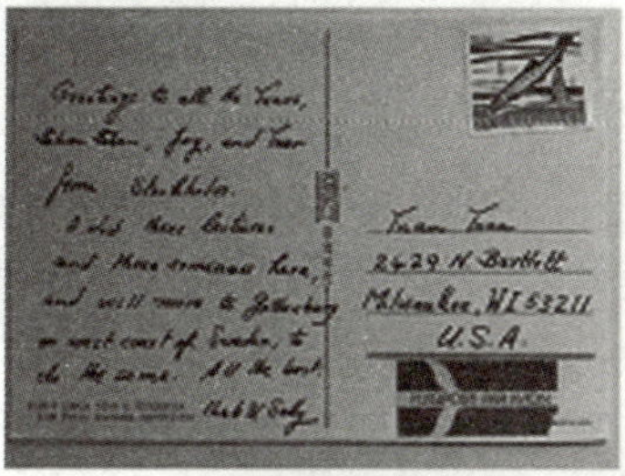

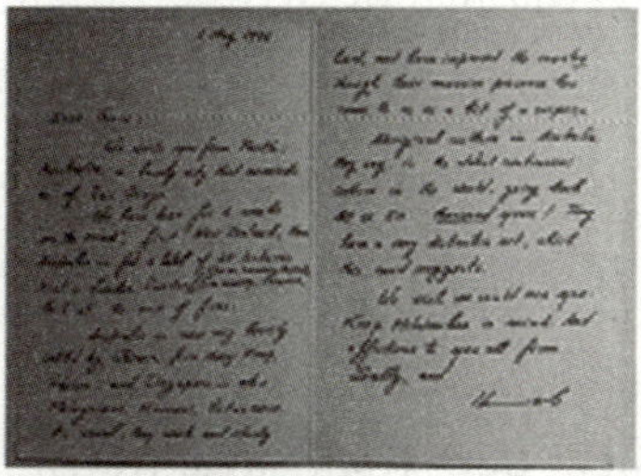

Hassan's lectures are famous internationally. I include three postcards among many we received from Ihab and Sally when they were abroad—one dated 2005, one 1996, and one around 1987 or 1988, almost ten years apart for each. These cards illustrate incredibly busy schedules of lecture tours of "a wandering postmodernist" at various universities and institutes around the world. No wander, Hans Bertens in *The Idea of the Postmodern: A History* fully credited Hassan as the one that fueled the postmodern movement via his lecture tours across the world and brought the postmodern ideas to the central stage of literary and cultural debates across disciplines.

Photo of Joy attempting to carry away the dictionary to the living room, July 1987.

Note 6. Ihab kept a rigorous daily routine of writing from morning till about 4:00. There was a big dictionary on the floor by his chair in his study.

Notes 7. The death of God is usually marked as a terminal event, but from a different perspective it could also signal an inaugural event. To some it is a ravaging ontological tragedy that, with either a "bang" or a "whimper" according to T. S. Eliot's "Hollow Men", ends the sublime illusion of the absolute subject and forecasts the catastrophic decenterment of the sovereign, autonomous, and transcendental self. That is to say, God, as the ultimate hegemonic framework that ontologizes the singular subject, elapses into a locus of void and, subsequently, the metaphysics of presence recedes into a haunted domain to house the ghostly subjects of absence. To confront this identity crisis, existentialists anchor their position decisively in the void to develop a pessimistic philosophy of despair in terms of self-loss, self-division, and self-alienation. Some thinkers are quick to follow Fukuyama's eschatology and resort to an "amort mythology", repeating after the death of God, with the death of Man, of History, and of the Self, (and more to follow), scandalizing the metaphysical homelessness and sensationalizing the ontological absence. Whereas, others in one way or another attempt to challenge this "mythology of the end" by exploring alternative directions, adventuring beyond the hauntology of absence into other locales, such as, heterologies. The postmodernists in particular are inclined to celebrate the death of God as a prime time for change. An end always signals the occasion for a shift of paradigm, a Copernican one probably, or as some contend, it signals an open space or infinite space.

Notes 8. Most postmodern theorists tend to suspend the concept of the self because in principle they deny any possibilities of language to install the subject in its ontological locus and the subject subsists on along the chain of signifiers. Jean-François Lyotard argues, for instance, that the subject has disintegrated due to the slippery effect of excessive signifiers. His famous *The Postmodern Condition: A Report on Knowledge* reiterates this position: "The social subject itself seems to dissolve in this dissemination of language games" (40). In other words, language games become the fundamental postmodern condition to recuperate the subject in terms of dispersion. The subject, in a postmodern context, has no interior except mosaic textures of interlinked linguistic networks. Derrida's *Positions* fully represents the typical post structuralist posture toward the current state of the subject. Derrida observes: "There is no subject who is agent, author, and master of *difference*. Subjectivity—like objectivity—is an effect of *différance*, an effect inscribed in a system of *difference*" (28). Thus, what is called "the subject" as an ontological category is actually constituted by various tissues of differences, and as such, the subject is meshed in an infinite network of word play, deferred and suspended in a chain of signifiers. Fredric Jameson, in

Postmodernism Or, The Cultural Logic of Late Capitalism, argues for a subject of "postmodern schizo — fragmentation as opposed to modern or modernist anxieties and hysterias" (372). Jameson's "schizophrenic" certainly echoes those ideas advocated by Deleuze and Guattari in their *Anti-Oedipus* and *A Thousand Plateaus*, both subtitled *Capitalism and Schizophrenia*. However, this is not on occasion to debate with scholars on this subject in various fields. A thorough evaluation of postmodern thoughts deserves a book by itself.

Note 9. Contemporary scholars have explored postmodern thoughts across all fields. Here are some examples: Linda Hutcheon's book, *A Poetics of Postmodernism: History, Theory, Fiction* (New York: Routledge, 1988), exams the complex issues of interweaving between history and fiction; Charles Jencks' *The Language of Post-Modern Architecture* (London: Academy Editions, 1977) and *The Story of Post-Modernism, Five Decades of the Ironic, Iconic and Critical in Architecture* (Chichester: Wiley, 2011) address issues of postmodernism in the context of architecture; Fredric Jameson's *Postmodernism, Or, The Cultural Logic of Late Capitalism* (Durham: Duke UP, 1991) discusses postmodernism in terms of cultural studies; and Jean-Francois Lyotard's *The Postmodern Condition: A Report on Knowledge* (Minneapolis: U of Minnesota P, 1984) focuses on interrogating the historical function of metanarrative and its death in the postmodern era.

Note 10. Readers might have noticed, I apologize if I quote

Hassan so frequently because I would like to, wherever appropriate, let Hassan speak for himself so we could hear him one more time.

Note 11. In an interview, when Cioffi mentioned that Hassan "coined the term 'postmodern' in reference to a certain kind of literature", Hassan declined the assumption, "No, I didn't coin the term. Some claim that a British painter called John Watkins Chapman used the term casually in the 1870s. Since then, Federico de Onis, Bernard Smith, Dudley Fitts, Arnold Toynbee, Charles Olson, Irving Howe, and Harry Levin have all used the term variously—with diverse meanings and degrees of insistence—before I did. But I guess I did stick with the term, and I did try to clarify for myself an emergent movement" (358). Therefore, Hassan is widely credited with initiating and launching an emergent movement and eventually developing an incidental term, "postmodern", into a distinct concept, a comprehensive system of ideas and a significant body of scholarship in regard to literature and culture in terms of postmodernism. In this sense, Hassan rightfully deserves the title, "the godfather of postmodernism".

Note 12. For the full list, please refer to "POSTmodernism" in Hassan's *The Postmodern Turn*.

Note 13. Hassan coined the term "indetermanence" (indeterminacy with immanence) in 1977 and frequently revisited, revised, and refined its meanings till the 2010s. Here are several versions of the concept with some alternations as it evolved during the course of several decades.

In "Globalism and Its Discontents: Notes of a Wandering Scholar" in Profession, Hassan revisited the concept of indetermanence:

> In 1977, I coined the term indetermanence (indeterminacy with immanence) to describe strong, contrasting impulses in postmodernism (Hassan, "Culture"). I meant to join, nondialectically, the deformative tendencies of that phenomenon (implying openness, fragmentation, decenterment, relativism, heterodoxy, among other cognate (terms) with its dispersive codes (involving dissemination, diffusion, interaction, rationalized procedures, semiotic projections by technological means). The neologism applied best to cultural postmodernism, its artistic forms. I did not envisage then it would become, with certain variations, a planetary fact(60).

In "Ideas of Cultural Change" in *Innovation/Renovation*, Hassan reiterated his position with a slight change:

> The first of these tendencies I have elsewhere called indeterminacy. But the tendency is really compounded of sub-tendencies which the following words evoke: openness, heterodoxy, pluralism, eclecticism, randomness, revolt, deformation. The latter along subsumes a dozen current terms of unmaking: decreation, disintegration,

> deconstruction, decenterment, displacement, difference, discontinuity, disjunction, disappearance, decomposition, de-definition, demystification, detotalization, delegitimation (28).

In "From Postmodernism to Postmodernity", Hassan elaborated his idea of indeterminacy:

> By indeterminacy, or better still, indeterminacies, I mean a combination of trends that include openness, fragmentation, ambiguity, discontinuity, decenterment, heterodoxy, pluralism, deformation, all conducive to indeterminacy or under-determination. The latter concept alone, deformation, subsumes a dozen current terms like deconstruction, decreation, disintegration, displacement, difference, discontinuity, disjunction, disappearance, de-definition, demystification, detotalization, delegitimation, decolonization(4).

In "Beyond Postmodernism? Theory, Sense, and Pragmatism" in *Rumors of Change*, Hassan listed "indeterminacy" at the top of the eleven features. For the full list, see *Rumors of Change*, pages 132-133.

Note 14. In July 1991, Ihab and Sally graciously hosted a farewell party for our family and warmly offered their maps, guides, and advise about our move from Milwaukee to San Diego. Ihab was quite torn at the moment, he said, both wanting

to keep me in Milwaukee and to let me go. Photo of Ihab showing me the details of his plan for our family's "journey to the West".

Note 15. Presently autobiography or memoir as a genre thrives as a popular mode of writing to engage the complex cultural conditions. For some of the founding theoretic books about autobiography, see: James Olney, *Metaphor of Self: Meaning of Autobiography*. Princeton: Princeton UP, 1972; James Olney, ed. *Autobiography: Essays Theoretical and Critical*. Princeton: Princeton UP, 1980; William C. Spengemann, *The Forms of Autobiography: Episodes in the History of Literary Genre*. New Haven: Yale UP, 1980. Great examples of current memoirs of hybrid nature are plenty, such as *The Borderland: La Frontera* by Gloria Anzaldua, for one. Situating travel and/or autobiographical writings in the context of postmodern theory, Hassan has contributed to redefining the genre and reviving memoirs in both ethnic studies and postcolonial studies.

Note 16. Hassan's *Out of Egypt* refuses any sentiments of nostalgia, in sharp contrast to Edward Said's *Out of Place: A Memoir* (New York: Vintage Books, 2000). See Alfred Hornung's article, "Out of Egypt, Out of Place: Humanist Crisis at Home in America" (339-349) in *Return to Postmodernism* edited by Klaus Stierstorfer, where Hornung explores critics' different stances about exile, diaspora, and the self in the postmodern and postcolonial world.

Note 17. Despite Hassan's opinions and other critics' observations, I think *Selves at Risk* is not merely "a passage" to get out of postmodernism; in fact, Hassan's analysis of quest heroes in American literature only reaffirms, in travel or quest, some of the fundamental tenets of postmodernism: displacement and decenterment of the self. Though he tends to consider *Between the Eagle and the Sun and Selves at Risk* departures from the postmodern studies, I personally see a close connection and an inherent continuity between his early writings on postmodernism and later works on quest, travel, and autobiography.

Note 18. In March 2004, at Santa Barbara, upon our invitation, Ihab was happy to accept the "informal" beloved title of "godfather" to Joanna (previously, Joy) and Erica while Sally simply claimed all of us to be her "godchildren". I was thrilled at that, being the "godfather of postmodernism", Ihab might as well recruit two more postmodernists of the next generation.

Photo of Ihab with Joanna and Erica in front of Santa Barbara Old Mission; photo of Ihab and me in conversation at a restaurant in Santa Barbara.

Note 19. Personally, I believe Hassan's later ideas of spirit inform a continuation of his intellectual quest along the line of postmodern thoughts. Rather than a departure, Hassan's new adventures in this area further expand rather than simply transcend postmodernism. It is a part of, not apart from, his continuous speculation of current culture in terms of a broader concept, "postmodernity".

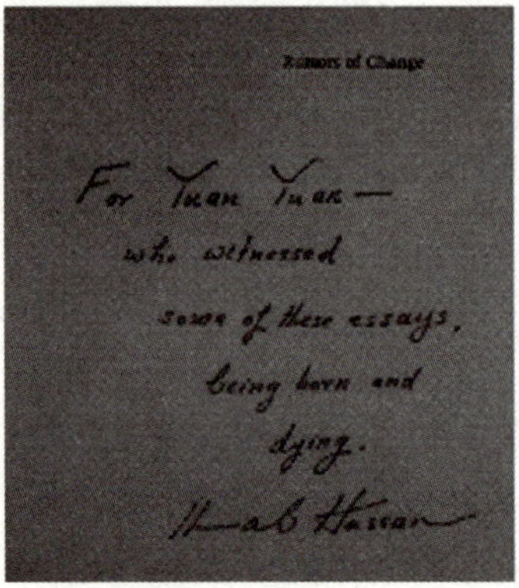

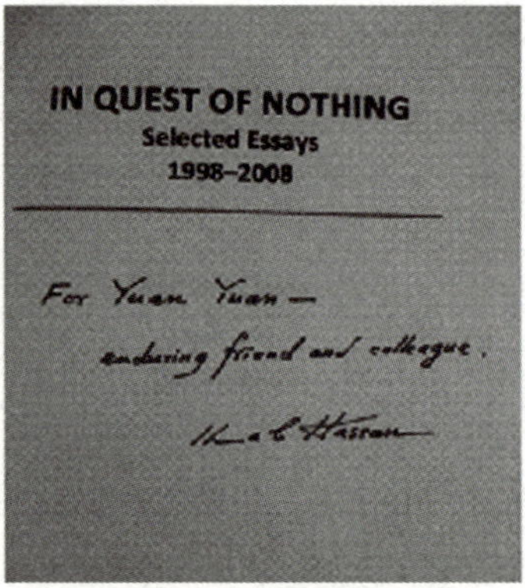

Note 20. In 2007 when Ihab was to donate most of his books to UWM library, he mailed a whole set of his books for me to keep and each book was individually inscribed. In *Rumors of Change*, Ihab wrote, "For Yuan Yuan—who witnessed some of these essays being born and dying". Four years later, in 2011, Ihab sent me his last book, *In Quest of Nothing*, in which Ihab simply inscribed, "For Yuan Yuan—enduring friend and

colleague". Since I left Milwaukee, Ihab occasionally sent me his manuscripts, sharing his most recent intellectual inquiries and enlightening me with his latest scholarly insights.

Note 21. April 1, 2015, the last of many photos I took of Ihab and Sally in their life time, against the background of the famous sculpture, at San Diego harbor, that celebrates eternal love and peace. Below is a photo taken in April 2014 at Dana Point, California where Ihab and Sally had a reunion with all their "godchildren".

from left: Yuan, Erica, Ihab, Joanna, Sally, and Shan Shan.

Works Cited.

Hans Bertens, *The Idea of the Postmodern: A History*, New York: Routledge, 1995. Print.

Frank L. Cioffi, "Postmodernism, Etc.: An Interview with Ihab Hassan", *Style*, 33.3 (Fall 1999): 357-371. Print.

Jacques Derrida, *Positions*, Trans. Alan Bass, Chicago: U

of Chicago P, 1972. Print.

Lerzy Durczak, "Ihab Hassan in Focus: An Interview with Ihab Hassan", *Web*.

Inigo Barbancho Galdos, "Literature Has Vanished in the Global World: Interview with Ihab Hassan", *Miscelanea: A Journal of English and American Studies*, 40 (2009): 97-102. Web.

Fredric Jameson, *Postmodernism Or, The Cultural Logic of Late Capitalism*, Durham: Duke UP, 1991. Print.

Ihab Hassan, "Counterpoints: Nationalism, Colonialism, Multiculturalism, etc. in Personal Perspective" in David Bennett (ed.), *Multicultural States: Rethinking Difference and Identity*, London: Routledge, 1998. 282-294. Print.

— *Between the Eagle and the Sun: Traces of Japan*. Tuscaloosa: U of Alabama P, 1996. Print.

— *The Dismemberment of Orpheus: Toward a Postmodern Literature*, Madison: U of Wisconsin P, 1982. Print.

—"From Postmodernism to Postmodernity: The Local/Global Context", *Philosophy and Literature*, 25. 1 (2001): 1-13. Print.

—"Globalism and Its Discontents: Notes of a Wandering Scholar", *Profession*, (1999): 59-67.

—"Ideas of Cultural Change" in Ihab Hassan and Sally Hassan (eds.), *Innovation/Renovation: New Perspectives on the Humanities*, Madison: U of Wisconsin P, 1983. Print.

— *In Quest of Nothing: Selected Essays 1998-2008*, New York: Brooklyn: AMS Press, 2010. Print.

—"Marginal Literature at the Exploded Center: An

Okinawan Instance", *World Literature Today: A Literary Quarterly of the University of Oklahoma*, (Winter 1977): 13-21. Print.

—"Of Truth and Lying—A Kenotic Essay", *An ABC of Lying: Taking Stock in Interesting Times*, Ed. Livio Dobrez, Patricia Doberz, and Jan Lloyd Jones, Melbourne: Australian Scholarly Press, 2004: 28-43. Print.

— *Out of Egypt: Scenes and Arguments of an Autobiography*, Carbondale: Southern Illinois UP, 1986. Print.

—" Postmodernism Revisited: A Personal Account ", *Amerikastudien/American Studies*, 43 (1998): 143-153. Print.

— *The Postmodern Turn: Essays in Postmodern Theory and Culture*, Columbus: Ohio State UP, 1987. Print.

—" Quest for the Subject: The Self in Literature." *Contemporary Literature* 29. 3 (Autumn 1988): 420-437. Print.

— *The Right Promethean Fire: Imagination, Science and Cultural Change*, Chicago: U of Illinois P, 1980. Print

— *Rumors of Change: Essays of Five Decades*, Tuscaloosa: U of Alabama P, 1995. Print.

— *Selves at Risk: Patterns of Quest in Contemporary American Letters*, Madison: U of Wisconsin P, 1990. Print.

—"Travel, Literature, Spirit: A Personal Meditation", *Journal X*, 5. 4 (Autumn 2000/Spring 2001): 183-191. Print.

Jean-Francois Lyotard, *The Postmodern Condition: A Report on Knowledge*, Trans. Geoff Bennington and Brian Massumi, Minneapolis: U of Minnesota P, 1984. Print.

Klaus Stierstorfer, ed. *Return to Postmodernism: Theory, Travel and Writing, Autobiography. Festaschrift in Honor of*

Ihab Hassan. Heidelberg: Universitatsverlag Winter, 2005. Print.

(原元:加州州立大学圣马科斯分校教授)

福克纳南方黑人家族研究[①]

李常磊

美国南方是一个由多民族、多种族构成的区域，发展至今，黑人已经成为南方最大的少数族裔。虽然美国南方黑人家族（家庭）作为真正意义上的社会组织的历史并不长，即使从内战结束以后算起，到目前也只有200多年的历史。在内战之前的南方社会中，黑人没有人身自由，长期处于被压迫、受歧视的地位，根本无法维持自己的家庭，更谈不上家族的组织活动；只有到了南方"重建时期"，黑人获得了一些自由之后才具有真正意义的家庭或家族组织。当然，在内战之前，南方处在十分恶劣的社会环境下，一些黑人通过多种方法成功建立了稳定的奴隶家族或家庭，依靠黑人传统文化扩大自己的亲属网，以此维系黑人传统的完整性，形成了自己家族的文化特征。这些家族多以女性为主，由母亲和子女组成，而父亲多为缺席，通常已被卖往其他种植园。这些黑人家族如同

---

① 本文是国家社科后期资助项目"威廉·福克纳家族小说的新历史主义研究"（项目编号：19FWWB004）和山东省社科项目"威廉·福克纳家族小说的历史书写研究"（项目编号：17CWWJ06）的阶段性成果。

南方白人家族一样,对南方社会的发展起到了十分重要的稳固和保障作用,影响或部分改变了南方的白人文化。

一、南方黑人家族发展史

美国南方传统黑人家族是一个相对封闭而又在时间上相对绵延不断的小的集团或体制。在南方历史动荡和社会迅速转型变化的时代里,黑人虽然历经波折,受到了身心摧残,但还是建立起自己相对稳定的家庭或家族组织,并与南方社会的发展保持着相对一致的势态,如婚姻关系逐渐增强,人口数量逐渐增多,必要生存权利逐渐增大等一个逐渐发展的过程。由于黑人在南方社会发挥的作用越来越大,黑人家族的重要性也越来越凸显出来。

黑人家庭是美国南方种植园社区的黏合剂,也是南方种植园奴隶最重要的生活组织。种植园奴隶家庭是在奴隶制特殊的背景下建立和发展的。内战前,种植园的黑人奴隶家庭始终受到奴隶主的干预,这种权力渗透并贯穿到黑人奴隶家庭生活的每一个方面,甚至决定着家庭的结合与分离。美国南方黑人被看作主人的财产,其婚姻和家庭没有法律保障,但黑人在特殊的生存环境中并未放弃这种最基本的权利,他们还是以自己的方式建立了家庭生活,并逐渐形成了奴隶制度下特有的家族观念和家族制度。美国南方奴隶家族的结构既不是完全根源于非洲的传统,也不是欧洲裔美国人家族模式的简单翻版,这种传统在一定程度上保持了非洲传统和风俗习惯,同时又把白人一些文化因素吸收到其家族观念中来并加以改造,形成了在美国南方奴隶制的特殊环境下特有的家族体系和家族观念。以婚姻关系为例,按照西方文化观念,婚姻是男女两性依一定法律、伦理和风俗的规定所建立起来的依附关系，是一定社会制度所承认的男女两性的结合，以此确定夫妻关系以及由此产生的父母子女之间的权利和义务。南方黑人家族为了适应奴隶主奴役和剥削而形成的一种特殊的生存策略，使黑人找到一种群体归属感和个体身份的认同。因此，在内战之前的婚姻关系完全取决于奴隶主的意愿，由奴隶主根据黑人男子在种植园的劳动给他指定妻子，所生孩子也是归奴隶主所有，黑人没有婚姻自由。美国南方所谓的“黑人家族”实际上是一个松散的血缘关系组织，并没有南方白人家族那样的真正含义。对此，福克纳虽然缅怀战前传统贵族的生活，但对这些家族对黑人奴隶的剥削和摧残给予了极大的谴责。这也从另一侧面反映了美国内战前后黑人在社会生活中的地位以及南方严重的种族问题。

在南方黑人奴隶观念中，家庭不仅仅指由丈夫、妻子和孩子组成的核心家庭，而是更广意义上的大家庭，即家族。这种家庭观念源于非洲悠久的历史传统，原因在于，虽然被贩卖到北美的非洲黑人没有把统一的西非文化带到美洲新大陆，但他们对家庭亲属关系的认识有着很多相似之处，非洲人把亲缘关系看作保持人与人之间关系的主要途径，其中一个部落中的每一个人都与这个群体中的其他多数人有着一定程度上的亲缘关系。他们的亲属体系非常庞大，日常活动往往是除核心家庭之外还有其他的亲属共同参与，如在一些非洲部落中，父母双方的成年兄弟姐妹，在抚养婴儿和料理家务方面都起着十分重要的作用。黑人把非洲大家庭的观念带到了北美，并将这些观念保持和发展，使之成为南方黑人奴隶制下维持社会群体感的一种重要手段。

由于不同的种植园奴隶主对黑人奴隶的组建家庭的态度不同，因此对黑人奴隶组建家庭的想法支持的力度也不尽相同。有的奴隶主不仅支持黑人建立自己的家庭，而且还提供经济上的支持,目的是为了获得更多的劳动力,赚取更多效益。可以说,生活在美国南方奴隶制的环境中,南方种植园一些黑人奴隶组建了自己的家庭,建立了自己的家族组织。黑人奴隶的文化正是通过一个个家庭或家族延伸出来的关系网得以传递。种植园奴隶家庭虽然不被法律承认,但对于奴隶来说却是最重要的生存机制之一。由于处在奴隶制的特殊环境,种植园黑人奴隶们一方面作为种植园社区重要的劳动力有着不同的分工和合作;另一方面,他们的家庭生活从婚礼到孩子的抚育,甚至到死亡后的葬礼都受到奴隶主权力的干预。即使面对各种各样难以想象的困难和阻碍,种植园时期的黑人奴隶一直努力创建和维系自己的家庭。内战前,许多种植园里的黑人的命名都非常重视家族血统的传承。许多黑人会以祖父母、父母或其他直系亲属的名字给孩子命名,有的也会用已故的孩子的名字。总的来说,黑人奴隶命名既保留了自己的传统文化,也受到了白人种植园主人权力的限制以及他们文化的影响。

奴隶家庭的力量是依赖于稳定的家庭构建,虽然黑人父母在家庭生活中权力和角色的发挥受到了种植园主人的严重干扰,但是父母在儿童的行为、态度、想法、价值观的形成中扮演着很重要的角色。美国南方黑人母权制家庭模式中主要分为三种类型:第一种类型为没有父亲的母权制家庭,这类家庭中的孩子跟从母姓,随母居住。第二种类型为有一个或几个短时存在的父亲的母权制家庭。这类家庭的父亲取决于是否能找到工作,能否挣到养家糊口的收入。第三种类型家庭为长期有父亲的母权制家庭。这类家庭虽然有父亲存在,但因其不能承担家庭责任,便无法维护做父亲的权威。母权制家庭的存在是美国几个世纪实行奴隶制历史的产物。作为奴隶的丈夫,被强制性地剥夺了做父亲的责任和权利。黑人男性的奴隶地位,使得他们往往不能成为家庭的赡养者,迫于无奈，黑人女性就被迫肩负以女性为特色的家庭模式。

二、福克纳南方黑人家族的历史特征

关于黑人历史问题，是美国南方历史书写的内容，也是南方文学书写的传统。然而，过去的南方文学在揭露和批判奴隶制和种族主义的时候，却往往从黑人和白人的二元对立出发，书写了白人奴隶主的残酷和黑人的屈辱，以及种族之间的对立，或表现黑人女性在种族和男权双重压迫下的苦难。由于置身于历史进程之外，并且处于社会边缘，南方黑人家族历史的书写一直被忽略。

福克纳在作品中对奴隶身份界定的一般模式是：理想的奴隶应该忠实于主人，而且要健康、清洁、恭顺、诚实、清醒、自制、愉快、勤劳、性情平和、有耐心、有礼貌、可靠和努力。奴隶主对奴隶的印象是：不诚实，不负责任，劳动不努力。主人希望奴隶服从主人的利益，有系统、有计划地劳动，绝对无条件地服从主人。福克纳对黑人家族的塑造反映了南方历史的真相，真实再现了内战前后南方那段恐怖但真切存在的奴隶制度。他用高超的想象、平淡而优雅的叙事给人们展现了不为人所知的这段历史，而这段历史无论对于奴隶还是奴隶主，对于其本人还是南方人，都是挥之不去的阴影。这种阴影萦绕至今，且会继续影响南方黑人的未来。通过黑人家族的文学表现形式，福克纳表达了他对南方历史和人性的深刻反思。

以福克纳《喧哗与骚动》中迪尔西家族为例，这个家族在约克纳帕塔法世系中始于迪尔西，家族成员包括迪尔西（Dilsey Gibson）、她的丈夫罗斯克斯·吉布森（Roskus Gibson）、大儿子沃什·吉布森（Versh Gibson）、小儿子 T. P. 吉布森（T. P.

Gibson)、女儿弗洛尼(Frony)、女婿和外孙勒斯特(Luster)等,负责服侍康普生家族或其他的白人家族,其中以迪尔西为重点,她是康普生家族的保姆,终生都服侍康普生家族。她的丈夫原先也在康普生家做工,后来看到这个家族罪孽深重,认为最终要遭到上帝的报应,因此放弃了在康普生家里工作的机会。此外,她的两个儿子和外孙陆续照看着康普生家的智障儿子班吉·康普生,可谓一代接着一代为白人家庭操劳。迪尔西的女儿嫁给了一个火车售票员,偶尔也到康普生家帮助其母亲照料这个家庭。

迪尔西自己的孩子分散在多个种植园中,但她却更关心着康普生家族的每一个人,细心地照料着家族中的每个成员,尤其是对班吉无微不至的照顾更是让人感动。她几十年如一日地照顾班吉的饮食起居,了解班吉的习性和爱好,当他哭的时候,迪尔西会想尽一切办法哄他,就像在照看自己长不大的孩子。她每次都会千叮咛万嘱咐地交代给自己的外孙勒斯特要好好照看班吉,对于勒斯特在照看班吉上的失误,她都给以严厉的批评,班吉的哭声在她看来就是勒斯特没有好好照看的结果。在小说中,只要有班吉的哭声后面都有迪尔西在质问勒斯特怎么惹到班吉了。迪尔西家族的经历反映了美国南方奴隶种植园经济时期、南方重建时期的发展历程以及存在的社会问题,福克纳通过对这个家族成员形象的塑造,颠覆了美国南方主流社会以白人为主、以男性为中心的历史,谱写了社会边缘人物非裔美国人的历史,通过众多小人物的书写,为人们展现了不一样的南方历史发展历程。

《去吧,摩西》①等作品中的尤妮思家族由三代组成,成员由女儿、孙女等构成。黑人家族以女性为主,这与南方黑人的家族构建

① 参见[美]威廉·福克纳:《去吧,摩西》,李文俊译,上海译文出版社 2004 年版。

有很大的关系。黑人基本上跟其母亲生活，因其家庭受到奴隶主的控制，无法决定自己的命运，因此，和母系亲属在一起的时间相对于父系亲属要久远一些。这是南方社会的真实反映。福克纳正是将目光投向南方传统作家或不屑关注，或难以发现，或识而不察的黑人家族，进行纵深开掘和独特的自我阐释，进而构筑出南方的历史，让微弱沉寂的黑人发出历史的声音，反映了南方奴隶制对人性的压抑和摧残。

奴隶制下的黑人家族妇女肩负起抚养孩子、照顾家人的重任。为了给孩子创造更好的生存条件，黑人妇女可以不顾及自己的尊严，因为她知道孩子比她的自尊更重要。蓄奴制直接剥夺了女奴的人身自由，也剥夺了她们成为母亲的基本权利。作为母亲的黑人女性在亲身经历奴隶制的残暴之后，心理产生极度的恐惧感。当意识到女儿将被奴隶主无情占有和蹂躏时，她们会采取暴力行为保护女儿，但是，这种行为又会对女儿造成伤害。因此，蓄奴制的创伤具有延续性，它对没有经历过蓄奴制的黑人女性同样产生消极影响。短篇小说《夕阳》里还有一个黑人家族，这个家族的女主人南希·曼尼可(Nancy Mannigoe)代表了传统的黑人女性隐忍的生存伦理观，这种伦理观是黑人女性基于自我保护而存在的。在这种伦理观的关照下，黑人女性对一切困境逆来顺受，缺乏独立的自我意识。南希作为黑人女仆，屡遭白人凌辱而怀了孕，数次向他人求救并哭诉，却没有得到帮助和同情；她在满足白人男性的兽欲的同时，还要背负自甘堕落的骂名。黑人女奴受到种族主义的压迫，同时又是男权制度的牺牲品。基于自己低贱的身份，南希无力反抗白人的侮辱；作为妻子的她，又为带给丈夫的屈辱与伤害而深深自责。他的丈夫耶苏知道妻子被白人强暴并怀孕的事实后，首先想到他被玷污的名声而非他倍受欺凌的妻子。由此可见，无论是白人还是黑人，都认可和接受种族主义和男权制度，这便是集体无意识的力量。在小说的结尾，深受奴隶制和男权思想影响的南希默默地接受了她的命运，她认为被耶苏惩罚是自己罪有应得。

在小说《沙多里斯》中服侍沙多里斯家族的黑人保姆埃尔诺拉(Elnora)对于白人统治者对黑人的奴役欣然接受，她将为主人世代服务视作荣耀，并竭力反对黑人特别是子女们为争取自由和合法权益而进行的斗争，将这视为大逆不道的行为。埃尔诺拉代表了南方众多逆来顺受的黑人，他们接受了被奴役的命运，麻木地过着服侍白人的生活。更为可怕的是，他们已经被种族主义和奴隶制洗脑，满足于被奴役、被驱使的生活，丧失了个体意识和独立意识，过着没有尊严、没有希望、没有未来的日子。

《去吧，摩西》这部关于美国黑人女性家族生活经验的代表作，除了揭露黑人母亲的生存困境之外，更加强调了黑人母亲在社会生活中所起的重要作用。黑人母亲用自己的坚韧和顽强保存了家庭的完整，保护并抚育了孩子，并使黑人文化得以继承和传播。黑人母亲不仅是养育者，更重要的是黑人文化的传承者。黑人妇女与文化传统之间存在一种天然的纽带，她们为守护、传播和继承文化传统默默地奉献自己的力量。

三、黑人家族忍耐精神与历史贡献

与同时代的作家尤其是南方白人作家相比，福克纳在种族问题上的立场是正义的，他对黑人家族的同情、对种族主义的谴责应该得到充分的肯定和赞扬。福克纳塑造了大量的黑人形象，尽力称颂他们身上的忠心、诚实、顺从等优秀品质。应该说，迪尔西是康普生家命运的见证人，又是福克纳希望的寄托。与康普生家爱的缺失相对的是迪尔西永不枯竭的温情。迪尔西是爱的象征，她的出现预示了人性复活的希望，她是文本中唯一的风景。“她的意义不仅仅是目击者。正如对康普生家族成员的关照一样，在客观上她延缓了康普生家族的崩溃。康普生家往日那气派的大宅院已经破败不堪，笼罩着一派惶恐惊乍歇斯底里的末日气氛，唯独迪尔西的厨房是沉稳可靠的避难所，仿佛是康普生家族这棵朽木上的鲜花。”①不同于康普生家里的主人们，生活在一个急剧败落又几乎是人人精神失常的贵族之家，迪尔西却能踏踏实实地干着事情。她用冷静的目光观察康普生家族的分裂，凭着爱、同情和怜悯为这个四分五裂的家庭收拾残局。她不卑不亢，疾恶如仇，勇敢地保护弱者。福克纳说：“迪尔西是我自己最喜爱的人物之一，因为她勇敢、大胆、豪爽、温存、诚实。”②面对杰生对小昆丁的暴行，她用自己衰老的身躯抵挡杰生挥动的鞭子；对智障的班吉，她的博爱甚至替代了母亲的角色，班吉生日时享受不到父母的亲情，迪尔西却掏出自己可怜的一点点钱给班吉买生日蛋糕。她忠心耿耿地把自己视为康普生家族的一员，为康普生家的不幸而哭泣：“我看见了始，看见了终。”她目睹了康普生家族的兴衰始末。

福克纳以内战历史事件与生活内容为中心，根据南方时代语境的变化，自由地书写自己对内战历史的理解，这样不只让读者看到了历史本身的丰富和复杂的一面，也给黑人家族叙事增添了艺术的魅力。迪尔西身上寄托了福克纳对人类的希望和信心，她的忠诚、忍耐、毅力和仁爱与康普生家族人物的病态形成了对照。因

① 唐璇：《〈喧哗与骚动〉的人物刻画》，《江西师范大学学报》（哲学社会科学版）2006年第3期。

② ［美］威廉·福克纳：《喧哗与骚动》，李文俊译，上海译文出版社2004年版，译本序第4页。

为在作家眼里,迪尔西体现着人性的复活。白人对黑人在政治、经济、文化上的排斥,使得黑人不仅在政治、经济上处于社会的底层,更重要的是在黑人心中造成了巨大的文化、种族自卑感。这种世世代代被罪恶、无知和耻辱所笼罩的非洲元素所带来的种族自卑感,加大了黑人与非洲文化的隔阂,以至于在20世纪中期的时候,许多黑人和白人一样都对非洲的历史和文化一无所知。福克纳笔下众多的"忠实仆人"形象则成为当之无愧的美学焦点。迪尔西与福克纳其他作品中的大部分"好黑鬼"形象相似,被赋予了普遍性的美德——忍耐与忠诚,但就个性而言,评论家倾向于将该形象与基督作类比,将其当作受苦受难的仆人。福克纳有意将小说背景设定在复活节附近,而将迪尔西的章节安排在复活节礼拜日当天,旨在呼应基督的复活与重生。故事前三章目睹了班吉的被阉割、昆丁的自杀、杰生的霉运和凯蒂贞洁的逝去,这些苦难最终都指向并期待一个救世主的出现。迪尔西的一章顺理成章地成为全书的枢纽部分,及时地扭转了前三章悲观绝望的基调。正如耐隆所说的:"迪尔西的忠诚已结晶成习惯,但在情感上她有幸并未被卷入康普生家族的癖性当中,与其白人主子家庭成员形成鲜明对比,她异乎强大。"①迪尔西拥有博大的爱,复活节当日,她坚持让班吉跟随自己去黑人教堂,女儿弗洛尼反对说:"我真愿你别老是带了他上教堂去,妈咪,人家都在议论呢。"而迪尔西回答说:"我可知道是什么样的人,没出息的穷白人。就是这种人。他们认为他不够格上白人教堂,又认为黑人教堂不够格,不配让他去。"②迪尔西的善

① 转引自唐璇:《〈喧哗与骚动〉的人物刻画》,《江西师范大学学报》(哲学社会科学版)2006年第3期。

② [美]威廉·福克纳:《喧哗与骚动》,李文俊译,上海译文出版社2004年版,第306页。

良是美的，穷白人对班吉的态度是不公的，然而敢于否定这种不公的迪尔西能够将班吉与常人一视同仁，其坚定的宗教信仰成为她“道德感”的“力量源泉”。

康普生家族早已丢失了作为基督教徒应有的希望，而承担整个家族复兴任务的中流砥柱的迪尔西，无疑成为南方人心中最后一道希望之光，绝望中的希望。在这个充满了颓败与衰落的康普生家族中，在这种摇摇欲坠、顷刻之间似乎就要倒塌的境况中，在这样一个死气沉沉的大家庭里，唯有老黑奴女佣人迪尔西是这个家庭赖以维持下去的支撑者，迪尔西像一根坚固的石柱，以勤劳和善良、忠诚和勇敢支撑它。她全然不在意会得到什么。她将宽容无私的爱奉献给了周围所有的人。迪尔西是爱的使者，她用她那无私纯洁的爱温暖着家族中的每一个人。她那高尚的人格、无私的精神和博大的仁爱将永远活在天地间。在她身上，我们看到了人性的光芒和人类的未来。迪尔西代表着人性美，在她身上散发着母性的光芒，虽是黑人奴隶但却义无反顾地担当起了父权社会的颠覆者。她的爱也给读者带来了希望，相信在这场社会变革中，会有美好的东西沉淀下来，一切疯狂和堕落都会被这场变革所埋没。

福克纳对于黑人家族的个人见解和叙述姿态与白人家族不尽相同，但其笔下所有的家族命运都殊途同归地走向了颓败、没落和消亡。他对这些家族命运的叙事方式各异，但在家族日渐式微并最终解体的过程中，并不像以前的南方作家那样对家族充满了憎恶与批判，或者根据政治斗争的需要对这种解体表示出乐观。相反，他对这些家族的毁灭寄予了无限的同情。作为处于社会等级最底端的黑人妇女，她们臣服于白人的统治，接受了被剥削、被压迫的命运，不仅放弃了对自己身体的支配，甚至放弃了主导自己灵魂的权益。《曾有过这样一位女王》中的埃尔诺拉就是具有代表性的一位黑人妇女。她忠心耿耿、吃苦耐劳，深得主人家的信任。对此，她也颇为满意，并将为沙多里斯家族服务视为毕生的骄傲。在老主人去世很久之后，她依然履行着当初的许诺：好好地照看珍妮小姐，并将此看作一项殊荣："我可以照顾她……我不需要别人帮忙……因为这是沙多里斯家里的事，上校去世前嘱咐我照顾她的，是他发的话。我用不着城里来的外人帮忙。"[①]由于长年生活于此，埃尔诺拉早已将自己视为沙多里斯家族的一分子，不仅照看主人的生活起居，还密切关注家族的声望。由于世代在沙多里斯家族为奴，并且深受母亲卢万妮亚忠心护主的影响，埃尔诺拉在奴隶制已被废除达半个世纪之久的时候，仍然甘心做个黑奴，并将自己和城里的黑人区别开。因为在她的眼中，像自己那样安分守己的黑奴才是"好黑人"，而那些背叛主人、终日在街上闲荡的黑人是背信弃义的"坏黑鬼"。由此可见，埃尔诺拉并不理解也不接受黑人为争取自由平等而做出的努力。恰恰相反，她认为黑人应该满足于自己奴仆的身份，一丝不苟地履行他们的责任，尽心尽力地为主人效力。在奴隶制和种族主义的压迫下，黑人尤其是黑人妇女的身心都备受摧残，她们的任劳任怨没能为自己赢得尊重，朴实善良也没能使自己获得肯定。白人主人所需要的不仅仅是她们的辛勤劳作，还要她们奉献出自己的身体以供其享用，还要她们出卖自己的灵魂以备其役使，渐渐地她们变成了一群没有自由、没有尊严、没有思想、没有希望的行尸走肉。

福克纳塑造了众多黑人个体和黑人家族，不仅关注了黑人个体的多舛命运，也关注黑人家族的历史发展。对于现实生活的打

① [美]威廉·福克纳：《献给爱米丽的一朵玫瑰花》，陶洁译，译林出版社 2001 年版，第 184 页。

击和痛苦，迪尔西有着超脱一般的理解，从来也没抱怨过命运对她的不公，劳苦和艰辛都能泰然处之。在迪尔西身上，福克纳所要揭示的绝不仅仅是“好奴隶”的爱，而是一种更为深广的人类情感。事实也是如此，迪尔西的生活充满了真诚，充满了自尊和爱心。尽管她作为一个黑人，作为美国南方被压迫的黑人种族的一分子，她是贫穷的，没有任何财产和社会地位，更谈不上有知识和学问，也没有作为现代生活的任何享受。但对她来说，生活是实实在在的，生活本身就是生命的过程，人在现世中的存在本身就体现出生命的荣耀和尊严。

福克纳作品展现的众多黑人形象，体现出了美国黑人通过努力奋斗可以走向成功，这种成功也否定了长久以来白人普遍认为的黑人无论从肉体上还是精神上的禀赋都低于白人的种族偏见。同时，又通过对黑人传统文化的挖掘，弘扬了黑人文化之美。这显然承担起了唤醒民族意识、重塑民族文化形象、增强民族凝聚力的作用。

（李常磊：济南大学外国语学院教授）

《地下铁道》中的或然历史与奴隶叙事[①]

李　锋

科尔森·怀特黑德(Colson Whitehead,1969～)的小说《地下铁道》(*The Underground Railroad*,2016)讲述了黑人女孩科拉逃离南方种植园、一路向北追逐自由的历险故事。与多数或然历史(alternate history)小说不同的是,这部作品并没有交代明确的历史分叉点,而只是营造了一个架空的历史世界——这个世界里的"地下铁道",不再只是一个隐喻,而是一个实体的铁路系统,每一段路程都有隐蔽的车站、专门的站长和乘务员,帮助黑奴逃往自由之地。该书的结构编排十分独特——全书共分为十二章,其中奇数章的内容是书中几个主要人物的背景与经历,构成一部时间上的列传;偶数章的内容则是科拉途经各地的遭遇,构成一部空间上的历险记。如此一来,人物与地点在书中交替出现、相互依托,共同构建起一个庞大的时空体系。

《地下铁道》因其奇妙的构思、娴熟的笔法以及对历史与当下的深刻关照,得到了极佳的专业评价和市场销量,出版后连续斩获

① 本文系作者主持的国家社科基金项目"当代美国或然历史小说研究:1945～2015"(项目编号:17BWW083)的阶段性研究成果。

2016 年度的美国国家图书奖、2017 年度的普利策奖和克拉克奖等重大文学奖项，并得到了奥巴马、奥普拉、厄普代克、斯蒂芬·金等人的高度赞誉和极力推荐。

一、实体铁道的真实与魔幻

为了写《地下铁道》，怀特黑德查阅了大量历史资料，并以此为据，在书中营造了一个极为真切的史实背景。例如，在书中每一个偶数章（对应着科拉向北逃亡的每一站）的开头，作者都会附上一张缉拿逃奴的真实告示，上面详细写着当事人的姓名、外貌描述、签发日期与地点，甚至包括具体的赏金数额。这些实实在在的信息，有如历史档案一般，给故事平添了一份厚重的历史感与可信度。

与此同时，作者又发挥丰富的想象力，赋予故事以相当的玄幻色彩。小说中最为突出的意象（也是其异于真实历史的“或然性”所在），当属贯穿全书的地下铁道。我们知道，历史上的“地下铁道”原本是指在美国内战前（尤其是 1810～1850 年），废奴主义者偷偷把黑奴从南方一站站输送到北方各自由州（也包括加拿大、墨西哥等地）的秘密路线以及沿途的藏身小屋；童年时代的怀特黑德曾以为“地下铁道”是一条条真实的铁路，直到小学四年级才了解其中的真相。当初的这一误解虽属无知，却为他日后的文学创作埋下了想象的种子。

在小说中，作者别出心裁，“用一种魔幻的手法把这条铁路嵌入了现实之中”[①]，使其虚中带实，难以捉摸。

一方面，由于历史上的“地下铁道”只是一个隐喻，并无实体性的存在，而小说中的铁路则纯属怀特黑德的艺术想象，无疑是没有

① 金衡山：《地下铁路的寓意》，《书城》2017 年第 3 期。

任何历史真实性的凭空想象。正因为此,书中对铁道与火车的描画,总是显得阴暗而神秘,带有一定的玄幻色彩:“台阶尽处是一座小型月台。巨大隧道黑洞洞的入口分居两端……铁轨想必是南北走向,从某个不可思议的源头出发,通往一个难以置信的终点。”① “火车头黑黑的,样子好丑,前面的排障器像一张三角形的大嘴巴,可是不会有什么动物脸上长着这样的引擎。”②

另一方面,相比于历史上作为隐喻的“地下铁道”,书中实体化的铁道和火车,无疑来得更为真切和实在,在叙事上也有其特殊的功能:(1)火车具有非常直观的空间属性和时间属性,更便于作者生动地表现主人公跨越各州的空间位移与时间推移,以及在此过程中的时空切换与意识流动。(2)延伸的铁路与疾驰的火车这一类具体的意象,可以作为黑奴的逃生欲望与自由意志的有形载体,给读者更加直观的阅读感受。(3)火车让逃亡过程变得相对简单和快捷,作者得以腾出更多的篇幅,用于表现沿途各州的社会问题,特别是黑人的悲惨境遇。

除此之外,实体化的地下铁道的存在,让书中的故事背景自然形成了“地上与地下”的二元世界,两者之间对比鲜明、反讽强烈——对于黑奴而言,地上世界宽敞明亮、光怪陆离,实则是一个充满禁锢的人间地狱;地下世界幽暗闭塞、褊狭局促,却能通达自由的新世界。地下铁道穿梭于这两个世界之间,寓意它“既是焦虑和恐惧的场所,又是修复和新生之所在”③。同时这也说明:所谓“自由”,其实与物理空间无关,也不仅仅是去除身体的束缚、结束

① [美]科尔森·怀特黑德:《地下铁道》,康慨译,上海人民出版社 2017 年版,第 75 页。

② [美]科尔森·怀特黑德:《地下铁道》,康慨译,上海人民出版社 2017 年版,第 78 页。

③ 承华:《穿梭时空女孩的创伤之旅:解读怀特黑德的〈地下铁道〉》,《外国语言文学》2018 年第 1 期。

物质上的匮乏，更多的关乎公平的权利与独立的人格以及精神的解放。

二、多重视角的万花筒

本书的奇数章(即第一、三、五、七、九、十一章)内容对应着几个主要人物的出身背景与人生境遇(包括科拉的外婆阿贾里、猎奴者里奇韦、内科医生史蒂文斯、救助过科拉的好心白人埃塞尔、共同出逃的伙伴西泽、科拉的母亲梅布尔)。这些以回溯为主的叙事，穿插出现在主人公科拉的逃亡经历中，犹如一部部相对独立的人物列传，从不同的视角展现出那个时代各色人物的众生相，也对故事主线形成了有力支撑。

1. 阿贾里：科拉的外婆阿贾里是来自非洲腹地的第一代奴隶，她被绑架后几经转卖，最终安顿在佐治亚的种植园。作者通过阿贾里这一个体的悲惨经历，展现了 18 世纪末 19 世纪初整个美国的奴隶贸易和种植园经济，也为全书叙事提供了必要的背景信息。这一部分连同贯穿全书的科拉逃亡经历，以及最后一章的梅布尔叙事，共同构成了一部完整的黑奴家族史。

2. 里奇韦：里奇韦是一个职业猎奴者，梅布尔和科拉这对母女先后成功出逃让他倍感耻辱，发誓一定要把科拉抓回来。尽管里奇韦在书中的定位是一个反面人物，但此人的本性并不邪恶，读者甚至会不时地被他强烈的敬业精神所触动。作者在这里极力展现出里奇韦作为“人”的一面，并非是要为奴隶制和猎奴者做任何道德上的辩护，而恰恰在说明：不公的制度足以将一个原本正直的人变为可怕的恶魔。

3. 史蒂文斯：作为一名外科医生，年轻时的史蒂文斯需要通过剖检尸体来提高自己的研究水平和手术技能，为此他曾参与盗坟和尸体交易，用卑劣的手段来实现崇高的目的，让读者实在难以对其进行简单的道德评判。此人性格和蔼、待人友善，却又从事着极为残忍的工作(即对黑人女性进行强制节育)，其人物功能与里奇韦有些相似，表明在罪恶的制度下，善良的个体同样会从事残暴的行径。

4. 埃塞尔：废奴主义者马丁的妻子埃塞尔是一个十分复杂的人物——作为一个家庭主妇，她对奴隶制的存废并不感兴趣，然而作为一个虔诚的基督徒，她又渴望将基督的圣言传递到非洲，来教化与拯救那里的"野蛮人"。埃塞尔起初对丈夫收留科拉颇有微词，但在对方害病时，她又悉心照料属于自己的"野蛮人"，并在最后为保护她付出了生命的代价，"埃塞尔"(Ethel)在古英语中具有崇高的意思，正如这一名字所暗示的一样，她最终通过受难实现了自己的升华。

5. 西泽：西泽是一个见多识广、精明能干的黑奴，一心想要逃离佐治亚的农场。他认为科拉母亲的成功逃离是运气使然，于是他便把科拉当作护身符，鼓动她跟自己一起逃跑。两人到达南卡罗来纳后，在机械厂上工的西泽对现状颇为满足，打算在这里继续待下去。然而不幸的是，他不久即被里奇韦抓获，并被当地白人暴民吊死。西泽的名字(Caesar)的发音同"凯撒"，似乎预示着他的中途早亡，哪怕身边有科拉这一护身符也无济于事。

6. 梅布尔：科拉始终不肯原谅母亲当初丢下自己、独自逃跑的举动。事实上，梅布尔在逃到半道时曾决定回来寻找科拉，但不幸被蛇咬伤，最终陷入沼泽而死。而科拉对此并不知晓，她对母亲的这份怨恨也就一直存于心头，让读者甚为遗憾和慨叹。这一类似"戏剧反讽"(dramatic irony)的情节设置，进一步增加了故事的悲剧色彩。"梅布尔"(Mabel)在拉丁语中含有"亲爱的"的意思，暗示了母女之间从未中断的情感维系。

除了以上六章中的几个人物外，小说中还有许多充满矛盾的角色，对读者的价值观与判断力形成强大的冲击。这其中既有落井下石、欺侮同类的黑奴，也有持守正义、舍己为人的白人——他们的存在有助于读者认识到那段历史的本真面目，对他们的解读也不能套用传统奴隶叙事中二元对立的简单模式（即“残酷的白人老爷”与“可怜的黑人奴隶”），而应当结合每个人物的人生际遇、心路历程和身份定位进行具体的案例分析。

例如，猎奴者里奇韦身边的黑人男孩霍默，虽已拿到解放证书并获得人身自由，却依然不肯离开主人，始终追随其左右，助其捉拿同类，而里奇韦也对这个男孩关爱有加，从而形成一种奇特的主奴关系。书中对霍默的一处细节描写尤具震撼力——“每天晚上，霍默都会一丝不苟，打开自己的小书包，取出一套小手铐。他把自己锁到车倌的座位上，钥匙揣进口袋，这才合眼。”[①]这种对主人的忠心不改、对自己受奴役身份的执着热爱，读来让人唏嘘不已，甚至难以置信，但在真实的历史中又的确不乏实例。事实上，这是一种类似于“斯德哥尔摩症候群”（Stockholm syndrome）的心理使然，即在长期奴役的状态下，被害者居然对施害者产生心理上的同情与依赖，甚至协助其加害他人。当然，作者的这种颠覆性写法，并非是将种族关系理想化，而是恰恰说明了奴隶制对黑人心理的摧残。

如果我们抛开偶数章里的主人公际遇，单看以上这些奇数章的话，这部长篇小说更像是一部《小城畸人》（*Winesburg, Ohio*, 1919）式的短篇小说集，各个人物的视角与经历互不相同，但又彼此关联，共同呈现出19世纪中前叶美国社会的复杂图景。

① ［美］科尔森·怀特黑德：《地下铁道》，康慨译，上海人民出版社2017年版，第227页。

三、多重地点的历险记

本书的偶数章(即第二、四、六、八、十、十二章)内容是科拉逃跑所途经的主要地点(包括佐治亚、南卡罗来纳、北卡罗来纳、田纳西、印第安纳、北方)。它们构成全书叙事的情节主轴,犹如一部空间上的游记与历险叙事,在讲述科拉逃生历程的同时,也全面呈现出内战前夕美国各地的社会样貌与风气。

1. 佐治亚:佐治亚是整个叙事的起点——科拉的母亲在数年前独自逃离种植园,抛下了年仅10岁的科拉,让她饱受主人的虐待和其他奴隶的欺侮;如今在另一个黑奴西泽的鼓动下,科拉决意逃亡,追寻自由。本章以高度写实又颇为克制的手法,客观展现了黑奴生活的惨厉,为主人公选择逃亡的决定提供了强大的动力。经过一番险象环生的奔逃,科拉与西泽终于坐上神秘的"地下列车",开启随后的奥德赛之旅。

2. 南卡罗来纳:南卡表面上是一个十分理想的避难所——当地政府雇用奴隶工作,为他们提供食宿、基础教育和医疗卫生,即使是流水线上的工作,也比在种植园的劳作来得更有成就感,以至于科拉一度想要放弃北逃,留在这里。然而,在博物馆里充当模特的屈辱,以及在医院的遭遇(白人医生对黑人男性进行防治梅毒实验,对黑人女性采取绝育措施),让科拉倍感不安,并在猎奴者到达此地后侥幸逃离。

3. 北卡罗来纳:北卡的形势远比南卡糟糕,这里的白人实施严酷的种族灭绝政策。科拉被好心的马丁夫妇隐藏在家里的阁楼上,只能透过小窗子观察外面的世界(包括白人集会、黑人被处以极刑等)。此时的科拉深感"无论是在棉田,在地下,还是在阁楼上的一间斗室，美国始终是她的监牢”[①]。数月之后，由于马丁家女佣的告发，科拉被抓住并交给里奇韦，而马丁夫妇也因为藏匿逃奴被市民们绞死。

4. 田纳西：里奇韦在押送科拉返回佐治亚的路上经过田纳西，此处刚刚发生了严重的火灾与瘟疫，造成大量的人员伤亡与财产损失。科拉起先将之视为上天对白人的诅咒和惩罚，随后才明白：这些灾难其实是“大自然一视同仁的结果，无关定居移民的罪恶”[②]，这显示出她的思维方式从感性到理性的转变。有几个年轻的黑人袭击了里奇韦的队伍，并放走了科拉，随后她一路逃到了印第安纳。

5. 印第安纳：科拉在印第安纳的瓦伦丁农场安顿下来，过上了安定和谐的生活，甚至跟一个叫罗亚尔的年轻黑人彼此相爱。在一次农场大会上，几位废奴主义者先后登上讲台各抒己见，不料大会遭到了白人的突然袭击，农场被焚烧殆尽，多人被乱枪打死，科拉也再次被里奇韦擒住。在科拉出逃途经的几处地方中，印第安纳无疑是相对最为理想的黑人家园，却遭到了最具毁灭性的打击，表明在当时的局势下，黑人自治只是一个虚幻的乌托邦。

6. 北方：科拉在被迫带领里奇韦观看地下铁道时，将其推下坑道，自己乘机跳上手摇车逃离现场。待她再一次来到地面后，并不清楚自己身处何地。一个赶马车去加州的好心黑人搭载了她，科拉思忖着此人的身世——“她很想知道他是从哪儿逃出来的，过去有多苦，走了多远的路，才把它留在身后。”[③]小说至此也就戛然

---

① ［美］科尔森·怀特黑德：《地下铁道》，康慨译，上海人民出版社 2017 年版，第 194 页。

② ［美］科尔森·怀特黑德：《地下铁道》，康慨译，上海人民出版社 2017 年版，第 242 页。

③ ［美］科尔森·怀特黑德：《地下铁道》，康慨译，上海人民出版社 2017 年版，第 344 页。

而止，作者故意没有交代主人公的最终结局。这一开放式的结尾，与其说是作者的后现代实验手法，不如说是在隐喻美国黑人群体的未来命运无法确知。

事实上，科拉所途经的每个州，其社会风气与政治局势都对应着美国种族问题的某一个侧面——这些问题，有的是在历史上确曾发生过的(如跨大西洋的黑人奴隶贸易)，有的属于时间上的移置(如书中针对黑人的梅毒实验，其实发生在20世纪30年代，而强制性节育主要发生在20世纪前中叶，而且并不仅限于黑人女性)，还有的则是不同政治理念的杂糅(如农场大会上针锋相对的政治观点，其实是在影射不同历史时期的几种民权思想)。作者在这里充分利用或然历史小说的创作自由度，将如此多样化的事件和观念全都并置在一个文本世界中，可以帮助读者从联系、发展的角度来全面审视美国的种族问题。

四、凝视中的权力关系

在科拉途经的几个地点中，最引人深思的当属南卡罗来纳——这里没有其他各州肆虐的暴力与公然的杀戮，白人与黑人和平共处，逃奴在这里可以获得就业岗位、基础教育、医疗卫生等待遇，俨然一派美好景象。然而，在这看似和谐的画面背后，却掩藏着更为隐秘而残酷的权力手段，表现为博物馆中参观者对黑人模特的凝视，医院中医生对黑人妇女的强制节育。

科拉在南卡期间，被安排到一家“自然奇观博物馆”充当模特，与其他两个黑人姑娘一起，按时间顺序再现黑奴历史中的三个代表性场景——“非洲腹地即景”“运奴船上的生活”“种植园典型的一天”，以此实现讲述美国历程、教育社会大众的目的。这项工作虽不算辛苦，却让科拉在心理上倍感不适：

> 对博物馆的参观者视而不见是一项艰巨的任务。孩子们捶玻璃,用粗鲁的方式对模特指指戳戳,在她们假装忙乎水手绳结时吓唬她们。大人有时冲着她们表演的哑剧叫嚷,做出评论,姑娘们虽然听不清,但那无论如何都不像好话。每隔一个小时,模特们便轮换一次角色,好让单调有所缓和,省得一个劲儿地假装冲洗甲板,打磨捕猎工具,爱抚木头番薯。[①]

科拉的这份不适,不单单来自工作内容本身的枯燥以及白人观众的无礼冒犯,还源于自己在橱窗中作为"被凝视对象"而产生的焦虑感。

在现代西方理论中,"凝视"(gaze)是一个非常重要的概念,它并不是日常意义上的长时间的、专注的"看",而是指主体"携带着权力运作或者欲望纠结的观看方法"[②]。在凝视的双方中,凝视主体可以借此表达内心欲望、施加心理压迫、行使权力规训,以此确立和巩固自己的权威身份;而客体在意识到自己沦为一个被观察和揣摩的对象后,便失去一定程度的自主性,并产生出一种焦虑感。

类似卡普兰(E. Ann Kaplan)的"帝国凝视"(imperial gaze)和穆尔维(Laura Mulvey)的"男性凝视"(male gaze),怀特黑德在小说中呈现的其实是一种"种族凝视"(racial gaze),即白人通过对作为"他者"的黑人进行观察(包括其身体、其劳作与生活方式等),获取一种心理上的优越感,树立自己作为"文明种族"的身份——为了证实自己的人性,白人会有意无意地将"他者"进行非人化和

① [美]科尔森·怀特黑德:《地下铁道》,康慨译,上海人民出版社 2017 年版,第 126 页。

② 陈榕:《凝视》,赵一凡、张中载、李德恩主编:《西方文论关键词》,外语教育与研究出版社 2006 年版,第 349 页。

动物化的设想,突出其原始、落后、愚昧的一面。由此可见,黑奴要获得真正的自由,仅仅去除掉身上的锁镣是远远不够的,还必须打破自身作为“非人”的身份定位,拥有自主选择的权利和文化上的尊严。

值得玩味的是,科拉在博物馆工作期间,想到了一个更适合自己性格的轮班次序,即反其道而行之,从“种植园”开始,经由“运奴船”再到“非洲腹地”而结束演出。这一前后颠倒的安排,犹如时光倒流,不仅颠覆了原先的历史版本,也给她自己带来了深深的慰藉——“在‘非洲腹地即景’结束一天的工作,总能让她迈入一条宁静之河。”[①]这份宁静,来自科拉因打乱官方话语而从中获取的满足感,也来自她内心的某种集体无意识,即所有黑奴对作为“根”的非洲祖地(及其所代表的自由生活)的本能向往;这份集体无意识,由于黑奴对悲惨的现实状况的强烈不满而变得异常活跃。

更为有趣的是,博物馆的玻璃橱窗并不是一个单向的凝视机制(如边沁设计的全景式监狱结构、福柯提出的监视体制等),而是可以相互对视、彼此影响的——身处橱窗里的被观察者也能透过玻璃清晰地看到外面的观察者,甚至采取一定的反制措施,行使属于自己的那一份权利。科拉即是通过这种“反凝视”的方式,用坚定而凶狠的目光紧紧盯住自己随机选定的个别白人参观者,令对方局促不安、踉跄退后。在作者看来,这种类似恶作剧式的回看其实具有非常重要的象征意义:

> 在束缚你的锁链上寻找有缺陷的地方。单独来看,每一环其实不算什么。但是连在一起,便成了强大的铁镣,虽有薄弱的地方,却让几百万人臣服。……这些人从个人来讲,并没

---

① [美]科尔森·怀特黑德:《地下铁道》,康慨译,上海人民出版社2017年版,第142页。

有迫害过科拉。但作为一个整体，他们就成了镣铐。如果她坚持下去，一点一点地破坏她在其中发现的薄弱环节，兴许能水滴石穿，绳锯木断。[①]

这番话，一方面道出了美国种族制度与社会偏见的巨大害处——大量生性善良的个体，完全可以形成一个罪恶的整体，残忍伤害那些无辜的非我族类；另一方面也在暗示，作为受害者的黑人，尽管无力马上改变这一局面，但应坚持抗争、步步为营，终有一天会瓦解这罪恶的制度与偏见。

五、美国的人权之殇

或然历史虽未曾真实地发生过，但却有着强烈的现实指向（有时在这方面甚至超过真实历史）。在《地下铁道》中，怀特黑德以充满想象的方式，讲述了一个真实可信的故事，直击美国历史上最黑暗、最不愿让人提及的部分，亦是美国人权曾经最为脆弱的部分——奴隶制度与种族主义。

作为美国立国之本的《独立宣言》明确指出：人人生而平等，造物者赋予他们若干不可剥夺的权利，其中包括生命权、自由权和追求幸福的权利。然而对南方各州的黑奴而言，这些权利根本无从谈起，因为他们并没有被作为人来对待。

小说中让人印象格外深刻的一个场景，是黑奴迈克尔能够熟练背诵《独立宣言》，虽腔调僵硬、不求甚解，但在没受过任何教育的黑奴当中，这已堪称奇迹。事实上，先前的主人教迈克尔背诵此文，并无意对他进行思想上的教化与启迪，只是为了从中取乐——

① [美]科尔森·怀特黑德：《地下铁道》，康慨译，上海人民出版社2017年版，第143页。

此人对南美鹦鹉十分着迷,于是尝试着教迈克尔背诵长文,因为他相信:“如果能教一只鸟学会打油诗,那么教一个奴隶记点儿东西,八成也行得通……黑鬼的脑子毕竟比鸟的大。”[①]将迈克尔与鹦鹉相提并论,明显是对黑人之“人性”(humanity)的否定,同时也在暗指:黑奴只能像学舌的鹦鹉一样,只学人言,不得人意。对于白人奴隶主而言,迈克尔的功能就是在有朋友来访时,出来背上一段《独立宣言》,博取大家一乐;当主人对此厌倦后,便把他卖到南方的佐治亚,最终被新主人手下的监工鞭打至死。科拉曾多次听到过迈克尔的背诵,虽然她对其中的含义不甚理解,但依然注意到其中的悖论:

> 她听不懂那些字眼儿,最起码大部分都不理解,但“生而平等”这几个字不能不引起她的注意。写出这些话的白人想必对此也不理解,因为“所有人”并不真的意味着所有人。因为他们夺走属于别人的东西,无论那是你能抓在手里的,比如泥土,还是你抓不住的,比如自由。[②]

这番话暴露出美国人权在历史上的局限与虚伪,即《独立宣言》虽然宣称所谓的“人人生而平等”,但其中的“人”,原来是有选择性的,而黑奴并不包括在内。

除了《独立宣言》之外,小说中常常提到的另一个重要文本就是《圣经》——无论是阿贾里还是科拉,都对圣经故事兴趣浓厚,并努力从中获取心灵上的慰藉(尽管她们对其中的寓意一知半解)。

---

① [美]科尔森·怀特黑德:《地下铁道》,康慨译,上海人民出版社2017年版,第37页。

② [美]科尔森·怀特黑德:《地下铁道》,康慨译,上海人民出版社2017年版,第132页。

然而，科拉在《圣经》里同样发现了针对奴隶问题的自相矛盾之处。她对收留自己的埃塞尔询问道：

> “这儿说的我没明白，拐带人口，或是把人卖了，或是留在他手下，必要把他治死。”科拉说，“可是后面又说，奴隶要顺服自己的主人——还要凡事讨他的喜欢。”把另一个人当作财产，这要么是罪行，要么是得到了上帝的恩惠。可是怎么还要凡事讨他的喜欢？肯定是哪个奴隶主溜进了印刷所，加上了这一句。[①]

面对这一疑问，即使是心地善良、同情黑奴的埃塞尔，也援引当时盛行的“含的诅咒”[②]说，来对此予以解释，甚至将黑人比作动物，排除在人的范畴之外：

> 它意思是说，一个希伯来人不能让另一个希伯来人做奴隶。但是含的子孙不属于那个家族了。他们受了诅咒，长了黑皮和尾巴。《圣经》里确实谴责了人对人的奴役，可是压根儿也没说到对黑人的奴役呀。[③]

---

① ［美］科尔森·怀特黑德：《地下铁道》，康慨译，上海人民出版社2017年版，第205页。

② “含的诅咒”(Curse of Ham)：根据《圣经：创世记》9：20～27记载，挪亚喝醉酒后，赤身裸体在帐篷里入睡，二儿子含看到后，告诉自己的两个兄弟闪和雅弗，闪和雅弗背过脸去为父亲盖上衣服。事后挪亚祝福了闪和雅弗，而对含非常生气，并诅咒含的儿子迦南，让其后人世代为奴。后来的部分基督徒据此认为，生活在非洲的黑人即是受诅咒的含的后裔，让他们充当奴隶，是上帝的意旨；在18～19世纪的美国，拥奴派分子也常用这个故事来为奴隶制进行辩护。

③ ［美］科尔森·怀特黑德：《地下铁道》，康慨译，上海人民出版社2017年版，第205页。

从埃塞尔的所言可以看出,白人对黑人的种族偏见,是何等的根深蒂固、难以改变,以至于在奴隶制被废除后,针对黑人的种族歧视依然长期存在于美国社会,一直延续至今。实质上,种族主义不仅仅是身体的束缚和权利的剥夺,更可怕的是观念上的歧视,因为其持续的时间更为长久,造成的社会分裂与精神创伤也更为严重。

历史(以及存在于历史中的人)具有内在的延续性,所以我们对个人的界定,不光要凭借其当下的行为,更要回顾和总结其过去的经历;对于群体而言亦不例外——每一个群体,都不可能摆脱对自己民族历史的记忆与想象而孤立存在,经历过严重创伤的民族尤其如此。所以,怀特黑德构思和写作《地下铁道》这样一部或然历史小说,或许就是想以一种另类的方式"还原"历史情境,继而引导读者重新"回忆"这一段苦难岁月,在此过程中"刷新我们对于这个世界的认识"(厄普代克语),并引发人们对当下世界的深刻反思。

(李锋:上海外国语大学教授)

玛丽莲·罗宾逊小说中的人文关怀[①]

李保杰　郝书苑

玛丽莲·罗宾逊(Marilynne Robinson,1943～)是美国当代著名作家,以其作品中对宗教相关主题细致入微的描写而著称,被誉为美国当今最具人文关怀意识的作家之一。罗宾逊是2013年国家人文奖章的获得者,授奖词称:罗宾逊博士的小说以及非虚构作品勾勒出我们生活中人与人之间的伦理关系,充分探索我们所身处的这个世界,并定义了"人之所以为人"的普世真理。

罗宾逊在文学创作中钟爱家庭和宗教问题,这同她的成长环境密切相关。玛丽莲·罗宾逊出生于美国中西部爱达荷州桑德珀恩特小镇的一个普通中产阶级家庭,父母都是虔诚的长老会教徒,家庭和社区的宗教氛围都较为浓重。1980年,她的小说《管家》(*House Keeping*)一举获得成功,获得美国笔会/海明威奖,入围1982年普利策小说奖,被誉为现代经典。罗宾逊最具代表性的作

---

① 本文是山东省社科规划重点项目"19世纪海上丝绸之路和华工海外流散的文学叙事研究"(项目编号:17BWWJ02)和国家社科基金后期资助项目"美国女性文学史"(项目编号:18FWW002)的阶段性成果。

品当属“基列三部曲”,包括《基列家书》(*Gilead*, 2004)、《家园》(*Home*, 2008)和《莱拉》(*Lila*, 2014)。这四部小说具有内在的相似性,即家庭主题和宗教主题,其中救赎和皈依是最终的目的。罗宾逊还撰写了大量的随笔和散文,如文集《祖国:英国、福利国家和核污染》(*Mother Country*: *Britain*, *the Welfare State*, *and Nuclear Pollution*, 1989)、《亚当之死:对现代思想的思考》(*The Death of Adam*: *Essays on Modern Thought*, 1998)、随笔集《儿时阅读》(*When I Was a Child I Read Books*: *Essays*, 2012)和《万物之道》(*The Givenness of Things*, 2015)。她在2009年获得了耶鲁大学“德怀特·特里讲师”项目(Dwight H. Terry Lectureship)资助,结束之后,她将耶鲁系列讲座的文稿结集出版,名为《心不在焉:自我的现代神话对内心的消解》(*Absence of Mind*: *The Dispelling of Inwardness from the Modern Myth of the Self*, 2010)。2010年,罗宾逊当选为美国艺术科学院的院士,时任美国总统的巴拉克·奥巴马十分喜欢她的小说,赞同其中“向善”“包容”等基督教核心思想,曾与她畅谈数小时,共同探讨美国文化传统和价值观等问题,这成为当时美国各大媒体争相报道的新闻。

一、宗教主题

玛丽莲·罗宾逊被誉为“后现代社会中的信仰坚守者”[①],宗教信仰是其“思想体系中的永恒指向和坐标”[②],“信仰”和“救赎”等是其小说的重要主题。她将宗教信仰视为人之本质和理解人生意义的根本:“我逐渐认识到,我的宗教,当然一般以上的宗教亦是

① 金莉等:《20世纪美国女性小说研究》,北京大学出版社2010年版,第267页。

② 金莉等:《20世纪美国女性小说研究》,北京大学出版社2010年版,第269页。

如此，能够也应该有助于突破这些限制，而从根本上说，这些局限最终归结于对于人之本性的狭隘界定以及在理解人生意义方面的不足。”[①]“爱”“回归”“重生”和“救赎”等是罗宾逊小说中常见的主题，这在“基列三部曲”中尤为突出。

《基列家书》采用第一人称叙述，是艾奥瓦州基列小镇上的牧师约翰·埃姆斯写给年幼儿子的书信集，带有布道风格的叙述正是围绕着基督教伦理展开。埃姆斯牧师写信时已经76岁，古稀之年的他回忆大半生的经历，讲述继承祖父和父亲的衣钵、献身宗教的历程，同时也回顾了与家族历史相关的美国内战以来的发展史，小说中个人的精神成长和国家的历史交织在一起。埃姆斯牧师见证了小镇上人们的生老病死，从而对生命有着非凡的感悟。在他年轻时，妻子路易莎因为难产去世，刚降生的女儿也随即夭折。他在之后的40多年孤身一人，直到漂泊无依的莱拉来到小镇，两人偶遇之后心灵相通，最终结婚。婚后儿子出生时埃姆斯已经年近七旬，他自知难以陪伴儿子长大成人，于是通过写信的方式，记录自己的过去和对孩子的期待与告诫。第二部《家园》以埃姆斯的好友罗伯特·鲍顿牧师离经叛道的儿子杰克的归家为主线，讲述鲍顿家族的历史和主人公的精神成长，深入地刻画了鲍顿家族的秘密与情感。小说开始，年近40岁的格罗瑞遭遇婚姻失败，回到基列镇照料年迈的父亲，因此见证了哥哥杰克的归家。第三部《莱拉》以埃姆斯牧师的第二任妻子莱拉为主要人物，讲述她从蒙昧到皈依的心路历程。小说情节从莱拉的出生、成长、随养母迪尔流浪，到她孤身一人来到基列镇，与埃姆斯牧师相识并结婚，最后以他们的儿子出世结束。故事情节与《基列家书》相契合，由此构建了三部曲的完整故事脉络。该作品采用第三人称主要人物叙事，

① Marilynne Robinson, *When I Was a Child I Read Books: Essays*, New York: Farrar, Straus and Giroux, 2012, p. 3.

对人物的心理刻画细致入微,时间、情节和人物的穿插错落有致,层层展开莱拉的身世,给读者以非同寻常的阅读体验。该作品斩获全国书评家学会奖,以及获洛杉矶时报图书奖等奖项,再次证明了罗宾逊这位杰出作家的实力。

这三部作品的人物和情节具有连贯性,互相填补了空白。《基列家书》的主线是埃姆斯牧师回忆自己的人生经历、与儿子罗伯特分享人生经验,其中穿插了两个次要人物:妻子莱拉·达尔和教子杰克·鲍顿,小说以杰克向教父埃姆斯牧师吐露心声并再次离家而结束,其中涉及埃姆斯牧师和妻子莱拉相遇相恋的部分情节。这两个次要人物在后面的两部作品中充当了主要人物:杰克成为《家园》的主要人物,莱拉成为同名小说《莱拉》的主人公。后两部小说都采用了第三人称主要人物叙事视角,将《基列家书》中缺失的部分补充完整,也从不同的角度对于"家园""救赎"和"爱"等主题进行了多方位的探讨。

与传统宗教主题的文学作品不同的是,罗宾逊的小说对后现代社会中"信仰"和"救赎"等主题进行了再思考,对于"如何获得救赎"以及"谁能够得到救赎"等问题加以重新阐释。这种思想在《莱拉》中有了更加具体的呈现。埃姆斯牧师的祖父是位特立独行的神职人员,他投身战争、参与到了杀戮和暴力之中,并因此失去了一只眼睛,因而外表有些骇人。他晚年时离家到堪萨斯传教,最终客死荒凉的异乡,但他留下的精神财富却广为流传,鼓舞着约翰·埃姆斯和基列镇的人们。然而,从另外一个角度看,他并没有尽到对家人的责任:他倾其所有帮助教众,从晾衣绳上取下衣物或者从床上拿走被子送给他们,儿媳因此不得不把家里仅有的少量现金四处藏匿;他将一家老小的生活置之度外的奉献精神被家人称作"比盗贼还糟糕、比家中失火还严重的灾难"[1]。虽然他声称一切

① Marilyn Robinson, *Gilead*, London: Virago Press, 2005, p. 35.

听凭上帝处置，但实际上真正为家庭操劳的还是约翰·埃姆斯的母亲。这也体现了罗宾逊对宗教生活与世俗生活矛盾的思索。

到了现代社会，“虔诚”和“信仰”有了更加复杂的含义，而“责任”的多维度性也愈加明显。莱拉的养母迪尔犯有盗窃婴儿罪和杀人罪：她将莱拉从生母那里偷走，后来还杀死追踪而来的莱拉的生父；更重要的是，迪尔对此没有悔过之意，拒绝忏悔，被捕后从关押所逃走。但是从另外一个角度来看，迪尔的存在却是对莱拉的救赎：迪尔挽救了莱拉的生命，给予她母爱，教会她生存技能，让她知道生命的尊严。对早年随迪尔四处流浪的莱拉而言，生活是否安逸、能否得到救赎并不重要，重要的是她能够和迪尔在一起：“即便迪尔永远迷失，莱拉也想在她身边，抓着她的裙裾。”[①]在迪尔被捕、出逃后，莱拉与她失去联系，需要独自应对生活，并最终获得救赎。正是有了和迪尔一起生活的艰苦经历，莱拉才能够泰然看待物质生活的匮乏而享受生活的本质，所以在婚后埃姆斯牧师因为年事已高而又无法给妻儿提供丰盈的生活而心怀愧疚时，莱拉并不以为意。同样，莱拉这个人物也不是传统意义上的“圣洁”女性，她的经历诠释了“救赎”的意义：小说隐晦地暗示了她非婚生子的身份，并且她在走投无路时曾卖身求生。尽管如此，她从迪尔那里学到了生命的尊严在于善良和本真：“我一直和异教徒在一起四处流浪。在我看来，他们和别人一样善良。不应该下地狱被地狱之火炙烤。”[②]无惧贫寒、勤劳工作成为莱拉的生活准则，对物质生活的淡泊使这位曾经蒙尘的女子带有了一种圣洁的光辉。正因为这样，埃姆斯牧师将莱拉比作圣经中的玛丽亚，而且小说的故事情节

---

① Marilyn Robinson, *Lila*, London: Virago Press, 2014, p. 21.

② Marilyn Robinson, *Lila*, London: Virago Press, 2014, p. 225.

也契合《圣经》中抹大拉的玛丽亚(Mary Magdalene)①的故事。莱拉的故事也引发了作者对于"救赎"的思考,即何为救赎、何以救赎。

二、社会历史

无论是《管家》,还是"基列三部曲",玛丽莲·罗宾逊的小说都取材于人们的日常生活,"家"成为核心的活动场所,也是小说人物心灵归属的象征,是作者致力于重新建构"灵魂"的证明。其中,家庭中亲子间的代际关系、现代社会对传统价值观的冲击等都成为书写的重点。

玛丽莲·罗宾逊虽然被誉为"人文关怀作家",但是这种人文关怀不能脱离开社会历史而独立存在。"基列三部曲"具有各自的社会历史背景:《基列家书》涉及19世纪50~60年代到1956年大约一个世纪间埃姆斯一家四代人的故事,以美国南北战争以来的社会为历史背景。《家园》集中讲述离家20年的杰克·鲍顿在1956年返乡看望暮年的老父,以及他对家园的重新认同,通过杰克和非裔女性黛拉·迈尔斯的爱情反映尖锐的种族矛盾和种族间事实上的不平等。《莱拉》通过莱拉的经历反映美国20世纪20年代到40年代中期的社会历史,以莱拉和养母迪尔颠沛流离的生活

① 在某些版本的传说中,玛丽亚是耶稣的门徒,在某些传说中玛丽亚被认为是一位耶稣救助的妓女。《圣经》中并没有花费太多的笔墨来描写抹大拉的玛丽亚,而且因为她的传记在一名妓女的传记后面,而被误认为是一个被耶稣拯救的妓女,但是实际上抹大拉是当时权倾朝野的便雅悯家族成员。她不仅是耶稣的追随者,更是耶稣的妻子,她追随耶稣修道,并成为有名的圣女之一。在《旧约》的福音书中,耶稣的门徒莱维说:"他(耶稣)爱她(抹大拉)胜过爱我们。"崇尚女权的耶稣甚至想让她建立和接管基督教。耶稣受难后,为了逃避罗马帝国的追杀、保全皇室血脉,抹大拉隐居法国南部,在那里生下了耶稣的女儿萨拉。这位被误解的圣洁女性是许多艺术家的珍爱,成为他们心中女神的化身。

透视阶级差别和下层人民的艰难生存。人文关怀、宗教信仰和救赎等主题紧紧嵌于社会历史的背景之中，从而使读者得以窥见人和宗教、人和自我以及人和社会之间的多层次关系。

阶级和种族问题是罗宾逊小说中突出反映的社会问题，和信仰问题相互交织，在四部小说中都得到连贯性的再现。《基列家书》的情节涉及一家三代人，故事具有历史感和时代感，结合了个人信仰和美国社会历史。19 世纪中期至 20 世纪上半叶恰逢美国发生重大变革，埃姆斯牧师的祖父致力于解放黑奴的运动，帮助从"地下铁道"逃亡的黑奴，后在内战中失去了一只眼睛；埃姆斯牧师则回忆起基列镇上曾经有过的几个黑人家庭，他们因为无法得到小镇居民的接纳、教堂被烧毁，所以被迫迁移到了别处。这说明即使在一百年以后，种族界限也并没有真正消除，人们依旧生活在彼此隔离之中；而祖父失去的眼睛代表了丧失的视力和判断力，象征奴隶制给黑人和白人都带来巨大的伤害。

种族问题在《家园》中更加明确地凸显出来。故事发生在 1956 年，正值民权运动前夕。虽然堪萨斯的布朗在诉讼州教育局的案件中获胜，但是这只是理论上诉求教育平等的开端，大多数州依旧实行《吉姆·克劳法》(*Jim Crow Laws*)，禁止黑白通婚、黑白学生同校。杰克·鲍顿爱上了黑人女性黛拉，但是他们的爱情得不到法律的许可和家人的承认，所以只能"非法同居"。杰克一家不得不偷偷摸摸地躲避房东和雇主，因为他们的夫妻关系被视为堕落、不体面的，后来终因事情暴露而失去了工作并触犯法律。黛拉的父亲是黑人牧师，但他并没有大爱精神或悲天悯人的普世情怀，而是对白人充满了偏见。同样，对于自己的父亲能否接受黑人儿媳和混血孙子，杰克也是心存疑虑，因而在回基列镇的一个多月里面，他始终没敢向父亲和妹妹道出自己的焦虑。当黛拉带着儿子来找杰克时，格罗瑞一时没有意识到他们是谁："但开车的是个黑人妇女,这是件稀奇事。基列没有黑人。"①杰克本人非常清楚:自己这种行为难以为世人所接受,所以也自认为"行为不端"。小说结尾时,格罗瑞对杰克妻儿的接纳便是"家园"的充分证明,而黛拉看到了杰克成长的地方,也打消了之前对他的一点疑虑:"黛拉满怀柔情地看了他曾经生活过的世界,所有的细节都在那儿得到了证实,证明他说的一句不假,而他的诚实的确一向是需要证明的。"②杰克一家对于家园的回归,正体现了家园之包容和保护本质的回归。小说通过呈现追求幸福和法律规训之间的矛盾,采用基督教中"浪子归家"的范式,实际讲述了两个不同版本的故事,最终合法化了个人对超越种族界限之爱情的追求。

《莱拉》则在阶级的视野下体现了对于"信仰"的思考。劳动营的领头人杜安直接对宗教权威发起挑战,在他眼里,上帝是不公平的,季节工人等底层民众并没有享受多少福泽,他们生活无依、四处流浪、风餐露宿,是一群被世界遗忘的人。他从来不去教堂,因为他认为教会骗取信众的金钱来供养神职人员。不过,杜安有自己的价值观,他相信人之间的平等,坚守传统的契约精神,所以雇主在提供工作机会时,他并不计较是否多干些活儿,从来都是尽职尽责完成任务:"这就是他们的尊严,忍受他们所能够忍受的一切,直到极限,不抱怨贫穷,不自怨自艾,因此孩子们能够在陌生人面前对大人恭恭敬敬。"③杜安所坚守的人人平等是基于人本主义的,他所谓的"人"是不附加社会地位和阶级身份的存在。在季节工人劳动营里,他们创造了这样一个精神的共同体:杜安和妻子恩爱有加,在贫寒中彼此给予温暖;大人们依靠打零工勉强度日,孩子们则在田野里与大自然为伴。因而迪尔从地里拔起的那颗鲜萝

① [美]玛里琳·罗宾逊:《家园》,应雁译,人民文学出版社 2010 年版,第 328 页。

② [美]玛里琳·罗宾逊:《家园》,应雁译,人民文学出版社 2010 年版,第 332 页。

③ Marilyn Robinson, *Lila*, London: Virago Press, 2014, p. 42.

卜的味道，久久回荡在莱拉记忆深处，那段岁月也成为她成长中的美好回忆。然而，这种精神共同体最终在资本攻势下轰然倒塌。随着大萧条的到来，季节工人难以找到工作，一群人的生计成为日日困扰杜安的难题，杜安所坚守的传统信条在现代工业社会受到了严峻的挑战。最终，为了给孩子填饱肚子，杜安去偷窃农场的鸡，并因盗窃被捕。被狗咬伤的杜安几近崩溃，摧毁他的并不是牢狱之灾，而是失去了的尊严。这些穷苦之人对于神灵没有信心，因为他们生活在被世界遗忘的角落中，“上帝对他们没有丝毫的兴趣”[①]。罗宾逊以此在阶级观照之下描写了底层民众对生活和前途的绝望和恐惧，追溯“无以救赎”背后的社会历史原因，并在宗教之外书写了底层人民的另一种信仰形式，即人与生俱来的情感和尊严。

玛丽莲·罗宾逊的人文关怀思想更加明确地反映在非虚构作品中。她在《亚当之死》中表现出对人类未来的极大关注。她对现代社会的进程进行了梳理，讨论“思想的自由”“想象力和社区”“爱”和“人类精神和良好社会”等问题，“对现代思想，尤其是达尔文主义进行了激烈的批判”。[②] 她认为“精神”和“灵魂”等话题不仅是成为文学写作的重点，而且也应该是人类追求的核心所在。在《万物之道》中，她再次对人文主义思想进行了详尽的阐释，提出人文主义的成就不仅在于重新发现古典的意义，同样也在于对他者文明的尊重：“对异教诗人和哲学家的尊敬和关注，对古代历史的研究，为适应现代目的而对古典内容进行的改编，都带有他们各自文化渊源的特点，同时也为几个世纪以来的教育和文化奠定了

---

① Marilyn Robinson, *Lila*, London: Virago Press, 2014, p. 235.

② 金莉等：《20世纪美国女性小说研究》，北京大学出版社2010年版，第268页。

坚实的基础,其影响延伸至今。”[①]由此可以看出,罗宾逊以作品中的基督教思想而著称,但是她的人文思想逐渐超越基督教的视域,扩展至所谓的“异教”,也是难能可贵的。

三、传统观念的重新建构

玛丽莲·罗宾逊在书写“信仰”和“爱”等基督教传统主题的同时,也对现代语境下这些理念的哲学化含义及其对人类生存的意义进行了思考。她说:“现代话语体系对于‘灵魂’一词真的是缺乏兴趣,然而在我看来,失去这个词意味着能力的丧失,不仅对于宗教,而且对于文学、政治思维和人类追求都是如此。”[②]但她同时也指出,灵魂作为造物主的杰作,其建构或者重建不是简单的“救赎”或者“迷途”,不可以仅从是否有感悟为标准来加以判断,人生的体验才是其中弥足珍贵的精华。罗宾逊认为,上帝是唯一的权威,任何人都没有资格对他人进行判断;可以说,这从侧面解读了她对于“救赎”的思考。在《亚当之死》中,她进而对宗教政治进行了明确的批判,提出:“某些人采用还原性的界定方式来解读效用和现实,将对真理的认知归功于原教旨主义的简单化,无法容忍与复杂性、模糊性和补偿性经历相关的事物。”[③]这种立场的结果就是,她一方面坚守了宗教上的本体论,另一方面也接受了后现代主义的解构思想,从而形成了罗宾逊式的宗教人文关怀理念,即在区分“信仰”和“宗教政治”基础上的人本主义。在《基列家书》中,罗宾逊借

---

① Marilyn Robinson, *The Givenness of Things: Essays*, New York: Picador Books, 2016, p. 3.

② Marilynne Robinson, *When I Was a Child I Read Books: Essays*, New York: Farrar, Straus and Giroux, 2012, p. 8.

③ Marilynne Robinson, *The Death of Adam: Essays on Modern Thought*, New York: Picador Books, 2005, p. 5.

埃姆斯牧师之口,多次强调了"权威"的含义。虽然埃姆斯感叹现代生活给传经布道带来了巨大挑战,人们甚至认为"宗教上的虔诚是愚昧无知的表现"[①],但是他最终也看到自己和"浪子"杰克有着本质上的趋同。

罗宾逊的小说描写日常居家的各种细微之事,通过看似平常的生活片段阐释心灵的归属。这种灵魂的归属可能会表现为对"家园"的追寻和建构,也可能表现为生活体验,但是无论是哪种书写范式,都带有罗宾逊式的鲜明宗教人文特征。《管家》和《家园》对"家园"进行思考,可谓罗宾逊小说的首要观照。这种思考呈现出多维度特征:家园既是安慰也是束缚,既为人们提供庇护,也让他们沉溺于幻想。可以说,这一系列小说中,几个主要人物都是在寻找家园:埃姆斯牧师追求精神归属,杰克寻找自我归属,莱拉和格罗瑞两位女性人物寻求安全感。这在次要人物的描写中同样得到了体现。例如埃姆斯牧师的哥哥爱德华早年在德国学习期间接受费尔巴哈的思想,开始对传统的信仰产生怀疑,他认为基列镇、家园皆是虚幻,使人们无法认清自己,所以他回国以后试图改造埃姆斯,让他摆脱"中西部人"[②]的狭隘和保守:"离开这里就意味着走出虚幻。"[③]《家园》的故事就是人们寻找家园的历程,集中体现在了杰克的历程之中。纵观几部小说,杰克一直是"害群之马"的形象,而《家园》也经常被解读为"浪子回头"的故事,《圣经》中浪子回头的故事被认作小说的叙事原型。然而,小说同时也对"浪子"形象进行了重构:这里"浪荡子"的含义与其说是"放浪形骸",还不如说是"流浪",杰克一直在流浪,寻找心中的家园和心灵归属。漂泊感和探寻精神使得他的追求带有了"离经叛道"的意味,而种族

① Marilyn Robinson, *Gilead*, London: Virago Press, 2005, p. 130.
② Marilyn Robinson, *Gilead*, London: Virago Press, 2005, p. 28.
③ Marilyn Robinson, *Gilead*, London: Virago Press, 2005, p. 30.

冲突的历史背景为他的寻找增添了厚重和悲情。

不只是杰克,罗宾逊小说中的许多人物,均带有不同程度的“流浪冲动”或者“流浪意识”。《管家》中的西尔维娅也是一个“流浪者”,她虽然回到母亲家里照看两个外甥女,但依然保留着流浪的“本能”,她和衣而睡,简单的包裹放在脚边,似乎随时准备再次踏上旅程;她不收拾家务,喜欢在湖边四处游荡,带着逃学的露丝到湖上看日出日落。杰克、莱拉、迪尔、西尔维娅、露丝等流浪者在寻找各自的归属,他们身上流浪本能的驱动力,可能源于个性发展和制度规训的矛盾,也可能来自传统和现代的矛盾,体现在个体对于规则的反抗或者是代际冲突。艾哈迈德认为《基列家书》反映出传统与现代的冲突,“体现了现代世界入侵所带来的冲击”[①],只是其语境是基督教的视域。埃姆斯牧师一家三代都是教职人员,他的舐犊之情从他写给儿子罗伯特的家书中可以得到证明,然而他可以肯定的是,儿子将来不会再入教职,家族传统必将走向终结。代际差别和时代背景下的价值观差异在鲍顿牧师父子身上同样得到体现:年轻一代希望社会变革,而老年一代则希望固守传统。儿子杰克阅读宣传共产主义思想的图书,支持黑人民权运动。但是父亲鲍顿牧师则不以为然:“没必要为那种骚乱烦恼。再过六个月,谁也不会记得还有这回事了。”[②]杰克的反抗来自他对规训的抗拒:“我总是疑心,笃信的人们计划着要拯救我。”[③]杰克从年少时本能自发的反抗,到他在跨行种族婚姻问题上的深思熟虑,正是流浪和寻找所造就的成长。归家时的杰克思想独立,吃苦耐劳;当然他依然有着诸多缺点,比如偶尔酗酒,甚至固执地拒绝家人的资助。当然,这部小说中叙述视角的有限性所缺失的部分,在《基列

① Fatema Ahmed, *Return of the Prodigal*, New Statesman, 2008, p. 54.

② [美]玛里琳·罗宾逊:《家园》,应雁译,人民文学出版社 2010 年版,第 97 页。

③ [美]玛里琳·罗宾逊:《家园》,应雁译,人民文学出版社 2010 年版,第 100 页。

家书》中得到了呼应:杰克偶尔酗酒的真正原因正是出于对家人的考虑,因为他不知道他们是否接受自己的跨种族婚姻。所以,“杰克的反叛性始终游移在接受传统与拥抱现代之间……现代性之革命性力量使杰克再次踏上离家之旅”①。杰克的“流浪”旅程实际上是不甘被命运操弄的抗争精神的外化体现。

罗宾逊的人文关怀思想和她的女性观照结合,典型地反映在了莱拉这一人物形象上。莱拉用孤独对抗社会的规训,她从儿时起就学会躲在桌子下向外张望;四处流浪时也常常在城外远远地看着万家灯火,所以孤独感是她看待世界的本能感受。迪尔的爱令她用心去体会世间珍贵的善良,用心底的温暖来陪伴孤独的自我。正因如此,婚后的她还会回到基列镇外面曾经栖身的窝棚,在野外静静享受内心的孤独和远离尘嚣的安宁。在窝棚里,她偶遇从家里逃跑出来的男孩,不顾自己怀有身孕,把大衣脱下来给他抵御夜间的寒冷。她能够理解杰克的流浪欲望,和丈夫一起同杰克促膝长谈。埃姆斯解除了对杰克的芥蒂,也理解了莱拉心中的安全感,从而意识到“寻找归属”是他们三个人本质上的共性,也是超越个体差异的人生之根本。可见,莱拉的存在使得埃姆斯的房子成为真正意义上的家园,让他每次对于回家充满期待。因此,《基列家书》也是埃姆斯牧师讲述自己获得心灵救赎、寻找世俗家园和心灵归属的旅程,正如他对儿子的谆谆告诫:“你的母亲从来不谈她自己。真的,从来没坦陈过她生活中有过怎样的悲伤。这就是她的勇气和骄傲,我知道你会尊重她的这一选择,同时也会记住,这需要你去非常非常温柔地对待她。”②这是文学形象展现出来的女性力量,也是莱拉所代表的人性之“圣洁”的理想。

---

① 胡碧媛:《家园模式的现代性救赎——评玛丽琳·罗宾逊小说〈家园〉》,《当代外国文学》2012 年第 3 期。

② Marilyn Robinson, *Gilead*, London: Virago Press, 2005, p. 156.

玛丽莲·罗宾逊就是这样一位坚守信仰并书写信仰的作家,她作品中的基督教色彩固然浓厚,但是她的书写从"宗教"观照拓展至"信仰"观照,摈弃了宗教政治对个体的制度化规训,关注人物的内心愿望和寻找历程。她的小说通过日常居家主题,提出对于"家园"和"救赎"的思考,在历史、种族和阶级的视野下,书写信仰的力量。

(李保杰:山东大学外国语学院美国现代文学研究所教授;郝书苑:山东大学外国语学院硕士研究生)

受害者变施暴者

——福克纳《押沙龙，押沙龙！》复仇欲火探析[①]

王秀梅

威廉·福克纳（1879～1962）的长篇巨著《押沙龙，押沙龙！》已成为20世纪无可争议的杰作，作者本人也认为“这是迄今为止一个美国人写得最好的一部小说”[②]。美国著名作家和出版家刘易斯·鲁平称这是塑造了迄今为止最伟大、最丰腴的南方的历史形象，也是世界上最伟大的历史小说之一。[③] 小说实际上围绕两个复仇的故事而展开，一是托马斯·萨德本以自己的才智和力量来报复社会对他的蔑视；另一个是被萨德本抛弃的混血妻子与儿女对他的报复。福克纳运用多样而特殊的写作手法，塑造了多个有血有肉的人物形象，他们出于各种原因对社会或对其他人充满仇恨，就好似一座座活火山，“复仇”的欲火在燃烧着每一个人，疯狂的报复最终导致父子反目、兄弟相残、兄妹差点乱伦的结局。究其

---

① 本文是国家社科后期资助项目“威廉·福克纳与莫言生态伦理思想研究”（项目编号：18FWW014）和山东省社科项目“威廉·福克纳家族小说的历史书写研究”（项目编号：17CWWJ06）的阶段性成果。

② ［美］达维德·敏特：《圣殿中的情网》，赵扬译，三联书店1991年版，第254页。

③ 参见［美］姚乃强：《福克纳研究的新趋势》，《外国文学评论》1993年第1期。

原因，正是罪恶的蓄奴制度导致了这一切人间悲剧的发生。

一

故事的主人公托马斯·萨德本尽管出生于贫穷的山区，但年幼天真的他一直过着无忧无虑的生活，并不知道人与人之间有高低贵贱之分。在那里，“谁若花力气圈出一块土，而且说‘这是我的’，那么这个人准是疯了；至于物品，别人拥有的不会多过你所拥有的”[①]。直到有一天，他替父亲去给种植园主送信时，看门的黑人奴隶命令他走后门，这使他感到非常震惊。他一个人躲到山里考虑了很久，突然意识到不仅白人和黑人之间有区别，白人和白人之间也有着天壤之别，而造成区别的原因在他当时看来就是一个人出身的贵贱、财富的多少和社会地位的高低。他突然感觉受到了莫大的侮辱，一个复仇的“宏伟蓝图”在他年幼的心里扎下了根，他要不惜一切得到比别人更多的财富和更高的权力，拥有比任何人更大的庄园，并建立一个永世相传的家庭王朝。他想用这样的方式来反抗社会的不公，报复那些曾经侮辱过他的人。

不久，他独身一人离开家乡来到西印度群岛，凭借自己的聪明和努力得到一个庄园主的赏识，在一次暴乱中救了庄园主，后来娶了他的女儿并生下一男孩查尔斯·邦恩，过上了优越而富足的生活。但萨德本不久发现妻子的祖先“有可能”来自非洲，妻子或许带有1/8的黑人血统。尽管他不说任何人都看不出来，但为了实现自己的理想，为了自己的家族不受任何玷污，他全然不顾妻子的感受和刚出生的儿子，毫不犹豫地离开新建的家而来到陌生的杰弗生镇，开始了第二次创业。

① [美]威廉·福克纳：《押沙龙，押沙龙！》，李文俊译，上海译文出版社2004年版，第219页。

短短几年间，萨德本利用一切手段获得了土地，通过剥削黑人的劳动建立了庞大的“百英里”庄园，成了当地首屈一指的大种植园主，并娶富商之女埃伦为妻，生下一双儿女亨利和朱迪斯。夫妻之间尽管没有什么感情而言，但在他看来这一切已足够了，他需要的就是一个传宗接代和挤进南方上层社会的工具，正如他所说：“我有过一个规划。为了完成它得要有金钱、一幢房子、一个庄园、要有奴隶和一个家庭——自然，也总得有位太太。”[①]曾有一段时间，他和家人过着衣食无忧，令外人羡慕的奢侈生活，并把儿子送到大学接受高等教育。但这一切却是建立在牺牲他人的幸福和剥削黑人和穷白人劳动力的基础之上，他的所作所为为他以后的生活埋下了隐患。他自始至终从没有把黑人看作人，只是一群会说话会干活能陪他打斗消遣的动物，是帮他建立王朝实现理想的工具，即使他的亲生混血女儿克莱蒂，虽然一天到晚服侍他，他却从没有承认这种父女关系，她也从没得到一点父爱。

当初不让他走前门，他就感到受到了莫大的污辱，现在他却拒绝承认带有黑人血统的亲生儿女以维护所谓的高贵血统，他居然没有感到一丝丝的不安，这一切在他看来都是理所当然。出乎他的意料之外，两个儿子居然在大学相遇并成为好友，二儿子亨利把“大儿子”邦恩带回家度假，并极力撮合妹妹嫁给邦恩。为了达到自己的目的，在明知严重后果的前提下，萨德本把邦恩的身世告知亨利，导致亨利枪杀邦恩后也逃离家乡。作为父亲的他，两个儿子一死一逃，却没有一丝一毫的忧伤，他那冷酷自私之心暴露无遗。萨德本的一生就是围绕他的“宏伟规划”，也就是为他曾受到的不公正的遭遇而报复社会，他报复的方式就是拥有比任何人都有更多的财富和更高的权力，建立更不平等的社会。他的梦想一度接

① ［美］威廉·福克纳：《押沙龙，押沙龙！》，李文俊译，上海译文出版社 2004 年版，第 257 页。

近实现的边缘,但南方经济文化的核心就是奴隶制,奴隶制不仅戕害了黑人,而且对白人也是一种伤害,所以萨德本就是奴隶制的牺牲品,他本人及其家族的毁灭就是南方历史的缩影,他的命运就是南方命运的象征。如果不是处在南方以白人为中心,注重血统和出身的文化背景下,他就不会那么看重自己的"规划"。南方一开始就因为实行奴隶制而受到诅咒,萨德本在报复社会的同时受到天罚也就是不可避免的了。他心中只有"规划",没有人性和最起码的道德观念,之所以受到惩罚,是因为他只是盲目地顺从了南方社会的价值规范。他把自己旺盛的精力和超人的才智投入一项注定要受到诅咒、要毁灭的事业之中。他从一开始的受害者摇身一变成为更加疯狂的加害者。

二

萨德本的二儿子亨利在大学里遇到了同父异母的哥哥邦恩,并很快成为无话不谈的好朋友,邦恩成了亨利崇拜的偶像。圣诞节时,亨利把邦恩带回了自己杰弗生的家,这促成了邦恩和妹妹朱迪斯的相见并相爱,除萨德本之外,家里所有人都非常支持这桩婚事。萨德本却整天忧心忡忡,在秘密去了一次南方之后,反对的态度更加坚决,却不给出任何理由。无奈之下,亨利甚至声称即便是放弃继承权也要支持邦恩,并一怒之下同邦恩一起离开了家,之后几年中亨利和邦恩的态度没有任何改变。为了达到自己不可告人的目的,萨德本最终告知亨利,邦恩带有黑人血统,这时亨利的态度骤然改变,反而竭力劝说邦恩放弃和朱迪斯结婚的想法。邦恩提出只要萨德本承认他们的父子关系,哪怕只是一个眼神,甚至不用说话,他都可以离开朱迪斯。面对亲生儿子邦恩,就这个再简单不过的要求,萨德本都不能满足他。邦恩为了得到生父的承认而拒不让步,甚至以娶朱迪斯相威胁;萨德本宁愿亲生子女乱伦也不肯承认他们的父子关系。萨德本和邦恩都不肯让步,为了阻止邦恩进入自己的家庭,亨利在家门口开枪杀死了邦恩,自己也畏罪潜逃,从而引发了一系列导致萨德本家族灭亡的事件。邦恩为了报复生父抛弃他们母子的行为却付出了生命的代价;亨利对邦恩前后截然相反的态度表明他也是一个不折不扣的种族主义者,为了报复邦恩也必须付出失去自由的代价,最后死于非命;萨德本因为种族歧视,一夜之间失去了两个儿子和女儿一生的幸福,王朝再次没有了继承人,宏伟的规划成了空中楼阁。

三

罗沙的姑妈出于自己 35 年仍然无法结婚的愤怒而形成了"对尘世上全部的男性至上原则(就是这原则使她姑姑 35 岁仍然是个处女)的活生生的控诉"①。一开始她就不同意萨德本和侄女埃伦的婚事,加上婚礼的举办遭到了镇上人的抵制,使他们家族名声受到影响,这更让姑妈憎恨萨德本。姑妈是"性格坚强、笃好记仇、从不松劲的女人"②,"即使事过十年还在为埃伦那门婚事的彻底失败而从事报复,以一条在蜕皮的蛇的盲目、无理性的狂怒,攻击全镇、整个人类,通过它的任何一个或是全体成员——兄长外甥女外甥女婿她本人全都在内"③。

而且,姑妈把这种一钱不值的愤怒全部灌输给幼小无知的罗沙。在姑妈私奔以后,罗沙如同继承了姑妈的衣服一样也继承了

① [美]威廉·福克纳:《押沙龙,押沙龙!》,李文俊译,上海译文出版社 2004 年版,第 52 页。

② [美]威廉·福克纳:《押沙龙,押沙龙!》,李文俊译,上海译文出版社 2004 年版,第 55 页。

③ [美]威廉·福克纳:《押沙龙,押沙龙!》,李文俊译,上海译文出版社 2004 年版,第 52 页。

其愤怒。受姑妈的影响,罗沙不自觉的憎恨萨德本,自始至终在整个叙述过程中从未用过萨德本的名字,而称他是注定要给自己和子孙带来灾难的祸根,是“邪恶的源泉和来由”,是“天堂不会要,地狱不敢收”的“该死的魔鬼”,是“恶棍”“吃人妖魔”“浮士德式的人物”,其目的就是要将他“魔鬼化”。她感情激烈,以偏概全,视瞬息为永恒,将萨德本确定为一个僵死的恶魔。她憎恨萨德本,因为是他把姐姐关在他的魔窟中,使她们姐妹不能相见。由于他的存在,她无法同姐姐生活在一起,这加剧了她的孤独感,她的少儿时代是在孤独封闭的环境中度过的;罗沙不原谅萨德本,另一个原因是萨德本不肯承认邦恩的行为导致她假想的未婚夫——她外甥女朱迪斯的追求者邦恩惨遭杀害,剥夺了她幻想中爱别人和被人爱的精神体验。而且,在姐姐死后,萨德本向她提出“试婚”的建议,卑鄙、令人讨厌的萨德本只是想得到一个男性继承人,而不是一个妻子,这极大的侮辱了她,并使她彻底丧失了组建家庭获得幸福的机会,所以激起了罗沙报复他的欲望。罗沙毅然决然离开他回到自己的家中,但求生的欲望促使她撕下淑女的面纱,以自我堕落和自我毁灭的形式报复这个使自己无法生存的不合理的社会,她 43 年鬼一般的室内生活和催人泪下的自白,叙说了一个因压抑而扭曲的女性的凄惨经历。在故事的结尾又是罗沙的出现打破了亨利相对安静的生活,因为误解,克莱蒂一把火烧掉了“百英里庄园”,她和亨利两人葬身火海。所以我们可以说,亨利实际上是罗沙愤怒的靶子,是罗沙间接杀死了亨利,替邦恩报了仇,同时报复了萨德本,使其王朝完全破灭。罗沙是被心理机制所左右,最终报复了萨德本父子。

四

按照弗洛伊德的理论,任何一种感情得不到满足即是一种压抑,无论是一种持久感情的被剥夺、一种习惯的被改变,还是一种业已平息的情绪再次骚动,都是压抑。如果发泄不出来,久而久之就会造成诸如复仇、除恶等各种各样的强烈愿望。人的任何情绪都需要发泄,文学是对情绪压抑的宣泄。《押沙龙,押沙龙!》中主要人物的性格都或多或少的不太正常。黑人对萨德本的侮辱使他受到极大的刺激,这一经历将伴随他一生。当他富裕之时,往日的贫困仍会在他心头盘旋,这也是一个转折点,他必须做点什么来发泄以前的不满和压抑;邦恩从小被父亲抛弃,得不到承认和父爱的他想找回属于自己的身份;罗沙的出生以母亲的生命为代价,父亲的自私、姑妈的怪癖、姐姐的漠然使她在缺失爱的环境中长大;萨德本那个卑鄙的"试婚"计划是压死骆驼的最后一根稻草,这激起了罗沙报复他的欲望。

总之,《押沙龙,押沙龙!》是福克纳的伟大作品,其伟大之处不仅在于作者成功塑造了一个白手起家、创造过辉煌、最终走向毁灭的南方典型人物——托马斯·萨德本,更重要的在于通过几个主要人物的塑造,把美国内战、南方发展史和第一次世界大战等众多历史题材有机地结合起来,反映了作者对美国南方所持有的特殊情感。几个主要人物看似都有点精神异常,究其原因是罪恶的社会制度使人扭曲,不健全的性格是在种族主义、白人至上、社会等级森严等基础上形成的。通过悲剧故事的叙说,作者控诉了不平等的社会给人造成的伤害,被压抑的情绪像火山一样喷涌而出,受害者变施暴者,家庭社会在循环的报复中变得支离破碎,最后大厦轰然倒塌。究其原因,奴隶制和种族主义是南方衰落的道德根源,只有消灭罪恶的蓄奴制,才能真正救民于水火之中。

(王秀梅:济南大学外国语学院教授)

马克·吐温的“撒谎”艺术

薛玉凤

人类对真理的追求是永无止境的，但在极力倡导真善美、抨击假恶丑的同时，却也从未停止过撒谎，尤其是善意的谎言。美国现实主义作家马克·吐温［Mark Twain, 1835～1910，原名萨缪尔·兰亨克莱门斯(Samuel Langhorne Clemens)］更是与谎言有着不解之缘。早在阿德顿·维吉、伊恩·莱斯利、乌特·艾尔哈特等心理学家对谎言进行专业研究之前一百年，马克·吐温就无论在理论还是实践层面，无论在现实生活还是文学作品中，都将撒谎上升到艺术的高度，并将撒谎艺术发挥到了极致。

一、撒谎艺术的理论构建

在题为“撒谎艺术的衰落”(“On the Decay of the Art of Lying”, 1882)的著名演讲中，吐温对撒谎艺术条分缕析，以幽默作家的身份对一群大佬嬉笑怒骂，真真假假，令人不得不服。吐温对撒谎的概念进行界定，对其普遍性、功能、种类及培养方式等进行详细阐述，使人眼界大开。

吐温声称撒谎是一种美德，是人类的“最可靠密友”，有着巨大功能，因此需要精心培养。他断言：“作为一种美德，一种天赋之才，撒谎是永恒的；作为必要时的一种消遣、一种慰藉、一种庇护……人的最可靠密友，撒谎是不朽的。”面对台下诸多训练有素的“撒谎专家”，吐温半真半假地说，撒谎是不可或缺的，世上需要明智的谎言，因此需要学校、父母、新闻媒体等精心而勤奋地培养，因为“谎言若是漏洞百出、不合科学，它往往就会像真话一样毫无效用”[①]。

吐温认为，谎言极其普遍，撒谎是人类固有的本性，人人都是撒谎者，时时处处都在撒谎，谎言各式各样。“人人都撒谎——每天都撒谎，每个小时都撒谎；醒着的时候撒谎，睡觉的时候撒谎；在梦里撒谎；高兴的时候撒谎，悲哀的时候撒谎。”[②]那些以为自己从不撒谎的人，只是对自己的谎言视而不见而已，这是人类文明的耻辱。

既然都得撒谎，那如何把谎撒得既善良又完美，撒出艺术范儿，是门需要刻苦训练的艺术：

> 我们的上策就是刻苦训练自己，使自己能把谎撒得既周全又明智；撒得出于善意而不是恶意；撒得能让别人受益而不是自己受益；要撒得健康，撒得仁慈，撒得有人情味儿，而不能撒得残忍，撒得伤人，撒得歹毒；要撒得漂亮，撒得优雅，而不能撒得笨拙，撒得粗劣；要撒得坚决，撒得直率，撒得彻底，还要翘首昂头，而不能撒得犹犹豫豫，撒得拐弯抹角，撒得战战兢兢，像是这个高尚行业丢了你的脸似的。唯有如此，我们才

---

① [美]马克·吐温：《来自地球的信》，肖聿译，中国社会科学出版社 2004 年版，第 276～277 页。

② [美]马克·吐温：《来自地球的信》，肖聿译，中国社会科学出版社 2004 年版，第 278 页。

能摆脱实话,它们叫人讨厌,如同瘟疫,正腐蚀着我们的净土。[①]

可见,在吐温看来,重要的不是真假,而是善恶。无论真假,有害的就该杜绝,有益的就该提倡。“我们不该提倡有害的谎话;我们也不该提倡有害的真话”,因为“有害的真话并不比有害的谎话更好”。[②] 重要的不是真假,而是利己还是利他,“若能用撒谎去做好事,人就应该总是撒谎”[③],如果为帮助别人摆脱困境而撒谎,连天使都会赞美他心地善良。让吐温哀叹的是,残酷的真话逐渐占了上风,而这些人之所以要说有害的真话,是怕说谎后灵魂不能得救,而那样的灵魂根本不值得拯救。

吐温提醒人们注意“无声的谎话”:“即使舌头不动,手、脚、眼睛和姿势也能表示出欺骗的意思——并且是有意的欺骗。甚至在布道的时候也是如此。”[④]无声的谎言等同于欺骗,即用缄默掩盖真相。许多冥顽不化的实话贩子都非常迷恋这种放纵,以为只要不把谎话说出来,就没有撒谎,完全是自欺欺人。

在吐温看来,撒谎是一门高贵的艺术,是一切艺术中最讲究的一种,比如礼貌用语就是用谎话堆积而成的,是生活中最普通、最实用、最常见的谎言,是美好而珍贵的撒谎艺术。礼貌谎言没有危害,却能免去生活中许多不必要的麻烦,需要善加培养。“讲礼貌

① [美]马克·吐温:《来自地球的信》,肖聿译,中国社会科学出版社2004年版,第283页。

② [美]马克·吐温:《来自地球的信》,肖聿译,中国社会科学出版社2004年版,第280页。

③ [美]马克·吐温:《来自地球的信》,肖聿译,中国社会科学出版社2004年版,第282页。

④ [美]马克·吐温:《来自地球的信》,肖聿译,中国社会科学出版社2004年版,第278页。

的最完美境界就是一座美丽的大厦;从地基到圆顶,它都是用善意而无私的谎话建造的,那些谎话无一不是外表华丽,金光灿灿。”[①]

在演讲结尾,吐温还不忘揶揄俱乐部的撒谎专家,说他们在撒谎方面经验丰富、成熟老到,因此当务之急是进行一番审慎的考察,看哪几类谎话最高妙、最有益,值得大撒特撒;哪几类谎话最好不撒,而区分它们的标准,自然是善恶。100多年后的今天,说谎心理学用无数实验论证了吐温的撒谎理论:谎言无处不在;人人都说谎,不止欺骗别人,也自我欺骗,“我们每天会用到5～200次程度不等的谎言”[②];谎言是一项重要的社交技巧,是人际交往中不可或缺的工具,在友情、爱情、事业等方面都扮演着重要角色;说谎是一种能力,是高智商的表现。“说谎是一件日常生活事件”[③],人们天生都是说谎能手。

二、撒谎艺术的现实基础

为保证自传最大程度的真实,吐温不惜将《马克·吐温自传》(*Autobiography of Mark Twain*, vols. 1～3, 2010～2015)推迟百年出版,但在自传中,他却多次坦诚自己对谎言的看法,并不遗余力地告诉读者:世界纷繁复杂,真实未必就是善,虚假未必就是恶。

演讲过去20年后,两个几乎一模一样的真实故事,一次次印证吐温的撒谎理论绝非空悬来风,而是有着强大的现实基础。吐

① [美]马克·吐温:《来自地球的信》,肖聿译,中国社会科学出版社2004年版,第280页。

② [德]乌特·艾尔哈特、威廉·尤能:《说谎心理学》,高会真、廉德冰等译,北京联合出版公司2015年版,第34页。

③ [英]伊恩·莱斯利:《说谎心理学:为什么不说谎,我们就活不下去?》,杨语芸译,湖南文艺出版社2013年版,第9页。

温在自传中全文引用的真实故事《天堂,还是地狱?》(*Was It Heaven, or Hell*? 1902)发生在豪威尔斯(William Dean Howells,1837~1920)的朋友身上,描述的就是同样的撒谎体系:病危母亲和病危女儿及陪伴在她们身边的人拼命撒谎保密,为的是让患者在忍受巨大身体折磨的同时不再承受精神之痛,临终前心情愉快。听好友讲述这个悲剧故事后,吐温很快将其以故事形式发表,没想到谴责他德亏的信件纷至沓来,但故事展示的正是他一以贯之的撒谎艺术的善恶标准:有益的谎言多多益善,有害的真话应该杜绝。

故事中36岁的年轻寡妇玛格丽特和16岁的女儿海伦及玛格丽特的两个67岁的老处女孪生姐妹姑妈原本过着"没有冲突,没有怨愤,没有吹毛求疵,也没有互相嫉妒"的"宁静的天堂"生活,却因海伦的一个善意谎言瞬间烟消云散,白白搭上一个花季少女的性命,令人扼腕叹息。两个一辈子不撒谎的姑妈之所以不顾医生的禁令,逼海伦去妈妈病榻前忏悔,导致海伦也染上致命的风寒,是因为在姑妈们看来,一是一切谎言都是罪过,假话应该杜绝;二是"责任先于一切,任何东西都不能免除一个人的责任,在责任问题上绝无妥协可讲"[①],而教育海伦是她们的责任;三是谎言会让她们失去灵魂,还有可能来不及悔过就死去。因而,即使为救人性命、救人灵魂,姑妈们也绝不撒谎。面对两个自私、迂腐、教条的姑妈,为母女俩看病的基督徒医生大发雷霆,他认为姑妈们卑劣可怜的灵魂不值得拯救,她们的虔诚既卑鄙、肮脏又自私自利;应该让灵魂为善事冒险,使灵魂高尚,这样就算丢了灵魂也无妨。医生一针见血地指出,两位老淑女满嘴仁义道德,嘴上从不撒谎,可她们一天到晚都在撒那"无声的谎言",她们"用眼睛撒谎,用虚假的语

① [美]马克·吐温:《来自地球的信》,肖聿译,中国社会科学出版社2004年版,第254页。

调撒谎，用放错地方的重音撒谎，用骗人的手势撒谎”，而这些出于伪善的恐惧心理而撒的谎与嘴上撒谎毫无二致。他宣称自己每天都“要撒上百万个谎”[①]，其他大夫也一样，人人都这样。在医生看来，撒谎不是医护人员的缺点，反而是难得的优点，这正是说谎心理学中强大的“谎言治愈力”，即发挥着“安慰剂效应”[②]的能治病的谎言。

两位老淑女被医生的话气得发抖，但为照顾可爱的侄女玛格丽特和被她们害惨的小海伦，她们不得不开始撒谎，竟都变成善用安慰剂效应的好护士，她们自己的精神面貌与健康状况也因此大为改善。在海伦病重及病逝后，她们甚至伪装海伦的笔迹，给玛格丽特写些充满爱意的小纸条。尽管每次撒谎后都心如刀绞、羞愧难当、忏悔不已，但这些谎言使饱受病痛折磨的可怜母亲始终以为女儿健康安宁，确保了一个母亲最后的幸福。姑妈们为撒谎而备受煎熬的良心总算有了回报，对她们来说，撒谎成了她们对母女俩的最后责任：面对责任，你别无选择。对吐温的开放式结尾，相信每个读者都自有公断：天国法庭会判决撒谎的姑妈们上天堂，还是下地狱？

《天堂，还是地狱？》不仅有故事原型，而且具有高度的预言性质，令人唏嘘。故事发表后，另一个几乎一模一样的悲剧故事很快发生在吐温身边：妻子莉薇因病去世，其间他们的小女儿吉恩因肺炎命悬一线，两个敏感的病人之间需要一个高度警觉、能应付突发状况的撒谎者，而这个艰巨的任务竟然落在从不撒谎的二女儿克拉拉身上，令吐温既惭愧又心疼。正如莉薇病逝前几周吉恩所说

① [美]马克·吐温：《来自地球的信》，肖聿译，中国社会科学出版社 2004 年版，第 258 页。

② [德]乌特·艾尔哈特、威廉·尤能等：《说谎心理学》，高会真、廉德冰等译，北京联合出版公司 2015 年版，第 105 页。

的那样:“克拉拉是唯一让母亲坚信不疑的人,因为克拉拉从未对母亲撒过谎,因此无论多么不可思议的谎言从她嘴里说出来,母亲都会深信不疑。”[1]吉恩所言不虚,在莉薇病重的22个月里,克拉拉每天照顾妈妈三四个小时,每天都需要用一打神圣的谎言来拯救母亲的生命、希望和幸福,而莉薇对克拉拉的话果真毫不怀疑,照单全收。可怜的母亲大概做梦都不会想到自打她生病后,从不撒谎的克拉拉几乎没对她说过实话。吉恩肺炎恶化、高烧不退时,克拉拉却满面笑容地对妈妈谎称妹妹正在雪中玩耍,转身还需要对吉恩撒谎,说母亲的病情没有恶化。那段时间,吐温家充满“喜剧、痛苦和悲剧”[2],全都焦灼不安,被蒙在鼓里的妈妈反而是最幸福的一个。为圆下一个又一个谎言,可怜的克拉拉吃尽苦头,多次险些穿帮,让她的老父亲几年后仍然心痛不已。吐温将撒谎艺术讲得头头是道,却是个可怜、笨拙的撒谎者,偶尔不小心冒出来的真话也一文不值,但为防他不小心泄密,他每天只能去妻子房间一次,每次只能待两分钟,其他时间只能通过纸条与妻子联系,一直到莉薇离开人世。真真假假,假假真真,真亦假来假亦真,这就是生活,为善而假的生活。

撒谎是艺术,是美德,需要历练,需要完善。无论是《天堂,还是地狱?》中的两个姑妈,还是莉薇病床前的女儿克拉拉,都为亲人的安危与幸福不得不牺牲自己的德行与准则,不得不迅速成长为满嘴假话的撒谎者。但这些善意的谎言非但不是恶的象征,反而是大善的标志,类似谎言每天都在医院上演。吐温的撒谎理论有着坚实的现实根基。

---

① Mark Twain, *Autobiography of Mark Twain* (Vol. 2), Berkeley: University of California Press, 2013, p. 103.

② Mark Twain, *Autobiography of Mark Twain* (Vol. 1), Berkeley: University of California Press, 2010, p. 105.

作为专业作家与著名演讲家，吐温直言自己撒谎成性，对撒谎颇有心得，有时候甚至分不清哪是真、哪是假：

> 我肯定自己对谎言比这个星球上的任何人知道得都多。我相信我是活着的人中唯一理性对待这个话题的人。七十年前我就熟悉它了。我说的第一句话就是谎言，我假装自己被钉扎了，其实根本没有那回事。从那时起，我就对这种伟大的艺术兴趣浓厚。从那时起，我就在修炼这门艺术，有时为取乐，有时为利益。直到今天，我有时都不知道该不该相信自己，不知道自己是否在撒谎。①

吐温非但不隐瞒自己的撒谎经历，甚至还鼓励、撺掇好友豪威尔斯撒谎，令人忍俊不禁。为和好友彻夜长谈，吐温写信邀请豪威尔斯到他家过夜，却又担心豪威尔斯夫人不同意，于是教好友撒谎："你能否告诉她，深夜回家总是让你很不舒服，或者诸如此类？这种事很容易博得克莱门斯夫人的同情，唯一的麻烦是你得一直撒谎下去，不能穿帮。"②吐温不惜现身说法，可见他在夫人面前撒谎是家常便饭，他很会利用夫人的同情心。同时，他还不忘提醒好友撒谎不易，要留意穿帮。说谎者要小心翼翼地避免自相矛盾；编造的故事要和已知事实相符；必须避免口误；必须记住之前说过的话；要控制自己的肢体语言，但又不能过度控制自己的行为举动，以免引起怀疑等，着实是一门艺术。在给好友的这封信中，吐温用"tell lies"(撒谎)这个双关语来表示"聊天""闲谈"，谎言果真无处

---

① ［美］马克・吐温：《来自地球的信》，肖聿译，中国社会科学出版社 2004 年版，第 280 页。

② ［美］马克・吐温：《马克・吐温信件集》(英文版)，世界图书出版公司 2011 年版，第 290 页。

不在。

三、撒谎艺术的文学再现

在心理学家看来,骗子、艺术家和疯子都是虚构症患者,而演员、剧作家和小说家虽不是说谎,但他们讲故事的艺术手法和说谎极其相似:都捏造情节,并要求观众或读者相信他们。不仅如此,"欺骗是许多作家喜闻乐道的题材"[①],马克·吐温更是如此。在吐温的生活中,谎言无处不在,在他所塑造的文学世界里,谎言更是威力无穷。小说本就是"虚构"的代名词,但它源于生活、高于生活,书中人物就像现实中的吐温一样,对撒谎情有独钟,也使无数读者陶醉在虚幻却又真实无比的文学世界里。

在吐温的多部作品中,善意的谎言无处不在,是吐温式幽默的一大源泉。这些谎言的主人公们有些主动撒谎,有些被动为之;有些撒谎成性,有些偶然而为;有些是自我导向——为自身利益而撒谎,比如为给别人留下积极印象、避免尴尬或避免惩罚;有些则是他人导向——为他人利益而撒谎。[②]

《汤姆·索亚历险记》(*The Adventures of Tom Sawyer*, 1876)的主人公汤姆是高明的撒谎能手,不仅屡屡得逞,还对撒谎颇有心得。他利用一个又一个别出心裁的谎言逃学、逃避姨妈的管教与惩罚,也善于利用各种谎言赢得伙伴们的信任与崇拜,甚至为自己谋利,就像那著名的刷墙故事。汤姆觉得人们都撒谎,至少他所见过的所有黑人都撒谎,而他自己所撒的谎,也不全是自我导

---

① 韩振恒:《从〈哈克贝里·芬历险记〉看马克·吐温对欺骗题材的表现》,《解放军外国语学院学报》1994年第5期。

② 参见[英]伊恩·莱斯利:《说谎心理学:为什么不说谎,我们就活不下去?》,杨语芸译,湖南文艺出版社2013年版,第10～11页。

向。他在学校代同学贝基受过，挨老师一顿鞭子，贝基的父亲撒切尔法官得知此事后对汤姆大加赞赏，说他为救贝基而撒的谎是"高尚、大度、仁爱的谎言"[①]，口气之热烈，恰如吐温在《撒谎艺术的衰落》中对善意谎言的大加赞美。哈克更是在《哈克贝利·芬历险记》(*Adventures of Huckleberry Finn*, 1884)的开篇就声称从没见过一句瞎话都不说的人，而该小说也被认为是"一部集各种欺骗之大成的书"[②]。汤姆和哈克的形象之所以深入人心，与他们口无遮拦、妙趣横生的谎言不无关系。

吐温的著名短篇《百万英镑》("One Million Pounds", 1893)也建基在诸多谎言之上，没有谎言就没有这个耐人寻味的传奇故事。濒临绝境的流浪汉亨利因为一张莫名其妙的百万英镑支票过上锦衣玉食的生活，帮朋友飞黄腾达，还赢得富家小姐的爱情，可谓一步登天。亨利并非有意撒谎，但他也从未主动澄清真相。面对那张真真切切的百万英镑支票，无人关心亨利是不是它的真正主人。恰恰相反，每个商家都立马堆起满脸媚笑，恨不得把所有东西都赊给亨利享用。亨利就这样凭着这张巨额支票畅通无阻，无所不能，金钱的万能地位被吐温展现得惟妙惟肖。

为亨利转运的是伦敦富家兄弟的一场赌博，而为艾德带来好运的却是个恶作剧。短篇《为艾德带来好运的玩笑》("The Joke That Made Ed's Fortune", 1897)的主人公经常被伙伴们嘲笑捉弄，却还是怀着一颗感恩的心，怀揣他们杜撰的推荐信到纽约找商业大亨。没想到歪打正着，大亨大为感动，艾德因此获得大亨的赏识，成为大亨新成立的烟草贸易公司的代表。对实情一无所知的

① [美]马克·吐温：《汤姆·索亚历险记》，成时译，人民文学出版社 2008 年版，第 211 页。

② 韩振恒：《从〈哈克贝里·芬历险记〉看马克·吐温对欺骗题材的表现》，《解放军外国语学院学报》1994 年第 5 期。

艾德对伙伴们感激不尽,把他们都招入公司工作,故事以喜剧告终。机会是为有心人准备的,若非艾德踏实、能干、友好、朴实,也许就真的只能被伙伴们当作笑料,即便有机会也是枉然。况且一切都源自他想去纽约旅行——当时就像环球旅行一样不得了的愿望。眼界决定命运,旅行有时会带来意外收获,这也许是吐温借这个谎言故事传递给读者的信息之一。

如果说亨利和艾德都是被动撒谎,那么短篇小说《与移风易俗者一起上路》("Travelling with a Reformer", 1893)的主人公则是主动利用一个又一个谎言,移风易俗,为大家谋福利,是典型的他人导向撒谎者。这是一位有着高度社会责任感的少校,有勇有谋有担当,爱管"闲事",爱较真,一次次巧妙利用高超的撒谎艺术——漂亮的权术,有效破除人们的种种陋习,维护自己及他人的自由和公民权利,令人心服口服。只要公众利益需要,少校每次都会理直气壮地谎称自己有大舅哥在董事会,问题立马迎刃而解,百试不爽,人们对权威的盲从嘴脸展露无遗。对于撒谎,少校的想法与吐温真是英雄所见略同:"为损人而说谎,为利己而说谎,这是不正当的。然而,为了有助于别人而说谎,为了有利于公众而说谎……就完全是另一回事了。"[①]事实正是如此,读者只会为少校的机智谎言叫好,不会因此觉得他德亏。

《康州美国佬在亚瑟王朝》(*A Connecticut Yankee in King Arthur's Court*, 1889)中来自19世纪康州科尔特兵工厂的工头忽然穿越到6世纪的英国亚瑟王朝,冒充大法师、魔法界的泰斗,利用日全食自救,后来当上亚瑟王朝的终身宰相,试图改变历史。《他是否还在人间》("Is He Living or Is He Dead?" 1893)中的艺术家们也是迫不得已,靠撒谎成名才得以养活自己。有权有势的

---

① [美]马克·吐温:《和移风易俗者一起上路》,叶冬心译,http://www.cnread.net/cnread1/wgwx/t/tuwen/000/020.htm[2020-6-17]。

人翻手为云覆手为雨，为所欲为，而无权无势的小人物无论如何努力，都无法获得该得的利益。无法实现梦想，只有通过投机取巧，梦想才能得以实现，甚至一步登天。吐温用他一贯的辛辣笔调，再次无情地揭露世态炎凉，其社会讽刺手法不漏痕迹，高明之至。这些都可谓是善意的谎言，无论自我导向，还是他人导向，对人对己都有益无害，是吐温所提倡的。而对恶意的谎言，吐温则猛烈轰击，毫不留情。

短篇名作《竞选州长》(“Running for Governor”, 1870)是美国式“民主”的一幅绝妙政治讽刺画，而其核心就是恶意的谎言，是作者所不齿和极力批判的。故事主人公“马克·吐温”代表独立党参加州长竞选，与污迹斑斑的两党候选人相比，他的最大优势是正派、清白，声望良好，可没过几天，伪证、偷窃、诽谤、贿赂等各种莫须有的罪名扑面而来，使他神经错乱、提心吊胆，最后不得不放弃竞选。在吐温看来，所谓“自由竞选”“民主政治”等冠冕堂皇的词汇，不过都是政客们争权夺利、相互倾轧的遮羞布而已。一个正直清白的老实人，很快被各种流言蜚语和无中生有的罪名所包围，众口铄金，使其精神崩溃，根本无法在竞选中胜出。人性中假恶丑的一面在美国竞选中展现得淋漓尽致。大到选举，小到报税，在美国人引以为傲的诚信体系中，恶意的谎言无处不在，《神秘的访问》(“A Mysterious Visit”, 1870)同样流露出吐温对现实的失望。对漏洞百出的美国报税制度，对肆意逃税漏税、为富不仁的富豪们，吐温毫不掩饰自己的厌恶与鄙视，讽刺与批评尖刻犀利，直中要害。

恶意撒谎，以谎治谎，以恶治恶，恶意的谎言在吐温的拟古小说《中世纪传奇》(*A Medieval Romance*, 1870)中对塑造人物、推进情节、决定故事结局更是起着意想不到的作用。男爵克鲁根施坦为攫取哥哥的公爵封号，不惜恶意撒谎，丧心病狂，无所不用其极，其他两个主要人物也都在撒谎，但其性质却又有所不同，需要区别对待。男爵杀人、造假、施计害人，十恶不赦，死有余辜，但他的女儿康拉德却是一个既可怜又可恨的人物。她从小被父亲胁迫，不得不与父亲同流合污，也属于受害者，值得同情。但28岁的她去行使公爵权力后，逐渐开始享受人们的追捧与奉承，直到被堂妹康丝坦斯穷追猛打也从无坦白的念头，甘愿充当父亲的帮凶，直至最后被戳穿，也算罪有应得。康丝坦斯比康拉德小10岁，本是父亲爵位的合法继承人，但未出生就被男爵叔叔算计，不仅失去继承权，还被叔叔的诡计弄得身败名裂，最后又被似乎情投意合的“堂哥”康拉德一再拒绝，起先是个不折不扣的受害者。后来，不明就里的她只因康拉德不接受她的求爱就指认康拉德为她孩子的父亲，也是以害人为目的的谎言，并非吐温所提倡。然而，故事以恶治恶的结局似乎告诉人们：“善有善报，恶有恶报”的良好愿望无法实现，善只有通过恶的方式才能得到善报。吐温对社会阴暗面的批判可谓是入木三分。

吐温那场惊世骇俗的演讲过去仅七年后，英国作家奥斯卡·王尔德(Oscar Wilde, 1854～1900)在文学月刊《十九世纪》(*The Nineteenth Century*)上发表对话体作品《谎言的衰落》(“The Decay of Lying”, 1889)，阐述其唯美主义思想，抨击现实主义与自然主义文学的“极端枯燥”乏味。王尔德认为撒谎是一种艺术，是一种科学，是一种社交乐趣。撒谎就是虚构、想象与创新，是艺术的正当目的与最高形式。撒谎的艺术是美的艺术，需要“最谨慎的研究和最无私的投入”①。为功利目的撒谎是可耻的，为艺术目撒谎则应大力提倡。王尔德与吐温异曲同工，将“撒谎的伟大艺

① [英]奥斯卡·王尔德：《谎言的衰落：王尔德艺术批评文选》，江苏教育出版社2004年版，第6页。

术”[①]发挥到登峰造极的地步。

小说本就是虚构作品，虚构中的撒谎更是谎言中的谎言。但无论是虚构的作品，还是虚构的人物有意无意的谎言，都是现实生活的折射。在这个谎言无所不在的世界，能把谎言塑造为艺术，并把撒谎艺术发挥到极致，为世界各地的读者带来欢笑与思考，是吐温对传统道德观的质疑与思考，也是吐温最大的真善美。

（薛玉凤：浙江理工大学外国语学院教授）

① Sam Sacks, “He'd been there before”, *Culture & Civilization*, November 2010, p. 62.

论梭罗隐居湖畔的功利主义思想

刘春芳

梭罗是美国浪漫主义文学的重要作家，他的代表作品《瓦尔登湖》以梭罗在湖畔的小木屋中隐居的生活为主要内容，展示了梭罗在迅速工业化和商业化的美国，为护持精神世界所作出的巨大努力。同时，作为爱默生的门徒，梭罗对爱默生的超验主义思想的传承与实践，也更加强化了梭罗的精神性和超越性。身为哈佛大学毕业生的梭罗，本来有着获得现世成功的可期前程，但他因受到爱默生思想的激励，义无反顾地选择了最简单、最俭朴的生活方式，去除了一切世俗的繁华与欲望，选择了到湖畔居住的生活方式，将自己塑造成自我精神的代言人。梭罗以极端的方式展示出与商业社会和世俗文化相对立的姿态，使他普遍被认为是追求纯粹精神与纯粹自我的代表人物，是对美国功利主义思想的背离与反抗。

梭罗选择远离俗世，孤身到瓦尔登湖畔的小木屋中，以极简的生活方式度过的两年时光，表面上看是其对物质世界的背弃，对于精神理想的坚守，是反物质、反功利的。然而，通过对梭罗隐居的原因、隐居的方式和隐居的目的的考量与梳理，深度挖掘其行为姿态的真实逻辑，揭示出梭罗隐居行为的功利主义思想内核。梭罗的隐居行为也因此成为美国功利主义文化的一种隐性推动，为美国功利主义思想的发展和繁盛增添了独特的形态。

一、隐居原因的功利因素

梭罗是在 1845 年 7 月 4 日开始到湖畔隐居的。从梭罗的日记和其他的传记材料中仔细梳理便可以看出，梭罗在决定到湖畔定居前一段时间可谓诸事不利，无论是家庭生活还是事业追求都遭遇了巨大的瓶颈，这使他在很长一段时间内处于低沉沮丧的状态。1840 年，梭罗向他倾心已久的艾伦求婚，不料却遭到了拒绝，让他内心大受伤害。有传记作者认为，这件事给梭罗留下了难以愈合的心灵创伤，甚至在一定程度上"封堵了梭罗的婚姻之路"①。

到了 1841 年，梭罗又紧接着遭遇了职业困境。他所工作的康科德学校被迫关闭，他甚至连谋生都成了问题。更令梭罗难过的是，1842 年，他的哥哥约翰因感染破伤风而突然离世，起因只是由于剃刀刮伤了皮肤。这突然的打击使得梭罗悲痛成疾，甚至无法正常生活，大约过了三个多月的时间他才渐渐恢复。然而祸不单行，1843 年，梭罗刚刚调整好身体和心情，打算到纽约去做家庭老师，而他所工作的家庭正是他最为崇拜的爱默生的兄弟威廉一家。原本梭罗一腔热情，充满期待，然而他却无法与威廉一家愉快地相处，他们之间的矛盾令梭罗再次陷入苦闷，他不得不离开纽约。1844 年，梭罗因与友人在公平天堂湾钓鱼之后煮鱼汤，造成了毁掉大片森林的大火灾，让他陷入了名誉危机之中，心力交瘁，不知如何自处。一系列的打击令梭罗的内心无比痛苦，在个人生活、家庭生活和事业道路接连遭受了重创的梭罗终于以非常决绝的方式选择了退到森林中隐居起来。

除此之外，梭罗父亲和哥哥的商业上的失败也给梭罗造成了

① [美]斯蒂芬·哈恩：《梭罗》，王艳芳译，中华书局 2002 年版，第 12 页。

较大的心理伤害。他的父亲和哥哥在当时的工商业发展大潮中，为了创业进行了艰苦的努力，但却遭遇了惨改，几至血本无归。他们的失败使梭罗对于工商业发展持抑制与不信任的态度。因此，他不但从不参与父兄的创业，而且认为他们一心致富的道德观念是错误的，是导致一切不幸，使人与人之间的关系恶化的根源。父兄的从商经历使梭罗对于商业社会产生了强烈的畏惧与厌恶心理，奠定了他日后逃离到湖畔的心理基础。可以设想，如果梭罗父兄在商业大潮中成为获得者、成功者，梭罗的人生也许会彻底改写。

梭罗隐居的诸多原因说明，梭罗的隐居行为并非出自内心深处对自我、对独立精神的执着追求，从本质上讲，这只是他逃避现实生活的打击，为自己寻求安身之所的必然选择，是他在各方面饱受生活的苦痛之后为自己的精神寻求的疗伤途径。他的隐居更多的是一种逃遁，是一种处理情感伤口的方式，具有不可否认的功利性原因。

梭罗的隐居是他为自己的生命之旅所开辟的另一条探索之路、疗伤之路、自愈之路。这个选择从某种意义上成全了他的一种姿态，即特立独行，使自己活成了一面旗帜的愿望。为此，他写下了许多文字，使自己的逃避之旅在文字中获得了深刻的观念意义和拯救意义，使他自己的出世行为神圣化为一种与众不同的生命实验，一种自我赋予的拯救世人于生存苦役的使命感油然而生。但问题是，这种使命感和拯救意义并非出自灵魂内部，因此梭罗根本做不到彻底而决然的隐居，在湖畔生活的同时，他依然较为频繁地继续进行着各种社交活动，从未间断对外界的密切关注。这种参与和关注随着梭罗内心伤口的逐渐痊愈而变得无法忍受，他便无法再安心于独居湖畔的生活了。梭罗最终于 1847 年 9 月 6 日结束大约两年的瓦尔登湖畔生活，以意气风发的状态重新回到社会中来。对于自己突然离开瓦尔登湖的原因，他只用模糊的笔墨一带而过："我离开森林，就跟我进入森林，有同样的好理由。我觉得也许还有好几个生命可过，我不必把更多时间来交给这一种生命了。"[①]如果说文字使他的隐居生活变得隆重而神圣的话，那么文字也使他的离开显得仓促而轻率。

除却令人沮丧的外部原因促使了梭罗的逃离，他选择湖畔隐居的内部动因却呈现出一种悖论。梭罗本人对于隐居生活本质上是不喜爱、不热衷的，他曾在《瓦尔登湖》中坦承自己对隐居生活的抗拒，对凡俗的社交生活的喜爱。

> 我却也不愿意去修行过隐逸的生活，除非是万不得已……我也跟大多数人一样喜爱交际，任何血气旺盛的人来时，我一定像吸血的水蛭似的，紧紧吸住他不放。我本性就非隐士，要有什么事情让我进一个酒吧间去，在那里坐得最长久的人也未必坐得过我。[②]

如果说生活的压力与不幸促使梭罗逃离到湖畔，那么其天性则说明其选择的内在意志。"梭罗认为，真正的向内探索是非常困难，也是有极高要求的任务。它需要的是超越自然的、将人引向精神真理的孤独之旅。"[③]明知向内探索的艰难而有意为之，梭罗表达的是一种生命意志，是为了某种外在诉求的达成。梭罗希望通过隐居的行为，来表达自己的某种认知和某种姿态。他的行为逻辑再次印证了其以实际目的为行动纲领的功利主义倾向，即为了

---

① [美]亨利·戴维·梭罗：《瓦尔登湖》，徐迟译，上海译文出版社2009年版，第283页。

② [美]亨利·戴维·梭罗：《瓦尔登湖》，徐迟译，上海译文出版社2009年版，第123页。

③ Ulf Schulenberg, *Romanticism and Pragmatism: Richard Rorty and the Idea of a Poeticized Culture*, New York: Palgrave Macmillan, 2015, p. 66.

最终目标的达成,他能够说服自己违背天性。从这个意义上说,他的隐居不是精神诉求的表现,而是树立姿态的一种需求,是个人为了达成某种目的的功利行为。

二、隐居过程的功利表现

梭罗在湖畔的隐居生活也并非像后人所传颂的那样纯粹。梭罗的天性原本并不向往隐居,因此他在隐居期间无法安心在湖畔孤独自处,也是可以理解的。事实上,梭罗隐居期间,从未做到真正远离俗世,也未曾真正实现孑然自处,独自与自然对话,达成纯粹的精神自由。

实际上,他的小木屋离康科德镇仅有两英里远(约 3.2 千米),这个小屋离爱默生的居住地就更近了,只有不到 1 英里(约 1.6 千米)的路程。也就是说,他只需步行 10 分钟就能到父母家中,只需步行 3 分钟就能到爱默生的家里。他在两年多的独居时光里,经常回到康科德镇的父亲家中去拿食物和其他用品,而且他的母亲和姐姐每周会给他送来补给。根据理查德·扎克斯所著的《西方文明的另类历史——被我们忽略的真实故事》中记载,梭罗的小木屋绝非他离世隐居的清静之所,他那里经常访客不断,在 1846 年 8 月 1 日,梭罗还曾在他的小木屋前举行庆祝年会,当时挤在这个小屋子里的人达到 25 位。康科德的人们也流传着一件关于梭罗的笑话,那就是“当爱默生先生摇响了晚餐铃时,梭罗就从林中猛冲出来,手里拿着餐盘排在队伍的最前面”[①]。而梭罗每次回到家

① [美]理查德·扎克斯:《西方文明的另类历史——被我们忽略的真实故事》,李斯译,海南出版社 2002 年版,第 19 页。

里就会“将家里装点心的坛子舔个干干净净”①。从这些记载可以看出，梭罗的隐居地点其实就是在离爱默生和家人不远的地方生活而已，他不但在基本生活资料上没有独立，在精神生活上也没有完全独立，他的隐居更多的是一种姿态。

在梭罗隐居期间发生的关于他的抗税的故事，也被后人演绎为一则为了争取个人自由而不惜抗税入狱的英雄传奇，而实际情况远没有传颂得那样威风凛凛，而是颇具滑稽色彩。如果把梭罗抗税的原因与宏大的反奴隶思想相连，自然会使他的行为具备了高尚而正义的内涵。而事实上，这是梭罗对税种的误解所致，因为他拒缴的税款只是地方税，与联邦税和州税没有任何关系，因此，这与奴隶制也便毫无关系。梭罗的拒缴本身并不具备更多的英勇性与传奇性。梭罗与收税员和监狱中的狱长都互相熟识，因此他的狱中生活根本谈不上艰难。第二天，他的姨母便替他还清了税款，他只在监狱中待了一夜。

梭罗的隐居及其在隐居期间通过拒税表达的反抗姿态，从本质上说都是面对社会问题、个体境遇和精神困境的一种功利性应对：通过隐居，他不但逃离了困顿挫败的生活，而且还能树立典范和标杆，使自己成为超验主义思想的践行者。通过抗税，他甚至能够使自己成为时代英雄。

从历史上看，苏格拉底同样是因抵制社会而入狱的人。但是，苏格拉底的反抗却带有极清晰的体系性和极深刻的哲学性。当时雅典监狱对苏格拉底的罪名是“亵渎神明”和“腐化青年”，而这项罪名背后体现的是苏格拉底与雅典民主派在其民主态度上的截然不同，是苏格拉底坚守自己的民主思想与逻辑体系的必然结果。最后苏格拉底拒绝和解，自愿赴死，同样是其对自己所坚持的哲学

① ［美］理查德·扎克斯：《西方文明的另类历史——被我们忽略的真实故事》，李斯译，海南出版社2002年版，第24页。

思想的最后支撑。他的死,本身是其对自身哲学体系的完善和对自身思想体系的坚持。或者说,他的死成全了他的思想,是理性和智慧的必然结果。而梭罗的反抗则不具备这种深刻性与逻辑性,否则他不会因为其亲人为其交税后而若无其事,更不会允许其亲人在之后多次为其交税。他的拒税只是一种姿态的表达,表达之后便与社会各安其所,既没有反抗的最后宗旨,更没有反抗之后如何建构起新型体系的思想基础。苏格拉底的反抗具有明显的超越性,是其哲学思想的一种体现方式,梭罗的反抗则没有思想意义和哲学意义上的超越性,也没有苏格拉底的哲学深度。梭罗的全部努力在于展示一种姿态:"他把个体发展视为社会的唯一目标,个人的道德感则是制度的唯一考验和最终保障。"①梭罗的抗税是一种纯粹的个体行为,是其通过隐居行为树立个体形象的一种途径。

学者们更多的将梭罗的反抗之举与印度的甘地进行对比,将梭罗的反抗行为与甘地的"非暴力不合作"在思想精神进行类比。而无论从行为范畴和目标指向来说,梭罗的反抗行为都无法与甘地的相提并论。"非暴力不合作"的斗争法是甘地在长期的斗争过程中形成的独特理论,他认为"非暴力"是人类的天性,动用暴力是动物性法则,而人则是非暴力的。正因为自身思想体系的支撑,他才在多次印度民族运动中,坚持用绝食等方式与英国殖民统治者对抗,拒绝暴力抵制。无论他的抵制结果成功与否,甘地都不可置疑地是成熟思想体系的执行者,是成熟的政治理论的践行者。他的思想体系在人类历史上也自成一家。梭罗的抵制行为与甘地相比,无论在其成熟性、体系性还是影响力上,都绝非同一层次和同一范畴。梭罗既没有成熟的思想体系所支撑,他的反抗只是一介平民的个体行为,是一个饱受生活挫折的人的自救行为,是大胆地

---

① Max Lerner, "Thoreau: No Hermit", ed. Sherman Paul, *Thoreau: A Collection of Critical Essays*, Englewood Cliffs: Prentice-Hall Inc., 1962, p. 21.

表达个体意愿与个体价值的行为。这种行为当然具备勇敢性和开拓性，无疑是对美国文化体系中大胆标新异的思想一脉相承，是其开拓新领域、尝试新方法的一种表现形式，但并不具备更加深刻的体系性与更加广泛的影响性。梭罗的反抗方式是个体的、应激的，没有苏格拉底的哲学厚度，也没有甘地的民族广度。梭罗只代表自己，或者说代表了美国的普通平民的抗争与情绪，是一种激情的外化。霍桑曾与梭罗有过接触，在霍桑的印象中，梭罗是"天性非常狂野的人"[①]，从这个侧面可以看出梭罗的性格特质，在其沉静的外表之下，他的天性还是非常不羁和狂放的，并不是可以深刻思考的人，而是激情难抑的人。因此抗税行为没有体系化的思维模式做支撑，只是梭罗强化个体姿态的一种随机反应。从这个意义上说，梭罗的抗税故事为其隐居行为笼罩了英雄主义和理想主义的光芒，极大地提升了其志在树立的高大形象。

这些看似还原了历史真相的记载与故事，在某种程度上打破了梭罗的精神典范的形象，破坏了其神话一般的光环与色彩。然而，这种还原究其根本只是事件表象的一种还原，而事件内核中所承担与传达的精神价值，却不是这些以具体数字和具体话语能够表现与揭示的。梭罗在瓦尔登湖畔的两年隐居生活也许并不像一些读者想象中那样孤独、与世隔绝和超然于世外，而梭罗的入狱经历也并不带有宁死不屈、大义凛然的英雄主义色彩。然而，正是这些并不具备完美光环的事件，仍然确定无误地展示出梭罗想要传达给世人的观点与价值。

① Nina Baym, Ronald Gottesman, Laurence B. Holland, *The Norton Anthology of American Literature*, New York: W. W. Norton & Company Inc., 1989, p. 1308.

三、隐居行为的功利指向

梭罗选择违背内心意愿在湖畔隐居的行为,在当时也属惊世之举,而他隐居的核心目的也是通过这种引人注目的举动,"进行经济独立的实验"[①],旨在为公众演示一种独立自主的生活方式,为美国文化的独立和自由提供最生动、最现实的例证。梭罗通过具体的实践进行思想展示,通过平实的文字宣扬理念,表现了清晰的现世利益诉求及功利思想。他的行为与美国的拓荒精神高度契合,传承了北美移民开拓未知、建构崭新天国的文化性格,对美国文化注重目的达成、注重实际效果的功利主义思想起到了丰富与推进的作用。

首先,湖畔隐居行为是梭罗的具体实践。梭罗认为:"无论多么古老的思想和行为方式,不经过证实就不能轻信。"[②]这句话体现了梭罗非常积极的实践精神,即一切都要经过自己的实践才具有可信度,不能简单地将古老的思想与传统继承下来。一切思想是因为其对实践有指导作用才有价值,存在的时间是否长久不是考量思想价值的尺度。而这种一切经过自己实践的思想背后,则是一种根深蒂固的功利主义思想,是一种选择有用的、可证明、可实践的行为的思想。梭罗将其湖畔生活的经历记录在著名的《瓦尔登湖》中,表达的是同一种观点,即衡量一切思想观念的尺度是看它是否有实际的效果作用。"他的艺术禀赋与扬基实用主义精神相结合,形成了一种气质与有机理论,使他对有抽象真理的实践

---

① Richard J. Schneider, "Walden", ed. Joel Myerson, *Henry David Thoreau*, Shanghai: Shanghai Foreign Language Education Press, 2000, p. 93.

② [美]亨利·戴维·梭罗:《瓦尔登湖》,王家湘译,北京十月文艺出版社 2009 年版,第 7 页。

不感兴趣。”[①]因此，与其说他的《瓦尔登湖》是一部散文，毋宁说它是“一种公开探索的实验报告”[②]。他认为：“一个哲学家不仅需要深奥的思想，甚至不仅是要建立一个党派，而是要热爱智慧的哲理，并按照它的要求过纯朴、独立、宽厚和信任的生活。不仅从理论上，而且从实际上解决生活中的一些问题。”[③]“解决问题”是梭罗这一系列论证的焦点，即他所信奉的思想，所坚持的理论，最终目的是解决问题，是对实际的生活产生具体的作用。“梭罗试图证明自我文化或者自我思潮，或者也许可以说是自我风格，都应该指向道德改良或者进步。这是一种道德责任意识，这种意识最终会促进社会改良。”[④]梭罗的隐居行为的确对他个人起到了解决问题的作用，同时也起到了向社会树立道德范式，引导社会关注自然、关注心灵、关注精神自我的作用。由此可见，梭罗进行孤独旅程的原因有着明确的社会指向和社会功用，他的目的是通过自我的行为方式唤醒社会改良的意识，其功利主义指向不言自明。

除此之外，梭罗在创作中也体现出功利主义目的。他的代表作《瓦尔登湖》的写作带有明显的功利色彩。梭罗在撰写和出版《瓦尔登湖》之前，曾经受过现实的打击。梭罗在瓦尔登湖居住期间，其创作的首部作品《康科德与梅里马克河上的一周》问世：这部作品于 1849 年由波士顿的詹姆斯·门罗出版。然而，这次出版最后证明只是一场出版界的灾难，当时一共印刷了 1000 册，“只卖出

① Leo Stoller, “Thoreau’s Doctrine of Simplicity”, ed. Sherman Paul, *Thoreau: A Collection of Critical Essays*, Englewood Cliffs: Prentice-Hall Inc., 1962, p. 38.

② [美]罗伯特·米尔德：《重塑梭罗》，马会娟、管兴忠译，东方出版社 2002 年版，第 99 页。

③ [美]亨利·戴维·梭罗：《瓦尔登湖》，王家湘译，北京十月文艺出版社 2009 年版，第 14 页。

④ Ulf Schulenberg, *Romanticism and Pragmatism: Richard Rorty and the Idea of a Poeticized Culture*, New York: Palgrave Macmillan, 2015, p. 66.

了 219 册,梭罗不得不向门罗支付了 290 美元的出版费用”[①]。这次出版的失败使得梭罗的《瓦尔登湖》的出版受到阻碍,詹姆斯·门罗取消了他曾经允诺的出版计划。这个事件对梭罗造成了一定影响,而他在对待《瓦尔登湖》的写作与出版时,显然接受了以前的教训。为了使《瓦尔登湖》顺利出版,梭罗根据读者品味和市场需求对创作方法进行了较大的改变。以清教移民为主体的美国文化市场,无论从主张勤俭朴素的信仰出发,还是从建设新大陆的具体使命来看,都不可能推崇和欢迎华丽精美的文学作品。于是,梭罗在《瓦尔登湖》开创了极为平凡朴实的文风,旨在受到当时读者的欢迎。及至梭罗离世之时,他又花费了巨大的精力将其发表过和未发表的作品一一作了整理和完善,并将其留给了寡母和一生未婚的姐姐,希望这些作品为家人带来收益。从梭罗的这些行为可以看出,他对物质利益的一贯关注,体现出他的行为背后的功利主义逻辑。

梭罗的隐居湖畔行为的功利因素,从根源上讲是对美国功利主义文化的传承与丰富。美国的移民构成、荒野生存、独立战争等建构历史,使得美国人必须去除与其生存目标没有直接关联的浮华表象,以个体的生存为逻辑起点的功利主义因此盛行。梭罗通过湖畔木屋的生活范式,承接了美国移民的拓荒精神,向大众做出在商业社会继续拓荒使命的示范,传递出与荒野精神相伴生的功利主义价值取向。正如北美移民是通过“五月花”号长途跋涉而来,梭罗则是到了距家乡几千米外的湖畔,他将湖畔隐居视作生命荒野的开拓。梭罗所努力挖掘的“是大多数人都认为是荒野废地,一眼看上去毫无价值的那些地方:都是那些地处边缘的荒郊野外、

① Walter Harding, “Thoreau's Reputation”, ed. Joel Myerson, *Henry David Thoreau*, Shanghai: Shanghai Foreign Language Education Press, 2000, p. 2.

人迹罕至之处。这些地方在任何人看来显然都是些丑陋的地方"[①]。这些被所有人忽略与放弃的丑陋之处,从某种意义上说更像是美国的象征,梭罗的行为是对美国这样一个崭新国家的致敬。他把所有的笔墨献给这些地方,既体现了他对美国的信心与热爱,又体现了他对于美国精神的一种诠释与传播——美国作为新的国家,能够展示给世界的就是其对"新"的热爱与崇敬。"新"对于他有着无可替代的至关重要的意义。"他厌恶任何衍生或者二手的东西……他站在智力与道德的最前沿,不断地挖掘并探寻拓荒者们最初的激情与迫切感。"[②]在新的疆域中探索新的价值观与道德体系,探索生命所可能具有的新的形态与观念,是梭罗的任务,也是美国的任务。

尽管有功利主义思想的存在,但却不可否认梭罗是美国浪漫主义作家中对物质追求最为淡泊的一位,事实上,他的确也曾将大部分精力用在完善精神方面。例如,他晚年时把精力都投入在植物学研究中,爱默生认为"他那些写作大部分根本就无法完成"[③]。也就是说,他并非纯粹意义上的功利主义者,他同时也有与现实利益无涉的精神追求。梭罗这种以精神追求出发,但未因此彻底摒弃现实的姿态,从某种意义上说,是美国作家普遍不可避免地带有功利主义色彩的根源之一,是美国社会的平民特色的体现,也是美国特殊的文化性格的体现。

通过隐居行为,梭罗的确如愿以偿地成为美国文化史上独树一帜的人物,他建在湖边的木屋已经演变为一种文化隐喻,表达着

---

① Andrew Menard, *Learning from Thoreau*, Athens: The University of Georgia Press, 2018, p. 118.

② Max Lerner, "Thoreau: No Hermit", ed. Sherman Paul, *Thoreau: A Collection of Critical Essays*, Englewood Cliffs: Prentice-Hall Inc., 1962, pp. 21-22.

③ Walter Harding, "Thoreau's Reputation", ed. Joel Myerson, *Henry David Thoreau*, Shanghai: Shanghai Foreign Language Education Press, 2000, p. 4.

一介没有地位、没有背景的平民对于个人价值的深度自觉。他通过彻底地拒绝喧嚣、拒绝社会、拒绝物质的方式,为美国浪漫主义文学注入了勇于开拓的新鲜元素。他独居湖边的生活方式,是对美国当时普遍生活方式的一种背离,是对新的生活方式的一种大胆尝试,是美国文化中的功利主义思想的一种继承和发扬,更是一种亲力亲为的展示与发扬。

(刘春芳:上海海洋大学外国语学院教授)

《灰色的马，灰色的骑手》中的创伤叙事

吕　惠

1918 年，西班牙流感肆虐全球，这场流感是世界现代史上最严重的瘟疫，全世界总死亡人数估计在 2000 万到 5000 万之间，美国是遭受瘟疫侵害最严重的国家之一，28％的美国人受到感染，约 67.5 万美国人死于西班牙流感，给一代人的心灵带来创伤。[①] 美国著名女作家凯瑟琳·安·波特就是无数感染了西班牙瘟疫，直面死亡的受害人之一，幸运的是，虽然当时已经被医生宣判了死刑，但是波特在染病半年后奇迹般病愈。20 年后，她以此次经历为基础，创作了著名中篇小说《灰色的马，灰色的骑手》。这篇作品是美国文学史上不多见的关于西班牙流感瘟疫的创伤叙事文本。

① Louis Kaplan, *American Exposures*: *Photography and Community in the Twentieth Century*, Minneapolis: University of Minnesota Press, 2005, p. 23.

一、《灰色的马,灰色的骑手》中的瘟疫创伤叙事

《灰色的马,灰色的骑手》作品最初发表于 1938 年,后被收录在第二年出版的同名小说集中。这部中篇小说取材于作者感染西班牙流感的亲身经历,是波特最具自传色彩的作品。作者本人在 1956 年的一次采访中曾经谈到这段经历:

> 我遇到了一个男孩,他是陆军中尉。……我们在一起的时光很短暂,我们彼此深爱着对方,可是我们太害羞了,总是进一步退两步。……后来,我因为西班牙流感病倒了,他们都放弃了对我的治疗,连报纸上都排印了我的讣告。我读过我的父亲和妹妹的通信,他们在商量如何安排我的葬礼。……我知道我快要死了。
>
> "那么那个男孩呢? 波特小姐?"
>
> "就是这个故事(指《灰色的马,灰色的骑手》)。……他死了。这是真实的故事。……
>
> 对我来说,我当时似乎真的死了,我死过一次了,在那之后我就再也不害怕死亡了。"①

值得注意的是,作者于 1918 年感染了瘟疫,但是直到 1932 年才动手写作《灰色的马,灰色的骑手》,发表时已经到了 1938 年。在病愈出院后,波特返回自己的报社继续工作,从未提及这场个人劫难。显然,波特是在有意识地压抑自己对于这场瘟疫的痛苦记

---

① *Denver Post*, 22 March 1956, 29C, quoted in Joan Givner, *Katherine Anne Porter: A Life*, Athens: The University of Georgia Press, 1991, pp. 127-128.

忆，但是记忆并没有消失。1932年，“她在瑞士的时候，看到窗外的群山，想起自己一战末期在科罗拉多州丹佛市所经历的一切”[①]。这才开始着手写作《灰色的马，灰色的骑手》，通过回忆，勇敢地面对这场瘟疫给自己带来的创伤。

在《灰色的马，灰色的骑手》中，作者采用了两种创伤叙事中常用的叙事手段：回忆和梦境。波特使用了大量与记忆相关的动词，比如“remember”“reminder”“memory”“forget”等，将压抑在潜意识里的痛苦回忆转成意识中的叙述。精神病理学是当代创伤理论的起源之一，其奠基人弗洛伊德认为，创伤性神经病患者“常在梦里召回其创伤所由产生的情景”[②]。可见，梦境也是回忆的另外一种形式。在《灰色的马，灰色的骑手》中，作者也大篇幅地使用梦境来叙述自己的创伤记忆。故事的开始就是女主人公米兰达充满各种死亡意象的梦境。米兰达梦见自己躺着的那张床“已经有太多的人死在这张床上了，有太多太多祖传的骨制品摆在壁炉架上”[③]。接着，她又梦见了一个陌生人，米兰达死去的亲人都喜欢“这个瘦长，浑身泛绿的陌生人”[④]。这个陌生人还骑着一匹灰色的马。灰色的马是死神的坐骑，而且这个陌生人面色苍白，显然，这个陌生人就是死神本尊。接着，米兰达梦见自己也骑上了一匹象征死亡的灰色小马，并且对灰色小马说，“我们一定要比死神和

---

① Joan Givner, *Katherine Anne Porter: A Life*, Athens: The University of Georgia Press, 1991, p. 280.

② ［奥］西格蒙德·弗洛伊德：《精神分析引论》，高觉敷译，商务印书馆2003年版，第122页。

③ Katherine Anne Porter, *The Collected Stories of Katherine Anne Porter*, New York: Harcourt, 1979, p. 269.

④ Katherine Anne Porter, *The Collected Stories of Katherine Anne Porter*, New York: Harcourt, 1979, p. 269.

魔鬼跑得快”[①],表现出强烈的求生欲望。米兰达从梦中醒来后,“一个词在她脑海中突然冒了出来,好像是响起一声警铃,大声警告她,让她想起她在睡梦中,而且只有在睡梦中高兴地想不起来的那件事情。战争,警铃提醒她。她摇摇头。她穿着拖鞋,两只脚懒洋洋地悬空摇晃着,她不由地想起坐在报馆办公室里她的办公桌上各种各样人的那副模样”[②]。

除了梦境和回忆之外,作者还通过米兰达片段式的、非线性的叙事来逐渐完成自己对于患病过程的记忆。当她从梦境回到现实,她回想起了这些天来自己是如何渐渐发现自己感染了可怕的西班牙流感的。“她回想起自己几天前就开始头火辣辣地、隐约地疼痛”,事实上几天前“黄昏就开始痛了”。[③] 后来,米兰达的症状越来越严重,最后终于病倒了。并且病情已经非常严重,意识开始变得模糊,作者以米兰达的角度回忆自己岌岌可危的状态:

> 她不出声了,毫不费力地在黑暗中越沉越深,最后她像一块石头似的躺在最遥远的生命底层,知道自己又瞎又聋,说不出话,不再感觉到自己身体的各个部分,完全摆脱对人生的一切关心。……一切理性的概念、合理的疑问、一切血肉联系和七情六欲都从她身上渐渐消失,化为乌有,只剩下一颗微小而光线强烈的生命的火星。[④]

---

① Katherine Anne Porter, *The Collected Stories of Katherine Anne Porter*, New York: Harcourt, 1979, p. 269. 典出《圣经·新约·启示录》第6章第8节:“我看到一匹灰色的马,骑在马上的名字叫作死亡。”

② Katherine Anne Porter, *The Collected Stories of Katherine Anne Porter*, New York: Harcourt, 1979, pp. 270-271.

③ Katherine Anne Porter, *The Collected Stories of Katherine Anne Porter*, New York: Harcourt, 1979, pp. 274.

④ Katherine Anne Porter, *The Collected Stories of Katherine Anne Porter*, New York: Harcourt, 1979, pp. 310.

这时就像很多濒临死亡的人一样，米兰达回忆起了自己的童年："她的回忆转到另一个地方漫游起来，这个地方她一开始是认识和非常喜欢的，现在只看得出一个个断断续续的情景。"①

在《灰色的马，灰色的骑手》中，作者通过回忆、梦境、非线性叙述的叙事等手法，不仅将个人的瘟疫创伤经历记录了下来，而且也记录了瘟疫对美国人民和社会，包括美国的医疗系统带来的巨大创伤，成功地把个人创伤和集体创伤连接了起来。正如美国历史学家阿尔弗雷德·克罗斯比所说："在所有文学作品中，《灰色的马，灰色的骑手》对 1918 年的美国社会状况进行了最为准确的描述"，"对历史学家也有借鉴意义"。②

二、《灰色的马，灰色的骑手》中的情感创伤叙事

和米兰达对瘟疫创伤叙事交织的是个人情感创伤叙事：自己深爱的青年军官亚当因为照顾自己染上瘟疫，在奔赴欧洲战场之后去世。这对于米兰达来说是巨大的伤痛，因为这种创伤还交织着对亚当的内疚。

米兰达和亚当是在她病倒前约十天认识的，两人很快陷入热恋，但是当时的亚当已经被征召，即将到欧洲战场参加一战。欧洲战场也是瘟疫横行，所以两人面临的危险是一样的，爱情是他们生活中唯一的快乐和希望。为了让分别前的最后时光过得愉快，两人都小心翼翼地避免谈及瘟疫和死亡的话题，但是瘟疫带来的死

---

① Katherine Anne Porter, *The Collected Stories of Katherine Anne Porter*, New York: Harcourt, 1979, pp. 298.

② Alfred W. Crosby, *America's Forgotten Pandemic: The Influenza of 1918*, Cambridge University Press, 2003, p. 318.

亡却无处不在。在散步的时候,他们"尽可能地继续他们的闲谈",而当送葬队伍不断地从他们眼前经过,他们已经无法回避时,亚当用"这种古怪的新疾病"来形容这场瘟疫,还说"别让它败坏我们的兴致"[①],以此来尽量减弱瘟疫带来的沉重的死亡氛围。

尽管亚当细心地避免提及或者少提及让他们不愉快的话题,但是他仍然无法把自己的恋人完好地保护起来。瘟疫和死亡仍然在不知不觉地逼近米兰达。米兰达的症状越来越严重,最后终于病倒了。但是由于病人太多,医院派不出救护车,也没有床位,所以亚当决定在米兰达的住所照顾她。这时,他们才不得不面对现实。亚当告诉米兰达:"真是要多糟糕有多糟糕,所有的剧院和几乎所有的商店和饭馆都关了门;街上整天都是出殡的队伍和救护车。"[②]两人在等待医院的救援过程中渐渐感到绝望,米兰达不由自主地想起了一首述说死亡的黑人圣歌,歌词中就包含着这篇作品题目中的死亡意象:"灰色的马,灰色的骑手,已经带走了我的爱人……"米兰达意识到自己可能死亡的危险,最后表达了自己对亚当的爱。万幸的是,米兰达最后终于等到了救护车,并被送到了医院接受治疗,但是情况已经十分危急。

就在米兰达濒临死亡的时候,亚当已经迫不得已地离开了她,开赴同样被瘟疫笼罩的欧洲战场。两个多月后,米兰达痊愈了,护士告诉她战争已经结束了。然而,战争的结束并没有给米兰达带来生命的希望和她渴望的爱情,她即将面临更大的精神打击。亚当的战友写信告诉她,亚当在欧洲战场死于西班牙流感。一开始,米兰达并没有表现出悲伤,因为她还不敢面对亚当已死的消息,心

① Alfred W. Crosby, *America's Forgotten Pandemic: The Influenza of 1918*, Cambridge University Press, 2003, p. 281.

② Alfred W. Crosby, *America's Forgotten Pandemic: The Influenza of 1918*, Cambridge University Press, 2003, p. 300.

理的保护机制使她有意识地逃避这一消息,“她把一封封信折好,放回原来的信封”[①]。然后,她装作若无其事地和护士、同事讨论起出院的安排。可是当她回到自己的住所,便再也无法逃避亚当死亡的事实了。曾经在这里,照顾他的亚当由充满生命力的青年士兵变成了幽灵,米兰达的心理遭到重大打击。不过,她努力克服痛苦,接受事实:

> 亚当好像一下子就来到她身边了,看不见却十分急迫地出现了。是一个幽灵,但是却比她还要生机勃勃。这是她内心为了欺骗自己制造的最后的谎言。虽然知道是假的,但是她还是不放弃这个谎言,不放弃自己痛苦愿望制造出来的假象。她说“我爱你”,然后颤抖着站起来,试图单凭意志力,使他出现在她的眼前。要是我能把你从坟墓中叫起来的话,我就会那样做。如果我可以看见你的幽灵,我会说,我相信……“我相信,”她大声说。“啊,让我再看一次。”房间里静悄悄的,空空如也,那个鬼魂离开了房间,被她冷不丁地站起身,大声地说话吓跑了。她清醒过来,好像刚睡醒似的。啊,不行,这样下去可不行,我再怎么也不能这样失魂落魄了,她提醒自己。[②]

弗洛伊德在自己的重要文章《悲悼与忧郁》中提出了两种由失去带来的心理创伤:悲悼与忧郁。两者产生的原因相似,都是“失去了所爱之人,或者说失去了替代爱情的抽象概念,如国家、自由

① Alfred W. Crosby, *America's Forgotten Pandemic: The Influenza of 1918*, Cambridge University Press, 2003, p. 315.

② Alfred W. Crosby, *America's Forgotten Pandemic: The Influenza of 1918*, Cambridge University Press, 2003, p. 317.

和理想等”[①]。两者有相似的表现，比如“极其痛苦的沮丧，失去对外界的兴趣，失去爱的能力，以及压抑自己的一切行动”[②]。但是，两者也有明显的不同。抑郁是指受创伤主体拒绝承认爱的客体的丧失，长期陷入孤立、内疚、冷漠等心理状态，无法自拔。悲悼则是指受创伤主体通过回忆，切断与所爱之人的情感联系，将自己的力比多投入到新的客体，这样“完成了悲悼的过程，自我重新变得自由，摆脱束缚”[③]。上一段的引文表明，米兰达已经通过回忆完成了对瘟疫创伤和情感创伤的讲述，释放了对死亡的恐惧、对爱人的内疚等负面情感，正如她自己说的：“我再怎么也不能这样失魂落魄了，她提醒自己。”[④]

在小说的结尾，作者描绘了一幅安静平和的情景：“再也没有战争，再也没有瘟疫，只有大炮停止后茫然的安静；合上百叶窗的房间没有吵闹的声音，街上空荡荡的，可以看到寒冷刺骨的明天的光亮。现在是做事情的时候了。”[⑤]这预示着米兰达已经完成了悲悼，摆脱了创伤，恢复了生活的信心。

---

① Sigmund Freud, “Mourning and Melancholia”, *The Standard Edition of the Complete Psychological Works of Sigmund Freud*, Volume XIV, London: The Hogarth Press, 1917, p. 244.

② Sigmund Freud, “Mourning and Melancholia”, *The Standard Edition of the Complete Psychological Works of Sigmund Freud*, Volume XIV, London: The Hogarth Press, 1917, p. 244.

③ Sigmund Freud, “Mourning and Melancholia”, *The Standard Edition of the Complete Psychological Works of Sigmund Freud*, Volume XIV, London: The Hogarth Press, 1917, p. 245.

④ Katherine Anne Porter, *The Collected Stories of Katherine Anne Porter*, New York: Harcourt, 1979, p. 317.

⑤ Katherine Anne Porter, *The Collected Stories of Katherine Anne Porter*, New York: Harcourt, 1979, p. 317.

三、《灰色的马,灰色的骑手》中的战争创伤叙事

虽然《灰色的马,灰色的骑手》整篇都是以米兰达的视角讲述了瘟疫和个人情感给米兰达带来的身体和心灵的创伤,但是通过米兰达的恋人青年军官亚当,这篇作品也完成了对战争创伤的揭示。《灰色的马,灰色的骑手》的故事发生在第一次世界大战期间。一战实际上是各帝国主义国家之间的政治、经济发展不平衡带来的恶果,而美国政府为了征召更多青年人入伍,全力开动宣传机器,鼓吹这是一场为了维护世界民主和正义的战争。但是,当成千上万的像亚当一样的青年来到欧洲战场的时候,他们只看到毫无意义的死亡,正如《永别了,武器》中的主人公亨利说的:"我没有看到任何神圣的东西,可没看到什么神圣的事,那些所谓光荣的事,也没有什么光荣。而所谓的牺牲,那就像芝加哥的屠场,只不过这里屠宰好的肉不是装进罐头,而是掩埋掉罢了。"①

这场战争最具有讽刺意味的是,成千上万的士兵不是死于这场"正义的"战争,而是死于瘟疫之手。西班牙流感和历史上其他瘟疫不同,受到感染的病人主要是年龄在 20～40 岁的青壮年,因此一战战场上的士兵在瘟疫中死亡惨重。超过 43000 名美国士兵死于西班牙流感,占美国士兵一战总死亡人数的 80%。② 而亚当正是这些被迫参加这场荒谬战争的一员。虽然他并不像有些青年人那样狂热地相信政府的宣传,但是也不得不离开生病的恋人,远赴欧洲作战。仅仅一个月之后,这个英俊、充满活力的年轻人就死于西班牙流感,用他的死亡证明了这场战争的荒谬。

---

① Ernest Hemingway, *A Farewell to Arms*, Oklahoma: Arrow, 1994, p. 165.

② Alfred W. Crosby, *America's Forgotten Pandemic: The Influenza of 1918*, Cambridge University Press, 2003, p. 206.

米兰达通过回忆亚当这名青年军官,来揭示战争给她和亚当,以及这一代青年带来的创伤。亚当和其他热心战争的青年人不同,他冷静理性,厌恶战争,厌恶政府的说教,敏锐地感觉到战争给人们带来的苦难。为了减轻死亡威胁的压力,同时也为了尽可能地享受与恋人米兰达在一起的最后时光,亚当和米兰达一样,动用了心理防御机制,避免谈及瘟疫和战争。在不得不提及的时候,也用"这种古怪的新疾病"来轻描淡写地形容这场瘟疫,还说"别让它败坏我们的兴致",以此来尽量减弱瘟疫带来的沉重的死亡氛围。[①] 在谈到战争的时候,亚当也是小心翼翼,比如他故意用戏谑的口气讲述他学习使用刺刀杀敌的情况;当米兰达说她要囤积食品和衣物,应付下一次战争的时候,亚当也尽量安慰她说:"我们这一回要把战争彻底消灭,而战争迟早会被消灭的,这就是我们未来的状况。"[②]尽管如此,对于战争和自己不可预知的未来,亚当是清楚的。他告诉米兰达,在欧洲战场,一队坑道工兵开始挖壕沟之后,平均寿命只有九分钟,还说,"那里的人像苍蝇一样死去"[③]。但是,在战争的巨大压力下,个人的心理防御机制是无力的,亚当最终还是没有能够逃过这一代美国青年的悲剧命运。

《灰色的马,灰色的骑手》也记录了战争创伤的另一层面,即对人们心理造成的创伤。一战扭曲了人们对传统理念,比如爱国和民主的认知。1918 年,美国宣布参战不久,政府不顾民众的生命,开动宣传机器,标榜参战是为了保卫世界的民主和自由,利用人们的爱国心强迫人民购买国债,支持战争。在报社的办公室,米兰达

① Katherine Anne Porter, *The Collected Stories of Katherine Anne Porter*, New York: Harcourt, 1979, p. 281.

② Katherine Anne Porter, *The Collected Stories of Katherine Anne Porter*, New York: Harcourt, 1979, p. 281.

③ Katherine Anne Porter, *The Collected Stories of Katherine Anne Porter*, New York: Harcourt, 1979, p. 281.

和同事被强迫购买爱国公债，还被强迫到医院看望受伤士兵，甚至在看剧的剧场都逃不过政府的战争宣传："战争，战争，结束战争的战争，为了民主，为了人道的战争，一个永远、永远永远安全的世界……为了互相向对方证明，并且向全世界证明我们对民主的信念，大家一起来买自由国债吧，别吃糖，别穿羊毛袜了。"①听着这些枯燥、虚伪、空洞的战争宣传，米兰达的病症加剧了，她说："我头痛……唉，他干吗不闭上嘴？"②可是，米兰达身边的同事都疯狂地购买爱国公债，参与宣传，却浑然不知自己的爱国理念被政府利用，也不知道，战争结束不久之后，他们就变成了"迷惘的一代"，悲悼传统信仰和信念的失落。

这场疯狂荒谬的战争还扭曲了人们对自己和他人身份的认知，这也是战争造成的心理创伤的一部分。和亚当一样，米兰达厌恶战争，对政府的宣传十分反感。她以薪金过低为由拒绝购买国债，但是，米兰达还是不能完全逃避无处不在的战争机器对人们造成的心理影响。在她终于被送到医院救治之后，由于当时米兰达的意识已经陷入混乱，自主的理性思维缺失，这时，那些政府的宣传开始侵入，扭曲了米兰达对自己和他人身份的认知。当米兰达看到德国医生希尔德谢姆的时候，一向反战的米兰达突然想象自己变成了士兵，而往日平和的医生突然变成一战中战场的德国敌人：

> 他的脸变成一个戴着德国钢盔的骷髅，一手拿着刺刀，刀尖上挑着一个在扭动的赤身露体的婴儿，另一只手提着一个

① Katherine Anne Porter, *The Collected Stories of Katherine Anne Porter*, New York: Harcourt, 1979, pp. 292-293.

② Katherine Anne Porter, *The Collected Stories of Katherine Anne Porter*, New York: Harcourt, 1979, p. 293.

> 大石罐,上面黑色的字体写着“有毒”。……米兰达一边尖叫,一边把两条胳膊举过头顶奔跑,她的声音引来了回声,传到她的耳朵里,像是狼嚎。希尔德谢姆是一个德国佬,奸细,德国兵,杀死他,免得他杀死你们。①

如果说《灰色的马,灰色的骑手》中的瘟疫创伤叙事和情感创伤叙事主要是为了通过回忆,起到治愈心灵创伤,更积极地面对生活的话,那么作品中的战争叙事则主要是为了警示现实,即类似一战的灾难很有可能再次降临。

凯瑟琳·安·波特虽然一生都未从政,但是对政治却有着敏锐的洞察力。20 世纪 30 年代早期,波特曾经去德国旅行,目睹了纳粹主义在德国的崛起。她敏锐地觉察到,在距离一战结束仅 20 年后,欧洲和全世界将会再次笼罩在战争的阴霾下。但是,在当时对法西斯主义绥靖政策占据主流话语的美国,波特只能通过她的文学作品和个人信件等个人叙事表达她对战争的担忧。1934 年,波特在一次采访中曾说道:“我无法告知这个国家的任何一位编辑我的想法。我不是记者,我不是一个靠政治观点出名的女人。即便我知道我要说的,即便我有证据,也很难让别人听见我的想法。……除了和别人交谈,没有人听我的想法。这让我感到很愤怒。我去过德国……我知道那里正在发生什么,可是没有人听我说这些。”②在一封私人信件中,波特重申了她个人反对两次世界大战的态度:“我不相信宗教的神秘性,也不存在是效忠于教会还是效忠于国家的矛盾,我仅仅作为一个纯粹的人,一个世俗的人,

① Katherine Anne Porter, *The Collected Stories of Katherine Anne Porter*, New York: Harcourt, 1979, p. 309.

② Joan Givner, ed., *Katherine Anne Porter: Conversations*, Jackson: University Press of Mississippi, 1987, pp. 178-179.

一个有着政治、道德、伦理理性的人,我坚信战争建立在自然罪恶的无底深渊之上。”[①]同年,波特发表了短篇小说《斜塔》,描述了德国极端民主主义横行的情形,警告人们:西方文明正像一座斜塔一样被纳粹摧毁。

波特之所以在20年后,也就是二战爆发前夕,才将自己在一战中的创伤经历付诸笔端,是因为她不仅想通过创伤叙事,彻底治愈瘟疫和一战给她个人带来的创伤体验。更重要的是,她希望通过从社会和历史层面更深层次地探讨创伤,来警示人类,防止相同的创伤体验重新出现。

四、结语

在《灰色的马,灰色的骑手》中,作者凯瑟琳·安·波特通过瘟疫创伤叙事和情感创伤叙事,达到了重构记忆,医治个人生命和情感创伤的目的。更难能可贵的是,作者将瘟疫创伤叙事、情感创伤叙事和战争创伤叙事交错连接,达到记录历史、警示后人的目的。波特为男主人公取名亚当,这个名字使读者自然而然地联想到《圣经》中人类的祖先亚当。这个人类祖先的化身因为瘟疫和战争死去。在死前,他这样评价人类世界的未来:“不会再有战争啦,难道你不看报吗?”[②]这是一句具有预言性质的反讽,警示人们不要相信报纸的宣传,战争和瘟疫很可能再次来临。就在《灰色的马,灰色的骑手》发表后仅一年,二战爆发,给人类带来的创伤比一战更加深刻。此后的近一个世纪中,战争和瘟疫在全球不同程度地爆

① Katherine Anne Porter, *Letters of Katherine Anne Porter*, ed. Isabel Bayle, New York: Atlantic, 1990, p. 351.

② Katherine Anne Porter, *Letters of Katherine Anne Porter*, ed. Isabel Bayle, New York: Atlantic, 1990, p. 281.

发,持续不断地给人类留下创伤。由此,我们更加认识到波特在《灰色的马,灰色的骑手》中对个人命运和人类命运的关照。这种关照加强了这部作品的思想深度,使其成为美国文学史上经典的创伤叙事文本。

(吕惠:外交学院英语系副教授)

论《螺丝在拧紧》中的幽灵书写

侯小山

《螺丝在拧紧》是美国小说家亨利·詹姆斯后期创作的中篇小说，1898 年首次发表于《科利尔周刊》(*Collier's Weekly*)。这部颇具争议的作品在詹姆斯的创作中具有重要的地位。金伯利·利德(Kimberly Reed)指出："没有哪部作品能够像《螺丝在拧紧》一样引发了如此激烈的分歧。"[①]小说讲述了一位来自乡下的女子到一个偏僻的庄园当家庭教师的故事。这位家庭女教师经常看到已死的前任总管和女家教的鬼魂，并认为这些鬼魂是来骚扰自己学生的(一个男孩和一个女孩)。为了保护学生，她要求学生不要与鬼魂来往。最后，女孩得病让管家带走，男孩被吓死了。

小说的情节看似简单，但引发的"有鬼"还是"无鬼"的争论至今不能平息。1938 年，蒙德·威尔逊(Edmund Wilson)在《亨利·詹姆斯的多重语义》中运用弗洛伊德的精神分析法分析文本，得出了家庭女教师是性压抑引发的神经官能症患者，鬼魂并非真

---

① Greg W. Zacharias, ed., *A Companion to Henry James*, Wiley-Blackwell, 2008, p. 100.

的鬼魂,而是她的幻觉。[①] 后来,在拉康和德里达的影响下,费尔曼解构了这一故事,认为"对于想要完全理解女教师或者她的故事的读者来说,女教师大部分的无意识是无法被触及的"。她告诫读者不要试图弄清《螺丝在拧紧》的神秘之处,而是要追踪故事发展的"重要轨迹"。[②]

近些年,幽灵批评的日益兴起为文学作品中关于鬼魂的解读提供了新的视角。在批评家眼里,幽灵已经成为一种隐喻,是缺场的表达形式和言说历史的策略。处于边界的幽灵自由出入各种场景,重复侵扰某人或某处,揭露了文本的过去、现在和未来。综观关于《螺丝在拧紧》的种种争论,评论家们大都聚焦于家庭女教师,通过分析家庭女教师的处境或心理来证实或证伪鬼魂,而书中两个鬼魂本身彼得·昆特和杰西小姐的形象却被很多评论家所忽视。然而,幽灵作为一种跨界的隐喻,模糊了过去与现在的界线,构建了一个介乎虚构与真实间的小说空间,诉说了那些曾被压抑、遗忘的个人历史和社会现实。亨利·詹姆斯在小说中通过对幽灵的书写表现了19世纪中后期阶级流动的大趋势,表达了他对中产阶级一心攀附权贵的关注。

一、被压制的"恶鬼":社会等级流动的悲剧

作为可怕的超自然之物,幽灵的显现表明被掩盖的事件存在着强大的生命力。他们超越时空,回归当下,意图言说不为人知的过去。朱迪斯·理查森认为:"作为一种特殊的或特定的社会记

---

① Edmund Wilson, "The Ambiguity of Henry James", *The Turn of the Screw*, New York: Norton Company, 1999, p.170.

② Peter G. Beidler, "A Critical History of The Turn of the Screw", *The Turn of the Screw*, ed., Peter G. Beidler, Boston & New York: Bedford/ St. Martin's, 1995, p.135.

忆,幽灵是创造历史的备选形式。在这段历史里面,通常被遗忘、抛弃或者压制的事件不管被看作害怕、悔恨、解释还是欲望都处于突出的位置。”[①]从文本表面来看,两个鬼魂生前的历史是被掩盖的。格罗斯太太和家庭女教师把昆特和杰西小姐视为邪恶恐怖的象征,扭曲了两人生前真实的经历。小说中大量充斥着大家对他们的道德评判。他们活着时是“声名狼藉”的“坏”仆人,死后是徘徊在布莱庄园,试图控制两个无辜孩子的心灵的“恶”鬼。我们抛开这些评价细读文本就能发现,两个鬼魂的具体死因在小说中就显得极其模糊。

在故事中,家庭女教师费了好大的劲才得知昆特的死因:“那一段罪恶的时间终于在一个冬日的黎明结束了,一个去上早班的工人发现彼得·昆特僵死在通往村里的大道上:人们解释说是他头上一道明显的伤口导致死亡的——至少在表面上如此,也许他离开酒馆后在黑夜中走岔了路,一失脚滑下了结冰的陡坡,造成了这道致命的伤口(事后的调查证明了这一点)。”[②]昆特的具体死因极其模糊而又充满矛盾。要知道昆特是个“个子高高,动作灵活,身材挺拔”[③]的年轻人。如此敏捷的年轻人摔死在路上似乎令人起疑,而且,“表面上”总是让人觉得另有隐情。他的伤口刚开始被描绘为可能是由重重一摔引起的,后来多数人还是认为,“他的一生中阴险狡诈,行事诡秘、邪恶,斑斑劣迹表明他另有死因”[④]。从

① Judith Richardson, *Possessions: The History and Uses of Haunting in the Hudson Valley*, Cambridge, MA: Harvard University Press, 2003, p. 3.

② [爱尔兰]詹姆斯·乔伊斯:《詹姆斯·乔伊斯短篇小说选》,戴茵、杨红波译,湖南文艺出版社 1998 年版,第 220 页。

③ [爱尔兰]詹姆斯·乔伊斯:《詹姆斯·乔伊斯短篇小说选》,戴茵、杨红波译,湖南文艺出版社 1998 年版,第 215 页。

④ [爱尔兰]詹姆斯·乔伊斯:《詹姆斯·乔伊斯短篇小说选》,戴茵、杨红波译,湖南文艺出版社 1998 年版,第 220 页。

文本中我们得不到昆特死的真正原因,一切都是带有极强价值判断的猜测。在格罗斯太太、家庭女教师以及绝大多数人看来,昆特的死是罪有应得,他为人太放纵,尤其是跟杰西小姐乱搞。

福柯在《规训与惩罚》中谈道:“在实际上,犯罪使个人处于整个社会对立面。为了惩罚他,社会有权作为一个整体来反对他。这是一种不平等的斗争,因为一切力量,一切权力和一切权利都属于一方。之所以如此,是因为这里涉及保护每个人的问题。之所以建立这种可怕的惩罚权利,是因为他在内部打击社会。他的行为不亚于一个叛徒,一个‘怪物’。社会怎么能不拥有控制他的绝对权利呢?社会怎么会不主张消灭他呢?”[①]昆特与杰西小姐乱搞的行为违背了当时的社会等级制度。虽然杰西小姐在外做家庭女教师,但她仍然可以被称作“淑女”,属于中产阶级的一员。她的社会地位比作为贴身侍卫的昆特要高。在世人眼里,分属于不同阶级的昆特与杰西小姐违反了当时的社会等级制度,败坏了整个庄园的名声。

在小说中,昆特与杰西小姐行为不端,自然成为邪恶的象征。昆特的死是罪有应得。家庭女教师一直在与昆特与杰西小姐争夺两个孩子的理由也出自对孩子道德意识的教育,她怕两个孩子被昆特与杰西小姐带坏。在极力劝说和询问昆特的情况时,家庭女教师就警告格罗斯太太:“他影响那两个纯洁、宝贵的小生命。”[②]根据社会的惩罚机制,昆特的行为与维多利亚社会的准则背道而驰,他理应受到惩罚,虽然他的死不明不白,但是对于大多人来说他的死是大快人心的。

---

① [法]米歇尔·福柯:《规训与惩罚》,刘北成、杨远婴译,三联书店 2003 年版,第 99～100 页。

② [爱尔兰]詹姆斯·乔伊斯:《詹姆斯·乔伊斯短篇小说选》,戴茵、杨红波译,湖南文艺出版社 1998 年版,第 217 页。

我们再来看杰西小姐的死因。杰西的死与昆特相比更加扑朔迷离。在家庭女教师再三询问下，格罗斯太太告诉她："她没有在这屋子里染病，至少外表看起来没有病。她在那年年底离开这儿回家去了，她说是回去休个短假。她干了那么长时间，也该给她放假了。那时我们还有个年轻姑娘——她留了下来当保姆，那姑娘心肠又好，人又聪明，在那段时间里是她照顾了两个孩子。可是我们那位小姐再也没回来，我正着急她怎么还没来呢，就听主人说她死了。"[①]主人从未告诉格罗斯太太杰西小姐的死因。整个文本也找不到杰西小姐的死因，只是格罗斯太太后来道出了杰西小姐离开的原因："她是没法再待下去了。想想吧，她可是家庭女教师啊！"[②]

细读文本，我们可以发现，格罗斯太太曾告诉家庭女教师："啊呀，小姐，你不是第一个，也绝不会是最后一个。"[③]格罗斯太太在给新来的家庭女教师暗指小主人很吸引女性时，无意地留下了与杰西小姐真正死因有关的线索。与新来的家庭女教师一样，杰西小姐肯定也是带着对主人的幻想和迷恋来到庄园工作。在新来的家庭女教师眼里，"他仪表堂堂，气宇不凡，风度迷人，和蔼可亲。不用说，在她心里，他是个殷勤备至的阔少，不过最打动她心扉，让她勇气顿生的，是他对她的态度——他认为她给他帮了一个大忙，他真是感激不尽"[④]。去年，主人待在布莱与当时的家庭女教师杰

① [爱尔兰]詹姆斯·乔伊斯：《詹姆斯·乔伊斯短篇小说选》，戴茵、杨红波译，湖南文艺出版社1998年版，第201页。

② [爱尔兰]詹姆斯·乔伊斯：《詹姆斯·乔伊斯短篇小说选》，戴茵、杨红波译，湖南文艺出版社1998年版，第227页。

③ [爱尔兰]詹姆斯·乔伊斯：《詹姆斯·乔伊斯短篇小说选》，戴茵、杨红波译，湖南文艺出版社1998年版，第196页。

④ [爱尔兰]詹姆斯·乔伊斯：《詹姆斯·乔伊斯短篇小说选》，戴茵、杨红波译，湖南文艺出版社1998年版，第190页。

西肯定有较多的接触。由于来自不同的阶层,两人的近距离相处自然会让杰西意识到主人不会和她结婚。对于她来说,社会等级制度是无法逾越的界线,她灰姑娘式的梦最终因主人的离开幻灭了。

但是,杰西小姐却走了另一条逾越社会等级的路,选择与社会地位比她低的昆特在一起。她将自己的爱转向了主人的贴身侍卫昆特,这样,她不仅违背了等级制度,也违背了父权制。这从格罗斯太太对她和昆特的评价中可以看出:"噢,地位不同,身份不同……她是一位小姐……可是他的身份却要低得多。"家庭女教师说:"他要做的事情也一定是她所希望的。"格罗斯太太脸上的表情说明事实的确如此,可是她有同时又说;"可怜的女人,她自讨苦吃!"[①]在昆特死后,杰西小姐在父权制的压抑下,她别无选择,只能自寻死路。

18世纪后半期,工业革命逐渐深入发展的同时,原有的财富结构发生了深刻巨大的变化。新兴的中产阶级开始与上层社会看齐,追求更高的阶级趣味和爱情。在当时的社会背景下,杰西小姐追求处于上层阶级的主人无可厚非,但是她与身份比她低的侍卫乱搞就是自甘堕落。当时的英国的国民意识就存在很强的攀附权贵的倾向。19世纪英国政坛的重要人物理查德·科布登就曾坦言:"我们是一个奴性十足的民族,眷恋并受贵族制度所驾驭。"[②]无疑,昆特和杰西是当时社会阶级流动大趋势的受害者。作为地位低下的男性,昆特不去追求贵族小姐,反而去追求意图攀附权贵的杰西。杰西小姐或许受到了主人的无情拒绝,但是她又转而与

---

① [爱尔兰]詹姆斯·乔伊斯:《詹姆斯·乔伊斯短篇小说选》,戴茵、杨红波译,湖南文艺出版社1998年版,第226页。

② Norman Gash, *Aristocracy and People: Britain 1815-1865*, London: Edward Arnald, 1978, p. 349.

昆特混在一起。她被社会抛弃的原因不在于攀附权贵的失败，而是她没有继续坚持，自甘堕落地向下一层阶级靠拢的举动。由此可见，亨利·詹姆斯借鬼魂揭示了当时阶级流动的趋势。

二、鬼魂归来：现世梦想的破灭

德里达在解读《哈姆雷特》中的幽灵时称："一切都开始于幽灵的幻象。更准确地说，开始于等待幻想。这种期待刹那间是让人不耐烦、焦虑和着迷：这个（这个事）最终会出现。亡魂将会到来。"[①]到了布莱庄园不久，家庭女教师就开始幻想着和她的梦中情人（主人）再次相遇。"当时我每日这么漫游时，心里常萦绕着一个念头：若像那迷人的小说所写，无意之中恰逢君临，该多迷人啊。此君应从小径转出，站在我面前含笑嘉许。"[②]然而，昆特的幽灵在塔顶的出现上打断了她不切实际的想象。"面对着我的那个人影，我多看几秒便认定，既不是我认识的人，也不是我心目中的那个形象。我没在哈雷街见过他——也没在任何地方见过他。此外，最为奇怪的是，当这个人影出现的那一刻，这地方似乎成了荒郊野外。"[③]家庭女教师一开始幻想着与梦中情人（主人）相遇，最终却等来了昆特的亡魂。蒙德·威尔逊认为："《螺丝在拧紧》的故事只是源自亨利·詹姆斯对其熟悉题材的一种简单变形：关于一位充满挫败感的英国单身女性的故事。我们可以很清晰地想起他也在

---

① Jacque Derrida, *Specters of Marx: The State of the Debt, the Work of Mourning, and the New International*, trans. Peggy Kamuf, New York and London: Routledge, 1994, p. 4.

② [爱尔兰]詹姆斯·乔伊斯：《詹姆斯·乔伊斯短篇小说选》，戴茵、杨红波译，湖南文艺出版社 1998 年版，第 204 页。

③ [爱尔兰]詹姆斯·乔伊斯：《詹姆斯·乔伊斯短篇小说选》，戴茵、杨红波译，湖南文艺出版社 1998 年版，第 205 页。

其他作品中常常描绘这样的女性,在外人面前,她们隐藏自己的内心情感,甚至不惜欺骗自己。”[①]小说中的家庭女教师心中充满了对爱情和地位的渴望。

仔细考察家庭女教师,我们可以发现,深受当时主流文化影响的她对昆特和杰西的鬼魂做出了极强的价值判断。她坚信,杰西小姐不该和地位低下的昆特在一起,这对身份不匹配的男女伤风败俗的行为几乎毁掉布莱庄园的清白。同时,家庭女教师还骄傲地认为她能替代杰西为主人效力,担负保护孩子的责任甚至获得管理庄园的权力。她的一厢情愿使她在与鬼魂的权力争斗中本能地贬低对方,她总是很轻易地从格罗斯太太的只字片语中证实自己的充满偏见的道德评判。

然而,杰西小姐所经历的事情直接预示了家庭女教师的命运。家庭女教师不可能意识不到这一点。因此,她挣扎于认清和否定现实之间。在潜意识的支配下,她既想发现杰西在布莱庄园的真实经历,又害怕和抵抗接受杰西小姐悲惨命运的最终原因。杰西身上发生惨剧就是她未来将承受的一切。但是,她一直选择了逃避,没有勇气也不愿意去直面现实。杰西小姐的鬼魂身份使家庭女教师能够在幻想中本能地自我保护,主观地贬低杰西。在这一过程中,家庭女教师就如哈姆雷特一样处在不耐烦、焦虑和着迷的状态中。

我们可以看到,鬼魂的出现一直在打破家庭女教师的幻想。昆特与主人之间形成了鲜明的对比。昆特的出现使整个地方都变得荒凉起来。他的到来在提醒家庭女教师:布莱庄园并没有她想象的那么美好,在主人背后存在着一种不为人知的神秘力量。杰

① Edmund Wilson, “The Ambiguity of Henry James”, *The Turn of the Screw*: *Authoritative Text*, *Contexts*, *Criticism*, eds. Henry James, Deborah Esch, Jonathan Warren, New York: W. W. Norton, 1999, pp. 170-173.

西小姐的幽灵的首次出现也同样打断了家庭女教师的幻想。在见到杰西小姐之前，家庭女教师觉得她就是孩子唯一的依靠："他们除了我一无所有，而我——哦，我拥有他们。这简直就是千载难逢之事，这事在我面前呈现出丰富的具体性。我是一座屏障——我要挡在他们身前。"[①]在这里，家庭女教师俨然把自己当作了两个孩子的监护人，保护着他们。

随后，当家庭女教师与小弗罗拉在公园玩耍的时候，杰西小姐的幽灵出现在湖对岸。家庭女教师一直不敢抬头看。"其时我再无怀疑，至少我深信，只要我抬起眼往对岸看去，肯定会看到我预料之中的东西。在那关头我的双眼紧紧盯着手中忙活的针线，此刻我再次感到了那股自我控制的力量，当时就是这股力量让我的双眼固定不动，直到我能镇定下来思考对策。"[②]正如昆特的出现一样，杰西小姐的出现也打断了家庭女教师自我标榜的孩子唯一"监护人"的幻想。其实两个孩子并不需要她。杰西小姐作为第三者的存在一直在注视着孩子们。就像她先前所意识到的："他们不需要我的参与，自娱自乐，他们似乎自个儿玩，把我当成一个积极的赞赏者。我在他们创造的世界里生活——他们却丝毫不需要进入我的世界，所以他们对我无所要求……"[③]因而杰西小姐的鬼魂在这儿也扮演了唤醒者的角色。她逐渐把家庭女教师从幻想中拉回了现实。

幽灵之所以能够引起主人公不安定的心理状态，是因为现实世界中存在危险的因素。小说中最终的危险因素来自主人。主人

① [爱尔兰]詹姆斯·乔伊斯：《詹姆斯·乔伊斯短篇小说选》，戴茵、杨红波译，湖南文艺出版社 1998 年版，第 220～221 页。

② [爱尔兰]詹姆斯·乔伊斯：《詹姆斯·乔伊斯短篇小说选》，戴茵、杨红波译，湖南文艺出版社 1998 年版，第 222 页。

③ [爱尔兰]詹姆斯·乔伊斯：《詹姆斯·乔伊斯短篇小说选》，戴茵、杨红波译，湖南文艺出版社 1998 年版，第 221 页。

作为一种不在场,是文中最大的幽灵。为什么主人自从去年离开布莱之后再也不去那里了?道格拉斯在介绍主人的情况时说道:“机缘巧合,竟轮到他来照料孩子,实在是令他大感吃力,因为他这种单身汉,既缺乏必要的经验,又无一丝一毫的耐心。他简直大伤脑筋,而且他自己也的确干下了一连串的傻事,不过对那两个可怜的小家伙,他还是格外心疼,尽了自己的心力……而他本人,只要一有机会,也亲自下乡去看他们。”①格罗斯太太在谈话中也提道:“他们两人全在这儿——去年的时候。后来主人走了,昆特一个人留了下来。”②由此我们可以看到,去年主人一直在布莱庄园,并且十分关心两个小孩,但是为什么他在一开始就给新的家庭女教师提出了非常奇怪的规定:“她绝对不可让他操丁点儿心,绝对、绝对不允许。发生任何事情都不得向他求助,向他抱怨,给他写信,一切问题均自理,所有费用由他的律师支付,她必须承担全部责任,让他不受打扰。”③他后来甚至都不愿抽空看迈尔斯的校长的来信。原因是:“这信,我认出来,是校长写出来的,而校长是个最烦人的家伙。请你去看信吧。你去跟他交涉。但记住千万别向我汇报。一个字也不行。我已离开!”④

主人前后的变化就显得非常蹊跷。起先,他对孩子关心爱护有加,到后来他不来庄园。他既不看孩子校长的来信,也不想知道家庭女教师怎么处理孩子的事情。主人在新的家庭女教师前的种

① [爱尔兰]詹姆斯·乔伊斯:《詹姆斯·乔伊斯短篇小说选》,戴茵、杨红波译,湖南文艺出版社 1998 年版,第 190 页。

② [爱尔兰]詹姆斯·乔伊斯:《詹姆斯·乔伊斯短篇小说选》,戴茵、杨红波译,湖南文艺出版社 1998 年版,第 215 页。

③ [爱尔兰]詹姆斯·乔伊斯:《詹姆斯·乔伊斯短篇小说选》,戴茵、杨红波译,湖南文艺出版社 1998 年版,第 192 页。

④ [爱尔兰]詹姆斯·乔伊斯:《詹姆斯·乔伊斯短篇小说选》,戴茵、杨红波译,湖南文艺出版社 1998 年版,第 197 页。

种表现都说明他现在对小孩一点都不关心，似乎在刻意避开回到布莱庄园的机会。考虑到孩子在杰西小姐鬼魂前很镇定，我们很容易想到杰西小姐生前和孩子之间的关系与现在的家庭女教师应该是一致的。那么，主人对孩子前后态度的变化就直接与杰西小姐有关。由此可见，故事中的幽灵并非像家庭女教师所说的是邪恶的象征，他们一直在提醒家庭女教师认清现实，远离主人。主人虽然“不在场”，可文本中处处透出他的“在场”。他不仅时时出现在女管家和家庭女教师的话语中，还牢固地占据着她们的意识，她们的一切行为都是为了他，为他着想，为他承担责任，为他开脱罪责，而谴责与自己处于同等地位的昆特和杰西小姐。如果说昆特和杰西小姐在生前是等级制与父权制的受害者，那么他们的幽灵出现在布莱庄园则是一种反抗的姿态。他们打破了家庭女教师的幻想，扰乱了深受等级制影响的布莱的生活。

两个鬼魂经常出现在湖边、塔楼和窗外。他们不进入房间，完全游荡在外。但是，他们一直骚扰着这所房子，这恰恰体现了他们的对社会性的反抗。“窗”在小说中是鬼魂“他者性”和人类“社会性”的分界线。房子是社会性的象征，窗户是连接内部世界和外部世界的界限。而布莱的房子地处乡下，外部世界就是自然界，没有束缚，是自由的象征。房子的焦点是两个小孩子，所有人都在尽心照顾着这两个孩子。但是，两个鬼魂却想方设法地使他们离开房子。弗罗拉和小迈尔斯晚上不睡觉，被鬼魂牵引着往房子外面跑。“她（弗罗拉）躲在窗台里（窗户朝外开着），藏得严严实实的，全神贯注，显然已无暇他顾。月色清朗、静谧，助了她一臂之力，这一事实也促使我迅速拿出对策。她在与我们曾于湖畔遭遇的那个幽灵正面接触，她一直未能与之交流，现在则可以做到了。”“但是，草坪上的那个却根本不是我想象中的人，不是我一心要去见的人。草坪上的那个——我看清楚后心中一阵恶心——正是可怜的小迈尔斯。”[①]最后,弗罗拉生病离开了布莱庄园,而小迈尔斯则死在了房子里。

从结局来看,两个鬼魂是胜利的。他们对家庭女教师深受社会主流文化的幻想进行了打击,使其幻想破灭。整个庄园也被他们破坏了。庄园的核心,弗罗拉和小迈尔斯一个离开了,一个死了。从表面上看,鬼魂似乎代表着邪恶。但细读文本,我们可以看到,他们也是等级制的受害者。变成鬼魂后,他们的反抗带有很强的破坏贵族自我保护阶级稳固性的色彩。亨利·詹姆斯在哥特小说《螺丝在拧紧》中深刻剖析了19世纪仍受贵族思想统治的英国社会现实。昆特和杰西小姐生前受到等级制度和男权思想的迫害,而死后以反抗者的姿态出现在布莱庄园,破坏了庄园的生活。在文本中,上层阶级的邪恶与鬼魂的邪恶交错。彼此相互对抗表现了19世纪末欧洲社会的动荡。

当幽灵向生者寻求死前的正义时,他们在时不时地提醒我们不可忘记过去被掩盖的事实。正是有了幽灵,我们才能更加关注自身,体验到自身的存在。被幽灵侵扰是生者内心蜕变的过程。这也是大部分评论家从精神分析的角度解读《螺丝在拧紧》中家庭女教师的原因。她的内心对于她自己来说既熟悉又陌生,是鬼魂恐怖的根源。艾弗瑞·戈登(Avery Gordon)认为:“鬼魂不仅仅是一个死的或者逝去的人,而是一个社会人。对它的调查能够带我们进入一个由历史和主观意识造就的地方。”[②]两个鬼魂被唾弃

① [爱尔兰]詹姆斯·乔伊斯:《詹姆斯·乔伊斯短篇小说选》,戴茵、杨红波译,湖南文艺出版社1998年版,第240～241页。

② Avery F. Gordon, *Haunting and the Sociological Imagination*, Minneapolis and London: University Of Minnesota Press, 2008, p. 8.

的背后是19世纪中后期阶级流动的大趋势。然而，亨利·詹姆斯又利用鬼魂的回归表达了他对中产阶级一心攀附权贵的关注。

（侯小山：山东大学外国语学院博士研究生）

辛西娅·奥兹克国外研究综述

张晶晶　李杉杉

辛西娅·奥兹克(Cynthia Ozick，1928～)是当代美国最重要的犹太裔作家之一,因其作品具有鲜明的犹太特性而被评论家称为犹太人的“后现代代言人”①。奥兹克于1966年发表首部长篇小说《信任》,迄今为止,共发表6部长篇小说、7部短篇小说集、9部随笔集及1部戏剧。伊芙·奥滕贝格(Eve Ottenberg)曾这样评价奥兹克:“她从未接近过最畅销作家的行列,但是在评论界却收获了广泛的好评。”②美国学界大名鼎鼎的人物哈罗德·布鲁姆(Harold Bloom)和希尔顿·克雷默(Hilton Kramer)都曾专门撰文点评奥兹克的作品。布鲁姆主编了现代批评文集系列之一的《辛西娅·奥兹克》(*Cynthia Ozick*，1986)并亲自作序。犹太研究领域的著名评论家露丝·R.维塞(Ruth R. Wisse)和大卫·瓦尔登(David Walden)亦曾对奥兹克的作品有所点评。美国学界对奥

---

① Jane Statlnder，*Cultural Dialectic*：*Ludwig Lewisohn and Cynthia Ozick*，New York：Peter Lang，2002，p. 225.

② Eve Ottenberg，“The Rich Visions of Cynthia Ozick”，*The New York Times*，10 April 1983，p. 46.

兹克作品的研究可以分为犹太主题研究、女性主义研究、创作风格研究和文学传承研究四大类。

一、犹太主题研究

奥兹克作为犹太人的身份奠定了其绝大多数作品的基调，她关注的主要话题包括与犹太人相关的各种议题，例如，如何才能避免触犯偶像崇拜的禁忌而成为一个真正的犹太人，犹太人在美国的生存状况和身份困惑，以及大屠杀的历史创伤和后大屠杀时代的信仰危机。因此，犹太主题研究是奥兹克研究领域的重中之重，也是读者理解奥兹克的必由之路。

奥兹克研究领域最热门的话题乃是其作品中展示的希伯来精神和希腊精神的冲突。奥兹克研究的领军人物伊莱恩·M. 考瓦尔(Elaine M. Kauvar)在其专著《辛西娅·奥兹克的小说：传统与创新》中研究了奥兹克多部作品的主题。她指出，希伯来精神和希腊精神之间的冲突、异教的诱惑和偶像的危险、同化的影响和后果、艺术家的懊恼和艺术潜在的危险都是奥兹克作品中不断复现的主题，已成为奥兹克的标志性主题。[①] 丹尼拉·法尔焦内(Daniela Fargione)在其博士论文《辛西娅·奥兹克和犹太文学：一个读者》中指出，奥兹克在1970年代写作的绝大多数短篇小说都聚焦在希腊精神和希伯来精神的冲突、异教和一神教的冲突、犹太教和文学的冲突之上。[②] 迪恩·J. 弗兰科(Dean J. Franco)在《重读辛西娅·奥兹克：多元主义、后现代主义和多元文化的相遇》

---

① Elaine M. Kauvar, *Cynthia Ozick's Fiction: Tradition and Invention*, Bloomington and Indianapolis, Indiana University Press, 1993.

② Daniela Farguione, *Cynthia Ozick and Jewish Literature: A Reader*, Diss. University of Massachusetts at Amherst, 2003, p. 14.

一文中指出:"数十年来,奥兹克坚持关注犹太道德律,以及与之共存的反偶像崇拜,在面对物质甚至审美价值时维护人性,这使得评论界普遍认同,奥兹克的重要主题就是希腊精神和希伯来精神之间的对立价值观。"[①]不仅如此,上述冲突已成为奥兹克创作的指导原则:米利安·希文(Miriam Sivan)在《自得其所:辛西娅·奥兹克小说中的人物刻画》一书中,分析了奥兹克多部小说中的人物,认为希腊精神和希伯来精神之间的分裂成为"奥兹克作品的指导原则"[②]。

奥兹克犹太主题研究的另一个重要方面是奥兹克作品的犹太道德观解析。薇拉·凯尔斯凯(Vera Emuna Kielsky)在《不可避免的流放:奥兹克眼中犹太人在异教社会生存的危险》一书中指出:"奥兹克打开世界的路径来源于她真诚的宗教视角,尤其是她的犹太视角。她的写作不是单纯地表现了犹太教义的字面意思,而是在直接的、不妥协的对峙当中表现了犹太教的精神,这种对峙来自犹太人所背负的摩西法律的道德重量,以及历史赋予犹太人的使命。"[③]邦尼·莱昂斯(Bonnie Lyons)在《辛西娅·奥兹克作为一名美国犹太作家》一文中提到,对奥兹克而言,"伟大的艺术必须要有道德的光环,一道微弱却发着白光的光环,一道救赎的光。在奥兹克自己的定义中,这救赎是改变生活的自由,并且暗暗地与命运抗争"[④]。莱昂斯认为,奥兹克"最基本的艺术和道德信条来源

① Dean J. Franco, "Rereading Cynthia Ozick: Pluralism, Postmodernism, and the Multicultural Encounter", *Contemporary Literature*, 1(2008), p. 56.

② Miriam Sivan, *Belonging too Well: Portraits of Identity in Cynthia Ozick's Fiction*, Albany: State University of New York Press, 2009, p. 8.

③ Vera Emuna Kielsky, *Inevitable Exiles: Cynthia Ozick's View of the Precariousness of Jewish Existence in a Gentile Society*, Diss. Arizona State University, 1985, p. 229.

④ Bonnie Lyons, "Cynthia Ozick as a Jewish American Writer", *Studies in Jewish American Literature*, 6 (1987), p. 17.

于犹太教的"*t'shuva*"这一概念,意指带来创造性革新和改变的能量"①。维克多·斯特德兰贝格(Victor Strandberg)在《希腊头脑/犹太灵魂:辛西娅·奥兹克的冲突的艺术》一书中揭示了奥兹克的思想和犹太道德之间的渊源,奥兹克作品承载的思想正是他称之为"生命!原则"(L'Chaim! Principle)的犹太民族精神,这是一种面对现实、寻求真理的精神气质,是犹太民族精神的写照。这种民族精神使得犹太人这一小小的族群成为世界民族之林中不可小觑的一股力量:在艺术、科学、政治、商业财经、司法体系等各个具体方面都不可忽视。② 艾米·克拉特卡(Amy Weintraub Kratka)在其博士论文《辛西娅·奥兹克的神圣审美观》中指出,"保持圣洁"③(Kedoshim Tihiyu)的劝告为奥兹克的艺术奠基,启迪了她关于道德想象力的观念,也成为她塑造人物的一个准则,同时也为她的作品赋予了犹太人的品质。苏珊·克林根斯坦(Susanne Klingenstein)在《"生活中的我不自由":作家辛西娅·奥兹克和她作为犹太人的义务》一文中提出,作家奥兹克为犹太人所做的是在犹太道德框架内写作,而犹太人奥兹克奉献自己的时间和精力,倾尽自己的才华为犹太人和犹太文明得以保存而写作。④ 珍妮特·伯斯坦(Janet Handler Burstein)在《辛西娅·奥兹克和艺术的叛

① Bonnie Lyons, "Cynthia Ozick as a Jewish American Writer", *Studies in Jewish American Literature*, 6 (1987), p. 17.

② Victor Strandberg, *Greek Mind/Jewish Soul: The Conflicted Art of Cynthia Ozick*, Madison: The University of Wisconsin Press, 1994, p. 47.

③ Amy Weintraub Kratka, *Cynthia Ozick's Sacral Aesthetic*, Diss. Boston University, 2005.

④ Susanne Klingenstein, "'In Life I Am Not Free': The Writer Cynthia Ozick and Her Jewish Obligations", *Daughters of Valor: Contemporary Jewish American Women Writers*, eds. Jay L. Halio and Ben Siegel, Newark: University of Delaware Press, 1997, pp. 48-79. Rpt. in *Contemporary Literary Criticism*, ed. Janet Witalec, 155, Detroit: Gale, 2002, pp. 206-220.

逆》一文中指出,尽管贝娄、马拉默德等其他犹太作家也意识到文化痼疾,并且质疑文字的救赎力量,但是对于审美与道德和宗教之间的冲突,奥兹克的见解是独一无二的。①

奥兹克作品的历史意识构成了其犹太主题的时间维度,也是奥兹克犹太主题研究的重要方面。彼得·鲍尔斯(Peter Kerry Powers)和珍妮特·库珀(Janet L. Cooper)均指出,奥兹克笔下的人物会编造个人或集体的历史。库珀认为,故事中人物编造的历史恰好展示了犹太历史的兴衰变迁,这导致了犹太身份的复杂性。② 然而,鲍尔斯却认为,小说人物篡改自己的身世恰恰反映了历史在后现代社会中的缺失——“奥兹克指责后现代写作技巧,在表面上制造了后现代当下的一种断裂,这种断裂直指当下的关键问题便是过去的缺失。”③但是,正是奥兹克意识到这种断裂,才使得她塑造的人物去主动追寻自己的历史,这让她的文本自身成为我们这个时代文化记忆的一部分——“她的文本自身已编织进了文化记忆之中,带领着读者来回穿梭,回到传统之中。”④考瓦尔也认为:“对于奥兹克来说,历史是必不可少的,但有了历史还不够:要想拥有未来,不仅要救赎过去,还要判断其意义。她的观点——‘历史是对事件的评判’——以及记忆的重要性都启发了奥兹克的

① Janet Handler Burstein, “Cynthia Ozick and the Transgression of Art”, *American Literature*, 59.1 (March 1987), p. 86.

② Janet L. Copper, “Triangles of History and the Slippery Slope of Jewish American Identity in Two Stories by Cynthia Ozick”, *MELUS*, 25.1 (Spring 2000), p. 182.

③ Peter Kerry Powers, “Disruptive Memories: Cynthia Ozick, Assimilation, and the Invented Past”, *History and Memory*, spec. issue of *MELUS*, 20.3(1995), p. 88.

④ Peter Kerry Powers, “Disruptive Memories: Cynthia Ozick, Assimilation, and the Invented Past”, *History and Memory*, spec. issue of *MELUS*, 20.3(1995), p. 95.

作品。”①

对奥兹克作品中大屠杀主题的探索是奥兹克犹太主题研究不可或缺的一部分。汉斯·博彻斯(Hans Borchers)认为奥兹克达到了大屠杀研究者伯杰(Alan L. Berger)对犹太作家的期待,后者指出“大屠杀是犹太写作的试金石”②。尽管奥兹克自己有诸多纠结,尽管从整体而言,作家还是不愿涉及这一领域,她依然将大屠杀当作中心议题。③ 事实上,在戴维·布罗纳(David Brauner)看来,奥兹克创作大屠杀题材作品触犯了双重禁忌,即犹太女性不能从事写作的禁忌和写作大屠杀的道德禁忌;但是奥兹克仍然打破禁忌,发出了犹太女性的声音。④ 不仅如此,她推动了大屠杀美学的发展。约瑟夫·阿尔卡纳(Joseph Alkana)指出,菲利普·罗斯(Phillip Roth)有关大屠杀的作品有两大特点,即对受害者心态的讽刺和对大屠杀经历的精确化,而奥兹克“超越了这些必需的、负面的步骤,拒绝感伤主义和普遍主义,发展出了一种更加复杂的后大屠杀文学审美”⑤。

---

① Elaine M. Kauvar, *Cynthia Ozick's Fiction: Tradition and Invention*, Bloomington and Indianapolis: Indiana University Press, 1993, p. xii.

② Alan Berger, *Crisis and Covenant: The Holocaust in American Jewish Fiction*, Albany: State University of New York Press, 1985, p. 192.

③ Hans Borchers, "Of Suitcases and Other Burdens: The Ambiguities of Cynthia Ozick's Image of Germany", *The Centennial Review*, 35. 3 (1991), pp. 616-617.

④ David Brauner, "Breaking the Silences: Jewish-American Women Writing the Holocaust", *North American Short Stories and Short Fictions*, spec. issue of *The Yearbook of English Studies*, 31 (2001), pp. 24-38.

⑤ Joseph Alkana, "'Do We Know the Meaning of Aesthetic Gratification?': Cynthia Ozick's *The Shawl*, the Akedah, and the Ethics of Holocaust Literary Aesthetics", *Modern Fiction Studies*, 43. 4 (1997), pp. 963-964.

二、女性主义研究

奥兹克的女性身份是影响其创作的另一个重要因素。由于犹太教传统乃至整个西方社会传统中的父权思想,奥兹克在成长道路上遭遇诸多性别歧视,因此她在作品中不可避免地探讨女性问题。就写作而言,奥兹克强烈反对用性别区分作家作品的做法,认为在男权传统下,女性作家的作品常常得不到认真公平的对待。对于奥兹克作品的女性主义研究也就成为奥兹克研究领域的重要方面。

奥兹克研究者一致认为,奥兹克是一位不折不扣的女性主义者。卡萨·波利特(Katha Pollitt)在《奥兹克的三个自我》一文中指出,奥兹克是坚定的女性主义者,且"作为女性主义的奥兹克是更加快乐的",她对弗洛伊德关于女性的观点进行了高超的反驳。[①] 考瓦尔也认为奥兹克是女性主义者,但不是激进的女性主义者,因为奥兹克并没有将女性的写作从经典当中割裂开来。此外,她认为奥兹克区分了后现代女性主义和经典女性主义;这一区分并未被广泛接受,甚至被曲解,被女性主义者所抨击。[②] 比恩斯托克·阿诺利克(Bienstock Ruth Anolik)在《利用假人,精灵附身:对犹太传说的女性主义改写》一文中指出,通过改写犹太神话中的假人传说,奥兹克等女性犹太作家希冀在男性支配的犹太书

---

① Katha Pollitt, "The Three Selves of Cynthia Ozick", *The New York Times Book Review*, 22 May 1983, p. 35. Rpt. in *Contemporary Literary Criticism*, ed. Jean C. Stine, et al., Vol. 28, Detroit: Gale, 1984, p. 352.

② Elaine M. Kauvar, "Notes toward Editing a Contemporary Writer's Letters", *Studies in the Novel*, 27 (Fall 1995), p. 409.

写传统中打开一个属于女性的叙述空间,找到女性在书写中的位置。[1]

作为女性主义者的奥兹克塑造了众多才华出众、卓然独立的女性形象,是评论者们关注的热点。莎拉·科恩(Sarah Blacher Cohen)指出,奥兹克笔下受过最好教育的角色通常是女性,她们拥有惊人的智慧、渊博的学识。[2] 希文在其专著中专辟章节,讨论奥兹克的女性角色,她指出:"奥兹克创造的女性人物解构了束缚并压迫女性数千年的女性形象中势不两立的圣母玛利亚和妓女的分裂。她们往往是身体和头脑并重的女性:思想的母亲,思想的恋人,恋爱中的思想者。她们没有被过时的得体的女性行为观念所绑缚,正如莉莉丝(Lilith)那样,她们不甘屈从第二。"[3]

此外,评论者还关注奥兹克作品中描写的特殊历史背景下的母女关系和女性经验。弗兰克·卡茨(Frank Katz)指出,《大披肩》是一部描写女性经验的小说,其中描写的女性经验是绝无仅有的。通常,女性在集中营遭受的三种身体变化,即性虐待和性凌辱、停经和绝孕的担忧、母性和生产,在小说角色身上均有所体现。罗莎遭纳粹军官强奸产下一女马格达,之后孩子被害,不仅剥夺了罗莎的母亲身份,还挑战了她的母性伦理,因为她亲眼看着孩子被害而默不作声。[4] 洛英也认为,《大披肩》中反映的母女关系是不同寻常的,小说中母亲角色对于主人公罗莎而言仍

---

① Bienstock Ruth Anolik, "Appropriating the Golem, Possessing the Dybbuk: Female Retellings of Jewish Tales", *Modern Language Studies*, 31.2(2001), p. 40.

② Sarah Blacher Cohen, *Cynthia Ozick's Comic Art: From Levity to Liturgy*, Bloomington and Indianapolis: Indiana University Press, 1994, p. 168.

③ Miriam Sivan, *Belonging Too Well: Portraits of Identity in Cynthia Ozick's Fiction*, Albany: State University of New York Press, 2009, p. 6.

④ Frank Harry Katz, *Screaming Laughing: The Functions and Varieties of Humor in American Holocaust Literature*, Diss. Arizona State University, 2000, pp. 83-86.

然是重要的,但在集中营的极端状况和泯灭人性的屠杀之下,主人公的母性遭到了残害,母亲不得不接受孩子被虐杀的命运而沉默自保。①

三、写作风格研究

奥兹克的写作风格研究是国外奥兹克研究的重要方面。斯特德兰贝里称奥兹克身上兼具希腊精神和希伯来灵魂,二者在她作品中完美融合,造就了奥兹克冲突的艺术。虽然她是犹太教的忠实信仰者,但是创作中的奥兹克是自由的,她并没有拘泥于犹太传统的一隅,作茧自缚。相反,身处两种文化传统之中的奥兹克,对于各种元素都信手拈来;无论是希腊神话还是犹太假人传说,万事万物皆备于创作,这造就了奥兹克兼容并蓄的创作风格。

善于运用魔幻和神秘元素,是奥兹克写作的鲜明风格。评论者们对此达成了共识,因为奥兹克的重要主题之一是现实和虚幻之间的冲突,奥兹克在表达这一主题时自然而然地使用了超自然元素和神秘主义元素,如劳伦斯·弗里德曼(Lawrence Friedman)所言:"无论奥兹克作品的基本主题是什么,她的故事都是虚实结合的。"②凯尔斯凯指出,奥兹克对神话和神秘主义元素的使用,增强了其作品的主题,"凸显了犹太后裔在美国焦虑不安的生存现状"③。洛英认为,奥兹克擅长运用神话和魔幻元素,其众多小说中有四部属于魔幻题材,都是其最优秀的作品。他指出,奥兹克痴迷于神话和魔幻元素,尽管她自己的小说常常传达

① Joseph Lowin, *Cynthia Ozick*, Boston: Twayne, 1988, pp. 106-107.

② Lawrence Friedman, *Understanding Cynthia Ozick*, Columbia: University of South Carolina Press, 1991, p. 122.

③ Vera Emuna Kielsky, *Inevitable Exiles: Cynthia Ozick's View of the Precariousness of Jewish Existence in a Gentile Society*, Diss. Arizona State University, 1985, p. 27.

的是相反的观点,即犹太教中关于写作的观点,"在思想和情绪上都要拒绝存在于造物主和被造物之间的神秘之境"①。然而,洛英并不认为这是西方传统对奥兹克的影响,而是奥兹克在面对文学困境时在两种冲突的解决方式面前的犹豫不决,从中产生了具有奇幻色彩的作品。② 由于对超现实元素的喜爱,评论者经常将奥兹克与奥康纳(Flannery O'Conner)进行比较研究。拉马尔·尼斯利(Lamar L. Nisly)宣称,"奥兹克和奥康纳通过使用魔幻和怪诞等元素,在描述神秘之物时让读者直接与神秘之物面对面",将他们引入一个现实的故事之中,目的是用可怕的不真实的场景让他们感到震惊,因此提醒读者现实往往就是神秘本身。③

评论者指出,奥兹克作品的另一个风格特征是其喜剧艺术。科恩在其专著《辛西娅·奥兹克的喜剧艺术:从轻率到礼拜》中分析了奥兹克作品的喜剧效果。她认为,源于对人性复杂的深刻洞察,奥兹克采取了一种轻松幽默的风格而非悲剧的风格来揭示人性不堪的一面。悲剧可以阐释人性最高贵的品质,而自然主义只能呈现人类动物性的存在。奥兹克通过喜剧创造了一个生动的世俗世界,生于其间的人总是在不停地犯错、忏悔,徘徊于地狱与天堂之间。④ 弗里德曼称《升空》(Levitation)"整体而言是对后现代写作的滑稽嘲讽"⑤。奥兹克的其他两个故事《嫉妒;或美国的意第绪语》(Envy; or, Yiddish in America)和《篡夺》(Usurpation)

---

① Joseph Lowin, *Cynthia Ozick*, Boston: Twayne, 1988, p. 78.

② Joseph Lowin, *Cynthia Ozick*, Boston: Twayne, 1988, p. 78.

③ Lamar L. Nisly, *Portraying Religious Mystery in the Fiction of Malamud, Percy, Ozick, and O'Connor*, Diss. University of Delaware, 1996, pp. 138-139.

④ Sarah Blacher Cohen, *Cynthia Ozick's Comic Art: From Levity to Liturgy*, Bloomington and Indianapolis: Indiana University Press, 1994, pp. 2-4.

⑤ Lawrence Friedman, *Understanding Cynthia Ozick*, Columbia: University of South Carolina Press, 1991, p. 122.

都属于此类风格,因为它们都在探讨作家生活和写作,这宣告了奥兹克作为纽约的犹太作家,在写作作家的生活中,“奥兹克可能意在打趣六七十年代风靡一时的自我指涉的小说,同时也因为她追随了一种已濒临死亡的风尚而自我打趣”①。弗兰克·卡茨(Frank Katz)也提到,奥兹克在描写人类极端状况的小说《大披肩》中使用女性作家惯常使用的幽默手法,以此攻击“标准”,即带给女性压迫和伤害的秩序。②

四、文学传承研究

尽管奥兹克自愿为犹太人代言,但是评论者仍然注意到奥兹克的作品中难以忽略的美国特性。尽管奥兹克作品中传承和表达的是犹太思想和道德律,但她在文学上的追随者却是美国文学的巨擘亨利·詹姆士;同时,她对 T. S. 艾略特以及现代派观点的传承也是美国学界关注的话题。

奥兹克曾经多次提及自己年轻时对詹姆士的模仿都不得而终,因此评论界认为她对詹姆士的师承关系是毋庸置疑的。爱德蒙·怀特(Edmund White)在《思想的大脑的图像》一文中指出:“任何不能反映内部或外部世界的艺术都不能激发奥兹克的兴趣,因此,奥兹克是詹姆士的忠实继承者。……和詹姆士一样,奥兹克也是一个道德家——不喊口号,不讲负面或积极的教训,而是行为

① Lawrence Friedman, *Understanding Cynthia Ozick*, Columbia: University of South Carolina Press, 1991, pp. 122-123.

② Frank Harry Katz, *Screaming Laughing: The Functions and Varieties of Humor in American Holocaust Literature*, Diss. Arizona State University, 2000, p. 82.

顺从于道德需求的一个人。”[①]弗里德曼指出,《信任》是一本詹姆士式的小说,不仅因为它在各个方面模仿詹姆士——“人物塑造、情景、主题甚至遣词造句都在模仿詹姆士的高度的严肃性”,而且“它对女性身份的关注……它的单一视角,它的主题阐释、风格和隐喻的复杂多样”。[②] 桑福德·平斯克(Sanford Pinsker)在《翻转詹姆士小说》一文中指出,奥兹克的新作《陌生的身体》(*Foreign Bodies*)“在所有詹姆士认为重要的地方发力。和《信任》一样,该小说处处模仿《大使》,尽管它有意将《大使》的国际主题完全翻转颠倒”[③]。

如果说奥兹克和詹姆士之间的师承关系显而易见的话,奥兹克和 T. S. 艾略特之间的关系则有些难以界定,研究者们对此也是见仁见智。平斯克在《奥兹克——唯美主义者》一文中指出,奥兹克是现代主义的支持者——“强调奥兹克的审美主义,我头脑中想到的是现代主义传统,那些缠绕着亨利·詹姆士、T. S. 艾略特、庞德、D. H. 劳伦斯等作家的矛盾和暧昧。”[④]阿诺德·班德(Arnold Band)在《舒适的杂糅——奥兹克的〈声誉与愚蠢〉》一文中指出,奥兹克“显然将自己看作是高雅的现代主义者,并哀叹其

① Edmund White, “Images of a Mind Thinking”, *The New York Times Book Review*, 11 Sept. 1983. Rpt. in *Cynthia Ozick*, ed. Harold Bloom, New York: Chelsea House, 1986, p. 129.

② Lawrence Friedman, *Understanding Cynthia Ozick*, Columbia: University of South Carolina Press, 1991, p. 30.

③ Sanford Pinsker, “Turning the Jamesian Novel Upside Down”, Rev. of *Foreign Bodies* by Cynthia Ozick, *Sewanee Review*, 119.3 (Summer, 2011), p. xliii.

④ Sanford Pinsker, “Cynthia Ozick, Aesthete”, *Partisan Review*, 69.2(Spring 2002), p. 206.

在当世的衰败"[①]。希尔顿·克拉默(Hilton Kramer)在《辛西娅·奥兹克向T.S.艾略特和高雅文化的告别》一文中指出,奥兹克在艾略特100周年诞辰时所作的"纪念性"文章中,对艾略特、现代主义、新批评和所谓的"高雅文化"进行了抨击,将艾略特拉下美国文学和文化的神坛,以此宣告与艾氏决裂。尽管奥兹克长期以来是"高雅文化"的主要追随者,此时她决心与这传统决裂,且宣布它的终结。[②] 马克·克鲁普尼克(Mark Krupnik)在《辛西娅·奥兹克:犹太的T.S. 艾略特》一文中指出,奥兹克深受艾略特的影响,并剖析了二者之间的谱系:二者都探讨宗教与文学的关系,尽管方式略有不同;两人都面临事业上的挫折——艾略特认为"浪漫主义沦为堕落的审美主义"是一战所致,他寄望传统信仰的恢复来重塑但丁代表的中世纪天主教;而奥兹克认为动荡来自20世纪60年代以来的主要运动,即政治上的激进主义和"为艺术而艺术"运动的复兴,她希望犹太作家从犹太传统中寻找犹太文学的新出路。[③]

评论界认为奥兹克与美国文学传统的渊源甚深。鉴于其对詹姆士和艾略特的传承,艾琳娜·维尔纳(Arlene Fish Wilner)在《作为艺术家的犹太美国女性:辛西娅·奥兹克和"白脸传统"》一文中,将奥兹克归类于美国的"白脸传统"(paleface)[④],即始于詹

---

① Arnold J. Band, "Comfortable Hybridity: Cynthia Ozick's *Fame and Folly*", *Jewish Social Studies* , 3. 2(1997), pp. 121-122.

② Hilton Kramer, "Cynthia Ozick's Farewell to T. S. Eliot and High Culture", *The New Criterion*, (1990): pp. 5-10.

③ Mark Krupnick, "Cynthia Ozick as the Jewish T. S. Eliot", *Soundings*, 74. 3-4 (1991), pp. 345-355.

④ Arlene Fish Wilner, "The Jewish-American Woman as Artist: Cynthia Ozick and the 'Paleface' Tradition", *College Literature*, 20. 2 (1993), p. 119.

姆士的“画室小说”，属于阳春白雪的文学传统；与此相对的是以惠特曼为代表的“赤颈传统”(redneck)，更多关注人的情感而非个人文化，属于下里巴人的文学，但并非就是粗俗的、缺乏教养的。此外，白脸传统珍视宗教信条，逃避现实，而赤颈传统拥抱自然，追求与自然合一。维尔纳指出：“考虑到奥兹克小说的智性化，毫无疑问她属于白脸传统，他们致力于观念的打磨、行为和道德之间的关联。”[①]克拉特卡认为，奥兹克与美国文学最深刻的的渊源在于她致力于将美学与宗教道德感结合。因此，她可以与霍桑(Hawthorne)、梅尔维尔(Melville)、狄金森(Dickinson)、贝娄(Bellow)和罗斯等一系列作家齐名。[②]

综上所述，国外奥兹克研究呈现出以下特点：首先，奥兹克研究深度和广度并重。研究范围囊括其作品中的犹太主题、女性议题、写作风格、文学传承等多个方面，同时在各个方面都进行了深度挖掘，具有极高的学术价值。同时，对于读者了解奥兹克作品提供了重要的参考。奥兹克对犹太主题的挖掘与贡献，包括对大屠杀叙事美学的超越，是当代任何一位犹太作家都难以企及的，可以说是美国犹太文学不可逾越的一座高峰。其次，文论研究和文学研究交叉。奥兹克研究中的一大特色是评论者用奥兹克自己提出的创作理念阐释她的文本创作，文学理论支撑文本创作，文本映照学理，相映成趣，凸显奥兹克高超的创作才能。奥

---

① Arlene Fish Wilner, “The Jewish-American Woman as Artist: Cynthia Ozick and the ‘Paleface’ Tradition”, *College Literature*, 20. 2 (1993), p. 122.

② Amy Weintraub Kratka, *Cynthia Ozick's Sacral Aesthetic*, Diss. Boston University, 2005, p. 46.

兹克用自己彰显犹太观念的文学创作开启了美国犹太文学写作的新方向。最后,外部研究和内部研究并行。美国学界除了对奥兹克作品本身进行多角度深层次的探析之外,将奥兹克放在美国文学传统之中加以研究;在承认奥兹克的犹太性的同时,并未忽略其突出的美国性,正是犹太性和美国性的深度融合造就了奥兹克的独特美学风格。

(张晶晶:北京体育大学国际体育组织学院讲师;李杉杉:北京体育大学国际体育组织学院副教授)

《芒果街，我自己的小屋》中的自我书写[①]

李晓丽

《芒果街，我自己的小屋》(*A House of My Own*: *Stories from My Life*)是美国拉美裔作家桑德拉·希斯内罗丝(Sandra Cisneros，1954～)于2015年出版的一部自传作品。凭借此书，希斯内罗丝获得该年度美国国家艺术勋章(National Medal of Arts)。全书共收录40余篇文章，其中多数为作者自1984～2014年发表于报刊的文章、做过的主题演讲和文选撰稿，中间还穿插了几篇从未付梓的文章和信件。这些散文体的文章被希斯内罗丝称为"迷失在我视线之外的小羊羔"，是她年近六十，向读者"宣示真实生活"、对自我进行重新评价和形塑的一种方式，共同展现了作家涉时间长河，对文学和人生的探索和体悟。[②]

---

① 本文是教育部人文社科项目"当代美国非裔小说中的生命政治书写研究"(项目编号：20YJC752008)和山东省社科联2019年度课题"赛珍珠作品中的儒家思想及其跨文化传播研究"(项目编号:19-ZZ-WX-05)阶段性成果。

② [美]桑德拉·希斯内罗丝:《芒果街，我自己的小屋》，程应铸译，南海出版公司2017年版，第14～15页。为叙述方便，以下简称《我自己的小屋》。后文涉及该书引文，如未加说明，只随文标注页码。

《我自己的小屋》与传统自传有着极大不同,并带有希斯内罗丝强烈的个人风格。与作家的成名作《芒果街上的小屋》(*The House on Mango Street*, 1984)极为相似,这部自传中的41篇小品文也是各自独立,没有遵循线性的时空顺序排列。从表面上看,作品没有形成一体的递进和严密的逻辑,碎片化和拼贴等后现代手法更是让叙事脉络显得模糊不清。但不可否认的是,与其他自传一样,《我自己的小屋》符合自传的基本特质。其叙事目标和核心始终围绕自传主的自我书写与身份建构展开。在略显杂乱的形式中,希斯内罗丝以自己独有的手法,依照自传的传统,"给生活加以一个模式,从中建构连贯故事",并在此过程中赋予了自我意义并实现了自我价值。[①] 本文试图发掘《我自己的小屋》所具有的自传文体特征和传统,同时透过碎片化的文本信息,提炼出希斯内罗丝自我书写的主题和脉络,探讨作家如何通过漫游者的自我阐释框架,如何借他人书写自己,以实现其身份建构与自我形塑。

一、自传文本特征

《我自己的小屋》虽然在形式上十分自由,体现了自传界限的开放性,但仔细看来,这部作品还是较为符合自传的界定标准。法国自传研究专家菲力浦·勒热讷(Philippe Lejeune)在《自传契约》中,对自传给出了一个基本定义:"某人以自己的生活为素材用散文体写成的后视性叙事,它强调作者的个人生活,尤其是其人格的历史。"[②]在此定义中,勒热讷对自传的语言形式、主题、作者情形和叙述者地位,明确了具体的指征。《我自己的小屋》虽然在形

① Roy Pascal, *Design and Truth in Autobiography*, London and New York: Routledge, 2016, p. 9.

② [法]菲力浦·勒热讷:《自传契约》,杨国政译,三联书店2001年版,第3页。

式上较为松散，文本信息稍显碎片化，但符合勒热讷定义的各项指征。书中收录的文章多采用散文体的叙事语言，所谈主题都直接或间接涉及个人生活及人格历史，绝大多数文章的作者、叙述者与主人公的身份保持了同一性。同时，每篇文章的写作时间都在事件发生之后，而且在每篇文章之前，作者又附加了一个前言，对文章的写作时间、背景加以介绍，必要时还加上了对文章写作时自我意识的解释甚至矫正，这些都保证了叙述的后视性视角，从而提供了自传书写所必须具备的一定的审视距离。

在满足自传基本要素的同时，《我自己的小屋》也对应了自传作家意图构建真实自我的写作动机。这部作品出版时，距离希斯内罗丝凭借《芒果街上的小屋》一举成名已有近三十载。三十年间，《芒果街上的小屋》的读者时常会揣度希斯内罗丝是否就是小说里的埃斯佩朗莎，她所写的众多故事是否是她自己的亲身经历。在该书的引言中，希斯内罗丝写道：

> 我让我的记忆在这里呈现，它是宣示我真实生活，并把它和我的小说区分开来的一种方式，因为在那里，似乎有太多对我的假定和虚构。（例如，有关于我死了的不真实谣传，就曾经在维基百科里报道。还有，不容含糊的是，我绝不像一份西班牙报纸描述的那样，是一个在蒂华纳卖淫的妇女，尽管它编造了一个动人的故事）我还不如来写一部自传，此刻我以不带任何偏见的形式，好比为自己编织寿衣，我提供我的个人故事，作为记录我自己人生的一个方法。(3)

在对待自传真实性这一传统问题上，希斯内罗丝的态度明确，在一开始就表明了整部作品处理事件的指向和内在核心：通过这样一个非虚构性作品，达到去除个人神话，袒露和解析真实自我的目的。诚如勒热讷所说:“公众认定自传是话语的一种私人形式,它被认定是一个真实的人的话语,这个人应该为他写下的文字负责,就像他为他的人生负责一样。”[①]因此,在自传的开端,希斯内罗丝就亮明了在自我阐释和认同过程中,自己作为自传作者而非小说作者的一种自知与自觉。

这种“自传契约”的订立,宣告了自我书写的真实性,但是不可否认,希斯内罗丝在选择和构架自传素材时,遵循了大多数自传作家都会遵循的原则,即让叙述尽量符合个人的价值判断和自我定位。书写自传的人,“总是有意无意地把对自己的叙述尽量符合自我的身份认定和道德评价,把叙述纳入自己的价值体系和思维模式”[②],“在自传中常常可以见到简约叙述和充分叙述的情况,作者对自己不愿意提起的事情或者是根本不提,或者是一笔带过,只做出简略的交代”[③]。希斯内罗丝似乎更加注重内心真实地呈现,更为关注的是自己作为拉美裔女性作家的自然身份和社会身份的构建。因此,在她选取进入这部自传的文章中,我们似乎很难看到太多牵涉她个人生涯过于细节性的描述,对于她的成长经历和感情经历在多数时候是一笔带过甚至是略过不提。但是,细节的模糊甚至缺失并不能抹消希斯内罗丝作为自传主的真诚和作品的真实性,因为作为自传主,她并不需要完全忠实于个人历史的精确性,进而将自己的一切和盘托出。《我自己的小屋》是作者努力看待和理解自己的生活之后的感悟,更是作者想要传达给读者的,她个人对记忆的解读与阐释。

此外,自传作品的对话性在《我自己的小屋》中也有明确的表征。作家现在的自我与过去的自我之间的对话,在两个时间维度

---

① [法]菲力浦·勒热讷:《自传契约》,杨国政译,三联书店 2001 年版,第 3 页。
② 杨正润:《现代传记学》,南京大学出版社 2009 年版,第 291 页。
③ 杨正润:《现代传记学》,南京大学出版社 2009 年版,第 294 页。

上完成。其一，入选这部自传作品的每一篇文章所写的时间都在所述故事之后；其二，作者置于每篇文章前的前言，作为副文本完成于自传的编选过程中。现在视角与过去视角之间的合力由此成为可能，每个人对自己过去的认识和评价总是变化的。因此，介于故事发生、每篇文章的书写以及前言书写之间的双重时间距离，使得作者能够在与过去的反复对话中重新审视自我，并不断完善对自我的理解。例如，在《唯一的女儿》(*Only Daughter*)的前言中，希斯内罗丝对文章写作的时间和当时的感受做了如下描写："下面是我在一九八九年的那个长夜里起床写就的。我获得那些荣誉的提名，当时我感到吃惊，现在依然在惊异之中，要知道，它们可能是一个人死后才能获得的殊荣。从那个时候起，我就有所感悟：绝望只是进程中的一部分，而不是终点。"(86)作家透过现在与过去的联通，将自己当下的体悟、反思和内省投射向了过去自我的经验世界，增强了自传文本后视性的叙事功能。

二、漫游者的自我阐释框架

在全书开始的引言中，希斯内罗丝将自己比作荷马笔下的奥德修斯，有意识地建立起漫游者的自我阐释框架，在自我寓言化中讲述生活经历和人格历史，向读者暴露和解释真实的自己。在自传书写中，自我寓言化铺设出的是一种自我语境，是作者自我成长历程中的精神产品，揭示的是作者给自我赋予的独特意义。希斯内罗丝在《海德拉屋》(*Hydra House*)一文中记录了自己第一次真正意义上的漫游。28 岁的希斯内罗丝"想成为一名作家，但除了旅行，不知道怎样来实现这个目标"(8)。所幸，一笔写作奖学金不期而至。她带着自己未完成的书稿来到位于希腊的海德拉岛，并在那里开始了边写作边漫游的生活。漫游的起点始于希腊，对应了奥德修斯的神话背景。当时的她认为自己会是在家中守望丈夫归乡的佩内洛普。然而,多年后,当她的足迹延伸到美国本土、欧洲和南美的许多地方,强烈的自我意识在漫游过程中被唤醒,并日益成熟。希斯内罗丝最终发现自己并非被动等待的佩内洛普,而是更像四处漂泊的奥德修斯,在长达30年的"奇异旅行"中不断找寻心灵的归家之路(30)。同时,奥德修斯的身份隐喻和漫游者的独特视角将其在多处漫游的经历串联起来,全书贯穿的行旅主题为专属于她的人生故事填充了丰富的个人意义。

希斯内罗丝在回忆父亲的文章中,对自己漫游者情结的源起做了说明。在某种程度上,父亲作为第一代墨西哥裔移民的离散心理促成了希斯内罗丝对于漫游的最初体验和认知。在《稻草变黄金》(*Straw into Gold*)一文中,她提到自己是从父亲那里"继承了他对漫游世界的爱好"(74)。被迫在美国定居的父亲常常由于思乡情切,在匆忙中退掉在芝加哥租住的房子,携妻带子返回墨西哥老家。归来后,又不得不在各个奇卡诺社区辗转,四处寻找新的住所。希斯内罗丝六岁前,时常在美墨两国间穿梭,并跟随父母经历"从一个奇卡诺公寓搬到另一个奇卡诺公寓的漫游"(74)。幼年的经历潜在性地形成了一种固有的行为模式,使得作家不抗拒也不惮于在跨越异质文化和不同边界的过程中,寻找并确立自我的身份认同,而这样的模式几乎贯穿了希斯内罗丝从离开出生地芝加哥,辗转一生到现居地圣米格尔的整个轨迹。

在希斯内罗丝对自己漫游动机的解释中,能够看出作家的每次"离开"都是以挣脱束缚为前提,表达了对现实秩序的某种不满与超脱。在一次访谈中她提到自己"与生活始终有种对抗性"①,

---

① 傅小平:《时代的低语:当代文学对话录》,新华先锋出版公司2020年版,第259页。

每一次打破局限的对抗行为，其背后的动机都是为了获取新的个人属性与人生定位。借由独立的生活，希斯内罗丝既能摆脱父权对其女性身份模式化的期待，又能在两性情感关系中占据主动地位，结束男性伴侣无谓的束缚和掠夺。希斯内罗丝是有六个儿子的墨西哥家庭中唯一的女儿，父亲对她的期待只是“成为某个人的妻子”(87)。在墨西哥文化里，“男人和女人只有通过结婚，否则不可以离开他们父亲的房子”，而希斯内罗丝毫不犹豫地用“双脚跨出我父亲的门槛”(73)。更糟的是，她在六个兄弟出门闯荡前就离开了家。“离开”打破了父权社会强加在墨西哥裔女性身上的禁忌，帮助她摆脱了奇卡诺社区里其他女性只能“将悲哀支撑在肘上，凝视窗外”(76)的消极命运，使她得以借助反学院派的书写将拉美裔女性不为主流文化所知的生命故事一一呈现。

在对职业生涯的回顾中，希斯内罗丝将离家和远行的漫游设定为她自我成就的一种必然模式和手段。作家梦虽然催生了希斯内罗丝的自我意识和对作家生活的向往，但即便是参加了爱荷华作家工作坊的学习，她“对于女性作家的生活状态”依然“所知甚少”(9)。一方面，身边的男性和白人女性因其固有的性别、种族和阶级偏见，对她的女性艺术家之路毫无帮助；另一方面，她对拉美裔前辈女作家和少数族裔女性主义学者，如格洛丽亚·安札杜瓦(Gloria Anzaldua)和切丽·莫拉格(Cherríe Moraga)，缺乏足够的了解和认识，进而造成了可供参考的精神榜样和成长模式的缺失。因而，希斯内罗丝只能凭借自己的努力，选择在不断地离去中“潜身于边境”，找寻自己的身份定位和“想象中的祖国”(210)。离别的这种行为“具有根本性的‘自我成长’象征意义”，希斯内罗丝必须“与先前的自我分手”[①],才能在求学、独居、旅行和写作中打破原有的自然属性和社会属性,并日益强大成熟起来。在某种意义上,《芒果街上的小屋》的成长主题在《我自己的房子》中得以延续。就像小说中埃斯佩朗莎最后所说的那样,“有一天我会把一袋袋的书和纸打进包里。有一天我会对芒果说再见。我强大得她没法永远留住我。有一天我会离开”[②]。希斯内罗丝在自传文本中记录了现实中的“埃斯佩朗莎”离开“芒果街”后,在各地漫游的生活经历和成长历程,以非虚构叙事补充了虚构叙事给读者留下的想象空间。

同时,希斯内罗丝走出奇卡诺社区的漫游让她获得了更广阔的社会视野,促使了她政治意识的萌发,并催生了她对抗阶级身份固化的努力。在《〈芒果街上的小屋〉十岁了》(“*The House on Mango Street's* Tenth Birthday”)一文中,希斯内罗丝回顾了在爱荷华作家工作坊时的经历,以及她创作《芒果街上的小屋》的动机。因为与白人同学在肤色、阶层和文化背景上的差异,希斯内罗丝敏锐地察觉到自己的“他者”属性,并一度陷入失声状态。研讨会上针对加斯东·巴什拉《空间的诗学》的讨论,使她猛然意识到家宅具有定义个体社会阶层属性的功能,而自己恰恰又缺失体面和功能完整的家宅空间。在对家宅的认知变化过程中,希斯内罗丝感受到居住空间的差异体现了社会阶级的分化。这样的认知转化为愤怒和借由文学书写发出“我自己的声音”的写作动机,《芒果街上的小屋》便是她与作家班和主流文学“对着干”时进行的“一场无声的革命”(121)。在她笔下,芒果街上的房子远非巴什拉所谓的“庇

---

① 邹兰芳:《想象的国度:现代阿拉伯童年自传及文化建构》,《现代传记研究》2014年第2期。

② [美]桑德拉·希斯内罗丝:《芒果街上的小屋》,潘帕译,译林出版社2006年版,第150页。

佑着梦想”，“保护着梦想家”和让人“能够在安详中做梦”的地方[①]，而是拘囿奇卡诺社区女性身心自由的场所。作家借由书写表达的既是自我也是女性群体挣脱枷锁的共同渴望，而这样的诉求从《芒果街上的小屋》一直贯穿到她的其他诸多作品。

在离家漫游中，希斯内罗丝还得到了在父母家享受不到的“奢侈”——完全属于自己的私密空间和对自我的探索。她从墨西哥文化给女性戴上的“无知和羞耻的双重贞操带”中挣脱（148），开始了解并学会对自己的身体、婚姻和生育负责。在墨西哥文化中，守护神瓜达卢佩圣母是天主教圣母和美洲土著女神相结合的产物，强调了“女性的忍让、付出、宽容和服从”，体现了“男性对女性的控制：女性婚前必须守节操，婚后隐忍持家、相夫教子”。[②] 希斯内罗丝无法忍受拉美女性对自己身体的沉默，并试图在重新审视瓜达卢佩圣母的过程中做出自己大胆的、颠覆性的解读：“卢佩，聪明的坏女孩，不是沉默和被动，而是在沉默中积聚力量。”（153）希斯内罗丝打破了传统自传的固有范式，即在将肉体和精神对立的柏拉图传统中，肉体在自传这一文类中的表现往往被压抑，甚至近乎抹消。希斯内罗丝认为，性体验是女性存在体验的一个重要部分。在颠覆灵肉二元对立中，她试图实现对女性他者身份的解构。因此，性别维度下的希斯内罗丝的漫游具有了“向外看”和“向内看”的双重视角。“向外”，她看到了奇卡诺社区男权文化对女性的束缚；“向内”，她看到并发掘了女性内在的真实与力量，而这些都建立在自由独立的漫游者身份前提之上。

---

① [法]加斯东·巴什拉：《空间的诗学》，张逸婧译，上海译文出版社 2020 年版，第 5 页。

② 李保杰：《从墨西哥女性原型看桑德拉·希斯内罗丝小说中女性形象的嬗变》，《天津外国语学院学报》2010 年第 4 期。

三、借由他人书写自我的叙述模式

在自传书写中,借由他人书写自我往往是对自我的一种映射。钱锺书在谈及传记写作时曾说:在写他人时,“不妨加入自己的主见,借别人为题来发挥自己”[①]。在容纳41篇文章的这部作品里,一共收录了15篇直接以他人为题的文章。希斯内罗丝族裔作家的特殊身份,使得她将关注更多投向前辈作家、活跃在拉美艺术圈和文化圈的人物。作家对于文学、艺术和族裔问题的认识与反思,在这些有关他人的文章中直接或间接地呈现出来。

在书中,希斯内罗丝介绍了多位对她文学创作影响深远的作家,以及自己对他们的理解和感悟。借由这些文章,希斯内罗丝完成了对前辈作家的致敬。与前辈作家的“对话”,让希斯内罗丝心智洞开,心灵得到抚慰,并且影响了她文学创作的主题和写作风格。那些她“亲身接触”过的,或是“从书页报刊上知道的”作家,被她视为文学家园里的“亲人”和文学创作的引路人(38)。这样的认同是她在对作家文本解读过程中,通过激活自己的想象力、直观力和感悟力,在与前辈作家的视域融合中达成的。在希斯内罗丝的创作生涯中,她曾受到“中坚的奇卡诺活动分子的攻讦”,她的作品被认为“还算不上真正的奇卡诺文学”(39)。阅读和聆听奇卡诺诗人路易斯·奥马尔·萨利纳斯(Luis Omar Salinas)的作品,让希斯内罗丝明白:一个奇卡诺诗人“不是一个咬文嚼字的浮夸诗人,也不代表什么理论学说”,而是“一个用心来写作的诗人,一个对人类怀着同情和悲悯的诗人”(46)。女诗人格温德林·布鲁克斯(Gwendolyn Brooks)所写的“食豆者”们“生活在逼仄的公寓里,

① 钱锺书:《写在人生边上》,辽宁人民出版社2000年版,第4页。

共用洗手间，没有足够的热水”(32)。受其启发，希斯内罗丝创造了属于她自己和整个墨西哥裔群体的“食豆者”们的故事。思想前卫的阿根廷文学大师郝尔赫·路易斯·博尔赫斯(Jorge Luis Borges)，曾出版过一本《梦见老虎》的集子，里面的故事“短小精致”，“像是百科全书的条目”(260)。恰是这本“介乎诗歌和小说之间的新体裁作品”，激发希斯内罗丝尝试在《芒果街上的小屋》“开创一种新的写作形式”(35)，打破“体裁与体裁之间的，写和说之间的，高雅文学和儿童歌谣之间的，纽约和想象的马孔多村之间的，美国和墨西哥之间的”，各种各样的界限(260)。这样的书写方式，让希斯内罗丝成为先锋的奇卡娜作家代表，并让《芒果街上的小屋》在历经 30 年岁月洗礼，依然充满浓浓诗意，绽放着熠熠光彩。流亡作家爱德华多·加莱亚诺(Eduardo Galeano)因为作品的政治性，曾两次被驱逐。希斯内罗丝将自己与加莱亚诺作品的相遇定义为一种“必然的缘分”(195)。那时的她正经历人生低谷，挣扎在生死边缘，而加莱亚诺的《火的记忆》拯救了她。在她看来，加莱亚诺的历史书写，从不平淡乏味。他的文字教给人们如何看透生死，看轻磨难，并始终保持做人的尊严。他严谨的写作态度也在提醒着希斯内罗丝：“为什么要写”(195)。这样的感悟，是希斯内罗丝在想象加莱亚诺深陷流亡境地，品味作品中的政治书写时慢慢获得的。希斯内罗丝对这些前辈作家的评价和接受被融入她作为作家的自我生成和形塑中，每一位单独篇章介绍的作家实际上投射出的是希斯内罗丝作家自我的某一个面向，它们共同构成了一个立体的拉美裔女性作家的主体形象。

除小说作家和诗人之外，拉美艺术和文化圈的多位音乐家、歌唱家和摄影家也是希斯内罗丝书写的对象。在不同于文学的艺术门类中，希斯内罗丝加深了对拉美文化和艺术传统的了解，对自己的族裔文化身份有了更多认同，并让她获得了独有的“人格、气质和生命意识”[1]。例如，在《致阿斯托尔的探戈》(“A Tango for Astor”)一文中，希斯内罗丝讲述了在她感到“迷茫、悲哀、消沉和懊丧的时候”，音乐家阿斯托尔·皮亚佐拉(Astor Piazzolla)的作品如何给予她生活和创作的指引(81)。作家将自己的经历、苦恼和情感带入了对音乐的聆听和欣赏，领会到美的东西和悲剧性的东西发生碰撞时产生的强烈的、迅猛的力量。她对于阿斯托尔音乐的理解不是外在的，而是内在于心的。在音乐中，她学会了要在工作中具备饱满的激情，要保持独立的人格，要勇敢和无畏。要将痛苦转换为咆哮，于她而言，就是诗歌和小说的创作。这样的信念，贯穿了希斯内罗丝对人生的理解，激发了她的诗歌创作和一部部作品的诞生。伽达默尔认为：“理解不是解释者对外在于他的一切文本及其作者意义的寻求和解释的行为方式，而是此在本身的存在方式。”[2]这或许能够解释，为何希斯内罗丝与阿斯托尔在面对面时，她唯一能说出的话是：“皮亚佐拉先生，你的作品，就是，我的人生。”(84)

当然，希斯内罗丝借他人抒发自己的叙述是一种相对“隐性”的模式。她个人作为文学创作者这一自我概念的发展和完善是在与他人的“对话”中被呈现出的，是一个透过文本信息的拼贴而被逐渐勾勒出的过程。因此，相较于直白地表明自己的文学创作动机、态度和手法，这样的呈现方式显然会给读者带来一定的挑战。但是，如此处理方式完全符合希斯内罗丝先锋作家的风格，同时也增加了这个自传文本阅读的趣味性，并为读者解读希斯内罗丝的自我书写提供了更多想象的空间。

---

① 刘小云：《阐释学的文本解读》，《求索》2010 年第 6 期。

② 朱立元：《略论文学作品的意义生成——一个诠释学视角的考察》，《中国社会科学》2017 年第 5 期。

《我自己的小屋》出版时,希斯内罗丝已步入耳顺之年。这部自传是作家对自己 30 余年生活和创作的回顾与思考,也满足了读者对作家的好奇与想象。如果说,希斯内罗丝的成长小说《芒果街上的小屋》讲述的是一个拉美裔女孩在贫困处境下,获得心智成熟的故事。那么,这本集子则勾勒了一位拉美裔女性作家,跨越种族和性别阻碍,在写作和生活旅途中,获得人生感悟,寻找精神家园的故事。书中,希斯内罗丝不断打破边界,如奥德修斯般,行进在了解世界和认识自我的旅途中,并用自己的方式诠释着这"大千世界"的"无限美好"(358)。她的自我书写实现了描述和构建自我发展的事实,并为自己的故事赋予意义的最终目的。

[李晓丽:山东大学(威海)翻译学院讲师]

亚裔美国文学之父赵健秀的共同体建构与操演性[①]

陈 永

亚裔美国文学之父赵健秀虽然一生饱受争议，但他对亚裔美国文学的创生和发展作出了不可磨灭的贡献，这无可非议。华裔学者卡尔文·麦克米林(Calvin McMillin)在帮助赵健秀将其分藏在三家图书馆的早年创作手稿编辑整理，尔后出版的最近一部长篇小说《大儿子的忏悔：伟大的华裔美国小说》“导言”部分说：“尽管赵健秀多刺的文风是故意而为之还是他的固有性格使然仍然值得商榷，但他所坚持的信念的力量和真诚不容置疑。”[②]然而，赵健秀多刺的文风究竟是故意而为之还是他的固有性格使然的疑点，评论界却鲜有探究，这一直是个谜团。纵观赵健秀一生文学创作和文学文化批评活动，有几个重要事件不容忽视。一是他在其1974年牵头编辑出版的具有开创意义的《哎呀！亚裔美国作家选

---

① 本文是山东省社科联年度项目“赛珍珠作品中的儒家思想及其跨文化传播研究”(项目编号：19-ZZ-WX-05)的阶段性成果。

② Frank Chin & Calvin McMillin, *The Confessions of a Number One Son: The Great Chinese American Novel*, Honolulu: University of Hawaii Press, 2015, p. 5.

集》中所推出的“亚裔感性”(Asian American sensibility)概念以及就谁应该成为“亚裔感性”的承载主体与第一代华人移民学者秦家骢展开的笔战;二是分别以他和其大学同班同学、著名华裔女权主义作家汤亭亭为代表的旷日持久的“赵汤之争”;三是他与著名非裔美国作家伊什梅尔·里德(Ishmael Reed)结成的生死同盟。学界对赵健秀与秦家骢的笔战从未关注过,更无人探讨过其与后来的“赵汤之争”的关系;也未曾有人研究过赵健秀从里德那里除了抵抗政治之外还学到了什么。此外,赵健秀的研究者,尤其中国学者,往往喜欢实读赵健秀的批评观点,却无法对赵健秀倡导的“亚裔感性”建构理论与其作品创作出现明显矛盾作出合理解释。本文试图从操演性视角探究赵健秀如何尝试形成各种知识共同体的可能性和如何通过结成知识共同体实现促进亚裔知识生产的根本目的。

一、“赵秦之争”的操演性本质

赵健秀等虽然感到定义的艰难,但他们在1974年编辑出版的《哎呀! 亚裔美国作家选集》“前言”中还是尝试着对力推的“亚裔感性”作出了如下定义:

> 我们的选集中遴选的作家都是亚裔美国作家。我们所说的“亚裔美国作家”是指菲律宾裔、华裔和日裔美国人,生于美国。他们从收音机里、电影荧幕上、电视屏幕上、漫画作品中以及白人文化推销者那里获得了中国和日本形象,在这些媒介中,黄皮肤的人总是被塑造为这样的形象:当他们受到伤害、情绪低落时,或者愤怒、诅咒、困惑时,他们会发出一声悲

叹、一声怒吼甚至一声尖叫——“哎呀!”[①]

赵健秀借由这群被50年来所谓真正的亚裔美国文学书写的出生在美国却被排除在其文化创造之外的亚裔的屈辱史,阐发自己的“亚裔感性”概念,发起亚裔文化抵抗政治运动。然而,细读该文可以发现,在序言中,“亚裔感性”一词一会儿使用单数,一会儿又使用复数,透露出编者们的某种犹豫不决。也就是说,编者们对于尚处于形成中的亚裔族群是否能够和应该生成一种共有的文化经验感受,以及亚裔族群内部是否应该同样也具有文化的多样性,存在着巨大的疑虑。但是,有一点是十分明显的,四位编者将亚裔新移民断然排除在他们的“亚裔感性”建构承载主体之外,这直接引发当年亚裔英文杂志《桥》(*Bridge*)执行编辑、第一代移民学者秦家骢与赵健秀之间的“笔战”。二人之间的争论开初以私人信件非公开的形式进行,后来该刊物的编辑们认为,二人的观点实际上代表着当时两种尖锐对立的意识形态,将它们公开发表对促进亚裔族群的形成至关重要,所以在征得二人的同意后,将二人的一共7封私人信件在该杂志上公开发表,从而使二人的争辩公开化。

在《哎呀!亚裔美国作家选集》中依照“亚裔感性”主体标准,编者们将林语堂和黎锦扬(C. Y. Lee)排除在该亚裔文学选集之外。然而,编者们又出尔反尔地将第一代华裔移民作家朱路易(Louis Chu)的小说《吃一碗茶》收录其中,这暴露出编者们坚持“亚裔感性”建构主体必须是土生土长的亚裔的主张的内在矛盾。不仅如此,赵健秀等对第一代华裔移民倪志伟(Victor Nee)的历史专著《老加州人:一座美国唐人街的文献调查》赞许有加,因为该书中记录了一个真实的唐人街。赵健秀还专门为将《吃一碗茶》收

① Frank Chin, ed., *Aiiieeeee! An Anthology of Asian-American Writers* (The Mentor edition), Washington, D.C.: Howard University Press, 1991, pp. xi-xii.

录进《哎呀！亚裔美国作家选集》和推崇倪志伟的历史专著与其主张的“亚裔感性”主体标准不一致进行了辩护：“在作家的出生地和是否具有真正的‘亚裔感性’二者之间，我们选择了在其作品中是否生成‘亚裔感性’作为衡量作家是否是真正的亚裔美国人的标准。”[①]其实，这种辩解十分勉强，何以断定其他亚裔新移民都不具有像朱路易和倪志伟一样的书写本真的亚裔经验的族裔文化价值取向？又何以断然肯定所有土生土长的亚裔就都具有‘亚裔感性’文化倾向？亚裔美国文学后来的发展更是证明了所谓“文学唐人街”亚裔作家们在内化主流社会要求亚裔接受的双重人格心理、内化“种族主义之爱”上，比林语堂和黎锦扬有过之而无不及。这也直接导致了赵健秀等主张的狭隘的“亚裔感性”建构主体理论的消解。

赵健秀和秦家骢的争执始于两人对美生华裔和新一代华人移民的关系问题的对立态度。赵健秀坚持以土生土长的亚裔为“亚裔感性”建构主体，这关键在于未能敏感地预料到1965年开始美国实施新的《移民和国籍法案》取消移民配额制后，亚裔新移民人口的急剧增加趋势会完全解构他试图明晰界定亚裔族群文化特质的努力。他的这种族群文化建构理念直接缘起于他对大量涌入的新移民的反感。在他看来，这些新移民只关注母国政治问题，而无意与土生土长的亚裔美国人一道，致力于解决亚裔社会内部存在的亚裔文化形象重建和现实生活中的种种急迫的经济和阶级矛盾问题，比如唐人街贫民窟、年轻人街头暴力犯罪和血汗制衣厂等。赵健秀等致力于“还我美国”(claim America)的捍卫族裔文化生存权的斗争，自然不满于只关心母国政治、受过良好教育美国化了的且动辄越俎代庖地代表亚裔美国群体发声的华人专业人士。赵

① Frank Chin, ed., *Aiiieeeee! An Anthology of Asian-American Writers* (The Mentor edition), Washington, D.C.: Howard University Press, 1991, p. xiii.

健秀申明:“我不是为我的出生权而斗争,我是为我的‘中国佬文化’(Chinaman culture)整体性而奋斗,这是一种被白人和来自中国的华人一直破坏的文化整体性。”[①]也许赵健秀对建构独立于主流文化又不同于中国本土文化的具有整体性和独立性的亚裔文化的“亚裔感性”理论有一定道理,但秦家骢对赵健秀的忠告在事后证明十分具有远见。他提醒赵健秀正视一个事实:“1970 年人口统计时,美国华人华裔人口总共五十万,其中一半为境外出生。而如今,每年有两万境外华人移民美国,你会发现你将越来越难以将自己与他们隔离开来。”[②]

如果没有当年亚裔人口构成的急剧变动,赵健秀甚至可以一直坚持“亚裔感性”的建构主体为土生土长的亚裔美国人。赵健秀口口声声要建构的“中国佬文化”本质上讲是一种反抗主流社会的新的族裔文化,其本身并不是对中国文化的完全拒斥,而是典型的少数族裔群体受到主流社会和华人新移民精英阶层挤压后,为了个人和群体生存而试图建构的强调内部融合的文化。然而,赵健秀认为,这种融合性文化只可能存在于第二代土生土长的华裔身上,所以他坚持认为移民父母是两种文化的断裂点,而秦家骢则认为移民家庭的父母是两种文化的连接点。深入分析后可知,在当年亚裔移民家庭中,父母普遍成了两种文化的断裂点的根源在于其土生土长的子女被迫接受了学校和主流社会强行灌输的对其父母一代人代表的异质外来文化歧视性观念,从而导致二代移民对母国文化的憎恨。

“赵秦之争”有一个巨大疑点,如果二人真的像他们往来信件

① Frank Ching, “Who's Afraid of Frank Chin, or Is It Ching?” *Bridge*, 2, 1972, p. 30.

② Frank Ching, “Who's Afraid of Frank Chin, or Is It Ching?” *Bridge*, 2, 1972, p. 34.

中表现得不共戴天，那很难让人相信的是赵健秀愿意将保存在自己手上的对方的信件交还给《侨》报编辑秦家骢，然后刊登发表。当时，同时在《纽约时报》任校样编辑的秦家骢和赵健秀二人作为文化界名人相互欣赏。此前，秦家骢曾建议赵健秀将他的一篇过于尖锐地批评三位白人批评家的文章进行修改以确保能够发表，但赵健秀坚持不做修改，恳请秦家骢将文稿转交《纽约时报》"周日戏剧"(The Sunday Drama)专栏编辑审稿。这篇文章据笔者考证应该是后来顺利发表的"别把我们圈禁在唐人街"(Don't Pen Us Up in Chinatown)。杂志《侨》在两期上刊登二人的信件原因之一应该是出于发行量的考虑。该刊物鼎盛时期的发行量也就 700 份，后来下降到 400 份，其中 40%为机构和图书馆单位订阅者。[①] 从出于扩大影响的角度考察，不难发现"赵秦之争"就是后来的"赵汤之争"的预演，因为与二人的 7 封信件同时刊发的还有两封曾被赵健秀破口大骂过的华裔历史学家宋李瑞芳和小说家张粲芳对赵健秀的批评的回应信件。这两封信件是编辑部约稿，与赵、秦二人的信件不同的是，此两封信件不似赵、秦二人的剑拔弩张，其口吻亦庄亦谐，对赵健秀极尽调侃。宋李瑞芳叫秦家骢不要被赵健秀耍弄，她和赵健秀其实是好友，在一次接受赵健秀采访时，二人还当面讨论过赵的坏脾气。赵健秀多次说秦家骢威胁要给赵寄一本宋李瑞芳撰写的华人历史图书《金山》，其实赵健秀早就当面向她要过该书，并让她签名。张粲芳的信件写得更幽默，她猜测赵健秀攻击她的原因可能源于赵健秀认为自己没有把他当回事。她在信中直接向赵健秀告饶："我已经相信他的写作具有原创性、启发性和争辩性。我相信你了，弗拉克；你也不用再反复提醒我了。我在此大声申明：赵健秀所说的'中国佬文化身份认同'特别具有原创

① William Wei, *The Asian American Movement*, Philadelphia: Temple University, 2010, p. 121.

性,它是对其他像他一样的华裔美国人吹起的号角。他对刻板形象的思想也是十分清晰的。他好斗,这也很健康,只不过他有时候会向本来尊重他的人也大喊大叫。"①很显然,这是肯定中夹带批评。张粲芳还调侃道:"如果赵健秀跟父亲交流出现障碍,我很抱歉,希望他饶了我,我也希望问题能够得到解决,那不是我的错。"②张粲芳说赵健秀是想把她变成攻击目标,逼她跪地哭着求饶,逼她承认赵说的一切都对。张粲芳怀疑赵是不是职业性地喜欢发火。在信中,张粲芳说她也跟赵健秀有多次通话和通信,赵健秀很固执,坚持认为张粲芳内化了陈查理的刻板形象,张坚称绝无此事。赵健秀总喜欢使用他的"中国佬英语",张说随他好了,但张粲芳怀疑这种语言是不是真的体现华裔经验的纯真语言。张粲芳在信件末尾提出了一个很严肃的问题:如果赵健秀认为有必要将自己与新移民区别开来,谁也无法使他改变主意,但如此一来,新移民就会遭受两次疏离。③

二、"赵汤之争"与"赵汤不争"

如上文所分析,赵健秀与秦家骢的"笔战"文化操演性的痕迹明显。细致考察亚裔美国文学文化发展史上的此次争鸣,很容易发现赵健秀真真假假的独特性格。他的戏剧家的文化操演天分或者恶作剧精灵精神早已显见,并非时至20世纪80年代末和90年代初编辑出版第二部亚裔文学选集《大哎呀!》时才被迫改弦更张,

① Frank Ching, "Who's Afraid of Frank Chin, or Is It Ching?" *Bridge*, 2, 1972, p. 36.

② Frank Ching, "Who's Afraid of Frank Chin, or Is It Ching?" *Bridge*, 2, 1972, p. 36.

③ Frank Ching, "Who's Afraid of Frank Chin, or Is It Ching?" *Bridge*, 2, 1972, pp. 36-37.

20世纪80年代末和90年代初的赵健秀是将这种操演性发挥得更加淋漓尽致。这种操演性的本质是真真假假、虚虚实实，以争论的形式主动与他人结成知识共同体。

1974年赵健秀等出版了《哎呀！》，虽然主流书评家们好评不断，但在亚裔批评界却没有激起一丁点儿涟漪。所以，在1991年出版《大哎呀！》时，他们重复对手使用的策略，即也像汤亭亭故意不听从赵建秀让她以小说文类出版《女勇士》一样蓄意挑起争斗。据该书编辑之一徐忠雄回忆："我们要出版一个《大哎呀！》，我们准备让所有人读了都见恼。我们就是要逼迫批评家们站出来告诉我们说错了，或者作出任何反应。"[①]十分明显，《大哎呀！》中由500页压缩为92页的长篇讨伐式序言"真真假假的亚裔作家一起来吧！"只有一个目的：向亚裔女权主义者发动更猛烈的进攻，从而刺激她们"作出任何反应"。

当时为数不多的大学开设了亚美研究课程，该学科仍然处于初创阶段，亚裔女权主义批评家们对赵健秀等的挑衅，既从个人生计出发，亦为亚美研究被边缘化所迫，她们选择发表文章和出版专著来积极应战，从而将原先在赵健秀和汤亭亭二人之间进行的"赵汤之争"演变成规模空前的族裔知识生产共同体。争论双方的口诛笔伐对攻以20世纪90年代为鼎盛期，如史蒂芬·H.隅田所言："这场争斗从1976年一直延续至今。它是一场极大地促进了亚裔美国文学生产的论战。很多人因参与这场'笔战'受聘，被解聘，获得终身教职，升职或者受到伤害。这场论战将本来对亚裔文学研究不感兴趣的人吸引过来，因为在研究中，他们发现人们讨论

① Shawn Wong, "*Aiiieeeee*! and the Asian American Literary Movement: A Conversation with Shawn Wong", *MELUS*, 29(3/4), 2004, p. 95.

文学犹如面临生死抉择。”[①]

不仅美国学者对立双方笔战不休，中国学者也加入战团。留美归国学者林涧在 2005 年 3 月 3 日《文学报》上的“何谓赵汤之争？赵汤不争；赵汤休争！”的“赵汤不争”论调引发国内学界的争论。[②] 肖画认为林涧明显“扬汤抑赵”，他借助对赵健秀持中肯态度的华裔学者黄秀玲，对“赵汤之争”的三个争论焦点，即“中国传统故事新编”“自传写作”和“性别争论”对该场论证进行了重读，其结论是“贯穿这三个角度的核心问题正是华裔作家在作品中表现的‘父权意识’……重识当年的‘赵汤之争’，从华裔作家内部的分歧解读父权意识对华裔作家创作的影响”，尤其是解读华裔作家作品如何“向美国文学经典靠拢”和“形成对话关系”。[③] 林涧一文批驳的对象是国内知名赵健秀研究学者徐颖果在 2004 年 3 月 3 日发表于《中华读书报》上的赵健秀访谈录《我不是为灭绝中国文化而写作的》。林涧的“赵、汤的基本立场是一致的”的判断是正确的，但她的“汤亭亭从未与赵健秀争过，从来是不屑于争的。汤亭亭从未写过针对赵健秀的文章”观点值得商榷。[④]

汤亭亭回应赵健秀的方式颇为奇特。首先，在出版社将《女勇士》书稿交由当时已经因为两部戏剧在主流剧场上演而成名的赵健秀审读后，二人之间就曾就该书是以小说还是自传文类出版以通信的形式直接争论过。[⑤] 可能汤亭亭和出版社故意逆赵建秀的

---

① Stephen H. Sumida, “The More Things Change: Paradigm Shifts in Asian American Studies”, *American Studies International*, 38(2), 2000, p. 102.

② 该文后收录进 2007 年 2 月出版严绍璗、陈思和主编的《跨文化研究：什么是比较文学》一书，原文在各大文献数据库中现已无法找到。

③ 肖画：《重读美国华裔文学中的“赵汤之争”》，《华文文学》2012 年第 4 期。

④ 林涧：《何谓赵汤之争？赵汤不争；赵汤休争！》，严绍璗、陈思和主编：《跨文化研究：什么是比较文学》，北京大学出版社 2007 年版，第 277 页。

⑤ *What's Wrong with Frank Chin?* Directed by Curtis Choy, performances by Frank Abe and Frank Chin, Chonk Moonhunter, 2005.

劝告而行，坚持以自传文类出版该书的原因是将赵健秀作为亚裔读者反映预先测试对象，基于赵健秀的强烈反对该书以自传形式出版推测以自传文类出版必然会引起关注。这一出版策略事后观之，固然是成功的，但也因为亚裔文化界的反对声浪过于强烈以至几近失控，汤亭亭被迫罕见地撰写《美国评论家的文化误读》一文以平息争议。这篇文章在很大程度上恰恰印证了赵健秀反对歪曲中国经典和华裔自传书写的正确性。除了发表该文之外，汤亭亭回应赵健秀批评的另一方式是出版宣扬华裔男性英雄主义的回忆、传说和事实混杂的《中国佬》和貌似调侃赵健秀的小说《孙行者》。细读最早出版于1989年的《孙行者》一书，笔者吃惊地发现，与其说该书是对理想主义者赵健秀的调侃，不如说是对赵健秀戏剧等文学艺术成就的礼赞。书中跟赵建秀一样生于龙年的垮掉派华裔青年惠特曼·阿新(Wittman Ah Sing)一心想成为华裔剧作家，他推崇关公、自比孙猴子，这完全就是赵健秀的人生经历写照和所持文化理念。惠特曼一心想将华裔聚拢起来，以恢复被迫中断了十年的华裔戏剧传统，并借此恢复华裔完全意义上的美国人的地位。全书高潮出现在最后一章"独角戏"，召集各阶层华裔排戏、演戏的惠特曼"是在界定一个社团，该社团将在演出期内每晚碰头。社团的建立并非一劳永逸，人们需要想象，实践，然后再加以创造。作为他周围的社团，我们将听他尽情地说，以此作为对惠特曼的奖赏和感谢。让他把心声全都倒出来，我们听他把要说的一切直截了当地讲出来。爆发和光火中的讲话太少"[①]。英文版原著在此段中反复出现的关键词是"community"，在当年出版的中文版中译成"社团"，其实它是指仍然处于形塑期的"华裔共同体"。中文版的该段最后一句系误译，应该译成"爆炸和燃烧太无声无息了"，意即在美国暴力是不可取的，语言才是最强大的力量，

① [美]汤亭亭：《孙行者》，赵伏柱、赵文书译，漓江出版社1998年版，第338页。

华裔要支持桀骜不驯的惠特曼和赵健秀为本族发声。汤亭亭借叙述者之口似乎在规劝与惠特曼一样敢于对台下白人观众怒吼的赵健秀,与主流白人社会要用语言协商:"惠特曼变了——变!——变成一位和平主义者。亲爱的美国猴王,别害怕。来,让我们拧着你的一只耳朵,亲吻你的另一只耳朵。"[①]汤亭亭借此在"规训"既令人讨厌又让人喜爱的"泼猴"赵健秀,劝他现实些。可以说,汤亭亭在《孙行者》中表达了对焦虑的赵健秀极大的理解。

"赵汤之争"更引人注目的是其后期赵、汤二人分别代表的亚裔文化民族主义者和亚裔女权主义者阵营长期的"笔战",但该"笔战"迟至1990年前后才大规模爆发,其爆发的时间节点并非偶然。当年积极参与"赵汤之争",随后占据美国诸多大学亚美研究中心位置的学者以20世纪80年代入职的亚裔女学者为主。为了当时该新兴边缘学科生存的需要和个人生计考虑,亚裔女权主义学者们并没有退路,她们视赵健秀等编辑的《大哎呀!》中长篇檄文的挑衅为天赐良机,积极应战,从而生产了大量族裔知识,并因此使得亚裔文学与亚裔文学批评走向良性循环。另外一个不可忽视的历史因素是,除了大量亚裔女学者入职外,20世纪90年代有大量亚裔青年就读大学,这给亚美研究课程和专业的开设提供了重要契机。[②] 亚裔大学入学人口中的女性比例增长迅速,1990年,亚裔女性在校人数首次超过亚裔男性,此后一直保持如此态势。[③] 在此难得的历史条件下,亚裔女权主义发展迅猛,亚裔女权主义知识生产者和消费者也由此产生共同体:亚裔女作家/女学者—亚裔女性

---

① [美]汤亭亭:《孙行者》,赵伏柱、赵文书译,漓江出版社1998年版,第377页。

② Mitchell J. Chang, "Expansion and Its Discontents: The Formation of Asian American Studies", *Journal of Asian American Studies*, 2 (2), 1999, p. 184.

③ Mitchell J. Chang, et al., *Beyond Myths: The Growth and Diversity of Asian American College Freshmen*, 1971-2005, Higher Education Research Institute, UCLA, 2007, p. 6.

读者。毋庸讳言,亚裔女性的关注问题与赵健秀等文化民族主义者的关注焦点的确有一定的冲突。林玉玲称:1989 年两部亚裔女性写作文集的出版直接导致亚裔文化界分裂为男、女两大阵营。[①]单从其中一本文集的标题"兴风作浪"(making waves)可知当年亚裔女学者快速提升学科地位的急切心情,甚至有些亚裔学者没有读过赵健秀的书也投入批评赵健秀的"战斗"。最为突出的例子是,1982 年在亚裔美国文学研究第一部理论专著《亚裔美国文学:作品及社会背景介绍》中对"赵汤之争"还持公允中立态度的亚裔美国文学研究泰斗级人物金惠经,在 1990 年突然以新的女权主义学者身份在《"这对冤家对头":亚裔美国文学中的男男女女》一文中对赵健秀提出尖锐批评:"被剥夺了父权制合法性带来的好处后,一些亚裔男子的反应是试图重新建立族裔文化领域的男性权威,并想通过使女权主义从属于民族主义关怀来使女性臣服。"[②]

"赵汤之争"有假戏真做的成分,美国学者应该是心知肚明的,但中国学者可能没有注意到此点。笔者研究发现,"赵汤之争"中双方观点均存有明显的漏洞,然而双方却从不揭穿。比如,赵健秀指责汤亭亭、谭恩美等女性作家继承白人自传文学传统,认同白人同化理论,向白人文化臣服,自传这种基督教忏悔文学不是中国文学传统。吊诡的是,备受赵健秀推崇的亚裔美国文学鼻祖水仙花姐妹都写过自传,不消说其他像韩素音和林太乙等以往华裔作家都写过自传,他极为赞赏的菲律宾裔美国作家卡洛斯·布洛桑(Carlos Bulosan)的《美国在心中》更是一部没有宗教色彩的自传。赵健秀还指责汤亭亭等人篡改花木兰的故事、灶神的传说,然而他

① 这两部亚裔女性写作文集分别为 *The Forbidden Stitch: An Asian American Women's Anthology* 和 *Making Waves: An Anthology of Writings by and about Asian American Women*。

② Elaine H. Kim, "'such Opposite Creatures': Men and Women in Asian American Literature", *Michigan Quarterly Review*, 29 (Winter 1990), p. 75.

自己的作品中对盘古开天、女娲补天、桃园结义等中国文学经典通过故意误读、篡改,与美国华人的历史结合从而赋予美国意义,其手法与汤亭亭等并无二致。对此类常识性认知,女权主义学者从未揭穿过。女权主义批评家们经常指责赵健秀建构亚裔女性英雄主义传统的同时,不知不觉地跌入他反对的白人男权主义窠臼,典型的证据是他的作品中缺乏对亚裔女性的人文关怀。赵健秀作品的历史背景基本是美国历史上《排华法案》实施时期的单身汉唐人街,让赵健秀塑造出令其反对者满意的女权主义人物形象,恐怕连金惠经本人也无法相信。此外,金惠经等对汤亭亭、谭恩美等作品中同样缺乏亚裔男性人物形象选择性失明,赵健秀等文化民族主义者也从未抨击过如此不堪一击的双重标准。

透过"赵汤之争"表面的争斗不难发现,双方经常走向合作,从而借争战结成亚裔知识共同体,进而在文学界和学界发出声音。赵健秀曾就亚裔历史学家罗纳德·高木(Ronald Takaki)是否有资格以其著作《从彼岸来的陌生人:亚裔美国人的历史》参加亚美研究协会图书奖评奖一事,在《亚美学刊》1990年第2期上发表文章《谁管理着亚美研究协会?》为高木受到亚美研究协会主席陈素贞打压打抱不平,金惠经等人也再次卷入该次论争。按理说,双方剑拔弩张,应该是老死不相往来,而2005年肯特·A. 小野(Kent A. Ono)主编的《亚美研究导读》将王灵智、陈素贞、金惠经评论高木著作的3篇论文和高木的回应文章一起放在第一部分"历史"中以形成问答关系,在"文学与女权主义"部分收录的是赵健秀针对汤亭亭等亚裔女权主义作家火药味特浓的《大哎呀!》序言节选和张敬珏完全支持汤亭亭女权主义文学风格的文章《女勇士对西海岸中国佬:华裔美国批评家需要在女权主义与英雄主义之间抉择吗?》1999年,黄秀玲主编的专论汤亭亭作品的论文集《汤亭亭的〈女勇士〉:教学用书》更是让人跌破眼镜地将赵健秀早前就发表过的挖苦汤亭亭、戏仿《女勇士》的短篇小说《中国最受欢迎的书》一并收录，此举再次证实了“赵汤之争”的文化操演实质。

三、赵健秀与里德的生死同盟

“操演性”（performativity）是言语行为理论（speech act theory）的核心术语，它起源于英语语言哲学家 J. L. 奥斯汀（J. L. Austin）唯一一本专著《如何以言行事》中的“施为语言”（the performative），它与描述语言（the constative）相对应。1955 年，奥斯汀一反传统语言观，即认为语言只是对外部世界描述的工具，提出语言也是一种行为，言就是行的新观点。学界普遍认为，奥斯汀的言语行为理论引发了 2000 多年来语言哲学研究的一场革命。奥斯汀在《如何以言行事》的第二章将文学语言认定为是“苍白的”寄生于日常言语行为之上的语言，因而将它排除在其研究范围之外。这个界定在多年后成为法国解构主义哲学家德里达的攻击目标。德里达认为，奥斯汀将日常语言与虚构语言对立，这是遵循自柏拉图以降西方语言哲学研究重视日常语言、轻视虚构语言的传统。正如西方逻各斯中心主义话语中的二元对立系统所显示的，我们总被潜移默化地灌输将事物作二元区分来更好把握事物的思想，比如好与坏、男人与女人、主体与客体、现象与本质、真理与谬误、日与月、善与恶、主流与族裔、本源与重复、日常话语与虚构语言等。而作这种二元区分的隐含话语的目的是，两个对立项的左边的一项总是处于支配地位，而后者总是从属前者。J. 希利斯·米勒是目前为止对奥斯汀将文学语言排斥在有效言语行为之外的观点批评得最为激烈的学者。在他的《文学中的言语行为》的第一章对奥斯汀的日常言语与文学言语的区分法进行了言辞犀利的批驳，他举出《如何以言行事》中诸多摘自文学作品的例子或具有文学性的举例，从而将奥斯汀设定的日常语言与文学语言界限彻底瓦解。[1] 正如何成洲所言,最终是朱迪斯·巴特勒从性别身份政治视角,将舞台表演理论与言语行为理论结合,从“施为语言”(the performative)演化出“操演性”(performativity)术语,使之大放异彩,引起文学、文化批评界等的广泛关注,从而成为人文社会科学的流行话语。[2] 由此,“操演性”具有了一体两面的特性,即日常言语行为的即时“施为性”和舞台、文学语言的长效“表演性”。赵健秀的文学批评和文本创作等文学言语行为正体现了这种虚虚实实的“操演性”。所以,说“赵汤之争”根本不存在是走极端的错误判断,同时完全实读赵、汤分别代表的对立双方的观点又会走向另一个极端。赵健秀最早是从他的铁杆盟友非裔作家伊什梅尔·里德学到了虚虚实实的文学言语行为策略,学会了坚守和妥协。

伊什梅尔·里德是赵健秀走上文学之路的恩人。赵健秀的第一部剧本《鸡笼中国佬》获得洛杉矶全美第一个亚裔戏剧团体“东西演员”(The East West Players)举办的戏剧创作比赛最高奖后,因为剧本表演难度太大且具有很大争议,该剧团无法将它搬上舞台。后来,加州大学伯克利分校的里德十分喜欢这部剧本,于是他将剧本辗转交给纽约美国地方剧场(The American Place Theater)艺术导演韦恩·汉德曼(Wynn Handman)才得以使该剧上演,赵健秀也因此一举成名。赵健秀和里德二人志趣相投,相互支持和影响,生成了被学界定义为“亚黑感性”(the Asian-Black Sensibility)的文学和政治生死联盟。这种联盟让主流文化界十分恐慌,他们利用白人、非裔和亚裔女权主义者来对他们以及他们的

① J. Hillis Miller, *Speech Acts in Literature*, Redwood: Stanford University Press, 2001, p. 46.

② 何成洲:《巴特勒与表演性理论》,《外国文学评论》2010 年第 3 期。何成洲将“performativity”翻译成“表演性”,学界也有人将它译成“操演”“操演性”“展演”或者“展演性”。笔者文中采用“操演性”译法,以为“操演性”将日常言语行为的“施为”与舞台和文学语言的“表演性”捏合在一起,与“performativity”更契合。

同道围追堵截。在1975年美国现代语言学会年会会场上，赵健秀和里德二人严词批评美国现代语言学会的一些成员，说他们不愿意阅读亚裔美国文学，并对犹太裔批评家们攻击非裔文学的发言进行反驳。随即，他们遭到了主流批评家们的抵制。加州大学尔湾分校犹太裔英语教授麦伦·西蒙(Myron Simon)给他们冠以“两个愤怒的族裔作家”头衔，并讥讽赵健秀是一位没有出版作品的作家(the unpublished author)，称“二人都不努力探寻难解问题的复杂答案”[①]。自此，两位都经历了来自主流文化界和后来的女权主义者阵营的辖制。但两人都没有选择退缩，而是更加“愤怒”且更加坚决地予以还击(counterpunch)，以至于在他们的支持者、中立派以及他们的贬斥者的批评中，两人的名字经常被一并提起。特别“有趣”的是，他们的贬斥者不时就会把二人一同拎出来“教训”一番。[②] 赵健秀受里德的愤怒政治(the politics of anger)影响至深，它使赵健秀处境艰难。里德时不时地对赵健秀等所谓亚裔文化民族主义者出手援助，比如里德牵线促成由霍华德大学出版社——一所黑人大学出版社——出版《哎呀!》。赵健秀任编辑的跨族裔文学艺术《新兵读物》卷三由里德所在黑人出版公司——庭鸟出版有限公司出版，这些都见证了二人和两个种族之间的友谊。在1998年出版的《刀枪不入的佛教徒及其他散文》扉页，赵健秀直接表示将该书献给里德，以表达他对里德的感激和景仰。

---

① Myron Simon,“Two Angry Ethnic Writers”, *MELUS*, 3 (2), 1976, p. 20. 白人出版社一直拒绝出版赵健秀的两部戏剧，一直到1981年，这两部戏剧剧本才由华盛顿大学出版社出版，所以“没有出版作品的作家”后来成了赵健秀对自己的尴尬身份的自嘲。

② 将二人一起分析的学者很多，比如克里斯托弗·A. 希恩(Christopher A. Shinn)在其收录于《非裔幽默、反语和讽刺：伊什梅尔·里德讽刺地说着》中的《兵法：伊什梅尔·里德和赵健秀以及美国非亚裔多元文化主义讽刺联盟》一文里就明确提出应该将二人放在一起研究，为的是更好地把握多元文化主义的历史和未来，不该将二人斥为20世纪60年代出道的异见人士。见该书第74页。

美国主流媒体中的黑人刻板形象总是吸毒者、贩毒者和强奸犯。同样,20世纪70年代及以前的主流媒体中亚裔男性则常为恶棍、性无能者或者唯白人马首是瞻的仆从形象,比如傅满洲和陈查理等,这使得对抗性书写成为必需,此乃赵健秀《鸡笼中国佬》中的泰姆转向欣赏非裔男性气质即操演"黑性"(perform blackness)的根本原因。如克里斯特尔·S. 安德森所言,赵健秀和里德一样是在抢夺主流社会对少数族裔的定义权,他赋予亚裔能动性和控制权,因为一直以来只有"主流社会享有定义权",赵健秀模仿里德的攻击性话语,也视白人主流社会为必须战胜的敌人。① 在接受中国学者蔺玉清的采访时,里德曾形象地描述自己对种族主义的反抗:"瓦特金斯(Mel Watkins)在《纽约时报》中说我的风格像阿里,'像蝴蝶一样飞舞,像蜜蜂一样蜇人'。但是,等我搬到现在的贫民区生活后,我变得更像泰森,我想要的写作风格能一拳把人的牙齿都打掉。我成为更加善于反击的拳击手,而不再是跳来跳去。"②里德在1988年出版的论文集《写作即战斗:三十七年的纸上搏击》的主标题是对拳王阿里的原话直接引用,赵健秀转而从孙子兵法和三国英雄故事中找到"生活即战斗"(Life is war)理念。

赵健秀的进攻目标一直是白人种族主义。所以,金惠经认为赵健秀"想通过使女权主义从属于民族主义关怀"有一定道理,但他并非是想让女权主义者臣服。自汤亭亭的《女勇士》未按照他的以小说文类建议出版之后,赵健秀的怒火部分地转向亚裔文学界内部目标。然而,赵健秀并非如林涧所言是出于妒忌心态才言辞激烈地攻击贬损本族的女权主义者。在此方面,美国多族裔文学

① Crystal S. Anderson, "Chinatown Black Tigers: Black Masculinity and Chinese Heroism in Frank Chin's *Gunga Din Highway*", *Ethnic Studies Review*, 26 (1), 2003, pp. 74-75.

② 蔺玉清:《多元文化主义的写作政治——伊什梅尔·里德访谈录》,《外国文学动态》2016年第1期。

学会刊物《美国多族裔文学》(*MELUS*)创刊参与人凯瑟琳·纽曼(Katharine Newman)的观察颇具洞见：

> 不少亚裔学者，尤其是女性，她们在环太平洋地区或国家接受过教育，现今在美国写作和教书。她们都是双语操用者，她们来到美国的时候正好这边有大学职位可供她们选择。她们的小说和自传出版后畅销；她们自然成了汤亭亭的党羽。她们无法欣赏赵健秀和他的盟友取得的成就——自然也理解不了革命者看到从未参与战斗的人成了胜利者后的沮丧。这两拨人根本不在同一个时区。①

“革命者看到从未参与战斗的人成了胜利者后的沮丧”这一句尤为贴切，直击问题要害。赵健秀等看到这拨女权主义者窃取了胜利果实后的愤懑、失落应该是难免的，但更为重要的是，女权主义者的关注点明显与赵健秀等的关注点不同。也就是说，她们严重干扰了赵健秀等“亚裔感性”文学文化建构运动进程，迫使他们停下步伐来澄清和解释本不需要澄清和解释的亚裔文化和历史知识，因为诸多第一代亚裔女权主义者移民对美国文化和亚裔美国历史理解相对肤浅，难有感同身受的体验。即使土生土长的亚裔女性对来自主流社会的种族主义与亚裔男性感受也不相同。不像亚裔女权主义者可以与主流女权主义者可以结成联盟，亚裔男性作为少数族裔男性，“与白人男性之间始终存在着无法逾越的鸿沟。亚裔男性的这种生存状态给他们的心理造成了极大的伤害，创伤是难以愈合的……在一定程度上，亚裔男性历史是被美国主流社会

① Katharine Newman, “*MELUS* Invented: The Rest Is History”, *MELUS*, 16 (4), 1989, p. 104.

'边缘化''女性化'的历史"[①]。正是亚裔两种性别对种族主义的感受差异悬殊,所以《孙行者》中南希和马利斯阿姨才会都觉得惠特曼"过于敏感了"[②]。

赵健秀将怒火部分地转向亚裔女权主义者的根本原因正是亚裔女权主义者与主流女权主义者的结盟。里德说:"其实视我俩为性别主义者的观点始于赵健秀批评汤亭亭和谭恩美等作家,而白人女性主义者把她们的书奉为《圣经》,甚至是她们背后的推手。白人女性主义者操纵(大学里的)妇女研究系,同时白人女性购书是书籍消费者。胡克斯提到,(白人女性主义者)告诉她要想成功就得为她们写作。"[③]主流社会出于辖制男性族裔作家和转嫁罪名的动机,怂恿女权主义者给坚持反对种族主义的里德和赵健秀很方便地贴上了"厌女症者"标签,但里德认为:"许多包含厌女主义思想的作品来自白人男性作家。我和赵健秀被猛烈地批评,是因为我们在媒体中没有多少权力,我们既不雇佣她们,又没法给她们奖金……赵健秀被孤立了,他的日子不好过。原因是他的族裔想要被同化……所以你不得不佩服赵健秀、徐忠雄等人,他们坚持华裔美国文化应该被保存下来。"[④]汤亭亭在《女勇士》之后虽然出版了不少作品,包括跟赵建秀等的文化民族主义同调宣扬华裔英雄主义的《中国佬》,但没有一部作品像《女勇士》一样受到主流读者的热捧,可见背后推手白人女权主义者力量的强大。赵健秀的两部分别于 1972 年和 1974 年上演的戏剧剧本白人出版社一直不愿

① 王建会:《"创伤"理论与亚裔美国文学批评——以亚裔男性研究为视角》,《当代外国文学》2010 年第 2 期。

② [美]汤亭亭:《孙行者》,赵伏柱、赵文书译,漓江出版社 1998 年版,第 354 页。

③ 蔺玉清:《多元文化主义的写作政治——伊什梅尔·里德访谈录》,《外国文学动态》2016 年第 1 期。

④ 蔺玉清:《多元文化主义的写作政治——伊什梅尔·里德访谈录》,《外国文学动态》2016 年第 1 期。

意出版发行，直至1981年才由华盛顿大学出版社出版，所以赵健秀被称为“没有出版作品的作家”。在此期间，它也成了赵健秀参加学术会议时对自己的尴尬身份的自嘲。

应该说，赵健秀从里德那里学到了族裔精神的坚守，有趣的是，他也从里德那里学到“操演性”之“表演性”技巧。被里德痛斥为白人女权主义者代理人的盖茨在他的专著《意指的猴子》中公开称“《意指的猴子》与《芒博琼博》之间有种共生关系”[①]，而里德在接受采访时也公开承认喜欢盖茨的《意指的猴子》和他的很多绝妙的思想。[②] 同样，赵健秀1999年中风苏醒后，好友徐忠雄对赵健秀说：“你其实很喜欢汤亭亭和谭恩美的作品。”[③]所以，里德的论文集《写作即战斗：三十七年的纸上搏击》的副标题中“纸上搏击”道破了玄机，既有真的抵抗也有咋咋呼呼的表演。

美国学者克里斯特尔·S. 安德森(Crystal S. Anderson)在其博士论文《绝非“难以准确定义”：美国非裔和亚裔小说中文学恶作剧精灵形象》中分析了两位非裔作家和两位华裔作家的作品中恶作剧精灵人物形象，其中两位华裔作家正是赵健秀和汤亭亭。安德森从西非、印度、北美和中国恶作剧精灵神话中得到灵感，界定出文学恶作剧精灵人物形象，他提出的介乎现代主义精灵感性和后现代主义精灵感性之间的本土现代主义感性阐释了少数族裔文学中反抗主流社会话语的族裔人物形象的连接作用：“展现出这种感性的恶作剧精灵小说人物承认占支配地位的主流文化和少数

---

① [美]小亨利·路易斯·盖茨：《意指的猴子：一个非裔美国文学批评理论》，王元陆译，北京大学出版社2011年版，第238页。

② Shamoon Zamir, “An Interview with Ishmael Reed”, *Callaloo*, 17 (4), 1994, p. 1147.

③ *What's Wrong with Frank Chin?* Directed by Curtis Choy, performances by Frank Abe and Frank Chin, Chonk Moonhunter, 2005.

族裔文化所占据的不同空间,但他积极地去调和这些对抗力量且同时坚守族裔文化价值观。”[①]其实并非如安德森所言,赵健秀的小说《甘加丁之路》中三位华裔人物都没有选择坚守华裔文化价值观,而是走向赵健秀最为推崇但现实生活中的族裔个体难以实现的自由地定义个人身份,倒是生活在现实中的赵健秀被迫协调着各种对抗力量并同时坚守族裔文化价值观,因此他是不折不扣的恶作剧精灵作家。巧合的是,赵健秀一直自比恶作剧精灵孙悟空。赵健秀与秦家骢“笔战”、与亚裔女权主义作家和批评家争辩,以及与非裔作家里德结成生死同盟,都是主动促成知识共同体。通过不同文类的创作实践、积极参与文学文化批评和给亚裔学生讲华裔故事等言语行为,赵健秀不断构建着“亚裔美国”。

(陈永:南京大学外国语学院博士研究生)

① Crystal S. Anderson, *Far from 'Everybody's Everything': Literary Tricksters in African American and Chinese American Fiction*, Diss, The College of William & Mary, 2000, p. 29.

由《紫色》探访美国黑人“自由呼吸的梦想”

刘 晶

一、黑白平权，大梦初醒

2020年5月25日，美国黑人乔治·弗洛伊德(George Floyd)遭遇警方暴力执法，被白人警察用膝盖抵住喉咙，呼喊着“我不能呼吸了”悲惨离世。弗洛伊德之死激发的愤怒引发了全美旷日持久的抗议活动，随后席卷全球；英、法、德、日、澳均举行大规模示威游行，反对种族歧视和暴力执法。

在这场声势浩大的声讨运动当中，美国民主运动领袖马丁·路德·金(Martin Luther King)的女儿伯尼斯·金(Bernice King)于5月29日发表的演说中宣称：“美国必须一次并永久地解决系统性种族主义及白人至上主义问题，而唯一能做到这一点的只有非暴力手段。暴力不是解决问题的办法。”[①]这一立场立刻遭到了不少质疑,有人问“她被人控制了吗?”更有人指出她以“高级黑人”身份代言所有美国黑人的不合法性。

谈及非暴力解决种族问题的策略,我们不禁会想起美国著名的黑人女作家艾丽斯·沃克(Alice Walker)。1962年,沃克受邀到金的家中做客。次年,她参加了华盛顿那场著名的游行,与万千人共同聆听了《我有一个梦想》(I Have a Dream)的演讲。“金领导的民权运动对艾丽斯的妇女主义思想的形成及创作有很大的影响。”[②]作为金的好友和支持者,沃克的作品剑锋直指美国种族歧视,与同为黑人女作家的托尼·莫里森(Toni Morrison)相比,沃克的文风更接近战斗檄文。她对黑人女性的性别问题和种族问题往往直抒胸臆,除了进行艺术创作以外,更利用文学文本作为阵地直接探讨两种问题的战略。作为非暴力抵抗运动的支持者,我们可以通过回顾沃克的思想来分析时下部分美国黑人民权领袖的思想。

艾丽斯·沃克的小说《紫色》(*The Color Purple*)以描述黑人女性的独特反霸斗争著称。她揭示了黑人女性面临的双重霸权——男性霸权和种族霸权。她指出,黑皮肤妇女需要在解决性别问题的同时开展反种族歧视的斗争,她们处于美国社会的最底层。本文暂且抛开性别问题,就《紫色》中的种族策略加以分析,探讨非裔美国女性对美国乃至世界种族问题的立场和解决方案。

---

① 《马丁·路德·金女儿就抗议发声:暴力不是解决问题的办法》,2020年5月30日,https://baijiahao.baidu.com/s?id=1668098801157053286&wfr=spider&for=pc。

② 孙永杰:《艾丽斯·沃克和她的〈紫色〉》,《世界文化》2013年第6期。

二、姐姐西丽——重建上帝

众所周知,《紫色》是一部书信体小说。文中除了姐姐西丽(Celie)和妹妹耐蒂(Nettie)在情节的中后部恢复通信以外,前半部分是西丽写给上帝的书信。如果书写行为是书写自己的身体,那么小说初始西丽的投寄对象是可疑的。此时的“上帝”是什么形式,什么形象呢?我们无从知晓。但我们知道,当西丽逐渐学会通过重新定义上帝的概念来重塑种族和性别问题,并在脑海里重新形象化圣经故事时,她随之改变了对自己性别角色和种族身份的看法。从此以后,西丽的书信便得到了整理和重建。

西丽的精神解放受到了同性爱人莎格(Shug)的指导。她逐步认识到,想象有形的外貌会使上帝沦为有限的实体,因为唯一有能力为神提供形体支撑的是白人。上帝“个子高大,模样挺老,胡子花白,满头白发”①的形象是有问题的。莎格控诉了白人意识形态伪造的宗教,指明上帝是根据男性和白人的典范描绘并宣扬的。“我发现我把上帝看成是白人,而且是个男人,我就对他不感兴趣了。”②作为替代,莎格创造了一个全新的概念,将神重置并重新定义了他的性别。她认为“上帝既不是她也不是他,而是它”。③ 消除上帝的具体形态,性别随之消失,主成为内在的实体。她告诉西丽:“上帝你心里,也在大家心里。……它不是你看得见摸得着的东西,不是跟别的东西,包括你自己在内的一切东西分得开的东西。我相信上帝就是一切。”④一旦上帝摆脱了形体上的限制,他

① [美]艾丽斯·沃克:《紫颜色》,陶洁译,译林出版社 2008 年版,第 130 页。

② [美]艾丽斯·沃克:《紫颜色》,陶洁译,译林出版社 2008 年版,第 131 页。

③ [美]艾丽斯·沃克:《紫颜色》,陶洁译,译林出版社 2008 年版,第 132 页。

④ [美]艾丽斯·沃克:《紫颜色》,陶洁译,译林出版社 2008 年版,第 131～132 页。

就可以遍布自然。莎格说：

> 我摆脱这个白老头的第一步是我在树木中发现了生命力；后来我在空气中发现了生命力；后来是在鸟背上；再后来是在别人身上。有一天我安安静静地坐着，觉得自己像个没娘的孩子，它突然来了，我觉得我是万物的一部分，不是跟万物毫无关系的、割裂的东西。我知道如果我砍一棵树的话，我的胳膊也会流血。[①]

诚然，企图驱散神的形体对于西丽来说是一项艰巨的任务。她意识到，莎格的建议将使她信仰一种全新的精神上的存在，但是上帝"白发男性"的旧形象却依旧顽固地抵制，抗拒被删除。莎格告诉西丽："如果你在做祈祷，而男人堂而皇之地一屁股坐下来接受你的祷告的话，你就叫他滚蛋。你就用魔法招来花朵、风、水、大石头。"[②]西丽曾经把自己想象成一棵树，以使自己对现实中的痛苦和虐待麻木。而后来正相反，新的理解要求她幻化成树以唤醒那些麻木的感官。她与世界之间的矛盾被重新积极而正面地调停。[③] 西丽在最后一封信中写道："亲爱的上帝，亲爱的星星，亲爱的树木，亲爱的天空，亲爱的人们。亲爱的一切。亲爱的上帝。"[④]这个清单表明，上帝的存在形式已经变得灵活和多元，他与一系列自然现象被一起界定。

---

① [美]艾丽斯·沃克：《紫颜色》，陶洁译，译林出版社2008年版，第132页。

② [美]艾丽斯·沃克：《紫颜色》，陶洁译，译林出版社2008年版，第133页。

③ Wendy Wall, "Lettered Bodies and Corporeal Texts", *Alice Walker: Critical Perspectives Pastand Present*, eds. Henry Louis Gates, Jr. and K. A. Appiah, New York: Amistad Press, 1993, p. 266.

④ [美]艾丽斯·沃克：《紫颜色》，陶洁译，译林出版社2008年版，第200页。

三、妹妹耐蒂——埃塞俄比亚主义

埃塞俄比亚主义来自《圣经：诗篇》(*The Holy Bible*: *Psalms*)中的一句赞美诗：“王子将要出埃及，埃塞俄比亚将向上帝伸出双手。”[①]埃塞俄比亚代表非洲，数百年来曾是圣人和立法者的光荣胜地。后来非洲人笃信异教，激怒了上帝，遂将荣耀赠予他人。出自《圣经》的这一节赞美诗暗示着：上帝必将宽恕非洲，并归还其曾有的荣耀。非裔美国人将自己的非洲传统和美国文化背景视为独特的优势，自发赋予了自身领导者的地位——他们正是带领“落后的”非洲重返基督教，并重现往日繁荣的“上帝之子”。“埃塞俄比亚主义为白人和美国黑人对非洲进行文明教化和宗教宣传提供了理论依据。”[②]

耐蒂在给西丽写的第三封信中首次提到非洲：塞缪尔(Samuel)、科琳(Corrine)夫妇和孩子们，作为美国和非洲传教协会的传教士，都在“准备去非洲传教，他们觉得这是他们的天职”[③]。美国黑人传教团以致力于帮助非洲儿童接受教育和基督教教育为己任，“虽然非洲人当年的文明要比欧洲人发达，但他们已经有好几个世纪一直过着艰苦的日子。……今天的非洲人民疾病缠身，无论精神还是体力都一蹶不振。他们信仰魔鬼，崇拜死者。他们不会读书也不会写字”[④]。考虑到兄弟般的友爱和仁慈，美国黑人传教士承担起他们认为无可争议的光荣使命，因为“埃塞

① *The Holy Bible*: *Psalms*, Book II: Psalm, 68: 31: “Prince shall come out of Egypt; Ethiopia shall soon stretch out her hands unto God”.

② John Cullen Gruesser, *Black on Black*: *Twentieth-Century African American Writing About Africa*, Kentucky: The University Press of Kentucky, 2000, p. 1.

③ [美]艾丽斯·沃克:《紫颜色》,陶洁译,译林出版社 2008 年版,第 87 页。

④ [美]艾丽斯·沃克:《紫颜色》,陶洁译,译林出版社 2008 年版,第 94 页。

俄比亚向着上帝伸出双手"[①]。

耐蒂传教非洲的动机暗含了一些潜台词:非洲是落后的;美国非裔传教士具有高度的责任感;埃塞俄比亚主义证实洲际文化宣传是合法的,因为它来自《圣经》。除了对非洲人悲惨的生活条件和空虚的精神施加怜悯之外,美国黑人也为非洲失去了曾经的繁荣文明而惋惜。从耐蒂的非美视野中观察到的非洲体现了美国黑人对埃塞俄比亚主义意识形态的信仰。耐蒂关于非洲的叙述清楚地表明了非裔美国人的排外主义,有学者认为它属于埃塞俄比亚主义的第五个意义。[②] 它指的是一种信念,即美国黑人是最有资格领导非洲和离散民众的领袖。这要得益于他们独有的在西方生活的经历以及基督教信仰。通常,这种排外主义导致美国黑人对非洲黑人极富自尊甚至傲慢,极大地加深了两族人民之间合作的矛盾。[③]

耐蒂对非洲大陆的(误)教育充斥着埃塞俄比亚主义、非洲主义话语以及白人帝国主义。她非常敬佩的老师比斯利小姐(Miss Beasley)曾经说过,这里是一个不穿衣服的野蛮人拥挤的地方。塞缪尔和科琳夫妇似乎了解得更多,有时也这样认为。"他们谈到他们为这些受践踏的人们所能做的种种好事。他们来自这些人,而这些人需要耶稣和医疗方面的好建议。"[④]回顾她和其他传教士们在教堂收到礼物的心情时,耐蒂激动地说:"大家都满怀希望,相信在非洲能做很多的事情。埃塞俄比亚就是非洲,这意义多么重大啊!"[⑤]值得注意的是,耐蒂热情洋溢的宣言表明,她将带着一种

---

① [美]艾丽斯·沃克:《紫颜色》,陶洁译,译林出版社 2008 年版,第 91 页。

② John Cullen Gruesser, *Black on Black: Twentieth-Century African American Writing About Africa*, Kentucky: The University Press of Kentucky, 2000, p. 4.

③ [美]艾丽斯·沃克:《紫颜色》,陶洁译,译林出版社 2008 年版,第 4~6 页。

④ [美]艾丽斯·沃克:《紫颜色》,陶洁译,译林出版社 2008 年版,第 89 页。

⑤ [美]艾丽斯·沃克:《紫颜色》,陶洁译,译林出版社 2008 年版,第 113 页。

固有的观念前往非洲大陆——埃塞俄比亚主义文本下的非洲落后、野蛮、残酷，迫切需要引领和启迪。塞缪尔也有一段话语证明了他依靠埃塞俄比亚主义的臆想来合理化自己的行动：“我们有一大有利条件：我们不是白人，我们不是欧洲人。我们跟非洲人一样都是黑人，我们和非洲人将为一个共同目标而努力：振奋世界各地的黑人。”①

到目前为止，我们可以说基督教化和文明使命实质上具有帝国主义动力，实际上与后来西方对非洲橡胶工厂的直接殖民侵略形成共谋，以“温柔的”方式强化了帝国主义侵略。非洲本土的原始和未开化对于帝国主义来说是一种罪恶。帝国主义国家不仅有权力，而且有义务去统治“落后的”国家。宗教是文化的重要组成部分，并未被排除在西方文明推进的过程之外。

四、西方目光注视下的非洲与本土抵抗

1. 目睹—认知—权力(Voir-Savoir-Pouvoir)

有学者认为，观看的欲望以及洞悉“未知”和“不可知”领域的渴望也将主体定位为男性。② 结合米歇尔·福柯(Michel Foucault)著名的认知/权力(savoir/pouvoir)的表述，我们得到了视野、意识形态与权力之间的关系。在福柯看来，认知就是权力。权力和知识通过话语结合在一起，而话语结构正是现实世界得以构建的基础。同样，爱德华·萨义德(Edward Said)也强调，在殖民话语中，了解和理解非西方世界的意志与凌驾那个世界的欲望是密不可分的。“自萨义德的观点问世以来，殖民话语被逐渐揭示

① [美]艾丽斯·沃克：《紫颜色》，陶洁译，译林出版社2008年版，第93页。

② Meyda Yegenoglu, *Colonial Fantasies: Towards a Feminist Reading of Orientalism*, Cambridge: Cambridge University Press, 1998, p. 90.

出来,欧洲认知殖民地的战略同时成为统治该世界的战略。”①

耐蒂重塑独立身份的过程也是定义“他者”的过程。在每一封书信里,她兴奋地提供了非洲的详尽描述,以告知有关这片神秘土地的“真实”景象。事实证明,这个“真实”仅仅是“她”的认识以及“她”对权力的掌控。在凝视、分析和走向权力中心的过程中,耐蒂享有两个优势:首先,作为美国人,她是比受压迫的非洲人更为“先进”的文化拥有者;其次,作为女性,她比塞缪尔更有特权去探索最隐秘的非洲女性生活。在耐蒂的书写中,非洲是一个令人不快的、原始的、落后的、以男性为中心的非洲,而她则在文化使者和女权主义火炬手两种优越的身份之间自由切换。

耐蒂想要了解非洲的渴望显露于她对知识的热爱中。耐蒂在写给西丽的信中,提到了她通过研究非洲实现自我教育的尝试。她对自己的“愚昧无知”感到震惊:“我从来没想到我无知到这样的地步,西丽。我对自己的了解简直是沧海一粟。”②耐蒂想要了解非洲的愿望通过旅非之前阅读相关书籍得到了暂时满足,有关非洲的知识令她充满了成就感。耐蒂在信中欣喜地说:“哦,西丽,天下竟然会有要我们掌握知识的黑人!他们希望我们成长,看到光明!”③

2. 耐蒂的西化努力与非洲本土抵抗

以“提升”为目标的传教活动遭到了非洲本土的持续抵抗,这是美国非裔精英始料未及的。晚年的塞缪尔回顾自己的一生,认识到他在奥林卡(Olinka)部落所做的努力是一场彻底的失败。他告诉耐蒂:“这一切看起来实在荒唐,我已经年近花甲,但我帮助民

① [美]艾丽斯·沃克:《紫颜色》,陶洁译,译林出版社2008年版,第49页。
② [美]艾丽斯·沃克:《紫颜色》,陶洁译,译林出版社2008年版,第89页。
③ [美]艾丽斯·沃克:《紫颜色》,陶洁译,译林出版社2008年版,第90页。

众的梦想却仍然是个梦想。……我们彻底失败了。”[①]塞缪尔和耐蒂并没有放弃宗教使命，但他们开始逐渐脱离父权制基督教，而向“非洲灵性”(African Spirituality)敞开大门。

耐蒂目睹了纽约哈莱姆地区的非裔美国人，他们崇拜非洲，而不是美国。她自豪地报道了在一个美国黑人教堂里，上帝是黑人。在对非洲奥林卡村落起源的叙述中，白人是非洲文化的附属产物。耐蒂满怀敬畏地记录了第一次看到非洲海岸的心情：“我的内心，我灵魂深处大受震动，好像有个大钟敲了起来，震撼我全部身心，我浑身战慄。”[②]

抵达非洲以后，耐蒂有一段描写生动地讲述了自己和塞内加尔妇女不期而遇的经过：

> 你没法想象村民们围着我们时脸上好奇的神情。她们开始只是瞪大了眼睛看我们，后来有一两个妇女摸摸我和科琳的裙子。我的裙子边因为连着三天在篝火旁煮饭，在地上拖得很脏，我都不好意思了。后来我看她们穿的裙子，我不再感到不自在了。她们很多人的裙子好像被猪在庭院地上拖过，脏得不成样子，而且还不合身。她们又往我们跟前凑过来一点点——没人开口说话——摸摸我们的头发，又看看我们的鞋子。[③]

从与非洲村落直接接触的切身体会来看，耐蒂起初打算与村民们友好互动，并向他们学习当地的历史和文化经验。但是，村民的反应令她转而关心起这些沉默的非洲女性如何质疑自己的身

① [美]艾丽斯·沃克：《紫颜色》，陶洁译，译林出版社 2008 年版，第 163 页。
② [美]艾丽斯·沃克：《紫颜色》，陶洁译，译林出版社 2008 年版，第 96 页。
③ [美]艾丽斯·沃克：《紫颜色》，陶洁译，译林出版社 2008 年版，第 101 页。

份。西方女性的文化身份在非本土文化的反视中不断遭遇危机。作为塞缪尔和科琳夫妇的随行人员,耐蒂的传教士身份经常受到当地人的质疑。有一次,她被问到是否是塞缪尔的另一个妻子;还有一次,她被塔希(Tashi)的母亲认作是这对夫妇的苦力。从这些经历中我们得知,其他文化背景的人们不断地挑战耐蒂西方自主女性的权威。

传教士确立泛非(Pan-African)意识固有的矛盾在性别领域浮出水面。塞缪尔觉得有义务向非洲妇女讲授一夫一妻制胜过一夫多妻制,尽管一个非洲男人的妻妾联盟要比一夫一妻制里的科琳强大得多。科琳时而因她与耐蒂的关系尴尬不清而郁郁不安。耐蒂同样自信满满地向奥林卡妇女展示文明国家的妇女向公共和私人领域的父权挑战,并取得胜利的成果。但是,奥林卡妇女也看到了她行动上和思想上显著的局限性:她是"传教士的苦工","可怜和藐视的对象"。简而言之,正如塞缪尔后来沉痛地意识到的那样,跨越种族和历史差异进行种族认同的过程,实际上是伪装成支持和提升的文化霸权体系。塞缪尔的自叙是《紫色》中唯一有幸(短暂)取代女性话语的男性叙事,这些文字揭示了他逐渐认识到自己的文化特权意识很浅薄。面对"守护"非洲文化免遭破坏之举的无能为力,塞缪尔和耐蒂开始重新定义服侍上帝的含义:"在非洲住了这么些年,我们心目中的上帝也跟以前不一样了。更有精神,也更属于我们的内心了。大多数人认为上帝应该像某样东西或者某个人——屋顶树叶或耶稣——但我们不是这样想的。我们不考虑上帝长得什么样,我们反而自由了。"[①]这一段描述可以和姐姐西丽重建的上帝概念相呼应。

① [美]艾丽斯·沃克:《紫颜色》,陶洁译,译林出版社2008年版,第178页。

五、艾丽斯·沃克的政治立场

尽管沃克对埃塞俄比亚主义和文化帝国主义的态度是否定的，但设计一个被教化成功的范例还是必要的。身为美国非裔精英的一员，她为这场跨国“支教”活动精心保留了一枚丰硕的果实——塔希。耐蒂将女权主义意识播种到非洲本土女孩塔希的心田，后者最终决定加入返美大团圆的队伍。耐蒂既是殖民主义抵抗者，又是殖民主义侵略者，她的种族独立需要一个“他者”。这一点可以从塔希自主接受奥林卡传统刺面可见。有学者指出，女性的刺面涉及面部疤痕，伤口表示对文化统治力量的奉献和臣服。疤痕表明产生了“外部性”，“目标或威胁”，这使主体的身份成为可能。奥林卡村民迫使年轻人参与这场仪式，将他们的身份认同刻在孩子的脸上。这是文明对身体宣示主权的显著表现：身体上的铭文将那个人限制在一种固定的文化中。[①] 刺面以后的塔希最初躲开了耐蒂和恋人亚当(Adam)的搜寻——伤疤代表非洲原住民的秘密，她的逃脱似乎使她躲过了西方的目光，也躲过了男性注视的目光。从耐蒂的角度来看，没有塔希就无法存在，因为她的自由新女性身份需要“他者”。最后，塔希随美国黑人一起返回美国，继续为整个美国黑人社区奉献“他者”的职能。

美国非裔黑人 Afro-American 的指代终究以最初的含义重现：《紫色》的后半部分并未将该复合词的非洲部分与在美国背景下以往被否定的积极部分相融合，而是将“非洲”带回到失望和不足的空间，最终被“美国”赋予的女性主义乌托邦淹没。

① Wendy Wall, “Lettered Bodies and Corporeal Texts”, *Alice Walker: Critical Perspectives Pastand Present*, eds. Henry Louis Gates, Jr. and K. A. Appiah, New York: Amistad Press, 1993, p. 265.

艾丽斯·沃克谴责“肤色主义”(Colorism),即仅基于肤色对同种的人群持有偏见或偏好的待遇。“肤色主义就像殖民主义、性别歧视和种族主义一样,阻碍了我们的发展。”[①]在她看来,美国黑人妇女和非洲妇女是血亲,是“同一个母亲的女儿,尽管被不同的父亲分开(用途相同)”[②]。作为黑白混血,沃克缺乏历史感,陷入了双重意识的困境。她转而寻求美国黑人和非洲黑人共有的种族传统——她的“漆黑的姐妹”[③]。这可以解释为什么她安排耐蒂去非洲复活种族血统。

遗憾的是,这个解决方案忽视了“黑色”本身的国家边界和文化意义。沃克抗议白人女性主义者替黑人代言,但讽刺的是,她本人也将自己的美国黑人经历作为所有黑皮肤妇女的普遍经历去理解。小说结尾通过建立一个由非裔美国人和非洲原住民组成的“女性主义者”社区,积极地提拔了土著女性。这个结局表明,掌握一手的资料和准确描绘非洲的意图并不能保证美国黑人作家与主流白人绘制明显不同的非洲版本。从事历险记、情感小说、旅行文学和其他类型写作的白人作家长期以来赋予黑人以固定的、明确的角色定位,选择这些类型写作的非洲裔美国作家须谨慎行事,以防重蹈覆辙。

著名黑人女权批评家贝尔·胡克斯(Bell Hooks)曾经对白人女权主义者所采用的大一统的声音提出了批判。她说:“通常,白人女权主义者的举动表明,直到她们代为指出,黑人妇女对性别歧视和男权压迫一无所知。白人女性认为,她们为黑人妇女提供了

---

① Alice Walker, *In Search of Our Mothers' Gardens*, San Diego: Harcourt, 1983, p. 290.

② [美]艾丽斯·沃克:《紫颜色》,陶洁译,译林出版社2008年版,第307页。

③ [美]艾丽斯·沃克:《紫颜色》,陶洁译,译林出版社2008年版,第311页。

‘客观’分析和‘解放计划’。”[①]白人妇女“对非白人参与者采取了屈尊的态度”,“这是她们(用来)提醒我们妇女运动‘是她们的’的一种手段”。[②] 同样地,沃克也提出了代表“所有”黑人妇女或有色妇女的主张,她使她们沦为美国黑人妇女强权话语的对象。沃克的思路表明,她没有彻底摆脱白人至上主义意识形态,而仍在抢夺“中心”和“权威”的地位。[③] 只要任何组织将“解放”定义为帮助被统治阶级与受压迫者取得社会平等,“它就对持续剥削和压迫‘他者’培养了深刻的兴趣”。[④]

弗洛伊德事件再一次把美国根深蒂固的种族问题抛在了世人面前。在跨越了21世纪五分之一的后现代,人类比以往更加频繁地向外太空发射先进的科技成果,然而我们的精神世界似乎并没有跟上这日新月异的步伐。人类对共用资源的争夺,对不同肤色人群的不公正待遇提示我们:时隔百年,马丁·路德·金的梦想仍然还是个梦想,我们仍需为这个梦想的实现付诸非凡的努力。

(刘晶:首都师范大学大学英语教研部副教授)

---

① Bell Hooks, “Black Women: Shaping Feminist Theory”, *The Black Feminist Reader*, eds. Joy James and T. Denean Sharpley-Whiting, Massachusetts: Blackwell Publishers, 2000, p. 140.

② [美]艾丽斯·沃克:《紫颜色》,陶洁译,译林出版社 2008 年版,第 141 页。

③ [美]艾丽斯·沃克:《紫颜色》,陶洁译,译林出版社 2008 年版,第 142 页。

④ [美]艾丽斯·沃克:《紫颜色》,陶洁译,译林出版社 2008 年版,第 144 页。

《新印度小姐》中的女性具象

张昕昕

女性具象是指对女性、国家和帝国身份的意识形态表达，通过将女性身体物质化，将女性身体的特质赋予女性身份，并将国家和地理女性化，使其具有女性特质，成为父权制或帝国制的从属。印度裔美国作家芭拉蒂·穆克吉（Bharati Mukherjee，1940～2017）在小说《新印度小姐》（*Miss New India*）中，通过人物塑造，建立女性（弱势）主人公身份与国家身体、地理身体的联结，揭露父权制度通过界定女性身体对女性进行压迫，而殖民主义通过界定国家身体、地理身体对殖民地进行压迫统治。文本作为男权制书写所需要的媒介载体，在父权制下也成为具象化的女性身体，沦为父权制压迫女性的工具和帮凶。然而，文本的具象也非坚不可破，作者通过在文本中使用斜体、书信和第一人称复数叙事这三种叙事策略，开发出女性可以表达真实自我、寻求主体性和身份的话语空间，鼓励女性反抗父权制的压迫。以此鼓励印度摆脱殖民主义的意识形态和价值观与时俱进，并在全球化时代敢于反抗美国新殖民主义的意识形态和话语霸权。

一、作为父权统治工具的女性身体勇敢反叛父权

《新印度小姐》中的女主人公安嘉丽生活的印度东北部小城高里普尔(Gauripur)依然是父权高于一切,安嘉丽的父亲虽然让女儿接受了大学教育,但这一切也仅仅是为她将来在婚恋市场找到一个好夫婿而作准备。安嘉丽从小成长的家庭就是典型的“母亲谦逊,父亲做主”①,父亲在家里拥有绝对的权威——“他那专横的语气,高高在上的举止,正是一个拿腔作势的父亲的角色。”②“安排安嘉丽结婚是他作为印度教徒的责任”③,他满心焦急地为女儿找一个女婿,以免她在此之前毁坏自己的名声,给整个家族蒙羞。为完成自己的使命,他一方面要女儿爱惜自己的身体和名誉;一方面,送她去上大学,甚至送她去英语辅导班,因为他认为“学好了英文意味着可以有更好的婚姻”④。甚至在等待相亲出嫁的日子里,她也被送去上英文课。父母安排安嘉丽所做的一切,不过是为了让她在婚姻市场上具有更高的价值,从而完成其父亲的责任,也兑现安嘉丽作为女儿的义务——嫁为人妻,生儿育女。在父权制家庭出生成长的安嘉丽完全没有选择的余地,而是父亲的财物,任由父亲安排她的生活和一切。

父权社会将女性身体商品化以维护其统治。露西·伊利格瑞

---

① Bharati Mukherjee, *Miss New India*, New York: Houghton Mifflin Harcourt Publishing Company, 2011, p. 24.

② Bharati Mukherjee, *Miss New India*, New York: Houghton Mifflin Harcourt Publishing Company, 2011, p. 9.

③ Bharati Mukherjee, *Miss New India*, New York: Houghton Mifflin Harcourt Publishing Company, 2011, p. 23.

④ Bharati Mukherjee, *Miss New India*, New York: Houghton Mifflin Harcourt Publishing Company, 2011, p. 20.

(Lucy Irigary)在《女性非一》(*This Sex Which Is Not One*)一书中,系统阐释了女性被商品化的现象和过程。伊利格瑞借用马克思的社会价值概念,解释父权如何通过将女性身体赋予交换价值和社会价值而剥削女性身体,压迫女性。女性商品化的前提则是女性身体具有男性所需求的生殖属性,女性身体因具有自然即生育属性而被赋予了社会即交换属性,这是女性身体被商品化的物质基础。[①] 具有生育属性的女性要成为商品还须具备交换属性,即被男性所欲求或需要,因此必须先对其进行投资才可进行交易。女性于是被培养成具有价值的身份,即"保留可使用可交换的一种抽象普遍的价值"[②]。商品化的女性身体具有两种状态:母亲和处女。前者通过生殖具有了男性难以超越的自然属性,而后者仅仅具有交换属性。女性价值的获得就是从交换属性过渡到自然属性的标准化过程。为保证交易能够顺利实现,男性须先对女性进行投资,在保证其保持处女之身的同时,使其为成为母亲身份做好准备,这是父亲对于女儿的责任。以此,女性被本质化,其本身具有的生理特征被强化成了女性特质。

将女性身体转化成使用价值和交换价值的过程开启了符号秩序。虽然女性不是话语的接受者,因而也无法接近表意系统,但是为保证流通的顺利实现,她们被赋予同男性一样的话语,单纯通过模仿男性语言保证社会秩序的建立。实际交易构成了男性对于女性的权力关系,确保了父权社会的正常功能,女性必须服从强加于其上的非处女即母亲的身份,而不被允许发展属于自己的个性。女性为继续待在表意系统内,被迫接受强加于其身的各种身份,从

---

① Luce Irigray, *This Sex Which is Not One*, trans. Catherine Porter and Carolyn Burke, Ithaca: Cornell University Press, 1985, pp. 176-179.

② Luce Irigray, *This Sex Which is Not One*, trans. Catherine Porter and Carolyn Burke, Ithaca: Cornell University Press, 1985, p. 181.

而成为父权制的共谋。这样一来，女性就被转化成了具有拜物教性质的物品，“女性就是菲勒斯权力的表征和流通，从而建立起男性之间关系”[①]。女性在男性之间的交换和流通维持了社会的运转，至少父权社会是如此运转的。

显然，小说的女主人公安嘉丽就被商品化了，她的身体被物化。19 岁的安嘉丽已经明白了这样的事实：

> 不要说星座不匹配，要求的嫁妆被拒绝，祖父的传闻，以及种性不规则等问题，女孩可能因为以下任何原因在欲求等级表上被减分：身材太矮小或太高大，皮肤太黑或太白，太丰满或不丰满，眼睛太大或眼珠颜色太浅，头发太卷，个人行为举止太大方或者太拘禁，学习成绩太好(表明太有野心)或太低(意味着作为生育机器的潜在风险)。当然，一份可观的嫁妆总可以解决这些问题。[②]

女性就像市场上被挑选的货物，挑选的标准从身材体重、外貌举止到教育程度，无所不包。对女性的物化在安嘉丽被父亲相中的女婿苏博德(Subodh)强暴的时候表现得淋漓尽致。他们初次约会的时候，“他解开内衣，评估她的乳房……她知道他的手在她的乳房上，使劲地揪，然后掂量着双乳，像小小的番石榴，然后她想起了那些她羡慕的女孩子，芒果样的乳房，香瓜样的乳房，刹那间一股腐烂的芒果的酸臭味从关闭的车窗弥漫进来，然后她看到在

---

① Luce Irigray, *This Sex Which is Not One*, trans. Catherine Porter and Carolyn Burke. Ithaca: Cornell University Press, 1985, p. 183.

② Bharati Mukherjee, *Miss New India*, New York: Houghton Mifflin Harcourt Publishing Company, 2011, p. 30.

许多被废弃的小屋和车的周围掉落的去了皮的芒果"[①]。安嘉丽深知这是对她的玷污,但也无从反抗。而她在遭受强暴的时候也丧失了交换价值,就像是一只腐烂的芒果。苏博德却认为这是"他的权力,他要知道自己选的是什么样的货物"[②]。

安嘉丽虽然在行为上顺从父亲的意志,但是内心深处却渴望摆脱父权制强加给她的身份和价值观。父亲给她的名字是"安嘉丽",而她自称为"安琪"(Angie)。前者在印度是一个典型的女孩名,是贤妻良母的代称,而后者是一个美国名字,代表着独立个性。安琪可以随意选择自己喜欢的服饰和音乐,而不是被自己的身份所限制,被父权所支配。安琪对于父权的反抗意识终于在遭受到未婚夫强暴之后彻底觉醒。因为身体在遭遇男权践踏的时候,她对自己的身体是拒斥的,处于克里斯蒂娃所说的"嫌恶"(abject)状态,她想要逃离父权制给她划定的身体界域。"回到家里,她想逃离那辆车,穿过客厅,径直回到卧室去呕吐。"[③]在她的身体被男性目光所审视、践踏之后,她终于意识到贤妻良母不是她想要的角色,她要追求家庭之外属于自己的幸福。因此,她离开父亲的家,离开了家乡,摈弃了代表父权制的旧印度。安嘉丽以此表达她拒绝与父权制共谋出卖自己的身体和身份,接受强加到她身上的妻子和母亲身份。她逃离家庭,到大城市去追寻自己的幸福,因此父权制下的家庭否认其存在。

---

① Bharati Mukherjee, *Miss New India*, New York: Houghton Mifflin Harcourt Publishing Company, 2011, p. 61.

② Bharati Mukherjee, *Miss New India*, New York: Houghton Mifflin Harcourt Publishing Company, 2011, p. 60.

③ Bharati Mukherjee, *Miss New India*, New York: Houghton Mifflin Harcourt Publishing Company, 2011, pp. 61-62.

二、作为国家身体的印度竭力摆脱英国的殖民统治

《新印度小姐》中的另一位女性角色明妮(Minnie)成长于英国殖民统治时期,对于帝国统治无限眷恋。明妮拥有的一幢具有安格鲁-印度风格的府邸由英国殖民者修建,在一群印度本土建筑中间可谓是鹤立鸡群。明妮是英国和印度混血,嫁给了英国人,自印度独立以来已有四年多,她再未踏出过府邸半步。每次与人谈起她的府邸,她都沉浸在往日的荣光中不可自拔:"这在历史上是十分重要的一座建筑,就像你的先辈确凿无疑地告诉你的那样,就在这间房间,就是用这些餐盘,很久之前,爱德华七世本尊和他的皇室成员,曾在此用餐。"[①]明妮说着一口标准的英式英语,行为举止俨然是帝国的遗孤,处处维护着帝国的统治秩序,这从她府邸里的管理风格上可见一斑,她对住在宅子里的租户颐指气使;奉行的理念是"所有的荣耀归于白芝浩(Bagehot)之名,愿它永不被辱没"[②],试图让宅子恢复帝国时期的荣耀。宅子是英帝国统治的象征,它的所有者明妮是帝国统治秩序维护者的身份,从不踏出宅邸半步意味着她拒绝接受现实,活在回忆里。在日新月异的班加罗尔,整个城市在重建之中,已没有了旧日的模样,只有这座府邸一成不变。

蕾妮·迪金森(Renee Dickinson)的"身体理论"(Corporeum)融合了女性主义、生态批评、后殖民和后结构主义理论,将女性身体和地理身体、国家身体以及文本身体联结起来。父权社会中的

---

① Bharati Mukherjee, *Miss New India*, New York: Houghton Mifflin Harcourt Publishing Company, 2011, p. 31.

② Bharati Mukherjee, *Miss New India*, New York: Houghton Mifflin Harcourt Publishing Company, 2011, p. 119.

女性身体边界由父权制界定,而殖民统治时期的地理区域和国家疆域边界则是由殖民统治划分的。在划定的边界内,女性、地理区域和国家疆域被书写、被本质化,同时被赋予相应的身份。在小说的序言中,作者将印度在父权制的浓重阴影、英帝国统治的遗留和全球化语境的三重影响下经历的嬗变通过地理的分布得到表达。在小说人物彼特所著的《经典的印度建筑:公共和私人》一书中,他写道:"从加尔各答(Calcutta)到旁遮普(Punjab),一直到海边,到孟买(Bombay),经过果阿(Goa)到南方,都是公共建筑和国家殖民者居住楼。"①这些府邸见证了英国统治印度的殖民史,今天仍是殖民统治的残存。如果说安嘉丽是印度父权制统治下女性形象的化身,那么明妮则是英帝国殖民统治下印度国家形象的化身。通过将国家身体女性化,印度女性和国家的命运紧紧相连,不可分割。英国殖民统治下的印度在面对殖民国英国时,就如同父权制下的女性,不得不委身于英国统治,放弃自己的民族特性、民族身份,成为具有英国性的殖民地,贡献自己的身体(资源),被代表父权的殖民者压榨、利用其身体。

安嘉丽作为反抗父权的代表,她的觉醒预示印度的觉醒。小说结尾,明妮的宅邸被租户雷乔(Rajoo)洗劫一空。在这场蓄谋已久的打劫中,雷乔组织了一帮年轻人,将宅邸里的古董家具,包括橱柜、沙发、梳妆台、储物箱、明妮祖父留下的钟,甚至明妮引以为傲的餐桌都拉走了,管家阿索克(Asoke)的亲戚也参与其中,他的女性亲戚甚至拉走了大米和食物。明妮在恐惧中撒手人寰,她余生留恋英国殖民统治,结果她的身体和她的府邸均被剥夺了价值。洗劫一空的府邸,赤身裸体死于恐惧中的女主人,二者再次被联系起来。赤裸的女性身体象征了在父权制社会没有任何社会价值和

① Bharati Mukherjee, *Miss New India*, New York: Houghton Mifflin Harcourt Publishing Company, 2011, p. 3.

交换价值的自然身体,而被洗劫一空的宅邸代表了殖民统治的影响已经日薄西山。

在小说序言中,作者借美国侨胞彼特·钱皮恩(Peter Champion)之口称印度的年轻一代是终将照亮印度的星火,"'你们身上有火苗——不要将它毁了,或消耗殆尽。印度是一个僵死的沉睡的巨人,但开始活动了。对我而言为时已晚,但是印度终将被照亮'。其中一个女性是安嘉丽·博斯"①。可见,作者从最初就已经通过火苗与光亮之间的联系将年轻女性安嘉丽和印度国家之间的命运巧妙地联结起来,女性成为国家形象的象征。这种关联贯穿小说的始终,在后记中,彼特再次说道:"'她身上有星火',感谢她以及千千万万个她,印度将势不可挡,甚至高里普尔(Gauripur)也将势不可挡。"②

在小说中,作者将女性身体和国家身体紧密联系起来,其背后依然是父权制逻辑在作祟。或许,既要脱离父权制的符号体系,又要表达女性话语是一对无法解决的矛盾,但是赋予女性作为照亮国家未来的新形象表达了作者改变女性形象的迫切愿望。彼特称女性是点亮这个国家的火花,这是对女性的赞美,是女性形象开始转变和提升的开端,表明了在飞速发展的印度女性的地位有所改观。安嘉丽的家乡高里普尔代表了落后的印度,那里母性和家庭生活依然被认为是女性的首要身份和职责;而大都市班加罗尔则代表了前进的印度,那里众多的安嘉丽们接受英语教育,工作和生活。她们代表了新的职业女性,在寻求自我独立和幸福的同时为印度的发展做出贡献,是印度的未来和希望。在与中国学者刘晶

---

① Bharati Mukherjee, *Miss New India*, New York: Houghton Mifflin Harcourt Publishing Company, 2011, p. 4.

② Bharati Mukherjee, *Miss New India*, New York: Houghton Mifflin Harcourt Publishing Company, 2011, p. 326.

的访谈中,穆克吉坦言,她很欣赏那些敢于在面对逆境的时候迈出步伐掌控局面的人①。

三、作为地理身体的印度难以摆脱美国新殖民主义

《新印度小姐》中另一位女性人物帕尔瓦蒂(Parvati)是印度归国侨民,从美国回到班加罗尔,建立企业并成为一个成功的商人,是当代通信机构(International Communicative Institute)的创立者之一。帕尔瓦蒂说着一口纯正的美式英语,对公司招募的印度各地来的女孩子进行培训,要求她们也会讲标准的美音,能够胜任接线中心的工作。帕尔瓦蒂有一个花园,花园里种植了多个国家引进的植物,"雨季后的花朵,成群的蝴蝶,还有时不时飞来的鹦鹉,虎皮鹦鹉和太阳鸟:关于这个花园的一切都是夸张的、奢华的。每一个在美元殖民地的人在植物方面都是具有竞争力的。花旗银行的斯里尼瓦桑(Srinivasan)进口了西伯利亚果树,休利特-奥卡德·古普塔(Hewlett-Oackard Gupta)将一个小型的印尼丛林移植了过来"②。前文已指出,当今印度的地理格局是父权制、帝国殖民统治和全球化三重影响下形成的;帕尔瓦蒂代表了全球化中的美国影响力。她的花园就是印度国家地理身体的象征,等待着美国的开发,而她就是花园帝国的管理者。"帕尔瓦蒂,戴着一顶宽大帽檐的帽子,穿着沾满泥土的围裙,带着一双手套,看上去滑稽可笑,用力地除草、松肥、修建着她那生机勃勃的帝国。"③帕尔

① 参见刘晶:《移民文学与〈新印度小姐〉——芭拉蒂·穆克吉访谈录》,《外国文学》2012 年第 5 期。

② Bharati Mukherjee, *Miss New India*, New York: Houghton Mifflin Harcourt Publishing Company, 2011, p. 284.

③ Bharati Mukherjee, *Miss New India*, New York: Houghton Mifflin Harcourt Publishing Company, 2011, p. 269.

瓦蒂的花园象征了印度在全球化时代遭遇的各种力量的塑造和冲击。美国是全球化语境下的新帝国，印度处于其新殖民主义的统治之下。

同帕尔瓦蒂一样，小说中的另一位美国归侨彼特也是美国影响力的代表。在全球化语境下，印度的女性化形象通过彼特和其同性恋人阿力（Ali）的恋情关系被强化。在他们的关系中，彼特是强势的一方，阿力是弱势的一方。阿力被赋予了女性化特征，他被称作“高里普尔最美的女人”[①]，他擅长跳舞和家务劳动。安嘉丽初次来到彼特家里的时候，“房间里毫无生气，就像是个仆人的宿舍”[②]。当阿力搬来和他同住的时候，他的房间焕然一新：

> 花团锦簇的彩陶花盆摆满了通往钱皮恩先生楼梯的狭窄走廊，天井上爬满了葡萄藤，楼梯上她叫不出名字的花儿香气沁人…圆桌上摆放着鲜花，桌布是彩色的，四面墙上都挂着画。屋里有两把看上去很舒服的藤椅和一盏落地灯。原本挂在钉子上的衣服现在都挂进了一架旧的木衣橱里，书架都沿着墙整齐地摆放到了卧室的壁龛处。彼特一人居住的时候，屋子里毫无生气，阿力的到来给房间带来了生气，阿力像个女人一样喜欢侍弄花草，他的女性特质在此流露出来。[③]

此外，两人的合照看起来就像是夫妇，彼特在他昏暗的小屋里读印度报纸，而在他身后的阿力则模糊不清，俨然一副仆人的扮相，“包

---

① Bharati Mukherjee, *Miss New India*, New York: Houghton Mifflin Harcourt Publishing Company, 2011, p. 41.

② Bharati Mukherjee, *Miss New India*, New York: Houghton Mifflin Harcourt Publishing Company, 2011, pp. 13-14.

③ Bharati Mukherjee, *Miss New India*, New York: Houghton Mifflin Harcourt Publishing Company, 2011, p. 14.

着头巾，穿着汗衫在刷碗"[①]。显然，在两人的关系中，阿力的角色就是妻子，"她"的工作就是家务琐事。他的女性化代表了印度的女性化。

印度不只是遭受父权制、英国殖民统治压迫的国家，在全球化的浪潮中，她同时还受到美国新殖民主义的影响。作者通过女性身体和印度地理身体的联合，凸显了新殖民主义对于印度的这种影响。殖民主义的影响似乎已经退去，然而新殖民主义仍然甚嚣尘上。小说的结尾，当安嘉丽回到故乡，再次参观了彼特的家。而此时的阿力"愈加年迈，(安嘉丽)坐在轮椅上几乎难以认出是阿力"[②]。阿力因为追求美貌，接受了整形手术，在手术失败后面对身体残疾的残酷现实。阿力的命运暗含了印度在与美国的较量中的悲观结局。穆克吉在接受采访的时候说，她曾经思考过印美关系这个问题。[③] 显然，作者对于在全球化语境下印度的结局也是不确定的。

四、作为叙事策略的文本身体反抗父权压迫

迪金森的"身体理论"指出，在父权制下，不仅女性身体被本质化，国家身体和地理身体也通过与女性身体的联结而被本质化。此外，文本也被具象化为女性化的文本身体。[④] 父权制度及其符

---

① Bharati Mukherjee, *Miss New India*, New York: Houghton Mifflin Harcourt Publishing Company, 2011, p. 42.

② Bharati Mukherjee, *Miss New India*, New York: Houghton Mifflin Harcourt Publishing Company, 2011, p. 328.

③ 刘晶:《移民文学与〈新印度小姐〉——芭拉蒂·穆克吉访谈录》,《外国文学》2012 年第 5 期。

④ Renée Dickinson, *Female Embodiment and Subjectivity in the Modernist Novel: The Corporeum of Virginia Woolf and Olive Moore*, New York: Routledge, 2009, pp. 1-2.

号体系通过语言设置对立，将母性价值强加给女性身体，同时将生理身体排除在话语体系之外。写作活动是填满空白纸张即文本身体的活动，同时给生理、国家和地理身体赋予人格和身份。写作方式揭示了思考方式，也表明构建身份的方式。例如，在现代主义作家的文本实验中，男性作家 T. S. 艾略特和庞德使用了一种厌食症式的写作风格，不仅意在去除文本身体，也因其多余而去掉女性身体。[①] 女性作家伍尔夫（Woolf）和摩尔（Olive Moore）则采用了松散、流动的审美，在他们的文本中，句子和段落仿佛漂浮在页面，有时候甚至通过意识流和冗余的文本形式流动至女性人物的头脑中，以此试图让女性身体重新进入文本中。

在《新印度小姐》中，作者通过将女性身体具象化以及将国家身体和地理身体具象化为女性身体，揭示父权制、英国殖民统治和美国新殖民主义对印度的影响和塑造。穆克吉诉诸多种叙事策略，为女性主体性的书写提供了一种新的路径。在文本中，作者使用斜体字表达主人公安嘉丽内心真实的声音和欲望、困惑和伤痛，同时通过书信体将这些想法表达出来，宣告自我的独立。此外，在小说的序言和后记中，作者使用第一人称复数叙事，试图与有着相同心路历程的读者产生共鸣，表达他们共同的诉求。

在小说中，作者在表达主人公安嘉丽的内心声音时，均采用了斜体。在父权制的压制下，安嘉丽不敢大声地表达自己内心真实的想法，但是作者在呈现新印度的新女性，想要她们的声音被倾听，因此她在文本中进行了大胆的实验，将表达作者内心隐秘想法的句子都用斜体加以处理。在家里面对她气势凌人的父亲和沉默寡言的母亲时，安嘉丽很少吐露真心，只是被动地接受他们强加给

① Renée Dickinson, *Female Embodiment and Subjectivity in the Modernist Novel: The Corporeum of Virginia Woolf and Olive Moore*, New York: Routledge, 2009, p. 15.

她的要求,然而她内心深处有一个微弱的声音在呼喊。例如,在父亲从征婚启事中为她挑选夫婿的时候,她内心的真实想法是:"他们真的认为这个店员配得上我吗?"[①]但她依然服从父亲给她安排的婚姻,因为她从小被灌输了作为女儿的义务。但事实上,她内心渴望能够掌控自己的生活。在她的老师彼特鼓励她离开家乡去大城市的时候,她误以为是彼特在求婚:

> 这是在求婚吗?她想,她差点大声说出来,想要帮助她。我愿意,我会让你幸福!接着他说道:"你应该去一个大城市。"她也曾常常想象着自己在孟买这样的大城市,或者在果阿的海滩上,然后她跟他说这些可能性。最后,甚至去美国,她想,尽管她不敢说出来,怕这会误导这邪恶的眼睛。
>
> …………
>
> 她想,他是要带我去班加罗尔吗?为什么不呢?我要去。转念又想:那我到底成什么样的女孩了?[②]

此时的安嘉丽刚刚遇到彼特,对他心生情愫,在她的内心深处,她只是希望有一个人能带她远走高飞。但是她又不敢表露心迹,只是在心理想象这一切并默默地说:我愿意,我要让他幸福!此时的安嘉丽内心还未真正觉醒,她认为摆脱父亲控制的方式是找一个心仪的男人结婚。

虽然彼特不能以安嘉丽幻想的方式带给她自由,但是他带给安嘉丽觉醒的勇气。在她得知彼特和阿力的同性恋情时,开始有

---

① Bharati Mukherjee, *Miss New India*, New York: Houghton Mifflin Harcourt Publishing Company, 2011, p. 21.

② Bharati Mukherjee, *Miss New India*, New York: Houghton Mifflin Harcourt Publishing Company, 2011, pp. 15-16.

了一些她从未有过的想法，这些想法也是用斜体呈现的：

> 他对待我就像是一个成人，她想。她将成人的身份强加于我。这就是成人的世界；这就是成人的交往方式。我理解了，但是我不该以任何方式回应。这看起来很奇怪，但又如此熟悉。他亲吻了他吗？我穿过了一堵隐形的墙，我不能再回去了。或许我就是鬼。头一次，她能够将这些表达出来，至少对她自己能说出来了：或许我不在这里，或许我什么也没看到。或许"安嘉丽"看到了，但是"安琪"没有看到。把自己一分为二让她觉得舒服。①

得知真相的她感觉自己穿越了一堵隐形的墙，她内心那个真正的自我开始浮现出来。通过这种书写策略，作者为主人公提供了一个反省自我身份和主体性的空间。但是此时的她仍然没有勇气表达自我。

最终，作者通过书信体让主人公表达出自己真实的想法。安嘉丽在遭受所谓的未婚夫的强暴后，终于决定要去大城市寻找梦想，她选择用书信和父母道别：

> 最亲爱的爸妈：
>
> 我不会跟任何人为我随便挑选的什么男人结婚，尤其不会跟这一个。如果我最终没有孩子，那就这样吧。你们看得明明白白，你们选择的这个男人玷污了我。他应该马上被送到监狱。我今天上午就要去巴特那(Patna)找我的姐姐了，她的名字你们却不愿再提。

① Bharati Mukherjee, *Miss New India*, New York: Houghton Mifflin Harcourt Publishing Company, 2011, p. 51.

> 等我安顿下来,我会再写信。这可能需要好几个月的时间。我已准备好在世界找到我自己的位置,求你们不要想着找我。①

安嘉丽不仅把自己的真实想法公开地表达出来,还采用了否定句表达强烈的决心,哪怕这会让她无家可归。她敢于说出强暴她的人该去坐牢,证明她已经敢于和父权制抗争。书信是文学中女性常用的表达自我心声的一种叙述形式。这封与父母的诀别信是安嘉丽到安琪蜕变的第一步,是她的独立宣言,标志着她与旧的价值观决裂的决心,标志着她拥抱新的价值观的开启。与斜体代表的微弱隐秘的声音相比,写信与父母告别是勇敢大胆的一步,象征着安嘉丽自我的获得。

在小说的序言和后记中,作者使用了第一人称复数叙事。序言开头便是:"年轻人在幻想着西方的时候,美国在他们的记忆中完全模糊,我们为美国痴迷,他们却受够了。"②"我们"指在新印度迅速成长的年轻人,与之相对的是西方的"他们",来自西方社会,在印度生活。之后叙述者虽然变为彼特的学生,但依旧沿用第一人称复数叙事:"当我们还是他的学生的时候,关于他我们唯一确知的是他来上课从来没有讲义。但他对我们的影响却犹如苍穹,挥之不去。"(2)彼特总是鼓励年轻人出去闯荡,并且承担了启蒙年轻人的责任,称年轻人是点亮印度的星火。

序言中的复数第一人称叙事在后记中再次出现,关于安嘉丽,叙述者说道:

---

① Bharati Mukherjee, *Miss New India*, New York: Houghton Mifflin Harcourt Publishing Company, 2011, p. 66.

② Bharati Mukherjee, *Miss New India*, New York: Houghton Mifflin Harcourt Publishing Company, 2011, p. 2.

> 老师告诉我们，去拜访我们的一位女校友，她已经离开了高里普尔，找到了一份工作，获得了老师常常跟我们说的成功。她的名字叫安嘉丽·博斯，我们很多人都记得她身材高挑，很外向，在比哈尔(Bihar)内地生活的众多孟加拉人中的一个。他说，她身上有“火花”，感谢她和万千像她一样的女孩，印度才蒸蒸日上。甚至高里普尔也蒸蒸日上。[①]

第一人称复数叙事表明了在全球化大潮下的印度，有千千万万和安嘉丽一样的年轻人，他们在新旧两种传统之间挣扎，而最终挣脱了陈旧的价值观的束缚，在新的价值观的鼓励下勇敢追求独立，追求幸福。同时，作者也希望和读者共鸣，激发出他们身上的火花，勇敢追求自我。

(张昕昕：北京外国语大学英语学院博士研究生)

① Bharati Mukherjee, *Miss New India*, New York: Houghton Mifflin Harcourt Publishing Company, 2011, p. 326.

“战斗的爱尔兰人”：论《尤利西斯》中的跨大西洋民族主义书写

王　蕾

民族主义书写是爱尔兰现代民族寓言《尤利西斯》(Ulysses)的重要主题之一，与之相关的“战斗的爱尔兰人”形象也几乎贯穿小说的始终。如都柏林城市空间中的“解放者”丹尼尔·奥康内尔的雕像，爱尔兰文化记忆中的古代英雄库胡林，媒介报道中的民族主义领袖巴涅尔，酒吧里民众口耳相传的芬尼亚勇士等。爱尔兰民族性中的战斗特质与爱尔兰屡受外族入侵的历史密切相连，乔伊斯在的里雅斯特讲学时曾指出：“看英国人占领前三个世纪的爱尔兰历史需要有强大的心理准备，内讧厮杀和抵御丹麦人、挪威人入侵的战斗……此起彼伏的战争将爱尔兰变成屠宰场。”[①]中古时期这段充斥着血腥杀戮的历史一直延续到近现代，使爱尔兰成为“一片战争之地，和平时期只是断断续续的插曲”[②]。可见，爱尔兰

---

① James Joyce, *Occasional*, *Critical*, *and Political Writing*, ed. Kevin Barry, trans. Conor Deane, Oxford: Oxford University Press, 2000, p. 113.

② Thomas Barlett and Keith Jefferey, introduction to *A Military History of Ireland*, ed. Barlett and Jefferey, Cambridge: Cambridge University Press, 1997, p. 6.

民族性中的战斗特质是抵御外族入侵和反抗英国殖民的历史产物,而非凯尔特民族的本质属性。

18世纪末,随着爱尔兰民族主义运动的兴起,“战斗的爱尔兰人”形象逐渐形成。由于英国殖民者对爱尔兰采取的污名策略以及流亡欧洲的爱尔兰民族主义者的影响,“战斗的爱尔兰人”形象在欧洲大陆得以深化,并成为爱尔兰族裔形象的一个重要组成部分。19世纪后半叶,爱尔兰大饥荒引发了大规模的移民潮,众多饥民横跨大西洋奔赴美国,“把爱尔兰历史播撒在地球的另一边”①。美—爱人士不仅深度参与了美国本土的民族主义运动,也为爱尔兰的民族主义运动提供了多维度的支持和帮助。历史学者大卫·格里森指出:“在美国,人们对爱尔兰人最普遍的刻板印象之一是‘战斗的爱尔兰人’。”②因此,乔伊斯在《尤利西斯》中的跨大西洋民族主义书写不仅揭示了爱尔兰民族性中战斗特质的成因,而且展现了美国民族主义运动热潮对爱尔兰族裔战斗特质的建构,从而体现了爱尔兰本土性与世界性互动关系。

一、大饥荒与绿色大西洋

1845～1851年,一场大饥荒席卷爱尔兰,造成了严重的食物匮乏,饥饿引发疾病、死亡和海外移民,导致当时爱尔兰的总人口骤减四分之一。作为爱尔兰历史的重要事件之一,大饥荒对爱尔兰的政治、经济、文化产生了深远的影响。大饥荒的起因在于马铃薯霉菌导致马铃薯大范围的歉收,引发严重的食物短缺。马铃薯

---

① [英]特里·伊·格尔顿:《历史中的政治、哲学、爱欲》,马海良译,中国社会科学出版社1998年版,第350页。

② David T. Gleeson, *The Green and the Gray: The Irish in the Confederate States of America*, Chapel Hill: University of North Carolina Press, 2013, p. 1.

是16世纪末由西班牙从美洲引入爱尔兰,由于爱尔兰的海洋气候和土地条件适合马铃薯的生长,种植面积逐渐扩大。1801年,英国正式通过了英爱合并法案,爱尔兰被并入大英帝国的版图,并饱受殖民征服和掠夺。从此,爱尔兰的农业种植结构演变为典型的殖民地单一作物种植结构,马铃薯取代小麦成为爱尔兰人的主食,"到1845年,爱尔兰总人口达到850万左右,其中470万人将马铃薯作为日常饮食的首选"①。

作为爱尔兰近代史的分水岭,国内外学者对大饥荒作出了不同阐释。一方面,以约翰·迈克尔(John Michael)和伍德汉-史密斯(Cecil Woodham-Smith)为代表的爱尔兰民族主义学者认为大饥荒的发生不仅是天灾,更是人祸。英国殖民政府所采取的无作为政策实质上是一种种族灭绝政策。因为"谷物大丰收,说明谷物是充足的,即使遇到土豆霉病,也能够支持爱尔兰全部人口"②。"五年内有一百万人死亡,一百万人移民,英国政府的政策是一种有意的灭绝政策,旨在保证爱尔兰无限期处于英国控制之下从而维护英国的政治利益……(英国)政府的危机处理不管是有意还是无心,都导致了饥饿。"③另一方面,以T. W. 穆迪(T. W. Moody)和R. D. 爱德华(R. D. Edwards)为首的修正主义学者倾向于以客观的无价值立场研究大饥荒的影响,破解民主主义学者所塑造的饥荒神话。他们认为,爱尔兰当时的人口密度和农业发展水平严重失调,英国政府已经在能力范围内采取了足够的措施,大饥荒的爆发不可避免。"1845～1852年发生的大饥荒……

① Austin Bourke, *The Visitation of God? The Potato and the Great Irish Famine*, Dublin: Lilliput Press, 1993, p. 52.

② Hugh F. Kearney, *Ireland: Contested Ideas of Nationalism and History*, New York: New York University Press, 2007, p. 271.

③ O'Heharty. P. S, *A History of Ireland under the Union, 1801 to 1922*, London: Methuen & Co. Ltd., 1952, p. 328.

不是爱尔兰历史上的第一次饥荒,也不是最后一次,只是爱尔兰漫长而苦难的历史中的一个时期。但因为这次饥荒的漫长周期和严重危害,在(爱尔兰)民众记忆中留下深刻烙印,受害者将其称为万恶之源,视其为民族压迫的表征……大饥荒值得被审视,但它不过是一个象征。"①

乔伊斯并未在《尤利西斯》中对大饥荒进行明确描述,但从侧面展现了食物严重匮乏以及农业种植结构单一对爱尔兰民众身心健康所造成的负面影响。首先,乔伊斯在小说中反复描述了"饥饿"的场景,"我的同族就成群结队地从饥饿的牢笼般的城里冲出来。他们手执剥皮用的小刀,奔跑、攀登、劈砍那满是肥厚的绿色脂肪的鲸肉"②。可见,爱尔兰底层民众迫于饥饿不得不哄抢被冲到岸上的鲸鱼肉以维持生存。其次,食物匮乏导致各种疾病泛滥。布鲁姆在都柏林街角看到一个小姑娘,"她看上去好像营养也不良。成天是土豆和人造黄油……这样,身体会垮的"(301)。与之相对,天主教神父"享受丰足的生活。神父的酒窖和食品库"(300)。由此可见,英国殖民统治和天主教会的压迫对爱尔兰本土民众的生活造成了严重的负面影响。

19世纪后半叶大饥荒的爆发,加之英国政府的无作为政策,爱尔兰本土民众,尤其是底层民众的生活难以为继。因此,大饥荒迫使一部分爱尔兰人移民海外谋求生活。大英帝国占领的北美洲自然资源丰富却缺少相应的劳动力,成为当时爱尔兰饥荒移民的主要目的地之一,攒钱买船票去美国成为许多贫苦爱尔兰人的出路,"1845～1854年间,大约有二百万人移民美国,约战爱尔兰全

① R. D. Edwards and T. D. Williams, eds., *The Great Famine: Studies in Irish History 1845-52*, Washington: New York University Press, 1957, p. vii.

② [爱尔兰]詹姆斯·乔伊斯:《尤利西斯》,萧乾、文洁若译,文化艺术出版社2002年版,第113页。后文中涉及该小说的引用均以尾注标注页码。

国人口的四分之一"[①]。搭乘移民船横穿大西洋对爱尔兰饥荒移民来说既是奔赴新生活的一种尝试,也是被迫融入美洲现代世界的一种探险。移民船原本是用来承载黑人在大西洋流域进行跨国活动的载体,爱尔兰学者凯文·惠兰(Kevin Whelan)据此提出了"绿色太平洋"[②]的概念。大西洋的历史由于爱尔兰饥荒移民潮的出现变得多彩,绿色大西洋中的爱尔兰饥荒移民成为黑色大西洋的续写,爱尔兰饥荒移民在美国落地生根,在积极参与美国本土民族主义运动的同时,也开启了爱尔兰民族主义运动跨越大西洋的流散历史。

二、瘫痪的中心与北美流亡者

爱尔兰民族性中的"战斗性"源于大规模系统性被暴力征伐的历史,大英帝国数百年的殖民统治更加深化了这种特质,"尚武""好战"等刻板印象也被逐步接受并吸纳为爱尔兰族裔的自我形象认知。乔伊斯曾指出:"当战胜国对战败国实施保证,战败国进行反抗从逻辑上并无可指摘之处。这是人性的自然反应。"[③]但他也同时指出,如果爱尔兰人默认他们天生就有战斗精神,那是因为他们想以此抵消对"国家的灵魂"已经"被几个世纪无用的斗争削弱"和"瘫痪"现实不满。[④]

---

① http://www.spartacus.schoolnet.co.uk/USAEireland.htm.

② Kevin Whelan, "The Green Atlantic: Radical Reciprocities between Ireland and America in the Long Eighteenth Century", *A New Imperial History: Culture, Identities, and Modernity in Britain and the Empire, 1660-1840*, edited by Kathleen Wilson, Cambridge: Cambridge University Press, 2004, pp. 216-238.

③ James Joyce, *The Critical Writings of James Joyce*, eds. Ellsworth Mason and Richard Ellmann, New York: Viking Press, 1964, p. 163.

④ James Joyce, *The Critical Writings of James Joyce*, eds. Ellsworth Mason and Richard Ellmann, New York: Viking Press, 1964, p. 171.

《尤利西斯》中详细描述了都柏林作为瘫痪的中心的情景,展现大英帝国高压殖民统治下都柏林民众日常生活的麻痹性以及爱尔兰本土民族主义者的内讧。一方面,英国殖民统治的暴力机器渗透至都柏林人日常生活的方方面面,皇家爱尔兰警察的身影遍布大街小巷,监狱、兵营随处可见,警笛声响彻昼夜。因此,小说中都柏林普通民众的民族主义救亡情结往往流于偏颇狭隘,自治派的报纸主编热衷于"来自马房的消息"(289),市民沉溺于在酒吧酗酒并追忆往昔。另一方面,民族主义者内部各执己见,"被外国政客巧妙地分裂了"[①]。橙带党、晓党、芬尼社、常胜军等民族主义团体各自为政,缺乏明确统一的战斗目标。"巴涅尔纪念碑的基石。衰竭。心脏。"(204)表明无冕之王巴涅尔在英国殖民者和爱尔兰民族主义内部的纷争共谋之下因急性肺炎导致的心力衰竭而死。可见,爱尔兰本土当时的民族主义运动遭受了严重的打压,民众的"战斗性"被迫转化为庸碌甚至是麻痹,而民族主义团体的"战斗性"也被打压得四分五裂。

与之相反,移民北美的爱尔兰族裔却表现出更为强劲的"战斗性"。巴涅尔 1880 年 3 月在美国圣·路易斯发表演说时着重指出:"相较于对身在美国的爱尔兰族裔发表演说,对爱尔兰本土民众发表演说时必须要采取更为强硬的语气。由于受到压迫和打压,爱尔兰本土民众需要鼓舞和激励;而身在美国的爱尔兰族裔的(战斗热情)则需要泼冷水降温。"[②]初代移民美国的爱尔兰人主要从事手工业、手工作坊、家务活等,笃信天主教使得他们顺利融入以清教徒为主的当地社会。大饥荒引发的大规模移民潮为当时美

① James Joyce, *The Critical Writings of James Joyce*, eds. Ellsworth Mason and Richard Ellmann, New York: Viking Press, 1964, p. 167.

② Michael Davitt, *The Fall of Feudalism in Ireland, or the Strong of the Land League Revolution*, London: Harper Publishers, 1904, p. 205.

国的工业革命提供了大量廉价劳动力,但是,爱尔兰移民融入美国社会的过程是痛苦的。后饥荒时代,由于跨越大西洋涌入美国东部沿海地区的爱尔兰天主教徒移民数量过于巨大,加之当时美国主体居民信仰清教,因此美国社会对爱尔兰饥民的同情很快转化为对天主教的敌对情绪。既没有一技之长,又没有买地的资本,爱尔兰饥荒移民只能聚居在城市贫民窟,从事社会底层工作,男性卖苦力,女性当保姆。

爱尔兰饥荒移民在美国面对艰难的生存困境和种族歧视,但是他们顽强地在美国生存下来。鉴于天主教信仰和爱尔兰口音,饥荒时代的爱尔兰移民群体一直被排斥在美国主流社会之外,甚至被贴上"怪异、贫穷、缺少教育、酗酒卖淫、犯罪率高"①的标签,"好战"也成为爱尔兰族裔在美国的刻板印象之一。但爱尔兰族裔凭借自身的坚毅在美国扎根,逐渐融入主流社会,并在各种工会中崭露头角,深度参与了美国本土的民族解放运动和现代化民主进程,有学者指出,美国独立战争的胜利离不开"流亡在美国的爱尔兰族裔"②。可见,美国的社会历史对于爱尔兰族裔的"战斗性"特质发挥着巩固和延续的作用。此外,爱尔兰族裔在美国站稳脚跟之后,也源源不断地向爱尔兰本土的民族主义运动输送了大量的资源,使爱尔兰本土的民族主义运动与北美的民族主义运动交相辉映,完成了爱尔兰族裔的跨大西洋流散历史。

三、血祭神话与美-爱民族主义回流

爱尔兰族裔的"战斗性"特质借由饥荒移民的奋斗和生活跨越

① 王辉云:《爱尔兰的土豆、大饥荒和移民潮》,《读书》2010年第8期。

② *The Proclamation of the Irish Republic* (1916), www.easter1916.net/proclamation.htm.

大西洋,在美国得到巩固和延续。同时,美一爱民族主义也通过不同渠道回流至爱尔兰本土,为被乔伊斯誉为"瘫痪的中心"的爱尔兰本土民族主义运动注入了新的活力。显然,乔伊斯意识到美-爱民族主义的跨大西洋回流。"战斗的爱尔兰人"形象随着饥荒移民跨越大西洋流传至美国,"回流至爱尔兰时明显是带着仇恨的"①。大饥荒引发了爱尔兰有史以来最大规模的跨大西洋人口流动,他们中的一部分人被贴上"流亡者"的政治标签而非普通移民,誓要"对那些造成饥荒死亡和棺材船的人进行血腥报复"②。美一爱民族主义者把激进的政治理念和筹集的专项资金从美国带回爱尔兰,最终促成了爱尔兰本土民族独立运动的高潮,后续一系列的民族自治运动,尤其是武装起义,"显然(是一项)跨大西洋活动"③。

乔伊斯在《尤利西斯》中着重描述了凤凰公园暗杀案和爱尔兰土地联盟两个事件,展现了爱尔兰族裔"战斗性"特质的跨大西洋民族主义流散书写。

首先,《尤利西斯》第八章"埃奥洛"中描述了美国报界对于凤凰公园暗杀案的报道,侧面展示了美-爱民族主义斗士如何借由美国舆论界为爱尔兰本土的民族主义事业争取世界范围的舆论支持。1882 年 5 月,英国政治家、时任爱尔兰事务大臣卡文迪和次官伯克在都柏林西郊的凤凰公园散步时被爱尔兰民族主义秘密团体"常胜军"成员刺杀。当时,爱尔兰民族主义立场报刊《自由人报》当时发表了文章,详细报道了凤凰公园暗杀案的始末,但只在爱尔兰本土范围得以流传,并未被外界得知。同时,英国《泰晤士报》发表所谓的"巴涅尔信件"影印件,暗指巴涅尔包庇凤凰公园暗

① James Joyce, *Finnegans Wake*, New York: Penguin Books, 1976, p. 112.

② Kerby A. Miller, "Revenge for Skibbereen: Irish Emigration and the Meaning of the Great Famine", *The Great Famine and the Irish Diaspora in America*, ed. Arthur Gribben, Amherst: University of Massachusetts Press, 1999, p. 189.

③ Terry Golway, "John Devoy and the Easter Rising", *Ireland's Allies*, p. 22.

杀案的凶手,妄图破坏当时巴涅尔在英国议会中所争取到的支持爱尔兰民族自治的英国政党联盟。但是,具有亲爱尔兰立场的《纽约世界报》迅速做出反应,“拍了封海底电报来约一篇特稿”并详细报道了“案件发生的地点……‘剥皮山羊’赶马车经过的路程”(272～273)。美国报业对凤凰公园暗杀案的转载和报道为巴涅尔在凤凰公园暗杀案事件中的公正立场正名,一举扭转了《泰晤士报》对巴涅尔的污名化,为巴涅尔重新赢得英国自由党人的政治同盟争取了国际舆论的支持。

其次,《尤利西斯》中描写了爱尔兰土地同盟的相关活动。自大英帝国对爱尔兰实行殖民统治伊始,土地作为最重要的农业生产资源之一,就成为大英帝国殖民当局与爱尔兰民众争夺的焦点。从十七世纪初开始,大英帝国政府就没收了爱尔兰北部的大批土地,并规定凡是迁居到那里的英国殖民者,只要宣誓效忠于英王,承认信仰新教的英王为宗教领袖,就能领到土地。从此,爱尔兰北部信仰天主教的农民便沦为佃农。大饥荒爆发后,大批英国商人抄底爱尔兰不动产,尤其是土地和房屋,造成大批失地农民和受到高价房租压迫的市民。《尤利西斯》第二章“奈斯陀”中迪希校长说:“我记得那次的大饥荒。你晓得吗,橙带党分支鼓励废除联合议会要比奥康内尔这样做,以及你们教派的主教、教长们把他斥为煽动者,还早二十年呢!你们这些芬尼社社员有时候是健忘的。”(87)此处,迪希校长将“芬尼社社员”一词作为激进的民族主义者的代名词。事实上,芬尼社的创始人之一詹姆斯·斯蒂芬斯主张推翻英国在爱尔兰的殖民统治,废除大地主所有制并建立共和国。1869 年 11 月,斯蒂芬斯因为内奸出卖而被捕,出逃后偷渡到美国,并被选举为美国芬尼社的领袖,组织美国芬尼社的爱尔兰成员进行多次起义。可见,流散至美国的爱尔兰族裔从未忘却爱尔兰本土的苦难历史,爱尔兰族裔的“战斗性”特质反而在美国得到前所未有的强化。

1879年8月,原芬尼社领导者达维特创办土地同盟,并得到爱尔兰各地民众和爱尔兰民族主义运动领导者巴涅尔的支持。10月,爱尔兰土地同盟正式成立,巴涅尔出任该同盟主席,达维特担任名誉书记,佃农、破产的小资产阶级和前芬尼社成员成为主要参与者,旨在将争取土地改革的农民运动与爱尔兰民族解放斗争相结合。巴涅尔和达维特频繁往返于爱尔兰和美国,为爱尔兰本土的民族解放运动争取资源,"尽管爱尔兰政治的中心在爱尔兰本土和英国,但爱尔兰民族解放运动成功与否的关键却在于提供资金和武器的爱尔兰裔美国人"①。纵观爱尔兰民族主义阵营,从联合爱尔兰人到新芬党都与爱尔兰裔美国人有着千丝万缕的联系。

19世纪末至20世纪初,爱尔兰裔美国人在美国社会逐渐受到主流社会的认可。一方面,一些爱尔兰后裔开始在美国政坛崭露头角,比如工人运动领袖皮特·麦奎尔(Peter McGuire)掌管波士顿政坛近半个世纪,詹姆斯·迈克尔·柯利(James Michael Curley)曾出任马萨诸塞州州长,阿尔·史密斯(Al Smith)曾出任纽约州州长等。这些大饥荒移民的后代通过大批加入公会,参加民主党,步入政坛,逐步提升了美国爱尔兰族裔的权益。爱尔兰裔政治家以极富煽动性的演讲和强硬的铁腕风格而著称,进一步加深了爱尔兰族裔"战斗性"的刻板印象。另一方面,1737年开始,爱尔兰裔美国人在每年3月7日会举行圣帕特里克节(St. Patrick's Day)游行,以彰显爱尔兰民族特有的文化传统。游行时,美国爱尔兰族裔会身着绿色服饰涌上街头,往往伴随过量饮酒和街头暴力事件。比如美国情景动画喜剧《辛普森家族》第八季第18集以戏剧化的形式反映了圣帕特里克节游行的场景,主持人反

① Una Ni Bhroimeil, "An American Opinion: John Quinn and the Easter Rising", *Ireland's Allies*, p. 207.

问道:“酗酒、暴力、毁坏公物——想到爱尔兰人是不是就想到这些?”[①]可见,“战斗的爱尔兰人”形象已经深入人心。

达维特曾指出:“爱尔兰必须通过流血、痛苦和牺牲来赢得自由。独立意味着革命、手染鲜血和冷酷无情。”[②]19 世纪末至 20 世纪初,随着新芬党和爱尔兰土地同盟在美国活动的不断深入,加之大英帝国在爱尔兰殖民统治的不断升级,爱尔兰裔美国人逐渐倾向于支持爱尔兰民族主义阵营的激进派,尤其是通过武装革命争取爱尔兰民族独立的政治理念。据统计,20 世纪 20 年代,约有 80 万爱尔兰裔美国人加入爱尔兰民族主义组织,转汇了超过 1000 万元美金以支持新芬党的革命活动,诸如此类“资助爱尔兰独立战争的资金”[③]才使爱尔兰独立成为可能。

《尤利西斯》的创作始于 1914 年,乔伊斯在 20 世纪初叶从侧面回溯了爱尔兰大饥荒的历史,以跨大西洋流散书写的方式回应了有关爱尔兰族裔“战斗性”特质的争议。一方面,乔伊斯为爱尔兰民族性中的“战斗性”正名,这是爱尔兰物质历史中的战争、殖民和压迫所导致的“反抗”,而非爱尔兰族裔“作为一个战斗种族的古老本能”[④]。同时,乔伊斯也通过《尤利西斯》中对爱尔兰本土狭隘民族主义者的自大、排外、内讧和暴力活动的描写,隐晦地表达了对这种“好斗”倾向的谴责。另一方面,乔伊斯通过《尤利西斯》中跨大西洋书写的暗线展现了爱尔兰裔美国人对爱尔兰本土民族主

① “Homer vs. the 18th Amendment”, *The Simpsons*, dir. Bob Anderson, 1997; United States: Fox, 2006.

② Robert Schmuhl, *Ireland's Exiled Children: America and the Easer Rising*, Oxford: Oxford University Press, 2016, p. 19.

③ Francis M. Carroll, *American Opinion and the Irish Question, 1910-23*, Dublin: Gill and Macmillan, 1978, p. 89.

④ Marion R. Casey, “Victor Herbert, Nationalism, and Musical Expression”, in *Ireland's Allies: America and the* 1916 *Easter Rising*, ed. Miriam Nyhan Grey, Dublin: University College Dublin Press, 2016, p. 170.

义运动的支持和参与,肯定了美-爱民族主义回流对爱尔兰民族解放运动的助力,从更为广阔的视角展现了爱尔兰饥荒移民在美国的生存历程,打破了爱尔兰族裔“战斗性”特质的刻板印象。

爱尔兰政府 1995 年举行了纪念大饥荒一百五十周年的活动,时任爱尔兰总统玛丽·鲁滨逊(Mary Robinson)在演讲时将爱尔兰大饥荒中的 150 多万移民称为爱尔兰“社会中的一笔遗产”①,饥荒移民构成爱尔兰历史上最大规模的移民输出,其中大部分移民至北美,他们在新世界的生存历程不仅完成了爱尔兰族裔的跨大西洋流散历史,重构了爱尔兰族裔的“战斗性”特质,也完成了爱尔兰本土性与世界性的互动。

[王蕾:山东大学(威海)翻译学院讲师]

① Mary Robinson, “Cherishing the Irish Diaspora”, an Address to the House of the Orieachtas, 2nd Feb. 1995, www. oireachtas. ie/viewdoc. asp? fn=/documents/address/2Feb1995. htm.

寻找家园的灵魂

——简论奥尼尔中期创作的归属主题

甲鲁海

尤金·奥尼尔的创作中期是其作品得到最多社会肯定的时期。这一阶段他尝试运用各种新的表现形式描写现代人的生存困境，注重对人物的内心世界进行深入探讨，其中一个重要的主题就是对人类归属感的探索，即现代人所面临的无所依托的精神状态。他曾说过："20 世纪，人类要有所归属。"他笔下的人物是一群没有家园的灵魂，他们处于身份危机中，找不到生活的目标所在，为了摆脱困境，他们做出了勇敢的尝试。无疑，在这些作品中，《天边外》《毛猿》以及《上帝的儿女都有翅膀》是比较突出的几部。

归属感是人社交中的基本需求，也是人类普遍的问题。它是"个体对自己有所隶属的一种心理体验，强调个体的自我感知，是个体被接纳和认同而产生的感觉"①。它影响着人的行为表现，因为人的自我实现是以归属感的需要为前提的。在他的中期作品

---

① 王锦：《归属感探析》，《西安文理学院学报》（社会科学版）2011 年第 4 期。

中，奥尼尔从身份、种族等方面细腻地揭示了人们对归属感的诉求。

在《天边外》中，天性浪漫的罗伯特与憨厚务实的哥哥安德鲁因为阴差阳错互换了角色。渴望去探索另一个世界的罗伯特为了爱情留在农庄上，却因为不善农事将农庄弄得一团糟，自己也穷困潦倒，身患肺病，奄奄一息，似乎只有在临终前获得了自由，去寻求自己真正的归属。而天生是个庄稼汉的安德鲁却成了一个投机商，虽然看上去挣了钱，却失去了朴实的天性，变得贪婪狡诈。在罗伯特眼中，安德鲁"失败得最彻底的"，因为他偏离了自己的身份，走上了邪路，注定要受到惩罚。

罗伯特具有诗人气质，他自己也承认："生活实际方面的事，我一分钟都没想过。"安德鲁是这样评价弟弟的："种田不是你的天性。"从自我归属感来看，罗伯特十分清楚自己的定位。然而，他因为心爱的姑娘放弃了航海的机会，但是在农场上，他的那些文采变得一无是处。更重要的是，他对天边外的渴望无法得到周围人的理解和认可，连看本闲书也要偷偷摸摸地进行。他为此遭到讥讽和怨恨，被认为是个游手好闲、好高骛远的人。虽然他一直在努力，但却把事情搞得更糟，甚至到了需要把农庄抵押出去的地步。罗伯特天生不是做农活的料，因而他在农场上得不到认同和接纳。由于无法实现自我价值，他一直缺乏归属感，过着"绝望消沉"的生活，与妻子反目成仇，遭到亲人的白眼，这正是他的痛苦所在。罗伯特寻求自我、寻求归属的努力以他身染肺痨病死农庄而告终，只有在临死前那一刻似乎才摆脱了俗世的羁绊，获得了自由，也最终找到了归属。通过罗伯特的境遇，奥尼尔试图表现出归属感的缺失给人带来的悲剧性结局。由于身份的错位，罗伯特无法与现实世界达成妥协，只能终日郁郁寡欢，沦为没有家园的灵魂。对他来说，死亡不是终点，而是自由的开始，到天边去，那才是他真正属于的地方。人们或许会认为罗伯特的命运可悲，因为他的理想、做法都是如此不切实际,但是,奥尼尔正是从中看到了一个被禁锢的灵魂终其一生寻求归属的悲剧意义。

如果说《天边外》是从家庭悲剧的角度反映人类对归属的追求,那么《毛猿》则主要体现了20世纪初工业时代大机器生产对人类带来的影响。通过处于社会底层的扬克的精神抗争,表现他对归属感的渴望。扬克的故事取材于奥尼尔早期的航海经历,正像剧作家本人总是感到没有归属感一样,扬克也处于一种无可皈依的状态。

扬克过去一直错误地认为自己有归属。他十分自负,认为是自己推动了世界运转,如果没有自己,世界就要停顿。扬克的这种盲目自信是建立在对生存世界缺乏认识的基础上的。他的傲慢无知使他无法正确地定位自己。然而,米尔德里德小姐的羞辱彻底粉碎了他的自信和乐观。他在第五大道见到了与邮轮截然相反的世界,意识到在上流社会眼中的自己是何等渺小。工友勒昂的话一针见血:劳动者用血汗创造出来的世界,可是在那里他们却成了非法的入侵者。当扬克试图加入世界产业工人联合会时却遭到无情拒绝,被摔出门去。最后,他到了动物园,对着大猩猩说:"我没有过去可想,也没有未来,只有现在——而那又不顶事。"他不无凄凉地自嘲道:"难道我们不都是同一个俱乐部——毛猿俱乐部——的会员吗?"最终,他发现自己的地位还不如一只大猩猩,因为自己既不在地上,又不在天堂,"受尽了夹缝罪"。扬克是大工业时代受尽压迫的社会底层的典型代表,被禁锢在地狱一般的炉膛口里,成为机器的囚徒。扬克是"现代人失去自我,找不到归宿的象征"[①]。

心理学家认为,人的社会性决定了他们渴求他人的承认和社会的认可,因为个人的能力和才华需要在社会中才能得到展现。

---

① 郭继德:《对西方现代人生的多角度探索——论奥尼尔的悲剧创作》,《文史哲》1990年第4期。

因此，人都有归属的需求，即隶属于一个群体，希望成为群体中的一员，并相互关心和照顾。如果人缺乏归属感，就会认为自己的人生没有价值，因此，寻求"归属"贯穿着扬克的悲剧。当他意识到自己没有身份、没有尊严的时候，他渴望找到在社会中的相应位置，最终他按照毛猿"团体的秘密方式"与大猩猩握手，死于它的拥抱之中。在那一刻他发出了绝望的呼喊："上帝，我该从哪里开始呀？又到哪里才合适呀？"扬克"……一步步后退直到最后一场找到了它"①——自己的归属。与《天边外》中的罗伯特一样，他似乎只有在死亡中才能得到最终的解脱和获得自由。扬克寻求归属的斗争或许看上去盲目和缺乏理性，然而，他的意识被唤醒了。无怪乎当世界产业工人联合会秘书将扬克说成是没有脑子的人猿时，扬克勃然大怒。他的例子告诉读者，沾沾自喜地生活在动物层次上给人带来死亡和毁灭，而转向内心世界寻求自我能为人们带来人生的意义。扬克说："那玩意是在你心里，它并不是你的肚子问题。吃饭——吃油炸面圈和喝咖啡——那跟它不相干。它藏得深着呐——在根底上呐。"藏在扬克心里的正是他的精神追求。剧本着力表现的"不是社会状况本身，不是劳资冲突、阶级压迫等社会现象的过程，而是……它的结果，即它给人的精神带来的创伤，在人的心理上的反应"②。扬克故事的一个重要意义正在于借此唤醒那些浑浑噩噩的灵魂。

有学者从生态伦理角度指出，扬克"代表着困境中的人类，他们缺少信仰……身心扭曲异化……走过了一条从自我膨胀到自我发现的艰难之路，在对所处伦理环境的认同和反思过程中，他们不

① Bogard Tavis, Jackson R. Bryer, *Selected Letters of Eugene O'Neill*, New Haven and London: Yale University, 1988, p. 107.

② 汪义群：《奥尼尔研究》，上海外语教育出版社 2006 年版，第 147 页。

断实现对于自身的突破,寻求摆脱自我毁灭的厄运”[①]。作为一个美国现代产业工人的代表,扬克由于对自己个体价值的错误认识,有着虚幻的自豪感,过着盲目乐观的生活。当他寻求归属的努力受挫后,他意识到自己不属于任何群体,找不到心理依托。他是劳动者和创造者,却得不到肯定、接纳和尊重,这正是扬克悲剧的重要原因。奥尼尔本人曾指出扬克故事的普遍意义在于:“扬克就是你自己,也是我自己,他是所有的人。”[②]

除了上述罗伯特和扬克的悲剧之外,《上帝的儿女都有翅膀》从种族角度描写了主人公吉姆寻求归属的斗争。作为一个迷失了自我的人,他从未在白人占主流的社会中找到属于自己的位置。他希望得到社会认可,然而黑人的身份似乎永远不可能让他出人头地。由于他的抱负,他在黑人伙伴那里到处遭人白眼,讥讽他不守本分,“你到底是个什么人?你以为自己是个什么样的人?”在那里,他屡遭排斥,指责他想用金钱使自己“变成白人”,这样是“绝对办不到的”。吉姆是一个夹缝中生存的人,无论在黑人还是白人那里都找不到归属。即便是他与心爱的白人女子艾拉结婚之后,两人之间也存在着无形的隔阂。他勤奋好学,可是却在考取律师资格的考试中屡屡受挫。而艾拉在嫁给吉姆之后,也找不到自己的归属。她以吉姆的黑人身份为耻,不愿出门,怕碰见自己的熟人。对她所爱的人吉姆,她表面上说他是“白人当中最纯洁的人”,而内心深处却盼望他在考试中“一千年也过不了关”。因为她天生的对黑人的优越感使得她不能容许吉姆出人头地。

吉姆渴望被社会所接纳,但是由于历史的原因,黑人一直处于

① 刘慧:《生态伦理视阈下扬克的悲剧》,《外国文学研究》2010 年第 3 期。

② J. L. Stylan, *Modern Drama in Theatre and Practice*, London: Cambridge University Press, 1981, p. 107.

“自卑和自毁的可悲处境”[①]，不能正确认识自己的民族文化，因而也就无法定位自己的身份。令人痛心的是，在很多情况下，黑人同时被自己的种族和白人所排斥。正如弗洛伊德指出的，吉姆的悲剧性结局表明：“黑人必须保持被压迫的状态，必须扮演低人一等的刻板形象，否则就会面临可能来自白人的暴力，提醒黑人自己的位置所在。”[②]一旦黑人试图超越这一界限，就会遭到严厉的惩罚。吉姆的困境在于，“黑人无法摈弃对自己黑人历史文化的继承，可他们人格身份的形成却是以白人作为榜样的”[③]。可以想见，一个人对自己的种族如果无法认同，那么势必会陷入一种“无根状态”[④]，在寻求归属的问题上会处于十分可悲的处境。

显然，奥尼尔肯定人的精神追求，无论他们地位如何，身处何处。人要寻求自己的所属，追求自己的归宿，这才是人生的终极意义。在奥尼尔来看，如果人只是随波逐流，不注重自己的精神追求，那么无异于行尸走肉。正如荣格所说，人类最基本的需求并不是生理需求，也不仅仅是简单的精神追求，而是找到在宇宙中的归属。上述作品正是奥尼尔对当时美国社会中重物质轻精神的做法敲响的警钟。或许，评论家温特的话能够很好地解读奥尼尔笔下那些找不到归属的灵魂：“他的角色生活在两个世界中：一个是实际的外部世界，另一个是无法满足、充满激情的欲望世界。后者是一个梦想者由于全部被禁锢的欲望而孜孜以求的。他愿意为后者

---

① 宋淑芳：《他者黑人——奥尼尔笔下黑人形象的文化与心理阐释》，《河南师范大学学报》（哲社版）2009 年第 5 期。

② Virginia Floyd: *The Plays of Eugene O'Neill: A New Assessment*, London: Continuum Intl Pub Group, 1985, p. 266.

③ 陶久胜等，《奥尼尔戏剧中的身份主题》，《南昌大学学报》（人文社科版）2012 年第 2 期。

④ 宋淑芳：《他者黑人——奥尼尔笔下黑人形象的文化与心理阐释》，《河南师范大学学报》（哲社版）2009 年第 5 期。

牺牲所有生命所赐予的一切,因为那里才有他梦想的真正现实。"①

综上所述,在他的中期作品中,奥尼尔从不同角度描写了一群迷失的灵魂在寻求归属的道路上所作的努力。通过这些人物的悲剧性结局,奥尼尔将人物的迷惘、孤独、失落、痛苦等复杂情感细腻地呈现出来,深刻揭示了20世纪初严酷的社会现实对人的精神世界所造成的影响。奥尼尔认为,人应该听从内心的召唤,勇敢地去寻找心灵的家园。归属感是一个内涵极为丰富的词,它除了包括对自己身份的认识、认同和接受,也包括与团体、社会和自然的关系。他笔下的主人公们渴望得到认可,渴望与他人、与周围环境建立和谐稳定的关系。然而,他们似乎不属于陆地,因为这里已经成为人与人对立的地方,不但有阶级的对立,也有种族的歧视。他们似乎也不属于大海,因为过去人与自然和谐共处的时代已经一去不复返。他们不再是《毛猿》中提到的所谓"自由人",那时人是"海洋的一部分……大海把一切都连接起来,结成一体"。他们与周围的世界格格不入,找不到属于自己的位置。他们寻求实现自我价值,却又处处碰壁。扬克等人的归属究竟在何处?恐怕没有人能给出一个明确的答案。然而,奥尼尔如同一位心理大师,关注着这些没有家园的灵魂,关注着人的心理状态引发的悲剧,启发人们的深刻思考,而这正是他的剧作普遍意义所在。

(甲鲁海:山东大学外国语学院副教授)

---

① Harold Bloom, *Eugene O'Neill*, New York, Philadelphia: Chelsea House Publishers, 1987, p. 5.

“博采众长，推陈出新”

——袁可嘉先生论艾略特诗与诗学①

黄宗英

袁可嘉先生在《半个世纪的脚印——袁可嘉诗文选》一书的《自序》中说：“20 世纪三四十年代是西方新诗潮和我国新诗潮相交融、相汇合的年代。在西方，艾略特、里尔克、瓦雷里、奥登的影响所向披靡；在我国，戴望舒、卞之琳、冯至和后来所谓‘九叶’诗人也推动着新诗从浪漫主义经过象征主义，走向中国式现代主义。这是一个中西诗交融而产生了好诗的辉煌时代。”②1988 年，北京的三联书店出版了袁可嘉先生的诗歌评论著作《论新诗现代化》，收录了他本人于 1946～1948 年在北京大学西语系任助教期间在当年沈从文主编的《大公报·星期文艺》《益世报·文艺周刊》和朱

---

① 本文为国家社科基金项目“比较视野下的赵萝蕤汉译《荒原》研究”(15BWW013)结项成果之一。

② 袁可嘉：《半个世纪的脚印——袁可嘉诗文选》，人民文学出版社 1994 年版，第 2 页。

光潜主编的《文学杂志》等报刊上，以“新诗现代化”为总题目，发表的20余篇文学评论系列文章。袁可嘉先生认为这是他“生平第一个创作旺盛期”。虽然为时短暂，前后不过两年时间，但是“有点生气”。由于这一时期袁可嘉先生在北京大学西语系主讲大学一年级英语课，教学工作“相当轻闲”，所以他“有许多时间搞写作和研究”。在袁可嘉先生看来，这一时期的中国新诗“现代化”有两个特点。首先，在诗歌主题思想上，诗人们既坚持反映重大社会问题，同时自由地抒发个人的心绪情感，而且力求个人感受与大众心志相互沟通，强调社会性与个人性相互融合，坚持反映论与表现论齐头并进。其次，在诗歌艺术方面，中国新诗“现代化”要求诗人们充分发挥形象思维的能力，寻求象征与联想的契合，让知性与感性融通，追求幻想与现实的交织渗透，强调继承与创新、民族性与世界性的完美结合。袁可嘉先生认为，这两个特点不仅使中国新诗“现代化”与西方现代派及旧式学院派诗歌在诗歌思想主题上有所区别，与西方单纯强调社会功能的流派有所区别，而且在诗歌创作艺术上，也使得中国新诗“现代化”与墨守成规或机械模仿的西方现代派有区别。[①] 然而，笔者认为，这两个特点颇有19世纪美国浪漫主义诗人惠特曼笔下《草叶集》中史诗性与抒情性兼容并蓄的特点[②]，因为惠特曼的特点就是“我辽阔博大，我包罗万象”[③]。而正如艾略特在《玄学派诗人》一文中所说的那样，为了再现一个复杂多样的现代西方世界，西方现代主义诗人同样被逼无奈，也只能变

---

① 参见袁可嘉：《半个世纪的脚印——袁可嘉诗文选》，人民文学出版社1994年版，第2页。

② 参见黄宗英：《惠特曼〈我自己的歌〉：一首抒情史诗》，《北京大学学报》(哲学社会科学版)2001年第4期。

③ [美]沃尔特·惠特曼：《草叶集》，赵萝蕤译，上海译文出版社1991年版，第149页。

得越来越包罗万象、越来越间接、越来越晦涩难懂。[①]

与此同时,在1947～1948年,袁可嘉先生还积极创作中国新诗,并且在沈从文、朱光潜、杨振声、冯至等著名作家主编的报刊上发表了20余首新诗。他主张中国新诗应该"走'现实、象征和玄学(指幽默机智)相结合的道路'"[②],并且想和一些诗友们一起将萌芽于戴望舒、卞之琳等20世纪30年代新诗诗人之手的新诗运动推向一个"与西方现代派不同的中国式的现代主义诗歌运动"[③]。20世纪40年后,袁可嘉先生把20世纪30年代中国新诗"现代化"的特点总结为"中国式现代主义",因为它在主题思想和诗歌艺术两个方面与西方现代主义诗歌"有同更有异,具有中国自己的特色"[④]。袁可嘉先生认为,20世纪30年代中国新诗诗歌理论具有其基本特点,比如,诗歌是由多种元素有机结合的一个整体;一首诗歌的成败与否取决于它的整体效果;诗歌与主客观因素紧密相连,不可缺少,甚至偏执一端;诗歌表现手法的现代化问题;等等。这些特点都受英美新批评派和现代诗的启迪和影响,但是它们不仅"参证了30年代新诗发展的得失",而且也是袁可嘉先生"用来考察中国新诗现状的一点心得"[⑤]。

在漫长的"半个世纪的脚印"中,艾略特似乎始终是袁可嘉先生关注的重点。早在1948年5月23日,袁可嘉先生就在《天津大

① 参见[英]托·斯·艾略特:《艾略特文学论文集》,李赋宁译,百花洲文艺出版社1994年版,第24～25页。

② 袁可嘉:《半个世纪的脚印——袁可嘉诗文选》,人民文学出版社1994年版,第574～575页。

③ 袁可嘉:《半个世纪的脚印——袁可嘉诗文选》,人民文学出版社1994年版,第575页。

④ 袁可嘉:《半个世纪的脚印——袁可嘉诗文选》,人民文学出版社1994年版,第2页。

⑤ 袁可嘉:《半个世纪的脚印——袁可嘉诗文选》,人民文学出版社1994年版,第2～3页。

公报》发表了书评文章《托·史·艾略特》,而40年后的1988年12月17日,袁先生又在《文艺报》上发表了题目为《艾略特:现代意识与传统文化的结合者》的文学评论文章。1960～1964年,为了响应“反资批修”的号召,批判当代资产阶级文艺思潮,袁先生连续在《文学评论》等报刊上发表文章,批判艾略特、新批评派、英美现代派诗歌和意识流小说。袁先生认为,这些文章虽然指出了以艾略特为代表的西方现代主义文学在思想意识方面的弱点,但是带有“政治上上纲过高,思想批评简单化,艺术上全盘否定”[①]的极端主义思潮的表现。更加“可惜”的是,1965年“文化大革命”开始后,袁可嘉先生有长达15年的时间没有机会写作研究,在他“44～58岁的成熟年代”留下了他写作生涯中的“一片巨大的空白”。直到1979年,他在政治上翻了身,他的笔头也随之“活跃起来”[②],重新开始研究和评论西方现代派文学,撰写了《欧美现代派文学概论》(1980)、《略论西方现代派文学》(1980)、《六十年代以来的美国诗歌》(1980)、《从艾略特到威廉斯》(1982)等文学评论文章,并且与董衡巽、郑克鲁合作主编了《外国现代派作品选》(第1～4册,1980～1985),与叶廷芳合作主编了《现代主义文学研究》(上、下册,1989)。

1979年,在后来收录《现代派论·英美诗论》的《欧美现代派文学漫议》[③]一文和后来收录《半个世纪的脚印——袁可嘉诗文选》的《略论西方现代派文学》一文中,袁可嘉先生在讨论西方现代派文学的艺术特征时,两次引用艾略特《窗前晨景》(“Morning at

---

① 袁可嘉:《半个世纪的脚印——袁可嘉诗文选》,人民文学出版社1994年版,第4页。

② 袁可嘉:《半个世纪的脚印——袁可嘉诗文选》,人民文学出版社1994年版,第5页。

③ 袁可嘉:《现代派论·英美诗论》,中国社会科学出版社1985年版,第69～70页。

the Window")一诗进行论述。这首诗的全文如下：

Morning at the Window

They are rattling breakfast plates in basement kitchens,
And along the trampled edges of the street
I am aware of the damp souls of housemaids
Sprouting despondently at area gates.

The brown waves of fog toss up to me
Twisted faces from the bottom of the street,
And tear from a passer-by with muddy skirts
An aimless smile that hovers in the air
And vanishes along the level of the roofs. ①

袁可嘉先生译文：

地下室餐厅里早点盘子咯咯响，
顺着人们走过的街道两旁，
我感到女佣们潮湿的灵魂
在大门口绝望地发芽。

一阵黄色的雾向我掷来
街后面人们的歪脸，
从穿着溅满污泥的裙子的过路人那里，
撕下来一个空洞的微笑，它在空中飘荡，

① T. S. Eliot, *The Complete Poems and Plays 1909-1950*, New York: Harcourt, Brace & World, 1971, p. 16.

朝屋顶那条水平线消失了。[①]

袁可嘉先生认为,“这首自由体小诗表达作者(一个天主教徒)对现代城市生活的卑微猥琐不胜轻蔑的思想”[②],然而作者“未作任何正面的陈述,而是完全依靠一连串的形象来暗示”:“盘子咯咯响”“潮湿的灵魂/在大门口绝望地发芽”“歪脸”“溅满污泥的裙子”“空洞的微笑”[③]等。在这首诗歌中,我们找不到任何说明性的文字,我们所看到的只是诗人“直截了当地用形象来表现他看不起城市中丧失了宗教信仰的心灵空虚——那伙灵魂霉得要发芽的人们”[④]。在笔者看来,诗中人“我”的视角和语气似乎都有点居高临下的感觉,仿佛他站在自家豪宅的屋子里或者阳台上,审视着周边的“窗前晨景”。他看到地面街上几位在都市豪宅的地下厨房里替有钱人家刚刚洗刷完锅碗瓢盆的女佣们。诗人艾略特在此的遣词造句十分讲究。在诗歌的开篇第一行,诗人并没有说“They are washing breakfast plates in basement kitchens”(她们正在地下室餐厅里洗早点的盘子),而是别出心裁地采用隐喻的手法直截了当地说:“They are rattling breakfast plates in basement kitchens.”我们可以把这第一行诗直译成:“她们是地下室餐厅里咯咯作响的早点盘子。”显然,艾略特笔下把那些忙于在都市豪宅的地下厨房里替人家洗盘子的女佣们直接比喻成“咯咯作响的早点盘子”的写法是一新招,让人耳目一新,也能看出诗人在使用17世纪玄学派诗人常用的“奇思妙喻”(conceit)手法。接着在第三行,诗人并没有直接写“我看到……”(I see ...)或者“我知道……”(I know

① 袁可嘉:《现代派论·英美诗论》,中国社会科学出版社1985年版,第69页。

② 袁可嘉:《半个世纪的脚印——袁可嘉诗文选》,人民文学出版社1994年版,第214页。

③ 袁可嘉:《现代派论·英美诗论》,中国社会科学出版社1985年版,第69页。

④ 袁可嘉:《现代派论·英美诗论》,中国社会科学出版社1985年版,第70页。

...)，而是选用“我感到……”(I am aware of ...)，仿佛诗中人“我”能够感觉到那些刚从地下厨房洗完早点的盘子，身上还散发着湿气和汗味，且疲惫不堪的女佣们身上所折射出来的一种“潮湿的灵魂”，而且诗人还让女佣们身上那种“潮湿的灵魂/在大门口绝望地发芽”。此处，“绝望地发芽”无疑是一种矛盾修饰(oxymoron)，一方面投射出生活在资本主义社会大都市里劳动女性的无奈和绝望；另一方面，又传达出这种社会制度下劳动人民对生命意义抱有一种无奈甚至是绝望的盼望。在《荒原》第一章《死者葬仪》的结尾处，有这么两行诗，其中艾略特也用到了“sprout”(发芽，长芽)一词：

> That corpse you planted last year in your garden,
> Has it begun to sprout? Will it bloom this year?[①]

赵萝蕤先生的译文为：

> 去年你种在花园里的尸首，
> 它长芽了吗？今年会开花吗？[②]

笔者曾经给这两行诗加过这么一个注释：“在古代传统的繁殖礼仪中，人们把神像埋入土中，以祈求丰年。耶稣和被绞死的神死后复活都与繁殖了的复苏有关，但是荒原中的人都不信教，即便见到耶稣也不认识。”[③]可见，《窗前晨景》一诗中这一“潮湿的灵魂/

① T. S. Eliot, *The Complete Poems and Plays 1909-1950*, New York: Harcourt, Brace & World, 1971, p. 39.

② 赵萝蕤译：《荒原》，黄宗英编：《赵萝蕤汉译〈荒原〉手稿》，高等教育出版社 2013 年版，第 41 页。

③ 胡家峦：《英国名诗详注》，外语教学与研究出版社 2003 年版，第 570 页。

在大门口绝望地发芽”的意象似乎印证了袁可嘉先生所谓“城市中丧失了宗教信仰的心灵空虚”,而那些“灵魂霉得要发芽的人们”居然构成了诗人笔下西方现代都市生活中这幅“窗前晨景”的主体。在艾略特看来,在第一次世界大战后的西方现代荒原上,“四月天”已经不是乔叟笔下《坎特伯雷集》开篇中那个著名的传统的万物复苏、大地回春的阳春四月,而是变成了一年四季中“最是残冷”(“the crullest month”)的月份:“它在/荒地上生丁香,掺和着/回忆和欲望,让春雨/挑拨呆钝的树根。”[①]在这些《荒原》的开篇诗行中,人们根本就看不到春的气息和新生的景象。同样,在这幅“窗前晨景”中,我们所看到的是“那伙灵魂霉得要发芽的人们”,似乎同样是一个虽生犹死,甚至是生不如死的现代荒原意象。在这首诗的后四行中,我们首先看到,向上朝着站在都市豪宅公寓窗前或者凉台上的诗中人“我”迎面扑来的是清晨映衬着大都市里棕褐色大厦的一阵阵“迷雾”(原文是“brown fog”);其次,向下诗中人“我”所看到的却是从都市地面街上人们那一张张“歪曲的脸”(twisted faces)上“撕下来[的]一个空洞的微笑”(aimless smile)。好一个“空洞的微笑”,没有目的,也看不到希望和生命意义!不仅如此,诗人艾略特还让这一空洞的、没有意义和看不到希望的“微笑”“在空中飘荡”。艾略特此处原文中使用的是“hovers in the air”,而英文单词“hover”的意思并非“飘荡”,而是像鸟儿一样“翱翔”。我们知道,在神创世之前,神的灵就已经在黑暗的“渊面”上“运行”(hover):

1In the beginning God created the heavens and the earth. 2Now the earth was formless and empty, darkness

① 赵萝蕤译:《荒原》,黄宗英编:《赵萝蕤汉译〈荒原〉手稿》,高等教育出版社2013年版,第27页。

was over the surface of the deep, and the Spirit of God was hovering over the waters.

1 起初神创造天地。2 地是空虚混沌，渊面黑暗；神的灵运行在水面上。[①]

然而，在现代西方大都市的"窗前晨景"中，诗中人"我"所看到的并不是一片生机盎然的繁荣景象，也感觉不到"神的灵运行在水面上"，而是那"漂浮"在空中的"一个空洞的微笑"，而且这一"空洞的微笑"很快就消失在了诗中人眼前的那一排排房子的屋顶线上。可见，艾略特笔下的这种意象并置叠加的手法似乎拉近了读者与社会的距离，让读者在阅读此诗的时候有一种身临其境的切身体验，因此比较容易体会到诗人对西方现代都市文明虚伪性的讽刺和揭露。袁可嘉先生认为，"这种方法用得恰当时可以增强艺术感染的力量，有助于克服概念化"[②]。实际上，这是现代派诗歌创作的一个重要艺术特征，即所谓"思想知觉化"的创作方法。在《玄学派诗人》("The Metaphysical Poets")一文中，我们能够看到艾略特对这种方法的一些相关描述："一种对于思想通过感官直接的理解"("a direct sensuous apprehension of thought")、"把思想重新创造为感情"("a recreation of thought into feeling")、"把思想转变为感觉"("transmuting ideas into sensations")、"把看法转变成心情"("transforming an observation into a state of mind")，以及"像你闻到玫瑰味那样地感知思想"("feel their thought as

---

① 《圣经·旧约》(中英对照·和合本·新国际版)，(香港)国际圣经协会 1998 年版，第 1 页。

② 袁可嘉：《现代派论·英美诗论》，中国社会科学出版社 1985 年版，第 70 页。

immediately as the odor of a rose")[①]。叶公超先生曾把艾略特对西方现代派诗人这种诗歌创作特征的描述直接翻译成:"诗人的本领就在于点化观念为感觉和改变观察为境界。"[②]

在袁可嘉先生看来,现代派的艺术手法发展迅猛,层出不穷,可谓五花八门,难以尽述。20世纪20年代后期出现象征主义诗歌,三四十年代出现意识流小说,六七十年代又出现荒诞派戏剧。然而,不论表现手法如何变化,现代派艺术家们似乎有一个共同的艺术追求,那就是袁可嘉先生所说的,现代派作家们"主张用'想象逻辑'代替'观念逻辑',强调用象征、联想和暗示来代替正面的叙述、解释或者说明"[③]。而这一现代主义艺术追求似乎从命题立意到表现形式的方方面面始终贯穿于现代派作品之中。诚然,在浪漫主义和现实主义的艺术作品中,我们也能找到作家们运用象征、联想和暗示的佐证,但一般具有较大的局限性,是针对某个明确的对象做局部的、间接的修饰,而现代派作家则是把象征、联想和暗示作为艺术创作的主导手法,作为作品的区别性本质特征,用来直接表达作者的思想感情。

同样是在1979年,在《略论西方现代派文学》一文中,笔者发现,当袁可嘉先生把《窗前晨景》作为例子来阐述西方现代派文学艺术特征的时候,他对艾略特"思想知觉化"的理论有了进一步的思考。那就是他把"思想知觉化"与"客观联系物"这两个抽象的概念捆绑在了一起:"这种'思想知觉化'更理论一点的说法就叫作

① [英]托·斯·艾略特:《艾略特文学论文集·玄学派诗人》,李赋宁译,百花洲文艺出版社1994年版,第20～26页。英文原文参见T. S. Eliot, *Selected Essays by T. S. Eliot*, London: Faber and Faber, 1932, pp. 286-290.

② 叶公超:《再论爱略特的诗》,陈子善编:《叶公超批评文集》,珠海出版社1998年版,第122页。

③ 袁可嘉:《现代派论·英美诗论》,中国社会科学出版社1985年版,第68～69页。

'思想找到了它的客观联系物'（艾略特语），情绪找到了它的'等值物'（庞德语）。"[①]虽然我们没有看到文章中对这一"捆绑"有进一步的阐述，但是我们能够看到国内文学批评家对西方现代派文学核心理论的研究，特别是对艾略特现代派诗学理论核心概念阐释的系统性正在不断深入。艾略特是1919年在《哈姆雷特》（"Hamlet"）一文中提出"客观联系物"这一概念的："用艺术形式表现情感的唯一方法是寻找一个'客观对应物'；换句话说，是用一系列实物、场景，一连串事件来表现某种特定的情感；要做到最终形式是感觉经验的外部事实一旦出现，便能立刻唤起那种情感。"[②]1990年，在《从现代主义到后现代主义——二十世纪英美诗主潮追踪》一文中，袁可嘉先生认为，尽管艾略特的文化政治思想是应当受批判的，但是，作为英美现代派诗歌的主将，艾略特在诗歌创作和诗学理论方面都做出了重大贡献。特别是艾略特早期提出的新古典主义理论观点在许多方面与象征主义理论并不矛盾。象征主义主张作家间接地抒发思想感情，而不是直接地表达作者的心绪，艾略特强调诗人应该"消灭个性"，诗歌创作就是一个"非个性化"过程；象征主义主张诗歌创作运用象征、暗示和联想的手法，艾略特提出在诗歌创作中寻求"客观对应物"，即"用一系列实物、场景，一连串事件来表现某种特定的情感"。艾略特早期创作的《J.阿尔弗莱德·普鲁弗洛克情歌》《一位女士的画像》（"Portrait of a Lady"）等诗篇之所以能够以嘲弄世态而著称，是因为他采用法国象征主义作家拉福格的会话体和讽刺语调与英国玄学派诗歌的机智特技相结合的手法，在挖掘诗中人物心理方面

① 袁可嘉：《半个世纪的脚印——袁可嘉诗文选》，人民文学出版社1994年版，第215页。

② [英]托·斯·艾略特：《艾略特诗学文集·哈姆雷特》，王恩衷译，国际文化出版公司1989年版，第13页。

体现出来开创性特殊效果和艺术深度。[①]

在袁可嘉先生看来,就艾略特的代表作《荒原》的思想内容和艺术手法而言,不论是在反映危机意识的深度和广度上,还是在创作手法的新奇和复杂方面,《荒原》都不愧是现代派诗歌的杰作。袁可嘉先生认为,艾略特在《荒原》的创作中,把第一次世界大战后丧失了宗教信仰的整个西方现代世界,从精神到物质比作一个以西方传统的圣杯传奇为背景的现代荒原,再现了西方现代荒原人的醉生梦死和道德败坏,最后盼望皈依宗教以求重生的主题思想。因为这一主题思想契合了战后西方迷惘一代青年人的悲观情绪,所以在西方诗坛风靡一时,引起了巨大反响,成为英美现代派诗歌的代表之作。此外,值得我们学习的是,袁可嘉先生画龙点睛式地总结艾略特《荒原》诗歌创作艺术方面的两个特点。第一,艾略特把诗歌创作与人类学、宗教神学及神话等学科相互捆绑了起来;不仅在诗歌中旁征博引,而且还给《荒原》作了 52 条注释,开创了后来为学院派诗人所继承的"博学诗"。第二,艾略特广泛寻找和应用"客观对应物",通过用典形成古今对比,相互衬托,借古讽今,让诗歌思想内容及其寓意不断向纵深发展;采用蒙太奇手法让他所摄取的现实生活镜头与历史传说相互映照,在读者想象中形成一种独特的、强烈的艺术反衬效果。[②] 由此可见,袁可嘉先生对"客观联系物"的认识和论述由早期的概念引用已经深入艾略特诗歌的诗歌文本释读,达到了形式与内容相互融合的高度。

1991 年,在《西方现代派文学的成就、局限和问题》一文中,袁可嘉先生又进一步把艾略特的"客观联系物"概念与艾略特在《传

---

① 参见袁可嘉:《半个世纪的脚印——袁可嘉诗文选》,人民文学出版社 1994 年版,第 344 页。

② 参见袁可嘉:《半个世纪的脚印——袁可嘉诗文选》,人民文学出版社 1994 年版,第 344 页。

统与个人才能》一文中所倡导的古典主义“非人格化”诗学原则及“历史感”的核心诗学理论联系了起来。众所周知，1926年，艾略特自称“在宗教上是英国国教式的天主教徒，在政治上是保皇派，在文学上是古典主义者”[①]。袁可嘉先生认为，艾略特的这番自我表白说明了他与传统的欧洲文学存在三个方面的紧密关联：第一，英国天主教历史悠久，艾略特的经院主义思想可追溯到中古时期。第二，保皇主义在英国同样由来已久，已经有300余年的历史，早已自成一个传统。第三，艾略特竭力推崇欧洲文化传统，反对浪漫主义诗歌创作中诗人的自我情感宣泄和个人中心主义，明确提出古典主义“非人格化”诗学理论和诗歌创作原则，认为诗歌创作不是诗人人格和情绪的宣泄，而是人格和情绪的逃避，并且提出了针锋相对的寻找“客观对应物”的诗歌创作艺术方法。[②] 我们知道，艾略特是美国人，1927年加入英国国教会，并且改入英国国籍。王佐良先生认为：“这也是一个迹象，表明20世纪发生于英国文坛的事情不少是由美国人发动的，小说上的亨利·詹姆斯，诗歌方面的庞德、艾略特就是较显著的例子。”[③]在文学上，他一方面称自己的代表性诗作《荒原》不过是他个人对生活发出的一通完全无关紧要的、带有节奏的牢骚[④]；而另外一方面，他在诗学理论上又强调诗人必须有一种“历史意识”，应该“消灭个性”，并且应该寻找“客观联系物”。可见，艾略特的诗歌创作与诗学理论带有明显的“反浪漫主义”特征，但同时与浪漫主义诗歌之间又存在着一种“似同

① 赵萝蕤：《我的读书生涯》，北京大学出版社1996年版，第27页。

② 参见袁可嘉：《半个世纪的脚印——袁可嘉诗文选》，人民文学出版社1994年版，第273页。

③ 王佐良：《英国诗史》，译林出版社2008年版，第448页。

④ 参见黄宗英：《抒情史诗论》，北京大学出版社2003年版，第69页。

而非同的复杂关系”[①]。我们无法把他归入浪漫主义传统,但是也不能把他纳入纯粹的古典主义文学传统,因为他不仅深切地看到了第一次世界大战后西方现代文明的深刻危机,而且创造了一整套全新的诗歌创作与诗学理论体系,为西方现代主义文学传统做出了重大贡献。或许,也正因为他看穿了西方现代文明的深刻危机,艾略特“更加坚决地要维护以罗马天主教为中心的西欧文明传统”[②]。有意思的是,袁可嘉先生对艾略特诗歌与诗学理论的论述充满着辩证唯物主义的观点。袁可嘉先生认为,艾略特著名的文学理论论文《传统与个人才能》一方面强调作家应该有历史感(historical sense),必须承认传统与现在的同时存在和相互作用;而另一方面,他又强调传统始终是一个动态的开放体系,既影响后代作家的艺术创作,同时又接受后代作家的反作用,因此虽然旧的传统影响新的作家,但是新的优秀作品同样可以改变旧的传统。[③]

总之,从艾略特诗歌创作艺术的视角看,艾略特的诗歌始终因其取材于现实生活之创新而闻名,但是他这种取材于现代生活题材的创新是一种基于意大利 13 世纪的古典诗歌、英国 17 世纪的玄学派诗歌和法国 19 世纪的象征主义诗歌之上的诗歌艺术创新。不仅如此,艾略特诗歌艺术创新包含了他采用现代口语会话和独白的创新,然而这种诗歌语言的创新又受法国象征派诗人拉福格的启发。此外,艾略特在《J. 阿尔弗莱德·普鲁弗洛克情歌》《荒原》等代表性诗篇的创作中注重诗中核心人物内心刻画,这也是一种创新,但是这种刻画诗中人物内心世界的手法却是采用 19 世纪英国诗人布朗宁的戏剧独白(dramatic monologue)。最后,艾略

---

① 张剑:《T. S. 艾略特:诗歌与戏剧的解读》,外语教学与研究出版社 2006 年版,第 24 页。

② 王佐良:《英国诗史》,译林出版社 2008 年版,第 448 页。

③ 参见袁可嘉:《半个世纪的脚印——袁可嘉诗文选》,人民文学出版社 1994 年版,第 273 页。

特机智尖刻的讽刺诗笔打破了英国浪漫主义及后来维多利亚时期呆板的诗风，让 20 世纪 20 年代的读者感到耳目一新，但是这种诗歌破格（poetic license）又仍然带有 17 世纪英国玄学派诗歌的明显痕迹。因此，袁可嘉先生认为，艾略特新的诗歌创作艺术实际上是“博采众长，推陈出新的结果”[1]。

（黄宗英：北京联合大学应用文理学院教授）

① 袁可嘉：《半个世纪的脚印——袁可嘉诗文选》，人民文学出版社 1994 年版，第 273 页。

《诗章》与布朗宁的“戏剧独白体”[①]

郭英杰　王 文

一

艾兹拉·庞德(Ezra Pound,1885～1972)是美国意象派诗歌领袖,也是颇有争议的美国现代派诗人、翻译家、批评家。他不仅特立独行,创作了不胜枚举的原创诗;而且喜欢标新立异,创造性地将中国古典诗歌、古罗马诗歌、盎格鲁－撒克逊诗歌等不同民族的世界名诗改造成属于他自己风格的诗。在对各民族诗人“有的放矢”的模仿和“别出心裁”的改造过程中,他对英国维多利亚时期的诗人罗伯特·布朗宁(Robert Browning,1812～1889)投注了大量热情和精力。虽然庞德对维多利亚诗歌颇有微词,但是对布朗宁的诗歌却有着特殊的好感。这是庞德诗歌创作“两面性”的一个方面。尤其是在他的史诗代表作《诗章》(*The Cantos*)创作的前

---

① 本文为陕西省社科基金项目“唐代诗歌与美国意象派诗歌的互文性研究”(项目编号:2014J11)和中央高校基本科研业务费专项资金项目一般项目(项目编号:17SZYB12)阶段性成果。

期，庞德曾经不遗余力地模仿布朗宁的"戏剧独白体"（dramatic monologue），同时进行大胆的创新和试验。

"戏剧独白体"被认为是一种特别的、独具艺术特色的文体形式，本来是剧作家根据剧情需要使用的写作技巧，后来被移植到小说、诗歌等创作领域。[①] 布朗宁在诗歌创作中擅长挖掘"戏剧独白体"的潜在价值。在他看来，诗歌中使用戏剧语言不仅在于表达某个特定的场景和行动，还在于揭示说话人的性格特征。这就与一般意义上的戏剧独白（soliloquy）有本质的不同：诗歌中的戏剧独白不在于说话者直接表达和转述了什么具体的内容，而是在诗学层面上如何将说话者与过去的历史事件进行理性嫁接，一方面不经意地隐匿作者的创作动机，另一方面邀请读者参与意义的建构。说话者（speaker）、听话者（auditor）和意义（meaning）的生成构成"三位一体"的立体关系。[②] 布朗宁这种独特的表达形式，在他书写的《男人和女人》（*Men and Women*，1855）、《戏剧人物》（*Dramatis Personae*，1864）、《指环和书》（*The Ring and the Book*，1868～1869）等作品中，都有淋漓尽致的呈现。评论家伊丽莎白·A. 霍维和格莱尼斯·拜伦把布朗宁的这种"戏剧独白体"界定为"一种人物抒情诗"，"一种借助特定的人物形象进行言语表达的诗"，具有思想呈现和意义阐释的双重价值和功效。[③] 至于如何恰如其分地将戏剧独白融入诗歌创作，发挥其潜在的作用，文体学家 M. H. 阿布拉姆斯在考察和研究布朗宁的诗学特点之后，提

---

① Glennis Byron, *Dramatic Monologue*, New York: Routledge, 2003, pp. 12-20.

② Philip Drew, *The Poetry of Robert Browning: A Critical Introduction*, London: Metheun & Co., 1970, pp. 5-9.

③ Elisabeth A. Howe, *The Dramatic Monologue*, Boston: Twayne Publishers, 1996, pp. 166-167; Glennis Byron, *Dramatic Monologue*, New York: Routledge, 2003, pp. 208-209.

出诗歌中运用戏剧独白的三个要素:

> 第一,至少有一个独立的人物角色,很明显不是诗人自己,发表的言辞构成诗歌整体的一个重要组成部分……第二,该人物角色与一个或多个其他人物角色相互关注和产生作用,但是必须通过听者的参与和理解,阐释他们在说什么和在做什么。第三,影响诗人选择和陈述者抒情表达的主要原则,旨在向读者揭示:该原则在某种程度上会加强文本的信息量、可信度以及陈述者在戏剧独白时呈现出来的气质和个性特点。①

这三个要素的提出使布朗宁的"戏剧独白体"成为有章可循的诗歌叙事手段。对于该艺术手段的潜在价值,既对传统(tradition)"无限痴情",又对现代(modernism)"不懈追求"的庞德不仅欣然认同,而且自觉接受。② 当然,庞德喜欢布朗宁还有一个重要原因,那就是他的独白体诗歌"充满思想,大胆讨论宗教、科学和政治"③。这在内容及风格方面都很合庞德的胃口。所以,在一段历史时期的诗歌写作中,庞德有意识地模仿布朗宁的"戏剧独白体",并在《诗章》里逐步地推陈出新,后来竟然成为《诗章》艺术殿堂当中不容读者小觑的一个风格和特色。

① M. H. Abrams, "Dramatic Monologue", *A Glossary of Literary Terms*, Boston: Thomson Wadsworth, 2005, pp. 70-71.

② Mary Ellis Gibson, *Epic Reinvented*, Ithaca and London: Cornell University Press, 1995, pp. 42-43.

③ De Nagy, N. Christoph. "Pound and Browning", in Eva Hesse, ed., *New Approaches to Ezra Pound*, Berkeley and Los Angeles: University of California Press, 1969, p. 87.

二

对于布朗宁的热爱，庞德并不隐晦；向布朗宁积极学习诗歌写作技巧，他也不掩饰。庞德在《诗章》第 2 章开篇就直言不讳地说：

岂有此理，罗伯特·布朗宁，
有且只有一本《索尔戴罗》。
但是谈到索尔戴罗，那么我的索尔戴罗呢？[①]

上述文字透露了庞德内心的一个愿望，那就是书写一部属于他自己的《索尔戴罗》(*Sordello*)——“但是谈到索尔戴罗，那么我的索尔戴罗呢？”对此，庞德没有直接给出答案，因为他想让读者在《诗章》里寻找。而且，庞德通过《诗章》旨在重塑一部风格迥异的、充满时代精神的《索尔戴罗》，并且力求在意蕴、宏旨及情节安排等方面“超越”布朗宁的《索尔戴罗》，以体现他独具匠心。或许，正是由于庞德对布朗宁以及《索尔戴罗》的喜爱，对于那些不了解布朗宁甚至不欣赏布朗宁的人，庞德表现出无可奈何的情绪，这从《诗章》第 48 章可以看出来：

没有好的沟通。在伦敦，
没有哪次愉悦的聚会让我感受到有好的沟通，
他们把布朗宁视为美国人，

---

① 本文中出现的译文未标注译者的均为作者自译，Ezra Pound，*The Cantos of Ezra Pound*，New York：New Directions Publishing Corporation，1971，p. 6.

说他在言行举止方面不像英国人。①

玛丽·爱丽斯·吉布逊认为:“从庞德发表作品开始,他就积极地想象他的作品可能面对的读者,(包括)他那个时代的以及未来的。”②事实的确如此,庞德以互文性的陈述方式调动读者的原型意识,是希望读者欣赏布朗宁的《索尔戴罗》之时,也在《诗章》中寻找另一个在风格方面与《索尔戴罗》有渊源关系,在内容方面却又与它大相径庭的作品。

不过,庞德在《诗章》写作时,并没有完全生搬硬套布朗宁的“戏剧独白体”形式,而是凭借先锋派诗人特有的实验精神进行创造和革新:

第一,“多声部”独白。

在《诗章》第 2 章,庞德写道:

海豹在悬崖边的水域嬉戏,喷着白色的圈
圆滑的脑袋,里尔之女,
　　　　　　毕加索的眼睛
在黑色的毛皮下面,柔软的海洋之女;
海浪在海滩的凹槽里流动:
“埃莉诺……”
　　　　　　可怜的老荷马瞎了,瞎得跟一只蝙蝠一样,
耳朵,耳朵能够听到海潮的涌动,那是老人低语的声音:
“让她回到船上,

① Ezra Pound, *The Cantos of Ezra Pound*, New York: New Directions Publishing Corporation, 1971, p. 240.

② Mary Ellis Gibson, *Epic Reinvented*, Ithaca and London: Cornell University Press, 1995, pp. 42-43.

回到希腊人中间，以免邪恶降临到我们头上
……”
船只在西奥斯着陆
　　　　　　男人们都想喝泉水
在岩石潭边，一个小男孩拿着未发酵的葡萄汁缓缓走来
　　　　　　“去纳克瑟斯吗？是的，我们会带你去纳克瑟斯，
一起走吧，孩子。”“不是那条路！”
“啊，那条路通往纳克瑟斯。”
　　　　　　我回应说：“它是一条笔直的船。”
……
里埃克斯说话了：“从现在开始，阿寇蒂斯，我的祭坛，
担心没有人祭拜，
　　　　　　担心没有木质的猫，
安心地与我的山猫待在一起，
　　　　　　给我的豹喂葡萄，
熏陆香就是我的香气，
　　　　　　葡萄藤在我的敬意中成长。”①

整个第2章本身就是一个戏剧独白。然而在该独白里，庞德却别出心裁地穿插了多个形象和多重声音：庞德写海豹(seal)在悬崖边嬉戏；由海豹联想到里尔的女儿、毕加索、海洋之女、老荷马；由海浪声联想到埃莉诺(Eleanor)和老人的低语；在老人的低语声中充满古希腊预言家式的呼唤和咒语；船只着陆，男人们饥渴的形象；岩谭边的小男孩、未发酵的葡萄汁、笔直的船；男人、小男

① Ezra Pound, *The Cantos of Ezra Pound*, New York: New Directions Publishing Corporation, 1971, pp. 6-9.

孩和"我"的对话;蓝色大海上里埃克斯(Lyaus)的自言自语;他自言自语的内容涉及祭坛、服役人、木质的猫、山猫、豹、熏陆香和成长的葡萄藤……如果原先我们认为该篇章只是布朗宁戏剧独白风格的翻版,那么现在我们无论如何也不能把二者直接联系在一起。尽管庞德刚开始的确是在模仿布朗宁,但是他的这种"多声部"独白已经充分表明他开始另辟一条新路径。而且,该路径卓尔不群。

我们再来看看《诗章》第74章,庞德书写了一个"话中话式"的独白:

世上多豪杰
　　　　下列都是我志趣相同的人:
写巨人的福特
　　梦想高贵的威廉
　　　　幽默大师詹姆斯唱道:
　　　　　　　"布拉尔尼城堡我亲爱的
　　　　　　　你如今只是一块石头"
谈数学的普拉尔
　　　　或爱玉器的杰普森
写历史小说的莫里斯
　　　　在浴缸中泡过两次的纽博尔特
　　　　　世上多豪杰。
　　　　　今日阴云蔽日
——"坐着别动,"科尔说,
"若你一动身上就叮当作响。"
年老的伯爵夫人还记得彼得堡的一个招待会
科尔认为或许还有一些(好的)交往留在
　　　　　西班牙,他愿常去那里吗?天哪,不!
　　1924年的观点

……

乔治大叔俨然一位发言人 万物皆流

(Pound 432-433)[①]

遭受牢狱之灾的庞德在“死囚室”(death cell)里生不如死。痛苦之余想起以前的朋友,包括作家福特(Ford Madox Ford,1873～1939)、诗人威廉(William Butler Yeats,1865～1939)、小说家詹姆斯(James Joyce,1882～1941)、作家普拉尔(Victor Plarr,1863～1929)、小说家杰普森(Edgar Jepson,1863～1938)、作家莫里斯(Maurice Hewlett,1861～1923)、诗人纽博尔特(Henry Newbolt,1862～1938)等。这些旧友每个人都是独立的“意象”:他们不是静止的,而是动态的;不只代表独特的风格特点,还发出独立自由的声音。这些声音叠加在一起,就是一部“多声部”的唱和:福特写巨人的故事、威廉梦想着高贵、普拉尔谈数学、杰普森迷恋玉器、莫里斯急着写历史小说、纽博尔特在浴缸泡两次澡,尤其是詹姆斯幽默十足地发出弦外之音:“布拉尔尼城堡……你如今只是一块石头。”而这些,也只是庞德戏剧独白时对过去的想象,还有“今日”的独白:“今日阴云蔽日。”“今日”的独白明显有更加新鲜的内容——科尔说:“坐着别动”,“若你一动身上就叮当作响”。这其实是以互文性的手法暗示庞德当时的身份和处境:戴着镣铐,死刑犯一个。不过庞德生性乐观,借伯爵夫人之口怀念彼得堡的招待会,似乎是想念那里的美味佳肴。当科尔即使有“好的交往在西班牙”,也不愿前往时,伯爵夫人发出“天哪,不!”的质疑声。时间定格在1924年,想象与现实合一。庞德此时还借用美国参议院“乔治大叔”,即乔治·廷克海姆(George Tinkham,1870～1956)的口

① [美]艾兹拉·庞德:《庞德诗选·比萨诗章》,黄运特译,漓江出版社1998年版,第18～19页。

吻,以“残篇”的形式说出希腊哲学家赫拉克利特的名言“万物皆流”(PEI IIANTA),意思是任何事物都不可能恒久,所以干脆丢掉幻想,回归真实。这明显是庞德互文式的自我告慰法,也是他“话中话”式的戏剧独白的一次伟大尝试。

艾伦·塔特总结说,庞德诗歌写作的秘诀是“对话”(conversation),所以《诗章》在不停地“说、说、说”。情况确实如此,庞德在《诗章》的每一部分都是对现实生活中非正式对话的模仿(imitation of a causal conversation)。“每一首诗章都有断流的情形,每一个好的对话都有一个几乎让人难以捉摸的高潮:因为没有独立的说话人,每一首诗章都是一个多声部的独白(a many-voiced monologue)。这就是《诗章》的做诗法。”①

第二,蒙太奇式的表达。

有评论家认为,庞德的《诗章》有三个对话主题:“古代社会、文艺复兴时期的意大利以及现代社会”②。然而,庞德是如何将这三个错综复杂的对话主题在戏剧独白的过程中连接在一起,之后形成一个有机整体,进而互文性地再现历史全貌的呢?我们认为,庞德的一个重要秘诀就是在艺术呈现方式上使用了蒙太奇式的表达。

为了说明问题,我们就以庞德《诗章》的三个对话主题“古代社会、文艺复兴时期的意大利以及现代社会”为例,来说明庞德在《诗章》戏剧独白过程中,确实任意自由地运用蒙太奇手法彰显其艺术特色。

关于古代社会蒙太奇艺术手法的运用,我们在《诗章》第52～

---

① Allen Tate, “On Ezra Pound's Cantos”, in E. San Juan, Jr., ed., *Critics on Ezra Pound*, Coral Gables, Florida: University of Miami Press, 1972, pp. 23-24.

② Allen Tate, “On Ezra Pound's Cantos”, in E. San Juan, Jr., ed., *Critics on Ezra Pound*, Coral Gables, Florida: University of Miami Press, 1972, p. 23.

61 章的《中国诗章》里有不少戏剧独白片段，如第 53 章：

夏朝！夏朝灭亡了！
　　因为冒犯神灵
让百姓疾苦
　　不是因你的美德
　　而是凭借成汤的美德
荣耀归属禹，治水的功臣
荣耀归属成汤
荣耀归属殷
追忆先王，创造新工具
　　五百年后文王继位
公元前 1231 年[①]

在该部分描述中，庞德有多幅图片的混搭：第一幅是夏朝灭亡，普通老百姓热情洋溢地欢呼。紧接着剪切到第二幅场景，揭示夏朝帝王没落的内因：“冒犯神灵”，“让百姓疾苦”。第三幅以对话的口吻与“你”探讨美德，实质上考察夏朝灭亡的外因：“不是因你的美德/而是凭借成汤的美德”，言外之意是有美德者得天下，无美德者失天下。第四幅歌颂“荣耀”，这里面又有三个并列场景：大禹治水，泽被百姓的荣耀；成汤灭夏，顺应民心的荣耀；殷商励精图治，奋发图强的荣耀。第五幅回顾历史，“追忆先王”，同时摆出历史发展的动因：“创造新工具”，顺应时代发展潮流。第六幅跨越时空到了五百年后，此时“文王继位”，翻开历史新的一页。第七幅定格历史，锁定旋律，指向让人遐想的“公元前 1231 年”。类似的例

① Ezra Pound, *The Cantos of Ezra Pound*, New York: New Directions Publishing Corporation, 1971, p. 265.

证还有《诗章》第74章:

在光之光中是创造力,
　　　　"是光,"埃里吉那·司各脱斯说。
　　　　如舜在泰山上
在祖宗的庙堂里
　　　　　　如同自神迹初萌
尧的圣灵,舜的
真诚,禹这位治水者的怜悯

监狱四角伏着巨兽般四座守望塔
　　在门口的三位年轻人
他们在我周围挖了一条沟
　　以免潮气咬蚀我的骨头
　　　　以正义赎回锡安山,
以赛亚说。不是放出去收利息,大卫王说。
　　　　　　　　　　　　　　　这个大畜生[1]

关于对文艺复兴时期意大利的蒙太奇艺术手法的运用,我们在《诗章》第8章捕捉到意大利人文主义者马拉特斯塔·西吉斯蒙德(Malatesta Sigismund)的几个特写镜头:

因为前面提到的著名的
米兰公爵
心悦诚服,同时希望前面提到的西吉斯蒙德大人

① [美]艾兹拉·庞德:《庞德诗选·比萨诗章》,黄运特译,漓江出版社1998年版,第11~12页。

可以进入佛罗伦萨最重要的社区
服务于民
……
为了进入社区的属地
　　　　　　　　或者托斯卡纳区的某个地方
正如为了使中央刑事法庭的十个成员喜悦那样
在那里以他自己的风格与他们相处，服务
于民
……
西吉斯蒙德，这个同盟者，冲破敌军防线
签署了条约，通过一扇大门
他们关上它，再打开另一扇大门，他于是说：
“现在你们抓我，
　　　　　就像在鸡笼里抓母鸡。”
……
那时候他才十二岁，西吉斯蒙德，
三年来无法交纳任何费用，
他的长兄无能为力；
就在那一年，他们在街道里打斗，
就在那一年，他离开家门去了切塞纳
　　　　　带回来征税款，
就在那一年，他趁着夜色横渡福利亚，然后……①

这四个特写镜头意味着四个醒目的蒙太奇式的片段。第一个片段聚焦“前面提到的著名的米兰公爵”，由他引出“前面提到的西

① Ezra Pound, *The Cantos of Ezra Pound*, New York: New Directions Publishing Corporation, 1971, pp. 29-33.

吉斯蒙德大人";两个"aforesaid"带给读者无限好奇和想象;要"西吉斯蒙德大人"进入佛罗伦萨社区干什么呢?答案是"服务于民"(in the service of the commune),"形成联盟抵御两个邻国";可见,这个带有无限悬念的"西吉斯蒙德大人"肩负着历史的重任,为他在后面情节的"圣贤"风度做好铺垫。第二个片段聚焦西吉斯蒙德进入社区属地的情形,由于不熟悉环境,初来乍到的他还以为到了"托斯卡纳区的某个地方";不过,他已作好准备,要与"中央刑事法庭的十个成员"一道,服务于社区人民。第三个片段聚焦西吉斯蒙德的勇敢无畏,在柏拉图(Plato)无法使锡拉库扎的暴君狄俄尼索斯(Dionysius)有所改变的情况下,不辱使命,"在安科纳的大门内""冲破敌军防线""签署了条约",还幽默地对敌军长官说:"现在你们抓我,/就像在鸡笼里抓母鸡。"第四个片段聚焦英雄人物西吉斯蒙德十二岁时的趣闻轶事,这明显是戏剧独白中的一个倒叙手法,企图还原西吉斯蒙德的早年生活。不过,庞德首先设置"风停息了片刻/夜幕慢慢降临到/一边"的自然背景,让人感觉身临其境;然后谈到他的经济状况及兄长,并且用三个并列的"And that year",说出他当年的"事迹":"在街道里打斗""离开家门去了切塞纳""趁着夜色横渡福利亚",这显然是一种"画中画式"的蒙太奇表达;最后的"and……"是庞德故意而为之的一种蒙太奇写作策略,省略的内容就是艺术手法上的"留白",希望读者在上述已知信息基础上,进行穿越时空的联想或者断想。

关于对现代社会的蒙太奇艺术手法在《诗章》里的运用,庞德更是标新立异,并以别开生面的方式铺陈和展开。实质上,庞德前面对古代社会以及文艺复兴时期意大利社会的蒙太奇式表达最终还是为了凸显现代社会的实际,通过比较说明现代社会的种种弊端,最后给人以警示:历史是一面镜子,现代人应该以史为鉴。在庞德心目中,现代社会真是丑劣不堪,比如《诗章》第 14 章中有这样的蒙太奇镜头:

语言的背叛者
以及印刷部门的流氓帮
还有那些为了被雇佣而说谎的人；
堕落者，滥用语言的人，
堕落者，唯利是图的人，
在感官的快乐面前折腰；

嚎叫，从一个印刷厂里的鸡舍开始，
印刷的咔嗒声，
干燥的尘土和杂乱的纸张吹过来，
恶臭、汗水、腐烂橘子的怪味，
粪便、全世界最糟糕的池塘，
神秘物质、硫黄酸，
优柔寡断的人，出离愤怒的人；
把珍珠宝贝扔进淤泥，
然后号叫着发现它们未被污染，
虐待狂母亲用衰老的躯体驱赶他们的女儿们上床睡觉……①

庞德认为，现代社会不可理喻是因为它充满“堕落”的“场景”：“充满语言的背叛者”“印刷部门的流氓帮”以及“那些为了被雇佣而说谎的人”。这些人都是使社会风气变坏的罪魁祸首，庞德在《诗章》中把他们叫作“perverts”。这其中有两个特写镜头：“滥用语言的人”和“唯利是图的人”，他们“在感官的快乐面前折腰”。紧

① Ezra Pound, *The Cantos of Ezra Pound*, New York: New Directions Publishing Corporation, 1971, pp. 61-62.

接着,随着一声"嚎叫"和"印刷的咔嗒声",另一个蒙太奇场景"从一个印刷厂里的鸡舍开始"。该场景包括多个并置的镜头,以及不同镜像的拼贴,包括视觉拼贴:"干燥的尘土和杂乱的纸张吹过来""粪便、全世界最糟糕的池塘""神秘物质、硫黄酸"和味觉拼贴:"恶臭、汗水、腐烂橘子的怪味"。现代人出现在这种肮脏混乱的场景,庞德给他们的特写镜头是"优柔寡断""出离愤怒";还有那些精神分裂症患者,他们"把珍珠宝贝扔进淤泥,然后号叫着发现它们未被污染",以及"虐待狂母亲",她"用衰老的躯体驱赶他们的女儿们上床睡觉……"这一切的一切如此荒诞不经,让人难免悲观厌世、丧失希望!

第三,碎片化艺术。

庞德的《诗章》是碎片化艺术的结晶,因为它充满各种碎片化的叙事。"几乎每一首诗章都以一些英雄人物的事迹、神话故事、典故的使用或者借助一种宏大叙事风格(grand style)进行抒情性的、生动的描述。"①在庞德《诗章》戏剧独白的文本世界,存在着文本内容的碎片化、逻辑思维的碎片化和表达形式的碎片化。

首先,就《诗章》文本内容的碎片化而言,在《诗章》第 77 章有这样的表述:

(舞蹈是一种媒介)
　　　　"归里返乡"
　　你是一个支撑肉体的小灵魂

点一小堆火焰给
跳庄严的芭蕾时保留一点光亮,这舞蹈从未在剧院上演

① Allen Tate, "On Ezra Pound's Cantos", in E. San Juan, Jr., ed., *Critics on Ezra Pound*, Coral Gables, Florida: University of Miami Press, 1972, p. 24.

完好无缺得和查士丁尼一世设计时的一样
　　　　在豪华车把他载过悬崖之前
　　　　　　帕德雷·荷塞已心中有数
　　　　　　　　　舟载其一而去
明了弥撒的含义，
　　　　学会其程序
圣体日的舞蹈　在奥赛尔
　　　　用的器具
陀螺，鞭子，及其他。[①]

细读上述文字，我们不难发现：庞德阐发的内容并不是他天马行空的想象，而是有互文性的出处和所指。比如，这几行中出现的有关舞蹈的描述，“源自米德(George Robert Stow Mead，1863～1933)登载在他主编的杂志《探索》上的一篇文章《中世纪教堂里仪式性的游戏与舞蹈》(1912)”[②]。庞德回忆得不准确，造成诗歌内容的残缺和“碎片化”。对照《诗章》原文，我们进一步认识到，上述引文中括号里的第一句应该是庞德对舞蹈存在价值的个人判断，即认为舞蹈是人们抒发情感、表达自我的“一种媒介”；“To his native mountain”(归里返乡)直接摘自米德的原文；而第三句“你是一个支撑肉体的小灵魂”原文是希腊语，庞德借此戏仿某个希腊评论家的措辞；“点一小堆火焰给/跳庄严的芭蕾时保留一点光亮，这舞蹈从未在剧院上演”应该是米德提及的中世纪教堂里仪式性舞蹈的客观描述，虽然该描述“完好无缺得和查士丁尼一世设计时

① [美]艾兹拉·庞德：《庞德诗选·比萨诗章》，黄运特译，漓江出版社1998年版，第81页。

② [美]艾兹拉·庞德：《庞德诗选·比萨诗章》，黄运特译，漓江出版社1998年版，第81页。

的一样”,不过仍然属于庞德记忆的残片,内容方面不成体系。基于前一句,庞德还互文式地联想到查士丁尼一世戏剧性的一幕,即“豪华车把他载过悬崖”;帕德雷·荷塞是帮助过庞德获得卡瓦尔凯蒂手稿影印本的西班牙牧师,像一位预言家一样对上述内容“已心中有数”;“舟载其一而去”原文是古英语“summe fugol othbaer”,出自英国早期的民间故事《漫游者》(*The Wanderer*)①。这又是庞德《诗章》互文性表达的一个例证。下文出现的“弥撒”“程序”“圣体日的舞蹈”“在奥赛尔/用的器具/陀螺,鞭子,及其他”也是米德《中世纪教堂里仪式性的游戏与舞蹈》内容的碎片,具有典型的中世纪宗教舞蹈的风格和特征。

其次,关于《诗章》逻辑思维的碎片化,在《诗章》第74章有这样的表述:

> 一天,云雾缭绕着泰山
> 　　　或在落日的辉煌里
> 　　　　　　同志无目的地祝福
> 夜间在雨沟里哭泣
> 　　　　　　　　是光
> 这场戏完全是主观
> 石头知道雕刻者给予它的形式
> 石头知道形式
> ……
> 无人
> 日落西山的人
> 钻石将不会在雪崩中消失

---

① [美]艾兹拉·庞德:《庞德诗选·比萨诗章》,黄运特译,漓江出版社1998年版,第81页。

即便它脱离其氛围
在毁于他人之手前他会先毁自己。[①]

在该选段中，庞德以“一天”的所思所想为基调，以戏剧独白体的方式呈现自己逻辑思维的碎片化。初读起来让人非常费解，不知所云。但是，细细品读，我们会惊喜地发现，庞德逻辑思维的碎片化有其特殊的功效，那就是充分彰显了庞德内在深沉的情感和复杂多变的情绪——庞德先是看到牢笼之外“云雾缭绕着泰山”，对于泰山是否存在“落日的辉煌里”不是很确定，因为他身处牢笼，所以用“或在”表示猜想；然后睹物思人，想到昔日好友（即庞德的俄语表达“tovarish”）以及他们“无目的地祝福”，禁不住黯然伤神；到了夜间，倾盆大雨，情绪反差更大：好友们曾经祝福他生活幸福，谁会料到他成了旷野里隔离人世的孤魂野鬼，被淋成落汤鸡，而且生不如死呢。想到这里，他伤心地“在雨沟里哭泣”。他渴望“lumina”，那会给他带来福音的“光”，然而他很快就发现“这场戏完全是主观”，不只暗示他的所作所为违背了所谓“世道”，而且暗示他一厢情愿地追逐虚无缥缈的理想世界和他那个“画好的天堂”。或许他应该像石头那样，因为“石头知道雕刻者给予它的形式/石头知道形式”，不该过于锋芒毕露、棱角分明。但是，谁会预见到现实是这样的呢？庞德用希腊哲人的语气说“无人”，一方面隐喻自己的身份是“奥德修斯”[②]，另一方面，实指当时“无人”知道他的苦闷和忧伤。他就像“日落西山的人”，但是又不甘心这样潦倒放弃。他于是希望像钻石那样，能够经受各种痛苦的考验，“不

① [美]艾兹拉·庞德：《庞德诗选·比萨诗章》，黄运特译，漓江出版社 1998 年版，第 14～15 页。

② 奥德修斯（Odysseus）说自己名叫“无人”，以捉弄一个魔鬼，参见荷马的《奥德赛》。

会在雪崩中消失/即便它脱离其氛围”。他也作好最坏的准备和最决绝的打算,那就是“在毁于他人之手前他会先毁自己”。由此看来,庞德在《诗章》中呈现出的思维逻辑的碎片化,其实是他内心世界某个特殊时刻情感表达的碎片化,可能是稍纵即逝的痛苦,可能是富于哲理的反思,可能又是二者的珠联璧合。但是不管怎样,庞德总有出人意料的戏剧独白。

再次,关于《诗章》表达形式的碎片化,在《诗章》第 82 章有这样的表述:

人,大地:一块符节的两半
而我将从中走出,不认识一个人
也没有一个人认识我
大地的婚姻　　她说,我的丈夫
大地生的,神秘
大地的体液淹没我
躺在大地的体液里;
躺在
劲风之中
沉醉于大地之伊科
大地的体液,强如退潮的
底流①

与文本内容的碎片化和逻辑思维的碎片化比较而言,庞德《诗章》表达形式的碎片化是非常显而易见的:行与行不对等,随意断裂和换行,言语输出支离破碎,等等。在上面 12 行的选段当中,如

① [美]艾兹拉·庞德:《庞德诗选·比萨诗章》,黄运特译,漓江出版社 1998 年版,第 193 页。

果说前3行是常规语序的表达，那么紧接着出现的2行则是“碎片”；第6、7、8行与第9、10、11行粗略一看有风格方面的对等性，但是它们明显属于意识流式的“碎片”；更何况，第12行的“底流”一词使该选段形式的碎片化更显突兀，同时作用于意义的碎片化。除了上面看到的例子，我们在《诗章》第13章、第25章、第39章、第53章、第68章、第74章、第86章、第91章、第102章、第105章、第108章、第110章、第113章、第117章等，都可以找到类似具有视觉冲击力的例证。比如，《诗章》第113章中的一个“碎片”：

肉体在灵魂之中
　　　　上升和折射的光明
　　　　　　　　　　黑暗被击碎，
　　　　　　　　　　　　　　碎片。
叶芝把象征建构在有圆柱的门廊之上
　　　　　　　　　　　　　　（巴黎）。
公牛凭借他体内的力量——
　　　　不是成为它的主人，
　　　　　　　　　　而是被奴役。
知道利息来自高利贷
（萨克·凯罗利，合适的价格）
　　　　　　在该范围内需要正义。[①]

在这里需要指出的是，庞德《诗章》表达形式的碎片化毕竟只是一个表象，其真实作用说到底是为思想意识和文本内容服务的。而且，庞德表达形式的碎片化有三个重要的功能：一是对传统诗行

① Ezra Pound, *The Cantos of Ezra Pound*, New York: New Directions Publishing Corporation, 1971, pp. 788-789.

和韵律进行颠覆,表达现代诗的品格;二是体现庞德诗歌语言及其表达的个性化,展现“我之为我”(for my own sake)的逻辑;三是呈现思维断裂的过程,并以意识流的方式进行传输和建构。对此,评论家大卫·帕金斯说得非常直截了当:“碎片化……从一开始就是《诗章》的基本特色”,也是“现代派诗歌的基本特色”[①]。

(郭英杰:陕西师范大学外国语学院副教授;王文:陕西师范大学外国语学院教授、博士生导师)

① David Perkins, “Modernism and after”, *A History of Modern Poetry*, Vol. 2, Massachusetts: Harvard University Press, 1976, pp. 227-229.

“当前最优秀的翻译作品”

——王誉公先生论赵萝蕤先生汉译艾略特《荒原》[①]

张军丽

1995 年 10 月 5～7 日，辽宁师范大学在美丽的海滨城市大连承办了 1995 年全国美国文学研究会年会，即全国 T. S. 艾略特研讨会。这一年不仅恰逢全国美国文学研究会成立 15 周年，而且正逢艾略特逝世 30 周年。北京大学赵萝蕤先生引用了叶公超先生为她 1937 年初版《荒原》中译本所写的序言中的一句话作为献给本次研讨会的题辞：“他（艾略特）的影响之大令人感觉，也许将来他的诗本身的价值还不及他的影响的价值呢。”[②]北京大学李赋宁教授给本次研讨会的题辞中写道：艾略特“重视诗歌的机智、精炼和形式的完美”[③]。时任全国美国文学研究会会长、山东大学吴富恒教授和南京大学刘海平教授给大会发了贺函。[④] 时任上海翻译

---

① 本文为国家社科基金项目“比较视野下的赵萝蕤汉译《荒原》研究”（项目批号：15BWW013）结项成果之一。

② 赵萝蕤：《全国 T. S. 艾略特研讨会题辞》，《外国文学研究》1996 年第 2 期。

③ 李赋宁：《全国 T. S. 艾略特研讨会题辞》，《外国文学研究》1996 年第 2 期。

④ 参见吴富恒、陆凡：《贺函》，《外国文学研究》1996 年第 2 期。

出版社总编汤永宽教授在开幕式讲话中说:《荒原》“史诗式的内涵与意蕴,它的形式结构的独创性,得到了文坛的确认”①。山东大学王誉公教授在大会闭幕式上作总结发言,肯定了“我国当前艾略特研究的最新成果”②。会议期间,成立了中国艾略特—庞德研究会(T. S. Eliot-Pound Society in China);辽宁师范大学吕文斌教授担任会长,担任副会长的有:山东大学王誉公教授、杭州大学朱炯强教授、中国社科院傅浩教授、南京大学张子清教授和中国社科院陆建德教授。《外国文学研究》1996 年第 2 期专门开辟了“T. S. 艾略特”专栏,刊登了 15 篇会议论文和一份由蒋洪新、孙永彬提供的“T. S. 艾略特作品译本、艾略特评价研究著作及论文目录”。在这些会议论文中,涉及艾略特诗歌艺术的论文有 3 篇:汤永宽的《艾略特诗歌艺术的独创性》、吕文斌的《T. S. 艾略特与意象派》和徐文博的《关于艾略特诗歌的用典》;涉及长诗《荒原》的论文有 6 篇:王誉公、张华英的《〈荒原〉的理解与翻译》、胡铁生的《论〈荒原〉的美学思想》、关福堃的《现代主义二重奏——〈荒原〉与〈尤利西斯〉》、傅浩的《〈荒原〉六种中译本比较》、潘玉立的《〈荒原〉中的现实主义倾向》和李颖的《〈荒原〉的意境》;涉及长诗《四个四重奏》的论文有 3 篇:蒋洪新的《印度思想与〈四个四重奏〉探幽》、张剑的《更深的沟通——〈东科克〉对现世生活的超越》、吕崇德的《对人生与永恒的沉思——〈小吉丁〉详析》;此外,还包括 3 篇讨论艾略特抒情诗和诗剧的论文:陈世丹的《〈枯叟〉的主题与结构试析》、王文的《生命哲学与〈大风夜狂想曲〉中的主题意象》和张强的《论〈大教堂里的谋杀案〉的非悲剧性因素》。在国内高级别外国文学类期刊上如此集中地针对一个作家发表 15 篇学术论文,这种情况实属罕见。董洪川在综述新时期 30 年国内艾略特研究的时候指出:“几

---

① 汤永宽:《开幕式讲话》,《外国文学研究》1996 年第 2 期。

② 王誉公:《大会总结发言》,《外国文学研究》1996 年第 2 期。

乎没有其他外国诗人享受过如此规模的待遇。"[①]

艾略特认为,我们的文化体系是多样和复杂的,而且描写这种多样和复杂的文化体系的诗歌艺术形式也应该是多样和复杂的,因此"诗人们的作品肯定是费解的"[②]。赵萝蕤先生认为,《荒原》晦涩难懂的主要原因是作者"引经据典太多",而且这些"典故盘根错节"、交叉渗透。[③] 由此可见,译者如何在译文中全面、正确、充分地反映原文诗歌并非易事。王誉公先生在对比翻译与创作本身时曾评价说,相比较而言,翻译比创作更难,因为创作是作者用母语写作,"而翻译是将一个思想和文学样式从一种文字转换为另一种文字的创造性活动",译者需要克服的"不仅有两种语言的困难,还有两种不同的社会文化所带来的种种困难"[④]。王誉公、张华英在其论文《〈荒原〉的理解与翻译》中指出:"赵萝蕤先生在《外国现代派作品选》中发表的《荒原》是我国当前最优秀的翻译作品。"[⑤]在该篇文章中,王誉公先生认为,"直译法"是赵先生"成功的关键",并且认为赵先生在"思想内容,诗歌形式和语言风格"方面,用现代汉语将原文表达得"清清楚楚,惟妙惟肖"。

现代主义诗歌因其变化多端的题材和语言,新颖奇特的象征和意象及含沙射影的语义表达等特点决定了"直译法"在诗歌翻译中的"主要地位"[⑥]。在谈到《荒原》这首诗的翻译时,赵萝蕤先生曾说:"直译法是能够比较忠实反映原作……使读者能尝到较多的

---

① 董洪川:《艾略特诗歌研究》,章燕、赵桂莲主编:《新中国60年外国文学研究》第1卷(上),北京大学出版社2015年版,第189页。

② [英]托·斯·艾略特:《艾略特文学论文集·玄学派诗人》,李赋宁译,百花洲文艺出版社1994年版,第24页。

③ 参见黄宗英编:《赵萝蕤汉译〈荒原〉手稿》,高等教育出版社2013年版,第3页。

④ 王誉公、张华英:《〈荒原〉的理解与翻译》,《外国文学研究》1996年第2期。

⑤ 王誉公、张华英:《〈荒原〉的理解与翻译》,《外国文学研究》1996年第2期。

⑥ 王誉公、张华英:《〈荒原〉的理解与翻译》,《外国文学研究》1996年第2期。

原作风格。”[①]因此,“这首诗很适合于用直译法来翻译”[②]。在评论赵萝蕤先生的“直译法”译文在句式结构方面的特征时,王誉公先生认为,赵萝蕤先生所采用的“变通”手法,即在基本保留原文句式结构的前提下,仅仅变动句中词语的位置,“是‘直译法’的灵魂,是译者的真功夫”[③]。王誉公先生以《荒原》正文前四句和“风信子女郎”一节为例进行说明。

四月是最残忍的一个月,荒地上
长着丁香,把回忆和欲望
掺和在一起,又让春雨
催促那些迟钝的根芽。[④]

王誉公先生评论到,在这四行诗句中,除第一句的英文句式符合中文表达习惯,因而按照语序逐字直译外,其他三句分别按照中文的表达习惯,将各分句中的修饰语作了必要的调整,捋清了分句的逻辑结构关系,达到了表意清晰的目的。比如,将状语“荒地上”(out of the dead land)提到该分句的句首,通过“把”字句和“让”字句分别把宾语“回忆和欲望”(memory and desire)和状语“春雨”(with spring rain)前置。

在笔者看来,“把”字句和“让”字句的运用及“长着”一词所体现的进行时态,不仅凸显了现在分词的主动意义,而且将原文拟人化修辞手法体现得淋漓尽致。黄宗英教授也高度评价了赵萝蕤先生的这几行译文,认为赵先生的译文不仅忠实于原作的内容和风

① 赵萝蕤:《我的读书生涯》,北京大学出版社 1996 年版,第 613 页。
② 赵萝蕤:《我的读书生涯》,北京大学出版社 1996 年版,第 613 页。
③ 王誉公、张华英:《〈荒原〉的理解与翻译》,《外国文学研究》1996 年第 2 期。
④ [英]托·斯·艾略特:《荒原》,赵萝蕤译,袁可嘉、董衡巽、郑克鲁选编:《外国现代派作品选》第 1 册(上),上海文艺出版社 1980 年版,第 89 页。

格,而且符合汉语的表达习惯,做到了“同义词(组)遣词准确”①。黄教授还注意到,诗歌原文前三行通过三个现在分词(breeding, mixing, stirring)的弱韵(feminine ending)断句,构建了“断续徐疾”的语调和节奏及句法结构的对仗,以凸显“孤独无序、焦躁不安的现代荒原人生命光景”②。译文中赵萝蕤先生通过使用近似分词——“长着”“把……(掺和)”和“让……(催促)”——并置行首的方法也成功实现了断句和排比效果,“做到了前四行的重音节数与原诗基本吻合,锁定了原诗的情致和节奏”③,取得了“形神并蓄的艺术效果”④。

王先生认为,四月“是苦难和复活的时间,是新生命开始萌动的时间”,四月之所以“残忍”,是因为“四月为了创造新生命,不得不破坏冬天(死亡)那死沉沉的平静”⑤。赵萝蕤先生直译译文“四月是最残忍的一个月”,恰到好处地体现了整章诗歌的主题“生命来自死亡和腐朽”⑥。

王誉公先生在评论“风信子女郎”(35～41 行)一节的译文时说,除第一行将时间状语“一年前”(a year ago)和“先”(first)分别提到主语“你”之前和之后外,其他“大多数诗行是逐字逐句翻译过来的”⑦。直译译文“我说不出/话,眼睛看不见,我既不是/活的,

---

① 黄宗英:《“晦涩正是他的精神”:赵萝蕤汉译〈荒原〉直译法互文性艺术管窥》,《北京联合大学学报》(人文社科版)2019 年第 3 期。

② 黄宗英:《“晦涩正是他的精神”:赵萝蕤汉译〈荒原〉直译法互文性艺术管窥》,《北京联合大学学报》(人文社科版)2019 年第 3 期。

③ 黄宗英、邓中杰、姜君:《“灵芝”与“奇葩”:赵萝蕤〈荒原〉译本艺术管窥》,《北京联合大学学报》(人文社科版)2014 年第 3 期。

④ 黄宗英:《“晦涩正是他的精神”:赵萝蕤汉译〈荒原〉直译法互文性艺术管窥》,《北京联合大学学报》(人文社科版)2019 年第 3 期。

⑤ 王誉公、张华英:《〈荒原〉的理解与翻译》,《外国文学研究》1996 年第 2 期。

⑥ 王誉公、张华英:《〈荒原〉的理解与翻译》,《外国文学研究》1996 年第 2 期。

⑦ 王誉公、张华英:《〈荒原〉的理解与翻译》,《外国文学研究》1996 年第 2 期。

也未曾死,我什么都不知道”[①],生动地再现了一位“呆呆”的男青年和一位“呆若木鸡”的少女四目相对的尴尬画面:“他们都停留在宇宙的静止点上,无法沟通彼此的思想感情。”[②]在“一年前你先给我的是风信子”一行的译文中,王誉公先生认为“‘是’字可有可无。加上它,汉语的意思显得通顺明白”[③],但是如果译文中没有“是”字,那么中文译文的句式结构与英文原文上更加吻合。笔者认为,增译“是”字似乎可以反映赵萝蕤先生在选择遵循原文句式结构“直译”的同时,也注重“变通”,强化上下文的逻辑联系:(收到的花是)风信子,(被叫作)风信子的女郎,(采花的地点是)风信子的园。本行的译者注指出,“风信子”象征春天[④],在这样一个美好的季节,男青年手捧代表暗恋之情的“风信子”来表白,盼望得到热情的回应,但结果是男女双方都瞠目结舌,一言不发,他们的爱情也就无疾而终了。“是”字的存在恰恰暗示了一丝讽刺意味,荒原上的人们相互之间缺乏理解、无法沟通、孤独而绝望。

除“风信子女郎”一节展现失败的爱情外,无爱或偷情的画面贯穿诗歌第二章和第三章始终。第二章“对弈”(77～172 行)为读者展示了两幅“荒原”上女人的情感世界:第一幅(77～138 行)里呈现的是一位上流贵妇,生活起居,富丽堂皇,但是神经紧张,不懂爱情,无法交流。王誉公先生在评论这部分时说,那些坐在“发亮的宝座”上的现代妇女“死气沉沉”,古时候“翡绿眉拉”反抗强暴的故事恰恰“反衬出现代女性思想感情的浅薄和贫乏”[⑤]。

---

① [英]托·斯·艾略特:《荒原》,赵萝蕤译,《外国现代派作品选》第 1 册(上),袁可嘉、董衡巽、郑克鲁选编,上海文艺出版社 1980 年版,第 91 页。

② 王誉公、张华英:《〈荒原〉的理解与翻译》,《外国文学研究》1996 年第 2 期。

③ 王誉公、张华英:《〈荒原〉的理解与翻译》,《外国文学研究》1996 年第 2 期。

④ [英]托·斯·艾略特:《荒原》,赵萝蕤译,袁可嘉、董衡巽、郑克鲁选编:《外国现代派作品选》第 1 册(上),上海文艺出版社 1980 年版,第 91 页。

⑤ 王誉公、张华英:《〈荒原〉的理解与翻译》,《外国文学研究》1996 年第 2 期。

王誉公先生以第105～110诗行的译文为例，表明在保住"英文诗歌的原意"方面，直译法"一字一句地紧扣原文"功不可没。[①]

……凝视的人像
探出身来，斜倚着，使紧闭的房间一片静寂。
楼梯上有人在拖着脚步走。
在火光下，刷子下，她的头发
散成了火星似的小点子
亮成诗句，然后又转而为野蛮的沉寂。[②]

王先生发现除了"楼梯上有人在拖着脚步走"一行中增译了"有人"一词外，第105～110诗行基本上是"完全直译出来的"，甚至是"死译"出来的，从而完整、全面地呈现了原文的思想内容和讽刺手法："那妇人在听到楼梯上的脚步声以后的行为（梳头）和心态（欲火炽烈）与室内沉静气氛形成鲜明的对照。"[③]王誉公先生还注意到，第109～110诗行中三个并列动词——spread(out)，glowed(into)和(would) be——的译文"散(成了)""亮(成)"和"转(而)为"，"恰如其分，既忠实于原词词义，又符合其语言环境"[④]。笔者认为，赵萝蕤先生采用直译法，通过寥寥数行栩栩如生地临摹了房间黑暗中焦急等待的"凝视的人像"(staring form)：听到楼梯间的声音后，她探身侧耳倾听，她的全部注意力都聚焦于外面，因而听不到房间里的任何声响，所以"紧闭的房间一片静寂"。当她确定楼梯上确有脚步声后，她心潮澎湃，连梳数次头发。

---

① 王誉公、张华英：《〈荒原〉的理解与翻译》，《外国文学研究》1996年第2期。

② ［英］托·斯·艾略特：《荒原》，赵萝蕤译，袁可嘉、董衡巽、郑克鲁选编：《外国现代派作品选》第1册(上)，上海文艺出版社1980年版，第98页。

③ 王誉公、张华英：《〈荒原〉的理解与翻译》，《外国文学研究》1996年第2期。

④ 王誉公、张华英：《〈荒原〉的理解与翻译》，《外国文学研究》1996年第2期。

赵萝蕤先生曾说,“我用直译法是根据内容和形式统一这个原则”[1],在翻译实践中,赵先生也忠实地实践着她对“直译法”的理解和感悟。笔者发现,在汉译《荒原》手稿中,赵萝蕤先生最初是把“使紧闭的房间一片静寂”(hushing the room enclosed)翻译成“紧闭的屋子更为静穆”[2]。对比定稿,手稿译文似乎没有把现在分词“hushing”的主动含义全面地表达出来,因而没有传神地勾勒出“凝视的人像”的侧耳倾听、翘首跂踵的行为和心境。此外,手稿译文中的“屋子”也没有定稿译文中的“房间”更吻合原文“room”的语义,手稿译文中的比较级“更为”是对原文的增译,但在达意方面似乎不如“一片”对原文“enclosed”的强化效果好。手稿译文中的“静穆”多形容“安静庄严”[3],与此处描写“欲火炽烈”之屋内女人的统一度不高,而定稿中的“静寂”一词更吻合原文“安静”的语义内容,更逼真地反衬出女人“倾耳细听”的专注度。

无爱或怯爱的画面在“对弈”一章的第二个故事(139～172行)中继续。王誉公先生发现赵萝蕤先生在翻译该部分时刻意模仿,使用“不乏粗俗字眼”的“现代汉语的日常用语”来传递原文对话中所使用的“粗俗的伦敦方言”:“打扮打扮”“镶牙”“看不得”“痛快痛快”“有的是别人”“瞪了一眼”“挑挑拣拣”“跑掉了”“别怪我没说”“真不害臊”“这么老相”[4]“脸拉得长长的”“打胎”“送了她的

---

① 赵萝蕤:《我是怎么翻译文学作品的》,《我的读书生涯》,北京大学出版社1996年版,第607页。

② 赵萝蕤译:《荒原》,黄宗英编:《赵萝蕤汉译〈荒原〉手稿》,高等教育出版社2013年版,第51页。

③ 中国社会科学院语言研究所词典编辑室编:《现代汉语词典》,商务印书馆2012年版,第692页。

④ 赵萝蕤先生将“这么老相”改译成“这么古董”,参见《外国文艺》(双月刊)1980年第3期。

命”“傻瓜”“得了”“缠着你”“干吗结婚”[①]，等等，从而表明赵萝蕤先生采用的“直译”手法不仅保留了原作的“基本语言特征”，也忠实于“当时人物的心态及其社会背景”[②]，更为读者生动地展示了一幅社会底层畏惧爱情、苦苦挣扎的画面。

无爱或偷情的主题在诗歌第三章中得到进一步发展。王誉公先生认为“火诫”(173～311 行)一章中的“火”有两层含义：第一层：“燃烧，表示色欲的破坏作用”；第二层：“精炼，表示净化的能量。”[③]王誉公先生引用诗歌第三章中对伦敦打字员与长有疙瘩的青年人之间的偷情行为的译文(249～256 行)，证明译文“准确表达了原诗的思想内容”[④]。

时机现在倒是合适，他猜对了，
饭已经吃完，她厌倦又疲乏，
试着抚摸抚摸她
虽说不受欢迎，也没受到责骂。
……
最后又送上形同施舍似的一吻，
他摸着去路，发现楼梯上没有灯……

她回头在镜子里照了一下，
没大意识到她那已经走了的情人；
她的头脑让一个半成形的思想经过：
“总算完了事：完了就好。”

---

① [英]托·斯·艾略特：《荒原》，赵萝蕤译，袁可嘉、董衡巽、郑克鲁选编：《外国现代派作品选》第 1 册(上)，上海文艺出版社 1980 年版，第 100～101 页。

② 王誉公、张华英：《〈荒原〉的理解与翻译》，《外国文学研究》1996 年第 2 期。

③ 王誉公、张华英：《〈荒原〉的理解与翻译》，《外国文学研究》1996 年第 2 期。

④ 王誉公、张华英：《〈荒原〉的理解与翻译》，《外国文学研究》1996 年第 2 期。

美丽的女人堕落的时候,又
在她的房里来回走,独自
她机械地用手抚平了头发,又随手
在留声机上放上一张片子。①

长有疙瘩的青年人"摸着去路"离开后,打字员竟然"没大意识到"她的情人已经离开,她甚至头脑中还闪过"完了就好"的念头,可以看出打字员是受害者,她丝毫没有享受到偷情的快乐,甚至这种无爱的关系对她来说是一种负担,所以才会有"总算完了事:完了就好"的如释重负的反应。在之后几行诗句的译文中,赵萝蕤先生特意采用了"机械地","随手"等字眼凸显打字员的麻木和冷淡。

王誉公先生总结了"火诫"一章所体现的现代诗歌的三个特点:从题材层面看,现代诗歌侧重描写"人类社会丑恶的东西",尤其是一战后青年一代生活的"空虚、荒唐",和他们"毫无意义的爱情,甚至是调情和奸情";从诗歌体裁层面看,现代派诗人注重使用"自由诗体,复调散文",喜欢尝试任何行之有效的诗歌形式;从诗歌语言层面上看,诗歌正逐步疏远"歌"接近"会话",凸显诗歌的"语言口语话"和"语言多样化"等特点。②

笔者认为,艾略特在描写这段毫无情感的偷情画面时,基本采用的是句式结构完整的散文式表达,平铺直叙,完全颠覆了诗歌在读者心中的形象。赵萝蕤先生准确把握了艾略特诗歌的这些现代派特征,用"口语化"、散文式的语言忠实地呈现了"荒原"中了无生气、毫无意义的"奸情"。王誉公先生高度评价了赵萝蕤先生不拘泥传统,敢为人先的翻译家精神,这一精神,在当时——一谈及英

① [英]托·斯·艾略特:《荒原》,赵萝蕤译,袁可嘉、董衡巽、郑克鲁选编:《外国现代派作品选》第1册(上),上海文艺出版社1980年版,第106~108页。

② 参见王誉公、张华英:《〈荒原〉的理解与翻译》,《外国文学研究》1996年第2期。

美诗歌，节奏、韵律等字眼就纷至沓来，一谈及诗歌翻译，意象、意境等词就跃然纸上——的大背景下，弥足珍贵："赵先生在译《荒原》的过程中，从不拘泥这些传统形式。她从实际出发，根据原作的特点，选用相应的形式和词汇，甚为完美地保留了原诗的思想和风格。"①诗歌翻译的最难之处当属诗味的保留问题，译者在保留诗歌形式的同时，往往损失了诗味，然而赵萝蕤先生的《荒原》译文"每每体现出形式与内容相互契合的艺术境界"②。

（张军丽：北京联合大学师范学院英语系副教授）

① 王誉公、张华英：《〈荒原〉的理解与翻译》，《外国文学研究》1996 年第 2 期。

② 黄宗英编：《赵萝蕤汉译〈荒原〉手稿》，高等教育出版社 2013 年版，第 16 页。

似同而非同的复杂关系

——张剑先生论艾略特的反浪漫主义诗学理论[①]

张　艳

T. S. 艾略特的诗歌“迫使人们重新认识英国诗歌发展史，迫使人们用一种新的眼光来看待17世纪的玄学诗派、弥尔顿和浪漫主义。同时他的作品更加深了人们对法国19世纪象征主义诗歌的认识，使人们更加意识到借鉴别国诗歌的巨大可能性及其对本国诗歌发展的重要作用”[②]。对艾略特诗歌和文学批评的引介不仅有利于中国读者理解和欣赏西方现代派诗歌，而且对于英语诗歌中译本的文学和文化价值研究具有重要的启示意义，对中国现代诗歌的发生和发展也产生了重要影响。

张剑先生于1996年出版的英文专著《艾略特与英国浪漫主义传统》(*T. S. Eliot and the English Romantic Tradition*)是国内

---

① 基金项目：国家社科基金项目“比较视野下的赵萝蕤汉译《荒原》研究”(项目批号：15BWW013)。

② 张剑：《T. S. 艾略特：诗歌和戏剧的解读》，外语教学与研究出版社2006年版，第1页。

第一本艾略特研究专著，完成于他在英国留学期间，书中收录了近300条注释与200多种参考英文原版文献。通过丰富翔实的第一手资料和例证，张剑先生向中国学者引介西方艾略特诗学理论研究的最新进展，探究了“艾略特的‘反浪漫主义’思想渊源，将艾略特的诗歌、戏剧与浪漫主义时期的诗歌作品进行比较，探讨它们之间的似同而非同的复杂关系，进而驳斥了将艾略特纳入浪漫主义传统的倾向和这种倾向带来的不良后果”[①]。张剑先生的研究推动了国内艾略特研究，促进了国内外艾略特诗学理论研究的交融，“标志着中国的艾略特研究真正直接与世界的艾学研究（T. S. Eliot Studies）接轨，参与了世界艾学研究的讨论与对话”[②]，同时对理解和推进现有国内以赵萝蕤先生为代表的艾略特诗歌译介和中译本研究具有重要的现实意义。

张剑先生注意到，自20世纪50年代起，以克尔莫德（Frank Kermode）、兰格朋（Robert Langbaum）、斯特德（C. K. Stead）、弗莱（Northrop Frye）等为代表的评论家开始重新思考艾略特与浪漫主义的关系，并倾向于作出艾略特“是对浪漫主义文学的继承”的评价。进入七八十年代，包括亚伯兰斯（M. H. Abrams）、哈特曼（Geoffrey Hartman）、米勒（Joseph Hillis Miller）、罗勃（Edward Lobb）、波恩斯坦（George Bornstein）、李茨（A. Walton Litz）在内的更多的评论家抛开艾略特诗歌理论的束缚，运用浪漫主义文学标准评价艾略特的创作。针对以上评论家总是试图将艾略特“描述为一个浪漫主义者或后浪漫主义者”的判断，张剑先生表示：“他们从浪漫主义研究中找来一套标准并以之将艾略特束缚于浪漫主义传统之中”的做法“似乎不失为”贬低和削弱他的成就

---

① 张剑：《T. S. 艾略特：诗歌和戏剧的解读》，外语教学与研究出版社2006年版，第24页。

② 董洪川：《“荒原”之风：艾略特在中国》，北京大学出版社2004年版，第185页。

的一种方式,因为当艾略特被视为一个浪漫主义者时,他只是一位“小诗人”。“因此,对艾略特成就的公正评价取决于对其传统的深刻理解”,“重新探讨(retrace)艾略特的传统并重新评估(reevaluate)他的诗歌”[①]成为张剑先生研究的重点。

艾略特在《传统与个人才能》中指出:“如果传统的方式仅限于追随前一代,或仅限于盲目地或胆怯地墨守前一代成功的方法,‘传统’自然是不足称道了。”[②]艾略特的传统不只是世代相传或从过去延续至今的东西,而是一种蕴含着“广泛得多的意义”的全新理念。对于“任何一个在25岁以上还要继续作诗人的人来说”,“历史的意识”不可或缺,因为“历史的意识”能够让诗人“不仅理解到过去的过去性”,而且还能理解“过去的现存性”[③],从而在过去与现在之间架构一座穿越时空的桥梁,进而完成与但丁、莎士比亚或荷马等西方文学传统中最具影响力的诗坛巨匠们的对话。一位作家或一部作品的完整意义涵盖他或它的“历史地位”与“当代价值”,即“过去因现在而改变正如现在为过去所指引”[④]。艾略特强调诗人要回归传统并从古典艺术经典中汲取营养,但在回归与吸收过程中,诗人与艺术家要以一种变化与发展的眼光看待可能出现在新作品与旧有的传统秩序之间的调整与适应问题。艾略特在《传统与个人才能》中提出:“现存的艺术经典本身就构成一个理想秩序,这个秩序由于新的作品被介绍进来而发生变化。这个已成

① 张剑:《艾略特与英国浪漫主义传统》,外语教学与研究出版社1996年版,前言。

② [英]托·斯·艾略特:《传统与个人才能》,李赋宁译,陆建德选编:《艾略特文集·论文》,上海译文出版社2012年版,第2页。

③ [英]托·斯·艾略特:《传统与个人才能》,李赋宁译,陆建德选编:《艾略特文集·论文》,上海译文出版社2012年版,第2页。

④ [英]托·斯·艾略特:《传统与个人才能》,李赋宁译,陆建德选编:《艾略特文集·论文》,上海译文出版社2012年版,第3页。

的秩序在新作品出现以前本是完整的，加入新花样以后要继续保持完整，整个的秩序就必须改变一下。”[①]这种改变是一个成长发展的过程，既是“精炼化”的过程也是“复杂化”的过程。一位成熟的诗人只有将个人的感情置于历史的长河中被传统以“种种特别的意想不到的方式”加以整体性地、有机性地组合才有可能创造出不朽的经典作品。

在张剑先生看来，艾略特个人成就与英国浪漫主义传统呈现出一种“似同而非同的复杂关系”[②]，艾略特对浪漫主义传统的批评与继承是矛盾的对立统一关系，既有排斥与斗争，也有贯通与发展，只有以辩证的眼光看待，才能对艾略特的艺术成就做出公正的评价。张剑先生并不否认浪漫主义对艾略特的影响，他指出：艾略特“在十几岁时就受到拜伦、雪莱和史文朋的影响，在他一生的创作中，艾略特对浪漫主义诗人可谓了如指掌，不仅在早年的诗歌带有他对丁尼生、济慈和罗塞蒂的模仿痕迹，而且在他成熟的诗歌中也可以找到一些能让人想起某些浪漫主义诗人的诗句”[③]。在《改变了的丁尼生》（“A Tennysonian Changed”）一章中，张剑先生透过艾略特的《歌：当我们穿过山丘回家》（“Song：When we came home across the hill”）、《破晓之前》（“Before Morning”）、《瑟西的宫殿》（*Circe's Palace*）等早期诗作以及《J. 阿尔弗莱德·普鲁弗洛克的情歌》（“The Love Song of J. Alfred Prufrock”）、《荒原》等经典诗作，从诗歌流露的“忧郁和哀伤”的情调、“庄严”（stately）的选词及大海、灵柩、尸体、坟墓、鬼魂等意象表达方面，展示了“丁尼

① ［英］托·斯·艾略特：《传统与个人才能》，李赋宁译，陆建德选编：《艾略特文集·论文》，上海译文出版社 2012 年版，第 3 页。

② 张剑：《T. S. 艾略特：诗歌和戏剧的解读》，外语教学与研究出版社 2006 年版，第 24 页。

③ 张剑：《艾略特与英国浪漫主义传统》，外语教学与研究出版社 1996 年版，第 16 页。

生式”对艾略特诗歌创作的影响。张剑先生指出:“似乎艾略特也从丁尼生和勃朗宁那里学到了戏剧独白:他早期最好的作品就是戏剧独白诗。”[①]接下来,张剑先生还以艾略特的《J.阿尔弗莱德·普鲁弗洛克的情歌》为例,指出诗中“让我们走吧,你和我,/当黄昏在天际慢慢展开”的诗行“让人想起许多浪漫主义时期的诗人,特别是华兹华斯的‘美丽的黄昏,宁静而自由’”[②]。不过,张剑先生在此所做的梳理与解读除了客观地展示了19世纪浪漫派到20世纪现代派诗歌从语言、修辞和感情等方面的密切联系与精神传承,更重要的目的是要把艾略特“放在浪漫主义的语境里去考察,那么,他与浪漫主义的差异和他的成就将会更清楚地表现出来”[③]。这也与艾略特的“传统观”不谋而合,传统不再是施加于个体的“令人窒息的压力”,而是成为“积极的力量”“灵感的源泉,加速心灵的成长与发展”[④],因为在艾略特看来,对于一部新的作品,在它与标准之间,“它看来是适应的,也许倒是独特的,或是,它看来是独特的也许可以是适应的;但我们总不至于断定它只是这个而不是那个”[⑤],这不恰恰就是一种“似同而非同的复杂关系”?

张剑先生称艾略特为“先锋”诗人,认为艾略特的到来“改变了英国文学的现存秩序,他通过诗歌和文学批评改变了一代人的文

① 张剑:《艾略特与英国浪漫主义传统》,外语教学与研究出版社1996年版,第27页。

② 张剑:《艾略特与英国浪漫主义传统》,外语教学与研究出版社1996年版,第27页。

③ 张剑:《艾略特与英国浪漫主义传统》,外语教学与研究出版社1996年版,第16页。

④ 张剑:《艾略特与英国浪漫主义传统》,外语教学与研究出版社1996年版,第234～235页。

⑤ [英]托·斯·艾略特:《传统与个人才能》,李赋宁译,陆建德选编:《荒原:艾略特文集·论文》,上海译文出版社2012年版,第4页。

学趣味，创立了一整套新的鉴赏标准。”[①]张剑先生梳理了艾略特在1917～1937年陆续发表的一系列文学批评论文：1919年，艾略特在《传统与个人才能》中提出诗歌的“非个性化”理论，强调历史的作用，主张“诗不是放纵感情，而是逃避感情；不是表现个性，而是逃避个性”[②]，认为华兹华斯在《抒情歌谣集·序》（*Preface to Lyrical Ballads*）中关于诗歌来自“宁静中回忆出来的感情”的理论是“一个不精确的公式”。同年，艾略特在解读《哈姆雷特》中指出“用艺术形式表现情感的唯一方法是寻找一个‘客观对应物’”，也就是说，艺术家在创作中可以通过“客观对应物”来表现个人情感的“非个性化”。较之浪漫主义诗歌，不难发现，浪漫主义诗人偏爱张扬的个性和炽热的情感，而现代主义诗人更多的是通过隐匿个人情感，逃遁个人的体验感受，赋予客体更多的内涵，以间接的方式引导读者去发现意义。1923年，艾略特在《批评的功能》一文中对浪漫主义做出“零碎”“幼稚”“杂乱”的评价，公开反对浪漫主义诗歌的“内心呼声”以及默里的浪漫主义批评标准。1933年，艾略特在《诗歌的用处与批评的用处》（*The Use of Poetry and the Use of Criticism*）中称雪莱像“一个伶俐的和富有激情的小学生”[③]。1937年，他在《诗歌与诗人》（*On Poetry and Poets*）中称拜伦只能成为“小学生的崇拜对象”[④]。张剑先生认为，以上观点“有效将艾略特变成一名浪漫主义的叛逆者”[⑤]，也印证了他对艾略特

① 张剑：《T. S. 艾略特：诗歌和戏剧的解读》，外语教学与研究出版社2006年版，第1页。

② ［英］托·斯·艾略特：《传统与个人才能》，李赋宁译，陆建德选编：《荒原：艾略特文集·论文》，上海译文出版社2012年版，第10～11页。

③ T. S. Eliot, *The Use of Poetry and the Use of Criticism*, London: Faber and Faber, 1934, p. 88.

④ T. S. Eliot, *On Poetry and Poets*, London: Faber and Faber, 1957, p. 196.

⑤ 张剑：《T. S. 艾略特：诗歌和戏剧的解读》，外语教学与研究出版社2006年版，第1页。

与英国浪漫主义“背离”关系(negative relation)的判断。

张剑先生指出,尽管艾略特的诗歌在语言、主题、意象表达上与浪漫主义诗歌看似有相同之处,但实则不同且内涵复杂。艾略特不赞成在诗歌创作中像浪漫主义诗人那样充分且直接地将热烈的感情流露出来,主张通过意象、事件、场景、典故、引语等一系列象征物将个体的主观抒情变为客观呈现,在体味、揣摩中引发所对应的思想情感,营造言有尽而意无穷的艺术境界。

以《J. 阿尔弗莱德·普鲁弗洛克的情歌》为例,这是一首特殊的情歌,在诗的开头“那么就让咱们去吧,我和你,趁黄昏正铺展在天际/像一个上了麻醉的病人躺在手术台上”[1]中出现黄昏、手术台、病人这一组“客观对应物”,这里的“黄昏”完全不同于威廉·华兹华斯在《这是一个美丽的黄昏》(“It is a Beauteous Evening”)中呈现的黄昏。在华兹华斯眼中,黄昏是美丽的,“宁静而从容”(calm and free),“像一位/因崇敬而屏住呼吸的修女”(as a Nun/Breathless with adoration),既本真纯朴、可爱可亲,同时又在极简的自然表象下蕴藏着“庄严”(solemn)与“圣洁”(divine)的神性力量,诗中静穆安详的氛围映照出和谐平静的心境。而《J. 阿尔弗莱德·普鲁弗洛克的情歌》中的黄昏却“像一个上了麻醉的病人躺在手术台上”,处于手术前麻醉状态,近乎死亡,为人控制和左右,而无丝毫反抗之力。“黄昏”幽暗的色彩烘染了气氛,困顿与迷茫的情绪蔓延开来,呈现一幅游离于生死之间的朦胧、混沌景象。接下来,“行人稀少的大街小巷”“廉价小客店”“满地是锯屑和牡蛎壳的饭店”展示了现代都市的凄冷、破败和肮脏。此刻,夜幕下的街巷被比作“冗长乏味的辩论”,隐藏着居心叵测的险恶目的;而“你”不得不要去面对令人困窘并茫然不知所措的麻烦。一种难以名状的

---

① [英]托·斯·艾略特:《J. 阿尔弗雷德·普鲁弗洛克的情歌》,汤永宽译,陆建德选编:《荒原:艾略特文集·诗歌》,上海译文出版社 2012 年版,第 3 页。

不安与担忧跃然纸上，使人无比忐忑，渲染出危机四伏的绝望情绪。张剑先生援引一位评论家的话强调，艾略特“唤起人们对黄昏所有的浪漫主义联想，目的在于‘彻底结束它们’”[①]。显然，艾略特笔下的情歌既没有浪漫主义诗歌的激情与自信，也不再是对美好爱情的憧憬与赞美，取而代之的是对现代社会丧失信仰、礼崩乐坏的描写，充满错觉与虚伪的自我欺骗，更像是心灵饱受煎熬的人在梦魇般的世界里发出的痛苦呻吟。

在此，张剑先生注意到艾略特对动物意象的喜爱，承载不同象征意蕴的动物形象出现在诗歌中，构成意味深刻的动物话语。正如黄宗英教授在《艾略特〈荒原〉中的动物话语》一文中提道：“利用各种动物话语（discourse of animality）来淡化诗歌中的主体意识可谓是艾略特一种有效的‘非个性化’创作尝试。”[②]艾略特在《J.阿尔弗莱德·普鲁弗洛克的情歌》中把黄雾（the yellow fog）比作一只猫，其中一连串的动词，如：“蹭（rub）、舔（lick）、流连（linger）、跌（fall）、溜过（slip）、围着绕（curl）、沉入睡乡（fall asleep）”赋予这只猫以慵懒散漫的形象：它“在窗玻璃上蹭着它的背”，“把舌头舔进黄昏的各个角落”，“在阴沟里的水塘上面流连”，“跌个仰面朝天”，“溜过平台”，“围着房子绕了一圈”，随后“沉入睡乡”。黄雾笼罩下的懒散似睡的空气，与第一诗节中像是麻醉在手术台上的病人一样的黄昏形成呼应。“猫”的意象惟妙惟肖地映射出普鲁弗洛克颓废、漫无目的的生活状态以及胆怯、矛盾、缺乏自信的心理状态。

张剑先生还以《荒原》中的“燕子”意象为例，指出“对于成熟时

---

① 张剑：《艾略特与英国浪漫主义传统》，外语教学与研究出版社 1996 年版，第 27 页。

② 黄宗英：《艾略特〈荒原〉中的动物话语》，汪介之、杨莉馨主编：《欧美文学评论选》，北京大学出版社 2011 年版，第 50 页。

期的艾略特来说,对丁尼生的引入已经不再是影响,而是反面例子"。《荒原》尾声部分:"我什么时候再是燕子——啊,燕子,燕子"一行诗让人联想起丁尼生的《公主》中的:"啊,燕子,燕子,你飞吧,飞向南方去吧……"丁尼生笔下的燕子有着柔软美丽的羽毛、清脆明快的啼鸣,它的温顺形象和善解人意让它成为人类的好朋友,与人类建立起亲近、友好的关系。正是基于此,丁尼生将燕子的呢喃声与喁喁情话相连,让燕子担当信使,寄寓情思,传递情人间的思念,奔放且热切的情感扑面而来。但出现在《荒原》的燕子却变了模样,正如张剑先生所指出的:"艾略特在将燕子这个意象引入他的诗歌之前,已经把'理想'的成分挤压干净。燕子不再是情人间的信使,也与浪漫的爱情毫无关联。相反,燕子与翡绿眉拉被残暴的国王奸污以及人际关系中肮脏的一面联系在了一起。"[①]根据奥维德的《变形记》,翡绿眉拉被姐夫蒂留斯强暴。翡绿眉拉将自己的伤心故事织结成一幅锦绣托人送给姐姐普洛克涅。普洛克涅在盛怒之下杀了儿子依贴士,煮熟了给丈夫吃。国王持刀杀死了姐妹俩,后来,姐妹俩都变成了鸟,翡绿眉拉是夜莺,姐姐变为了燕子。[②] 艾略特通过这个悲剧性的神话影射第一次世界大战后两性关系的混乱和道德的沦丧,反映了当时西方世界颓废、悲观和病态的精神状态。

张剑先生在书中第十三章提道:艾略特在他 14 岁生日当天收到一本精美的《美洲东北部的飞鸟手册》(*Handbook of Birds of Eastern North America*),对于这份特殊的生日礼物,艾略特表现出浓厚的兴趣,在书中"把他所认识的鸟都打上了一个勾:鹌鹑,

① 张剑:《艾略特与英国浪漫主义传统》,外语教学与研究出版社 1996 年版,第 27 页。

② 参见黄宗英编:《赵萝蕤汉译〈荒原〉手稿》,高等教育出版社 2013 年版,第 167~169 页。

鸫,麻雀,金翅雀,等。那时的他是一个好奇的、对外界的美很敏感的孩子,当然鸟也与童年的天真和幸福联系在一起”①。在《荒原》的原注(第五章《雷霆的话》第357行)中,艾略特也提到他曾在魁北克州(Quebec Country)亲耳听过画眉的叫声。根据《美洲东北部的飞鸟手册》的记载:“这种鸟最喜欢住在深山僻林里……它的鸣声并不以多变或洪亮著称,但它的声调的甜纯、易节的优美则是无与伦比的。它的‘滴水歌’确实值得赞赏。”②由此可见,各种各样的鸟的形象出现在艾略特的诗歌中并非偶然,而是与他从小对鸟的“痴迷”有着密切的关系。对于儿时那段快乐时光的美好记忆奠定了艾略特未来诗作中对鸟的形象与意义的界定:“无论是《枯叟》中迎风展翅的海鸥,还是《荒原》中在松树林里唱‘滴水歌’的寄居鸫;无论是《圣灰星期三》中那不折的翅膀,还是《东科克》结尾处在无垠的海水上飞翔的海燕,还是《烧毁的诺顿》中以翅膀反射阳光的翠鸟,它们都代表了一种正面的价值。”③在这里,通过以鸟为代表的动物意象及其构成的动物话语,艾略特打破了诗人在诗歌中对于诗歌意义的直接阐述,激活了读者的想象力,从而极大地扩展了诗歌所蕴含的深刻寓意。可见,通过“观察动物话语来解读《荒原》也许算得上是在寻找那种文中所不存在的内涵……它们不仅表现了诗中人个性消失的戏剧化艺术效果,而且也表现了这个‘零碎整体’中动物话语的特殊艺术表现力”④。

面对波恩斯坦、李茨等评论家针对艾略特后期诗歌中出现的

---

① 张剑:《T. S. 艾略特:诗歌和戏剧的解读》,外语教学与研究出版社2006年版,第178页。

② 黄宗英编:《赵萝蕤汉译〈荒原〉手稿》,高等教育出版社2013年版,第219页。

③ 张剑:《T. S. 艾略特:诗歌和戏剧的解读》,外语教学与研究出版社2006年版,第179页。

④ 黄宗英:《艾略特〈荒原〉中的动物话语》,汪介之、杨莉馨主编:《欧美文学评论选》,北京大学出版社2011年版,第54页。

“快乐元素”(happy evidence)就将艾略特归类为一名后浪漫主义诗人的评估,张剑先生予以反驳。虽然传统的星星、玫瑰、花园、喷泉等意象继续出现在艾略特后期诗歌中,且艾略特早期诗歌中的各种技巧和手段并不再使用,但这并不意味着他“反对浪漫主义的主要武器已经不复存在”。而恰恰相反,艾略特通过将诗歌中的意象进行多重类比,使用哲学和神学的一些概念追溯传统,对他所经历的体验和感受进行思考。这种“超验”的本质正是艾略特在其后期诗歌创作中创造出来的一种全新的诗歌表达方式,既是对个人追求精神升华过程中经历的折磨和煎熬的再现,也是他对“传统”所作的颠覆式的阐释与崭新的表达。

综上所述,张剑先生对艾略特与英国浪漫主义之间“背离”且“似同而非同的复杂关系”的判断与阐释推进了国内学者对艾略特的“反浪漫主义”诗学理论的深入研究,对于进一步挖掘艾略特诗歌和戏剧作品的历史与当代价值意义深远。同时,对于当下国内艾略特诗歌翻译以及中译本的比较研究具有重要的借鉴意义。

(张艳:北京联合大学应用文理学院基础教学部副教授)

文学翻译是文学接受

——董洪川先生论赵萝蕤先生汉译艾略特《荒原》[①]

崔鲜泉

四川外国语学院的董洪川先生先后撰写并出版了博士论文《“荒原”之风：T. S. 艾略特在中国》[②]及期刊论文《赵萝蕤与〈荒原〉在中国的译介研究》，介绍赵萝蕤先生翻译《荒原》的历史背景，将文学接受理论运用到翻译批评当中，指出“文学翻译是文学接受”[③]，并且引用了袁可嘉先生的评论：“赵译《荒原》是译介到我国的第一部西方现代派力作”[④]，充分肯定了赵萝蕤先生汉译《荒原》的历史功绩。

英国著名文艺批评家理查兹说：“翻译很可能是整个宇宙进化

---

① 基金项目：国家社科基金项目“比较视野下的赵萝蕤汉译《荒原》研究”（项目批号：15BWW013）。

② 董洪川先生在四川大学文学与新闻学院攻读比较文学与世界文学专业时的博士论文，于2003年9月完成，并于2004年由北京大学出版社出版。

③ 董洪川：《“荒原”之风：T. S. 艾略特在中国》，北京大学出版社2004年版，第119页。

④ 袁可嘉：《现代派论 · 英美诗论》，中国社会科学出版社1985年版，第24页。

过程中迄今为止最复杂的一种活动。”[①]各种各样的翻译理论层出不穷。近年来,越来越多的学者认识到译者的主体性对译本的重要作用,将接受理论运用到翻译批评当中,由此出现了翻译的接受理论。文学接受理论于20世纪60年代兴起于联邦德国,其代表人物是伊赛尔(Wolfgan Iser, 1922～2007)和尧斯(Hans Robert Jauss, 1921～1997)。他们强调文本与读者的关系,将文学批评研究的重点从作者与文本的关系转移到文本与读者的关系上。文学接受理论强调文学作品是一个过程,即从作者到文本的创作过程及文本到读者的接受过程。而将接受理论运用于文学翻译批评上,就可以把文学翻译也看作是一个过程。这一过程包括三部分:第一,作者到文本的创作过程;第二,译者对文本的翻译过程;第三,译本到读者的接受过程。[②] 文学翻译的接受理论,突出译者的主体作用,逐渐受到国内学者的青睐。不少学者开始将接受理论运用于翻译批评当中,董洪川先生也是其中之一。在他的论文《“荒原”之风:T. S.艾略特在中国》中,董洪川先生系统地阐述了他的翻译接受理论的观点。

董洪川先生认为,“文学翻译就是文学接受”。他的理由有三点。第一,大多数人是通过文学译本接触外国文学作品并接受其影响的,因此译本是外国文学接受的起点。第二,译者首先是接受者。译本具有双重意义,它既是传播的开始,更是接受的结果。第三,翻译是两种文化交汇后碰撞出的火花,故而研究外国作家作品在一个国家的接受就必须研究译本。因此,艾略特诗歌和文学评论文章的翻译是中国接受艾略特诗论及其诗歌作品的有机部分。

---

① Edwin Gentzler, *Contemporary Translation Theories* (Second Revised Edition), Clevedon: Multilingual Matters, 2001, p. 14.

② 参见卞建华:《文学翻译批评中运用文学接受理论的合理性与局限性》,《外语与外语教学》2005年第1期。

董洪川先生认为,在探讨《荒原》的汉译时,“接受语境、译者主体性、误读、创造性叛逆等自然成为讨论的话题”①。

接着,从翻译历史的角度,董洪川先生阐述道:“一部翻译作品的成功既有社会外部环境的作用,也有译本本身的作用。”②《荒原》是现代派诗歌的代表作。它旁征博引、艰深晦涩,给翻译者带来了极大的困难。尽管如此,赵萝蕤先生1937年初版《荒原》中译本仍然取得了巨大成功。1939年,林语堂先生主编的《西洋文学》就发表邢光祖的书评,称“赵女士的这册译本是我国翻译界的‘荒原’上的奇葩”③。此后,长达半个多世纪,中国学界对赵萝蕤先生的汉译《荒原》褒扬声此起彼伏。

董洪川先生认为赵译《荒原》的成功,一个原因是艾略特不仅在当时西方文学界的地位如日中天,而且被中国文坛广泛接受;另一个原因是“中国自身文学发展的内在需求”④。赵萝蕤先生当时认为《荒原》是西方现代派诗歌的代表作,值得向中国读者介绍,会对中国诗坛产生积极正面的影响。赵萝蕤先生说:“我翻译《荒原》曾是一种类似的盼望:我们生活在一个不平常的大时代里,这其中的喜怒哀乐,失望与盼望,悲观与信仰,能有谁将活的语言来一泻数百年来我们这民族的灵魂里至痛至深的创伤与不变不屈的信心。”⑤由此可以看出,赵萝蕤先生翻译《荒原》是希望中国的文学界能够学习借鉴艾略特的创作风格,促进中国诗坛的进一步发展,

---

① 董洪川:《“荒原”之风:T. S. 艾略特在中国》,北京大学出版社2004年版,第120页。

② 董洪川:《“荒原”之风:T. S. 艾略特在中国》,北京大学出版社2004年版,第134页。

③ 赵萝蕤:《我的读书生涯》,北京大学出版社1996年版,第2页。

④ 董洪川:《“荒原”之风:T. S. 艾略特在中国》,北京大学出版社2004年版,第136页。

⑤ 赵萝蕤:《艾略特与〈荒原〉》,《我的读书生涯》,北京大学出版社1996年版,第18页。

具有很强的现实意义。

此外,译者接受是“整个文学接受中最为独特的部分”[①]。董洪川先生认为其独特的原因有三点:一是译者的接受可以通过译本反映出来;二是译者接受又受到特别的约束,比如译者需要考虑读者、出版社等;三是严肃的译者对原作的解读是经过深思熟虑、反复斟酌的。在文学翻译中,译者不仅是原作的读者和接受者,同时也是译作的作者,对原作进行再创造和改写。董洪川先生总结了赵萝蕤翻译《荒原》的三点启示意义:一是“信”字为先;二是参阅大量文献、文学作品,充分挖掘用典,增加译者按,即译者注释;三是运用灵活的“直译法”。

董洪川先生提到,在接到翻译《荒原》任务之后,赵萝蕤先生选择了比较理想的《荒原》版本,“首先对《荒原》进行了全面而深入的研究”[②]。众所周知,《荒原》典故繁多、旁征博引,涉及 50 多部文艺作品,运用了 7 种语言,“晦涩正是他的精神”[③]。艾略特曾经对此发表过评论:“诗的晦涩是由于略去了链条中的连接物,略去了解释性和连接性的东西,而不是由于前后连贯,或爱好写别人看不懂的东西……”[④]赵萝蕤先生为了忠实于原作的风格和思想内容做了多方努力。《荒原》体裁多变,因此赵先生对译文体裁反复琢磨,希望“以体裁和文风的多样性从形式上辅助再现诗中采用的不同国家与时代的语言、体裁及包孕复杂文化内涵的典故”[⑤]。赵萝

① 董洪川:《“荒原”之风:T. S. 艾略特在中国》,北京大学出版社 2004 年版,第 137 页。

② 刘树森:《赵萝蕤与翻译》,赵萝蕤编:《荒原》,中国工人出版社 1995 年版,第 4 页。

③ 黄宗英:《“晦涩正是他的精神”:赵萝蕤汉译〈荒原〉直译法互文性艺术管窥》,《北京联合大学学报》(人文社科版)2019 年第 3 期。

④ [英]托·斯·艾略特:《四个四重奏》,《荒原:艾略特文集·论文》,上海译文出版社 2012 年版,第 233 页。

⑤ 赵萝蕤:《我的读书生涯》,北京大学出版社 1996 年版,第 10 页。

蕤先生还参阅了大量文献和相关作品，以便找出诗人略去的链条中的连接物，来克服《荒原》晦涩难懂的困难，这一点从她增加的译者中按可以看出。

董洪川先生认为，通过“直译法”，赵萝蕤译出了《荒原》的情致。他以赵译《荒原》第1～18行为例来进行说明。董洪川先生认为，赵萝蕤先生的译文不仅保留了原诗的意象，准确地表达了原作的思想内容，并且与原诗的节奏保持一致，译出了原诗的情致。此外，通过灵活的“直译法”，赵萝蕤先生译出了《荒原》的语言风格。《荒原》集高雅与低俗于一身，既有歌剧片段也有打油诗之类的粗俗诗行，既有戏剧独白也有下等人的不雅对话，既有日常口语，又有优雅的书面语，还有粗俗的俚语，即什么都可以入诗，有大俗也有大雅，使得诗歌语言风格多变。赵萝蕤的翻译努力再现了原诗不同的语言风格。董洪川先生以原诗142～151行为例来进行说明。他认为原诗这几行在句法、语汇、节奏上都是典型的口语风格，赵萝蕤先生的译文也同样用了口语和俚语，努力再现了原诗的口语特征，忠实传达了原诗的风格。[①] 此外，董洪川先生还以《荒原》第五章为例，表明赵萝蕤先生的译文在形式和意义上较好地再现了原诗。[②]

总之，董洪川先生认为：“赵译本《荒原》就整体而言，确是一部难得的佳译。译者不仅对原作理解透彻，对原作的艺术价值做出了正确的判断，而且在译文中也较为成功地找到了两种语言的结合点。特别是站在文化交流的角度看，赵译对艾略特在中国的接

① 参见董洪川：《“荒原”之风：T. S. 艾略特在中国》，北京大学出版社2004年版，第141页。

② 参见董洪川：《“荒原”之风：T. S. 艾略特在中国》，北京大学出版社2004年版，第141页。

受起到了巨大的历史作用”[1]。

（崔鲜泉：北京联合大学应用文理学院基础教学部副教授）

① 董洪川:《“荒原”之风:T. S. 艾略特在中国》,北京大学出版社 2004 年版,第 144 页。

尤金·奥尼尔作品中的中国想象

何亦可

尤金·奥尼尔(Eugene O'Neill,1888～1953)是美国戏剧史上具有划时代意义的剧作家,他在戏剧创作中"自觉地从中国传统文化和思想中汲取思想和艺术创作的养分"①。当奥尼尔遭遇了宗教信仰危机和价值危机时,他将目光投向了东方,寻求他心中的精神价值,最终找到了与自己心灵契合的道家思想。奥尼尔于1937年在加利福尼亚州离海不远的山沟里仿中国建筑风格建造了一座小别墅"大道别墅",并收藏了《道德经》和《庄子》,更说明他对中国文化的热爱和对道家思想的崇拜。从大量的客观事实和多位著名学者的研究来看,奥尼尔一生始终对东方思想文化有浓厚的兴趣。随着他对东方以及中国的想象不断地发生变化,他对道家思想的接受和理解,是一个不断修正和完善的过程。在这个过程中,他对"无为""循环"和"回归"等道家思想的理解和阐释逐渐加深,这不仅影响了他的生活方式和人生态度,而且渗透和融入他一生的戏剧创作之中。

---

① 刘海平:《中美文化交流的杰出使者——纪念尤金·奥尼尔逝世50周年》,《外国文学研究》2003年第4期。

“国家形象源于对自我与他者、本土与异域之间的关系。”[①]中国形象经常出现在西方文学作品中,反映了西方人对中国的认知,同时也映射出自身的心理状态,他们希望从塑造的中国想象中找到解决问题的方法。作家创作出来的异国形象受到集体想象的影响,并随着认知、思想变化而变化,因此西方对中国的想象也一直在变化。20世纪上半叶的欧洲深陷世界大战的泥沼,此时的西方将希望投向东方文明,很多文学作品将东方描绘成世外田园,充满智慧、宁静又质朴的理想国,一个遥远的乌托邦。奥尼尔也不例外,他所塑造的中国形象在西方国家具有巨大的影响力。本文通过研究奥尼尔早、中、晚作品中的中国想象的变迁,在郭继德老师[②]、刘海平老师[③]等相关研究的启发下,来看其对中国道家哲学思想的接受和吸收的过程。

一方面,“中国”一词其实很早就出现在奥尼尔的早期创作中,较为显著的有《天边外》《泉》等剧本。但早期作品中的中国只是个“遥远,神秘,令人向往”但不可名状的模糊概念。直到在他中期的剧本中,中国才逐渐成为有确定地理位置和文化历史背景的国土。奥尼尔用书本上读到的和被他理想化了的“中国”来反观、批评令他十分生厌的美国拜物主义。以马可·波罗来华经商为题材,揶揄美国商业社会的大型讽刺剧《马可百万》就是突出的代表。奥尼尔在“大道别墅”完成的后期作品中几乎再没有提到过中国,中国也不再是世外桃源的代表,但中国哲学思想已经完全渗透入这些作品,由外化转为内化,例如《进入黑夜的漫长旅程》《送冰的人》等。

---

① [法]达尼埃尔·亨利·巴柔:《从文化形象到集体想象物》,孟华主编:《比较文学形象学》,北京大学出版社2001年版,第118～152页。

② 郭继德:《奥尼尔戏剧在中国的接受与影响》,《山东外语教学》2012年第3期。

③ 刘海平:《中国文化与美国戏剧篇》(英文),《中美文化的互动与关联》,上海外语教育出版社版1997年版,第68～90页。

另一方面，在人物类型、主题思想还有戏剧样式上，早期剧本都采用西方与东方二元对立思维，截然区分“天边外”与“天际内”“美”与“丑”“现实”与“幻想”“真实”与“谎言”“喜剧”与“悲剧”等看似对立的概念。[①] 但到了中后期，奥尼尔打破了二元对立的传统思维，从阴阳相对到相反相成，让简单的对立在更高的层次上融合，因而使剧本达到了一种难以企求的悲剧的超然与冷静。东西文化在这些作品中得到了较好的融合。正是由于这种自然的融合，奥尼尔的后期作品才使人耳目一新，给人以新的震撼。

一、“中国梦”：早期作品

奥尼尔作品中出现最早的中国形象可以追溯到《天边外》(1918)、《加勒比群岛之月》(1918)、《泉》(1921)，这均属于他早期的作品。20世纪初，他对中国的了解更多是通过译介书籍，而非亲身经历，所以中国在他的剧本中蒙上了一种接近神秘主义的色彩，更多是通过他的想象而虚构的形象。而且剧本中的人物希望到中国附近的某个海岛上去生活，以此看作是解脱痛苦的唯一途径。同时，他对道家无为思想的阐释也开始萌芽。

《天边外》是奥尼尔第一部在百老汇上演的戏剧，故事讲述了兄弟二人错位的人生。弟弟罗伯特是一个具有忧郁诗人气质、沉迷幻想的人，他不满足于家乡的生活，希望终有一日能到“天边外”去冒险拼搏，得到更好更理想的生活。“远方未知的美在呼唤着我，我从书中读到的东方神秘和魅力在呼唤着我，需要广阔空间的

① 参见刘海平：《中美文化交流的杰出使者——纪念尤金·奥尼尔逝世50周年》，《外国文学研究》2003年第4期。

自由,为的是探索天边外隐匿的神秘是什么。”[1]而哥哥朱利安则与其相反,完全是一个扎根在土地上的务实青年。当罗伯特即将实现自己的梦想,踏上追寻天边外的路时,他爱上了哥哥的心上人露丝,最终放弃了天边外的理想,走上了哥哥的道路,哥哥痛失所爱后,无奈走上了弟弟本该要走的路。巴柔认为,一个作家通过对异国的描述,表达其所向往的一个空间,在这个空间里想象着“他者”,并进行自我审视。剧中,中国只是一个天边外的所在,一个臆想,没有具体详尽的细节描述。它充满了神秘的色彩,中国是模糊广阔的天边外的一个地方,但是充满了奥尼尔的情感和想象,它不是地缘概念上的中国,而是一种作者的思想和情感寄托。

《泉》的主人公也希望到“东方某个遥远的地方——中国、日本或是某个别的国家——总之是一个被大自然隔开的某个极其宁静的地方”[2]。剧作发生在西班牙 15 世纪末,著名冒险家胡安拥有远大的抱负和雄心壮志,但却忽略身边的爱情,并拒绝贵族维森特夫人的真情表白。之后,他从摩尔诗人那里了解到东方青春泉的事情,并跟随哥伦布去东方探险。奥尼尔塑造了一个具有“浪漫的冒险精神”的主人公,他一直有着“中国梦”。在这部剧作里面,“中国”有大墙围起来的村庄,里面黄金遍地,还有神圣的树林和林中那青春之泉,还有奇装异服的“中国诗人”。这便是奥尼尔对中国地理的全部想象。胡安弥留之际,他的生活状态体现出无欲无为的道家内涵,“消瘦的面孔显示出一种崭新的气质,那是心灵深处的平静带来的安详”[3]。胡安便是早期奥尼尔对道家思想“无为”

---

① [美]奥尼尔:《奥尼尔文集·天边外》第 1 卷,荒芜译,人民文学出版社 2006 年版,第 336 页。

② [美]奥尼尔:《奥尼尔文集·泉》,郭继德、甲鲁海译,人民文学出版社 2006 年版,第 359 页。

③ [美]奥尼尔:《奥尼尔文集·泉》,郭继德、甲鲁海译,人民文学出版社 2006 年版,第 360 页。

的理解与体现。奥尼尔希望能在中国这样的神秘国度摒弃欲望，寻觅宁静。胡安受伤后平静度过了最后的时光，他放弃所有个人欲望，像天真的孩子一样生活在道院里并去世。胡安希望死后能够融入大自然中，他在内心呐喊："要是去世了，将会融入万千美丽中，这是幸福的起航。"①此历程中，他经历恐惧死亡，但最后又坦然面对死亡的到来。人生较天地的永恒不过须臾一瞬，他认为自己只不过是世界永恒循环中的一滴水而已，世间万物均按照各自的规律运转。

在奥尼尔早期作品中，中国始终作为西方社会的对立面、"他者"存在，他以东方的善来批判西方的恶。20世纪初，西方社会物质主义盛行，精神价值日益失落，人性异化不断加剧。精神价值的危机和宗教信仰的丧失，成为当时西方人日常生活中面临的十分尖锐的现实问题。生活在这"上帝已经死去"的世界上，人们迫切需要寻求一种新的上帝，以弥补他们精神家园的困境。许多有识之士把目光转向东方，希望在古老的东方文化中寻找某种精神价值。奥尼尔即是其中一位，"跟他同时代的许多艺术家（诸如庞德、艾略特以及海塞和阿尔多）一样，奥尼尔把精神上的困境看成传统西方文化的产物，因而必须在东方式的平和宁静当中寻找慰藉"②。他说："我心中有一种理念，美国其实并非最成功的国家，而恰恰是一个大失败……它的主要思想是把拥有外界事物看作拥有自己的灵魂。美国是个典型，因为这些事发生得突然，同时又发生在这个拥有庞大资源的国土。正因为人们已无法在当代西方文化中发现生命的意义，因此只好远眺东方或许转世投胎只是奢望，

① ［美］奥尼尔：《奥尼尔文集·泉》，郭继德、甲鲁海译，人民文学出版社2006年版，第360页。

② Ernest Griffen, *Eugene O'Neill: A Collection of Criticism*, New York: McGraw-Hill, 1976, p. 35.

但至少可以为他们在失去一切之后，找到一个心灵的栖息之所。”[①]如詹姆斯·罗宾森所言：“如同今天许多美国人一样，奥尼尔经历了对本土文化的深刻异化。跟众人一样，他掉头东去，沿着早期基督教教会和现代浪漫派哲学家艺术家的足迹和道路东行。跟他们一样，他毫不保留地接受了他在那儿发现的人生哲理，因为他仍然是个西方人。然而他的心灵魂魄由此而得到深化。”[②]

二、“到中国去”：中期作品

在奥尼尔早期剧本中，中国只是个“天边外”，“遥远，神秘，令人向往”但不可名状的模糊概念，在中期的剧本中，它才渐渐成为有确定地理位置和文化历史背景的国土，成为剧本叙事的中心。如《马克·百万》(1927)就以具化的东方为背景，不再是臆想抽象的地方。中国从边缘走到了中心，从幕后走到了台前。而奥尼尔早年去中国的夙愿在1928年10月终于得以实现，他从上海踏上了中国这个文明古国的土地，这对他中后期的创作起到非常重要的作用。中期另一个变化表现在，早期剧本都采用二元对立思维，截然区分“天边外”与“天际内”“美”与“丑”“现实”与“幻想”“真实”与“谎言”等看似对立的概念。但到了中后期，奥尼尔打破了二元对立的传统思维，阴阳对立的成分减弱了，和的氛围浓厚了，这是因为他借鉴了道家思想中阴阳互换的概念，从阴阳相对到相反相成，体现的是相克相生、万物对立统一的道家观念。

老子对世界的本原问题在《道德经》得到这样的论述：“道生

① 汪义群：《奥尼尔研究》，上海外语教育出版社2006年版，第155页。

② [美]詹姆斯·罗宾森：《尤金·奥尼尔和东方思想》，郑柏铭译，辽宁教育出版社1997年版，第24页。

一,一生二,二生三,三生万物。万物负阴而抱阳,冲气以为和。”[①]这里概述了事物发展的规律万物之中包涵“阴”和“阳”两种相对的力量或方面,例如生与死,善与恶等都是并存的,但又不断地向相反的方向发展。老子的“祸兮福所倚,福兮祸所伏”就精辟准确地论述了祸与福相互转化的关系,即“物极必反”的发展规律。老子还十分强调“冲气以为和”,即对立冲突的双方最终要发展到和谐统一,才能“天地相合以降甘露”,才能“清静为天下正”[②]。老子提出阴阳“对立统一”的辩证关系,庄子后来也提出了“一清一浊,阴阳调和”的看法,进一步发展了老子的这一思想。《马可百万》的剧情和人物安排,都是按照东方与西方、男性与女性、争斗与服从、阴与阳、生与死等这些概念的意义来安排的,体现的是非生即死的、万物对立统一的道家观念。

奥尼尔在《马可百万》中集中写了东西方文化价值观念的冲突,特别是将“东方的静虚的唯灵论和西方的破坏性的物质主义进行了对比”,他利用阔阔真公主和马可这两个人物作为这两种文化和人生哲学的代表:阔阔真作为一名女性,是被动的,注重精神上的追求,是中国思想中“阴”型人物;而马可作为一名男性,是好动的,追求理性,是“阳”型人物。受拜金主义影响、商业化恶习濡染的马可无法理解阔阔真的真挚而深厚的感情。在两种观念的冲突中,马可作为胜利者活了下来,阔阔真成为失败者而殒命,但她因为心中有爱,所以从死亡之中找到了永生。故她说:“我爱过,尔后死了;我现在有爱了,又活了。”[③]这句话就把两个对立的“阴阳”人物代表糅合在一起了。西方的冒险家就成了被征服者,而东方的

① 《老子》,中华书局 2013 年版,第 2 页。

② 李湘雅:《解读道德经》,人民文学出版社 2006 年版,第 132 页。

③ [美]奥尼尔著,郭继德编:《奥尼尔文集》第 3 卷,人民文学出版社 2006 年版,第 10 页。

女性变为征服者了。剧中的忽必烈被称为是"苍天的儿子,土地的君主",他是阴阳对立又统一的典型例子,因为他一个人兼有阴阳两方面的特征,成为"天地合一"的代表。面对阔阔真的尸体,忽必烈有这样一句台词:"孕育你的子宫和埋葬你的坟墓是协调的。"[①]这暗示了她的生与死是一个循环,旅程的结束意味着她生命的完结,但她的葬礼却像是庆祝她的重生。于是,教士们高呼:"死亡比生命更加真实。"

奥尼尔将东方宁静的精神至上和西方喧嚣的物质至上进行了鲜明的对比,表现出作者对东方文化的向往,对中国恬淡无为的传统哲学的推崇。文学评论家霍斯特·费伦茨在《〈富商马可〉、奥尼尔的中国经历与中国戏剧》中指出:"奥尼尔像他的同时代人埃兹拉·庞德一样,相信东方能够给西方提供某种迫切需要的准则……他希望用道家的所谓的'出世'的思想来医治西方物质主义的病根。"[②]在奥尼尔看来,西方尽管表面上繁荣和成功,但背后却是道德的沦丧、灵魂的丧失,整个社会都处于迷茫之中。而道家的恬淡、清净、无为思想,吸引着当时许多试图消除西方社会种种弊端的人士。

三、"不说老庄而老庄精神在焉":晚期作品

奥尼尔后期作品中几乎再没有提到过中国,中国也不再是世外桃源的代表,中西方的文化冲突也减弱,因此西方的评论家大多认为奥尼尔创作前期和中期东方神秘主义色彩浓厚,但其晚期剧

---

① [美]奥尼尔著,郭继德编:《奥尼尔文集》第3卷,人民文学出版社2006年版,第98页。

② [美]霍斯特·弗伦茨:《〈富商马可〉、奥尼尔的中国经历与中国戏剧》,龙文佩编:《尤金·奥尼尔评论集》,上海外语教育出版社1988年版,第318页。

作是他对东方思想的退避与对西方基督教思想的回归。本文却认为其晚期作品如《长日入夜行》《送冰的人》等中的东方理念不仅没有削弱,反而得到了前所未有的加强,中国哲学思想已经完全渗透进这些作品,充满着道家思想的张力。东西文化在这些作品中得到了较好的融合,尤其是道家提倡的"返璞归真""无为""人生如梦""天人合一"的哲学思想在晚期剧作中得到了充分的体现。"'道'对他来说,已不仅是他反复琢磨过了的哲学思想,而且是身体力行过了的实在经验。道家思想悄悄地潜入了他的作品的主题、结构、人物和风格之中,在一定意义上还决定了他对创作题材的取舍。"[①]本节以《进入黑夜的漫长旅程》为例来说明这一问题。

《进入黑夜的漫长旅程》是一部现代家庭悲剧,它细致地刻画了人物复杂的心理活动和矛盾冲突,认为一个人的现实存在和他的未来命运都是由他过去的所作所为决定的,逃避过去的一切努力都无济于事,人们所能做的就是认命。奥尼尔的这种宿命论和独特的悲剧意识,揭示了他对生活意义的追求、对人类精神迷惘的理解以及对命运的顺其自然。《进入黑夜的漫长旅程》的情节结构就体现了道家的循环思想。剧本的题目"进入黑夜的漫长旅程"预示着昼与夜的交替和循环,也暗示剧情发生在现在(现实)和过去(往事)的转换和循环之间。随着白昼的推移,雾的意象反复出现;剧中人时而出现在现实中,时而出现在对往事的回忆中:"他们的爱与恨、怜悯与责难、关心与批判反复并交替出现。"[②]

奥尼尔在剧中大量地运用了雾和大海的意象,来强调人的希望以及梦想实际是虚幻的,用来掩盖内心的空虚。他借爱德蒙的

① [美]詹姆斯·罗宾森:《尤金·奥尼尔和东方思想》,郑柏铭译,辽宁教育出版社 1997 年版,第 3 页。

② 李顺春:《尤金 · 奥尼尔戏剧创作的道家视界》,《苏州大学学报》(哲学社会科学版)2009 第 5 期。

口说出了他对“空”的热爱:“我喜欢待在雾里……一路上我没有遇到一个人影,一切看上去、听起来显得虚无缥缈,没有一样东西是本来的面目。我就喜欢这样……独自一人在另一个世界里。在那儿真假难辨,整个人生都被遮盖起来……雾和海连成一片,分不出彼此,我觉得自己是在海底行走,仿佛很久很久以前就沉在大海中。仿佛我就是个雾中的鬼魂,而雾就是海的鬼魂。然而做一个鬼中之鬼,倒使你感到内心平安。”①在另一个世界中,鬼魂是可以亲近的,这种认知在西方哲学中很少出现,但是在道家思想中却非常普遍。因为生死从来就不是对立的,而是循环交替的。庄子在《大宗师》第五篇的最后一句话是“成然寐,蘧然觉”②,用酣睡与醒觉的隐喻说明出入死生轮回的“无往不可”之状。奥尼尔通过剧中人物之口表达了他对老庄“无为”思想的向往。

奥尼尔晚期戏剧作品的“主题思想,主人公价值观和人生观以及整个剧本的象征使用和情节结构”③,无不散发着浓郁的道家思想。在奥尼尔后期的戏剧作品中,道家的“无为”思想融入奥尼尔戏剧之中,并与剧本的环境、人物、思想和性格等融为一体,以至F. 卡品特(Frederic Carpenter)称奥尼尔后期的戏剧作品为“超脱的剧本”。奥尼尔的创作理念与道家思想相互融合,尤其表现在戏剧中的人物类型、主题思想、精神境界等方面。正是道家思想对奥尼尔跨越时空的影响,才使其作品有“思想的深度、内容的广度和艺术的巨大魅力”④,这在美国戏剧史上前所未有的。

---

① [美]尤金·奥尼尔:《奥尼尔集》,三联书店1995年版,第1024页。

② 陈鼓应:《庄子今注今译》,中华书局2001年版,第167页。

③ [美]詹姆斯·罗宾森:《尤金·奥尼尔和东方思想》,郑柏铭译,辽宁教育出版社1997年版,第3页。

④ 郭继德:《奥尼尔的戏剧创作与中国哲学思想》,《山东外语教学》1994年第2期。

奥尼尔在作品中对“中国”的想象，反映出西方社会的自我形象，可以看出中国文化对世界文明进程发挥着重要作用。奥尼尔剧作中的中国形象正是他提供给西方世界的一剂“救世良方”，宁静淳朴的“田园牧歌”式的“中国”是奥尼尔用以批判西方物质主义的乌托邦想象。其笔下的关于中国的形象，是一种正面的、褒义的表述，奥尼尔的创作正是这个时代的社会心态的反映。奥尼尔剧作中的中国形象的真正意义在于为西方观众提供了一面可以反观自身的“镜子”。尤金·奥尼尔对中国戏剧和中国文化的想象、思考和借鉴，在中美两国的戏剧发展史上留下了浓墨重彩的篇章。

（何亦可：山东师范大学外国语学院讲师）

编后记

《美国文学研究》(2020)即将付梓，回顾近20年的历程，百感交集。文集自2002年出版，至今整整十辑，一直由郭继德先生担任主编，每一辑的编后记也都是郭先生亲自撰写。然而这一次却非比寻常：就在此文集的编辑出版过程中，郭先生驾鹤西去，未能看到付出多年心血的这一事业再结的硕果。2020年6月初将文稿交与出版社不久，郭先生因身体抱恙而入院治疗，其间一直牵挂着文集的出版事宜。8月底郭先生突然病情加重，于9月10日教师节凌晨溘然长逝，为他钟爱的教育事业奉献了终生。因此，此次的编后记由我来撰写，将此文集集结前后的诸多经历分享与美国文学研究界的师长同仁。

文集的第一篇是加州州立大学原元教授怀念恩师伊布·哈桑教授的纪念文章，梳理哈桑思想的特质及形成历程，呈现大师的熠熠风采。诚然，文章学术之厚重非旁人所能探及，而能够得到哈桑教授终生关爱的弟子恐怕除了原元老师也别无他人。令人感慨的是，哈桑先生早于郭继德先生5年辞世，也是在9月10日，中国的教师节这一天。文集借此致敬两位先生，感谢他们为中美文化和学术交流做出的卓越贡献。

值得欣慰的是，学术传统得以传承，中青年学者成长起来，学术新秀也开始崭露头角。黄宗英教授和他的团队在诗歌研究领域成就卓著;李常磊教授和他的团队在不断推进福克纳研究,成果丰硕;薛玉凤教授、刘春芳教授、李峰教授等学者已经在各自的领域获得较高的赞誉;更年轻的学者思维活跃,研究视角新颖,研究选题独特,涵盖瘟疫及相关的创伤叙事、幽灵叙事、生命书写、共同体意识等批评范式,充分体现了学术的传承和创新。

文集的出版得到山东大学外国语学院的支持、美国文学研究会领导的关心和全国文学研究同仁的信任,在此一并表示感谢。

山东大学美国现代文学研究所李保杰

2021 年 4 月